CUCKOO

FOREVERMORE

Leonard K. Szymczak

EVANSTON PUBLISHING, INC.
EVANSTON, ILLINOIS 60201

This is a work of fiction. The characters and events portrayed in this book are purely fictional and any resemblance to real people or incidents is coincidental.

Australian measurements and weights were changed to be more accessible to American audiences.

EVANSTON PUBLISHING, INC.
1571 SHERMAN AVE, ANNEX C
EVANSTON, ILLINOIS 60201

Printed in the U.S.A.
10 9 8 7 6 5 4 3 2 1

Library of Congress Card Catalog Number:
95-61433

ISBN: 1-879260-37-9

Cover art and design by Dorothy Kavka

This book is dedicated to all those
inspired to dream
who have mustered the courage
to turn a dream into reality.

ACKNOWLEDGMENTS

Many people have influenced this book making it impossible to mention them all. However, I wish to give special thanks to the following:

To Lenel Moulds and Maureen Lawson, whose advice and encouragement helped make this manuscript a published reality.

To Marylou, Melissa, and Nate Szymczak, who patiently witnessed and supported the long, involved birthing process.

To my editor, Dorothy Kavka, who provided guidance and astute recommendations.

To Melissa Wessell, who assisted with the revising and proofreading.

To my family, who provided the life experiences that shaped me into a teller of stories.

To Maria Szajewski, George Ortenzo, Audrey Jones, Dr. Bernard St. George, Bill Motlong, Marcus Galanos, my men's groups, The Writing Workshop at the Journalist Club, Sydney, and Family and Mental Health Services/ Southwest for their support and valuable contributions.

SYDNEY, AUSTRALIA

🦃

FRIDAY, JANUARY 7, 1994

I slipped on the stairs as I frantically hurried to my six o'clock appointment with Melody Mill at Sydney University. For the past 18 months, ongoing therapy with the University counselor had become my salvation. Prior to seeing her, I had dissolved into a series of panic attacks. The very thought of completing my thesis had immobilized me with waves of anxiety. The text had been close to being finished, but doubts plagued my rattled mind. Who would ever care about my study "The Operant Conditioning Response with Rats Subjected to Frequent Immersions in a Water-Filled Maze"?

As the pressure to complete my thesis intensified, so did my procrastination. My parents became furious. They saw my career and all their money going down the drain. When the departmental advisor joined my parents in harassing me, I became a nervous wreck. After my third panic attack, I began sinking like one of my rats in the tortuous maze.

Thank God for Melody Mill. Not only did she help me understand my performance and separation anxieties, but, more importantly, she led me to the light at the end of the tunnel. I was finally able to complete my Ph.D. thesis, albeit much later than scheduled.

I entered the waiting room and heard the secretary announce my arrival.

"Peter Pinowski is here."

When I entered Melody's office, I was greeted by the sweet fragrance of apricot potpourri and a soft, gentle voice. "I was wondering if you were going to make the appointment. I didn't know if you were affected by the bushfires."

"We're lucky the fires missed most of the western suburbs. They're predicting dry, hot weather for the weekend though, and my ma's pretty nervous about it all. But even a bushfire wouldn't stop me from seeing you. I have so much to tell you..."

"Take it easy, Peter," soothed the 40-year-old counselor with long copper hair. "Sit down... Relax..."

The warm, tender sound of her words calmed my very soul. Even her decor evoked a sense of tranquility. A settee with cushions the color of straw embraced my body while pictures of birds adorning the walls captivated my mind. My favorite was the yellow-winged honeyeater stuffing the gaping mouths of her young brood.

"Are you ready to start your new job on Monday?"

"I'm feeling pretty anxious about it."

"That's normal, Peter. Just remember how much progress you've made."

I gazed on Melody's full breasts nestled beneath a peach blouse. Her very presence across from me made me feel nurtured, cared for. I breathed a contented sigh and leaned back into the cushions. My mind drifted to my recent fantasy about our relationship becoming more intimate. Even inquired about Melody's personal life from a lecturer. She wasn't married and had no children. Her life was devoted to clients. I remained her most ardent admirer.

Melody leaned forward. "I must reiterate once more. Since you've received your degree and have found employment, our counseling will soon terminate."

As if smacked by an emu's egg, my head reeled. "I... I'm not ready. There's so much to work through. This morning I dreamt a giant wedge-tailed eagle was attacking me. Its razor sharp claws were clenching my testicles."

"Peter, I've been telling you for the past two months that our therapy must end. You're no longer attending the University. The Counseling Department caters for students. I agreed to continue with you only through the transition period. Even now, I shouldn't be counseling you."

I glanced at the honeyeater feeding her chicks. I wasn't strong enough. I desperately needed her encouraging words.

My mouth gaped. "I... I could sign up for a part-time course."

"You know that's merely avoidance."

"So what? I can't make it without you."

"I believe you're more than capable."

"How many more sessions can I have?"

"We've gone over this a number of times, Peter. We have another session in two weeks and then our final session, one month after that. You keep resisting termination. It's time you were weaned from therapy. I'm confident you can fly on your own."

I protested at being pushed out of the nest. It wasn't fair! "What if I have another anxiety attack?"

"If you have any difficulties, you already have several names of private therapists."

I didn't want another therapist. I wanted my Melody. Why the hell did I ever complete my thesis?

"Just a few more sessions?"

She shook her head. "After today, I can only give you two more appointments."

"Please? I won't survive!"

She merely offered a benevolent smile which I took as a hopeful gesture that she might just reconsider. At the moment, I thought better of pushing her on the matter. There was ample time between now and the next session for her to soften her stance. Who knows, I might even have a relapse.

"Now let's review your progress. Your panic attacks have stopped completely. While you're 28 years old and still living at home with your parents, you've made some important inroads on your way toward independence. The fact that you're starting a new job is most encouraging. Remember, it will be normal to experience some anxiety about the unknown."

"The unknown wouldn't be so scary if I knew that our sessions could continue, at least for a few more months."

"Peter, if you want to keep our therapy alive, now is the time to take seriously the notion of journaling. When you express your thoughts, feelings, conversations, and events of the day, you, in effect, become your own therapist. It will help you release your frustrations. Remember, I won't be available after our last session."

"I don't know."

"Two weeks ago you mentioned to me that you were given a new computer."

"An Apple Macintosh. It was a gift from my parents for graduation, Christmas, and my next birthday."

"Use the computer. If you get nothing else from therapy, I want you to start your journal. Today!"

"You know I procrastinate. You, yourself, told me I'm anal retentive."

"No more excuses, Peter. You need to do this, now."

I sank back into the settee and glared at the pictures of birds.

"Peter, look at me. I want you to make a commitment to journal." Her voice softened as she reached out for my hand. "Do this for me. Please."

A warm glow emanated from my heart as I stared into her hazel eyes. How could I resist?

"To misquote an overused saying, 'I guess today will be the first journal entry of the rest of my life...'"

MONDAY, JANUARY 10, 1994

The double-decker train rumbled across the Sydney Harbour Bridge. I spotted black smoke blowing from the north, indicating that the devastating fires which had erupted over the weekend were still not under control. Firefighters had reported they were waging a battle with a spot fire in the Northern Suburbs Crematorium. Ashes were turning to dust.

The weekend bushfires were one of the worst natural disasters inflicted on Sydney. It had wreaked havoc in the outskirts of the northern and southern suburbs and the Blue Mountains. There were horrific reports of fireballs leaping over houses. Thousands had to be evacuated. Several lives were lost and more than 100 homes were destroyed. I ironically thought of the poet Dorothea Mackellar and her anthem to the bush, "I Love a Sunburnt Country." With the current drought conditions, our country was well and truly getting burnt.

I checked my digital watch—8:31a.m. I took a deep breath and reassured myself that I would arrive at work in time for the nine o'clock start. Fire or no fire, I couldn't be late on my very first day. I distracted myself from worrying further by gazing below at the harbor. The blistering summer sun sparkled off the white tiles of the

Opera House while ferries and hydrofoils left trails of sea mist as they journeyed to and from Circular Quay.

8:53 a.m. The train dropped me off at the lush northern suburb of Warrawee. Figured the Aboriginal name, meaning "come here," had to be a good omen. The suburb had been left untouched by flames.

I jogged past the frangipani trees laden with aromatic white and yellow flowers on toward the Royal Prince Andrew, the largest and oldest hospital in Sydney. The newly completed nine-story building, which now serviced most of the medical wards and operating theaters, jutted tall in the sky like a concrete stalk. I scurried past the eucalyptus trees and towering palms on the manicured grounds which had fortunately escaped being charred. Before me loomed an antiquated stone building, the site where destiny had provided my career opportunity. I shuddered at the thought that the structure, built before the turn of the century, could still be housing ghosts of convict laborers.

Panting and puffing, I rushed into the Department of Child and Adolescent Psychiatry with two minutes to spare. As it turned out, it didn't really matter. The department director, Dr. Gerard Smelder, arrived 45 minutes late for my welcoming interview. The overweight, gray-haired child psychiatrist, who I guessed to be in his early 50s, quickly informed me he was long overdue for a meeting to discuss the hospital's response to the fires. Ten minutes was all he could spare.

A barometer floating in a model ship adorned his mahogany desk. He moved the ship half-an-inch. "I expect my staff to cooperate fully," he declared. "Welcome aboard!"

He handed me a folder with forms to complete, a timetable, and a booklet on hospital procedures, then ushered me to my office. As he departed down the hall, he added, "See you at the 11 o'clock management meeting. My room."

I mumbled, "Glad to join the crew."

My tiny room was no larger than a steward's cabin. Overhead fluorescent lights illuminated white antiseptic walls, an old brown laminated desk, two black plastic chairs, and a gray filing cabinet. I peered through the sole window which had wire mesh embedded in the glass. A lofty evergreen stood outside the screened-in verandah. Not exactly a room with a view. I decided that a few posters plus a potted plant to hide part of the scuffed beige linoleum might brighten up the office, not to mention my spirits.

At 11 o'clock, I emerged from my cubicle and headed for the case management meeting. Nervous about joining the other staff, I remembered one of Melody's anti-anxiety techniques. I calmed myself by taking long, deep breaths, then walked nonchalantly into Dr. Smelder's plush office. Musk aftershave and pipe tobacco permeated the air. The shiny mahogany desk was accented with matching bookcases and coffee table, and the red leather executive chair left no doubt this was the control center of our commander-in-chief. On the wall hung a warm, welcoming picture—a group of ducks flying overhead in V-formation with a hunter hiding in a boat aiming his rifle.

The chief was sitting on his couch next to an attractive blonde in her mid-20s whom I later found to be the social worker, Leela Hennessey. She was smiling politely as he gesticulated with his pipe. The contrast of the two looked outrageous. I mean, here was this older, oversized psychiatrist wearing a brown herringbone jacket at least one size too small, slouching over this young gorgeous bird with a bright yellow dress. I had a mental flash of a vulture talking to a canary. His bulging eyes hidden behind black-rimmed glasses gazed longingly into narrow slits surrounded by chartreuse eye shadow.

I gazed lustily at the social worker and found myself wondering if her panties were lace or cotton, yellow or blue. I became green with envy that she was listening to Smelder and hadn't even noticed that I had taken a chair in the room.

"All right, Gerard. Let's get this show on the road," announced a short burly woman barging into the office. "It's after 11 and I've plenty of work to do."

I stared open-mouthed at Maxine Benton. A psychiatric nurse in her 50s with red-rinsed hair, she was dressed in white and built like a footballer.

She bellowed, "I just took a call from a man whose wife drowned in a swimming pool, trying to escape the fire. Their children need immediate crisis counseling. According to some reports, there's a lot of fire ahead of us. We need to be prepared."

"Take it easy," said Dr. Smelder. "I've already discussed our role in the community with the administration. We'll provide counseling back-up for families with children and adolescents who've been affected by the disaster."

"Where is everyone?" blared Maxine. She caught my eye. "You must be the new psychologist."

I nodded meekly. "Peter Pinowski."

"I'm Maxine, the psychiatric nurse. Been in this department longer than I care to remember. If you need any help settling in, give us a yell." Before I could answer, she thundered, "Here's our team!"

The rest of the staff, each carrying a mug, shuffled into the room. I shook hands with a pastoral care counselor named Henry Snart and nodded to Theresa Ramadopoulos, the child psychologist. An Indian psychiatric intern with an unpronounceable name passed around a plate of doughnuts.

Dr. Smelder placed his ebony pipe in the crystal ashtray. "Peter, these management meetings take place every Monday morning. Like everyone else, you can use the time to receive assistance on difficult cases."

Everyone smiled at me in a strange sort of way. It wasn't a glad-to-have-you-here welcome. It was more like it's-going-to-be-fun-watching-how-you-cope welcome. My lips were already parched and my armpits were drenched. I forced a half-smile.

"We have to plan our response to the bushfire disaster," said our commander. "But first, is there any urgent case that needs to be discussed?"

Maxine's husky voice echoed, "Yes, Heidi Wentworth."

After Smelder nodded his approval, she continued, "This 15-year-old girl was recently hospitalized for anorexia nervosa. We have to agree on a treatment plan. I don't want a ball's up like we had with the last anorexic."

Dr. Smelder reached for his pipe. "Let's address the issue of eating disorders, shall we?" He tapped the tobacco with a metal prod and stared my way. "As we all know, anorexia is a family dynamic involving an enmeshed relationship between a mother and daughter. Their identities become fused," he added, then, lighting a match, glanced at Leela Hennessey who fluttered her eyes and flashed a smile.

Maxine snapped. "Who's going to see the client?"

"Now you hold on. We have a new face here. It's important he understand the dynamics."

The commander turned my way. "How much do you know about eating disorders?"

"I'm... uh... only familiar with the articles you published." Frankly, his articles were boring and his interventions made him sound like a pompous messiah. However, at this stage of my career, honesty would be akin to suicide. "I was impressed with how clearly you portrayed the family dynamics. Could you elaborate on the theory?"

Dr. Smelder drew an endless puff on the ebony stem.

"With anorexics, the enmeshed relationship between the mother and daughter must be disengaged..."

I reached for a glazed doughnut.

"... conflict must be brought out into the open. Differences need to be acknowledged and accepted."

"You can't discount the unconscious link between nourishment and impregnation," said Theresa Ramadopoulos.

I gulped and stared at the olive-skinned child psychologist whom I guessed to be in her 30s.

She stroked the starched collar of her white blouse. "Oral satisfaction is unconsciously equated with intercourse."

I stopped munching my doughnut.

"The anorexic must face her sexual impulses which are feared yet desired. Eating, when pleasurable, is fraught with guilt. Individual therapy can help her understand that any increased sexual feeling will kill the desire to eat."

This Born-Again-Freudian would kill anyone's appetite!

"That's approaching it very psychodynamically," said Smelder. "We don't want to get all caught up in these intrapsychic concepts, now do we? Working with the entire family to implement systemic shifts is the only way to facilitate immediate change in the shortest span of time."

Maxine blurted, "I agree with Theresa. Heidi needs individual therapy. You can do that systemic bulldust to the family, but when it comes down to it, this 15-year-old is plain hungry to talk to someone."

"I don't think individual sessions will help," he pouted. "This anorexic needs family therapy."

Theresa tried to reason. "Couldn't it be possible that individual therapy might provide Heidi with confidence to be more expressive during family sessions?"

The chief fidgeted with his pipe. "If there are too many therapists, the client won't know which direction she's supposed to change."

"Only if the therapists are pulling in opposite directions like that last case," huffed Maxine. "You can't convince me individual therapy wouldn't be of some benefit."

"I agree with Gerard," added the luscious Leela, toying with her blonde strands of hair.

Like a ping-pong game, the arguments were batted back and forth. I wondered if anyone thought about asking Heidi what she needed. At any rate, I sure as hell wasn't about to raise that issue. Keeping a low profile today was a high priority.

Eventually Henry Snart, the pastoral care counselor, moved to diplomatically resolve the conflict. "There are good arguments on both sides," he said as he removed a piece of lint from the lapel of his gray suit. "Surely we don't want to give our new colleague the impression that we can't compromise."

While the tall, priestly 40-year-old figure waited for a response, his eyes kept shifting like floating ping-pong balls. Following those dancing discs made my head spin.

The Indian intern broke the silence. "Couldn't family therapy be supplemented by individual therapy and assessed in several weeks?"

Now why didn't I say that?

Dr. Smelder pondered while he tapped his pipe on the ashtray. "We might just give it a whirl. Leela and I can work with the whole family while our new psychologist here can see the anorexic. Besides, Pinowski needs a few clients. He can provide us with an individual assessment at one of our future meetings. Now, if no one has any objections, we have to discuss our response to the fires. But first, let's adjourn for a quick cuppa."

Before I could answer, everyone bolted to the kitchen for tea and coffee. The wry smirks on the departing faces told me I had just received my rite of initiation. During the break, I remained in shock and watched Dr. Smelder put away three chocolate doughnuts, two cups of coffee, and a Kit Kat. Discussing anorexics must've given him an appetite.

Later in the day, alone in my cubicle, I pondered over my two cases assigned at the management meeting. In addition to Heidi Wentworth, I was allocated the Tortelli family with an eight-year-old boy with encopresis. I cursed my misfortune. First, I was shoveled a girl who wouldn't eat, then I was dumped with a boy who couldn't stop shitting.

To make matters worse, Dr. Smelder instructed that I see the Tortellis as an entire family. I wasn't about to disagree. Took me half an hour to build up the confidence to phone them. When I finally reached the mother, I had great difficulty explaining through her broken English why I needed her 10-year-old daughter, Maria, at the session. She couldn't understand how Maria could help Angelo stop soiling his pants. Wasn't sure myself. I finally convinced her to bring everyone. "It's hospital policy," I informed her.

On my way for the compulsory medical, I surveyed the vast hospital complex with its squash courts, sauna, and swimming pool. I was overjoyed when I heard that they had table tennis—a real man's game. All I needed was a partner.

I completed my first day with a medical examination to formally confirm my appointment. Blue eyed, brown haired, and 5'11", I weighed in at 174 pounds with a slight bulge in the middle from too many of my mother's *pierogi*. Other than the childhood tonsillectomy, nearsightedness was my only medical flaw. My brown plastic frames, while somewhat battered, served me in good stead. The medical verdict: fit for duty.

I was going to visit Heidi Wentworth on the pediatric ward, but it was close to five o'clock—quitting time. Tomorrow was another day.

I picked up the afternoon paper as I headed for the train station. Thank God, the worst of the bushfires seemed over. Homeowners were allowed back on their property and most of the affected highways were now open.

I traveled south across the Sydney Harbour Bridge and spotted the seven-story-high Big Dipper roller coaster at Luna Park. The laughing clown's face which marked the entrance to the amusement park made me smile. I had, in fact, survived my first day.

"*Piotr... Piotr...Jest godzina siódma*. It's seven o'clock."

I hid my head under the pillow, hoping to catch a few more winks. The sweltering heat baked the room while Blackie's wet nose feverishly nudged my face. Truly one of the family, the 10-year-old crossbreed—labrador, doberman, cocker spaniel and God knows what else—was desperate to be taken out. He eagerly brushed his jet-black coat against the bed. The piercing chirps of the starlings outside told me I would get no further rest.

"*Piotr, Wstawaj Szybko!* Hurry, get up!"

"*Tak! Tak!* I'm up, I'm up already!" I stamped on the floor to let her believe I was up and about. Ma was forever crusading about not being late. At times like this, moving into my own flat seemed the sensible thing. Then again, who would my parents have to worry about? Besides, I enjoyed the comforts of home. What with my older sister, Stella, married and living in Melbourne, I had my parents all to myself. Theresa, the Born-Again-Freudian, might think it all too Oedipal, but what the hell. I had my own room, two loving parents, continental food, friends, and now a good job. What more could a bloke want?

"*Piotr!*"

"Yea! Yea!"

I leaped out of bed before the human alarm clock could barge in to screech in my ear. Besides, Blackie's prancing was becoming more urgent.

I hurried his visit with the neighborhood trees and dashed back for a quick shower. In the rush, damn near took off my upper lip shaving. I frantically collected my briefcase, gave the Macintosh computer a love pat, and rushed into the kitchen.

"Don't have much time to eat, I'm in a rush."

"*Usiasc!* Sit!" ordered my mother. "Next time, get up when I call you. Here's your prunes."

"I only want corn flakes."

"Cold cereal's not enough. I cooked some eggs."

"I'm running late!"

"A working man needs a big breakfast," she said. "Your Pa's left long ago."

"Yea, okay, but hurry up. I don't want to be late."

"Don't forget your dirty clothes. Put them in the hamper."

"Yea, yea." If, heaven forbid, Ma pegged clothes on the line after nine in the morning, her housecleaning schedule would be ruined.

"What's the latest on the bushfires?" I asked.

"My prayers have been answered. Most of the homes are safe. There's still a few fires in the national parks so you better be careful. I packed your lunch–tuna sandwiches, carrot cake, and some bananas."

I wolfed down my breakfast and stuffed the large paper sack into my briefcase. Bloody hell! It was almost eight o'clock.

I flew out of 23 Orpington Street with Ma's parting words echoing in the background.

"Take an apple for the train!"

I checked my watch–9:03–as I walked into the reception area. Theresa Ramadopoulos was already picking up her files. Wearing a frilly white blouse and cherry-red skirt, she noted my arrival with a smile.

"How was your first day?" she asked.

"It'll take awhile to settle in, but I'll be all right."

"Peter, your upper lip is bleeding."

I touched my face.

"Damn, I cut myself shaving. Must've opened up when I dashed from the train and collided into that bloke. At least the blood matches my crimson tie. Better get cleaned up."

Like a real twit, I headed for the toilet.

I swung open the door and found myself staring at the social worker, Leela Hennessey, nonchalantly combing her blonde silken hair. Don't think I'll ever get used to our unisex loo. Too embarrassed to share the sink, I quickly slid into a cubicle and concentrated on emptying my bladder on the side of the bowl to create a muffled effect.

I was relieved when she left. I stopped the bleeding with a small piece of toilet paper. I combed my hair and straightened my tie. Now I was ready for my second day.

Later that morning, I caught up with Theresa in the hallway. "My Polish blood often becomes uncontrollable."

The child psychologist gave a serious stare. "I take it humor is your form of making contact?"

"Yea, well, er, I like cracking jokes. Must be hereditary. My father's a great practical joker. He's the one who decided on the name, Peter, probably for the initials."

"It sounds like your father's humor was at your expense."

"Just as well our last name wasn't Urbanski. Having smelly initials would've killed me."

"Beneath the humor, you seem to have a lot of feelings about your name."

"Haven't really thought about it very much," I lied. "You probably get razzed about Ramadopoulos."

"Occasionally. I'm currently resolving my internal conflict about being Greek in an Australian culture."

"Oh..."

The olive-complexioned woman became more pensive. "Your Polish heritage seems important to you."

"My father always told me there were two types of people–those that were Polish and those that wished that they were Polish."

"There you go again with your humor. Can't you be serious?"

I took a step backwards. "What do you want to know?"

Theresa combed her long fingers through black curly hair. "Did your parents migrate here after the war?"

"They initially came to America back in 1957 and stayed in Chicago 14 years before moving to Sydney. My father wanted to join his brother in business. I was six when we migrated here."

She edged nearer. "That's similar to my background. I was seven when my parents moved from Greece 29 years ago. The upheaval created incredible emotional turmoil. As the eldest child, I was expected to learn English and translate for my parents."

"Fortunately, I didn't have that problem. I just remember talking a little different than the other kids."

"That can affect your whole identity."

I took a further step backward. "How do you like working at Prince Andrew's?"

Her silent stare told me she knew I had changed the subject. Thank God, she didn't mention it.

"I've enjoyed most of my 10 years here," she said. "I don't care for the underlying tension and conflict. As you've probably observed, Gerard expects everyone to practice family therapy. I happen to believe clients have a right to individual psychotherapy. I've been in analysis for the past two years and it's made a dramatic difference in my life."

I wondered whether she had a sense of humor before she lay on the couch.

"How often do you go?"

"Three times a week. I'm finally delving into my core emotional issues."

"Pretty expensive issues."

"Not when you view it as an investment in personal growth. Have you ever been in therapy?"

Revealing inner secrets in a public hallway was not my idea of a friendly morning chat. "I don't think my mind could stand being any more healthier." I spotted the wall clock. "It's almost 10 o'clock! We'll be late for the family therapy consultation."

"Might as well comply with Gerard's decree," she sneered. "Everyone must attend."

The chairs in the conference room were arranged in a semi-circle facing a whiteboard and TV monitor. Theresa and I joined Maxine Benton at one end of the room while, at the other end, Dr. Smelder, with his familiar scent of musk and pipe tobacco, was talking on the phone next to Leela who sported black fishnet stockings and a smart burgundy dress. Henry Snart and his dancing eyeballs were scanning a case file, and Violet Struthers, a semi-retired psychiatrist, was jabbering away at the mustached Surjit Bhullar, the dark-skinned psychiatric intern.

Fifteen minutes late, the highly paid family therapy consultant, Dr. Frank King, entered. His muscular build, black shirt, and matching trousers looked more the part of a priest-boxer than a child psychiatrist. The tiny white flakes dotting his shirt suggested he was in desperate need of a strong dose of dandruff shampoo.

"G'day! Sorry I was late, but the Harbour Bridge was bumper to bumper. The fires have mucked up the traffic. Does anyone have a pad I could use?"

Hoping to make a good impression, I offered mine.

"Who wants to present?"

Eyes plummeted. A pregnant pause lasted forever until Henry Snart, the lanky pastoral counselor, fidgeted with the buttons on his gray suit and announced, "I'll discuss the Jackson case."

"Good on ya!" cried the 45-year-old eminent psychiatrist. "Show us the family genogram."

Henry Snart drew symbols on the whiteboard. Women were portrayed as circles and men as squares.

JACKSON FAMILY

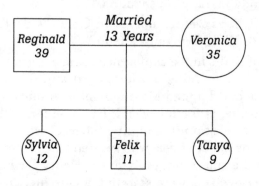

"Who's the presenting problem?" asked Dr. King.

"Tanya refuses to attend school and her temper tantrums are uncontrollable. She also wets the bed, but that isn't a major concern for the parents. According to Mrs. Jackson, bed-wetting runs in the family. She herself wet the bed up until she was 14."

Maxine blurted, "I suspect Mr. Jackson has experienced many a wet dream."

Everyone cracked up–except Henry. He just rambled on, "Tanya presents as overweight and immature and acts more like a four-year-old. Felix and Sylvia can't stand her because she bosses them around. The father's a window cleaner and is fairly ineffectual with the children while Veronica, the mother, worries constantly about her daughter."

The consultant kept scribbling on my pad. "How many sessions have you had?"

"Two with the family and one with Tanya."

"Why did you see Tanya separately?"

"During the initial family interview, she refused to speak. I thought she would feel less inhibited on her own."

Dr. King groaned. "That was a crucial error, Hank. They sucked you right into their system. You colluded with them by focusing on the pathology of the child rather than the family. That move stole your therapeutic thunder. Always remember: you're in charge of the therapy–not the family."

Beads of perspiration settled on Henry's brow. Felt sorry for him, yet was grateful. Rather him than me.

"Let's see if we can salvage this case. Do you have a video?"

"Only the first session. I haven't had a chance to review it."

"No worries!" said Dr. King, brushing the white flecks off his shoulder. "We can review it together."

Henry's eyes did a pirouette. "It's an old session. I'm not sure it will be helpful."

"Rubbish! We can all learn something. I want everyone to watch for interactional sequences–who does what to whom, when and how."

The pastoral care counselor reluctantly exited then reemerged with a video. "Which part do you want me to show?"

"Whack it in the VCR and see what's playing."

The family burst on the screen in living color. Mrs. Jackson was sitting next to her nine-year-old daughter, Tanya. Both appeared depressed and grossly overweight. A weedy looking father with a strawberry birthmark on his left cheek sat passively across the room. I immediately thought of Jack Spratt and his wife. The other two children occupied the gaping space between them.

Henry was sitting next to Tanya and talking to the mother. "How long have you been having these difficulties with Veronica?"

"You mean Tanya, don't you," answered Mrs. Jackson.

"Sorry. Yes. I meant Tanya."

"Stop it right there," shouted the consultant. "What did we just see?"

Henry mopped his forehead. I doubted whether "extra dry" deodorant would've helped today.

Gerard pointed his pipe at the television monitor. "It's obvious Snart's confusion about the names reflected the mother and daughter's enmeshment. With the father emotionally and physically distant from his wife, Tanya's behavior is serving to bring her parents together."

"Excellent hypothesis," praised Dr. King.

Our commander smiled like a Cheshire cat.

"Any other ideas?"

Another silent pause. I wasn't about to share any of my hypotheses even if I had some.

"What about you, Theresa?"

She responded rather hesitantly. "I believe... the child is suffering separation anxiety. She's involved in a hostile-dependent relationship with her mother whom I suspect had a very dependent relationship with her own mother."

"Don't forget Mr. Jackson," joined Maxine, the psychiatric nurse. "Most fathers of these school phobics opt out and leave the hard work for the mother. This bloke's a wimp. Probably couldn't even get it up. The poor wife's burnt-out from coping on her own."

Dr. Smelder stepped in. "Those comments aren't very systemic. We're interested in how problems are maintained in the family. Right, Frank?"

All eyes turned toward the teacher.

"Gerard has a good point. Analytic interpretations aren't all that useful. As family therapists we must identify the dysfunctional family patterns and then change the sequences of behaviors."

Theresa and Maxine uttered not a word. I could well imagine, however, what their scarlet faces were saying.

"Play more of the session, Hank."

The TV flickered: the drama unfolded like "The Days of Our Lives."

The obese mother shouted hysterically, "Tanya refuses to get up in the morning. I can't make her go to school–God knows I've tried. She won't budge. Just watches TV all day. Sits like a lump."

Henry asked, "Don't you like school?"

"Ugh, ugh," answered the lump, shaking her head.

"What don't you like about it?"

She shrugged her shoulders.

"You don't like anything about school?"

"Ugh,ugh."

The therapist turned toward the father. "Have you tried taking Tanya to school?"

Mr. Jackson sighed. "I give up now. When I see my Tanya on the floor, I get cross and yell. Her mother screams at me to back off. So I let her handle it."

"Do you want your husband to help with Tanya?" asked Henry.

"Of course! I want him to talk to our daughter, but he starts screaming and threatening her. That only makes it worse. She gets upset, then I get upset."

Tears welled in her eyes.

Henry offered her the Kleenex. "You seem pretty upset."

"I don't know what to do," whimpered Mrs. Jackson. "Reggy and I fight about Tanya all the time. He storms off to work muttering about cleaning his damn windows."

"How do you feel about that?"

"Alone. So..." Her whimper turned to sobs.

Tanya started crying. Felix and Sylvia sniffled. More tissues were drawn. The father just stared at his shoes.

"We've seen enough," announced Frank King abruptly.

The black-clothed figure marched toward the whiteboard and, with red marker in hand, began writing.

1. When Tanya feels smothered by her mother, she rebels with temper tantrums. The mother, feeling helpless, looks to her husband for support.

2. The father responds by yelling at his daughter. She feels attacked and then seeks the aid of

her mother who then chastises the husband for not caring.

3. The father, feeling defeated, passively withdraws by working harder at his job cleaning windows which becomes a metaphor—he's on the outside looking in. His wife, feeling more isolated, again turns to the youngest daughter who responds by staying home from school.

He tossed the marker in the tray. "The pattern, repeated time and again, has become a vicious cycle."

Dr. Smelder raised his writing pad. "My hypothesis is practically the same."

"Good on ya!" cheered the consultant.

Since Dr. King had my note pad, I had a great excuse for not knowing anything.

"Considering the difficult nature of the case, I suggest we work paradoxically. What do you think, Gerard?"

"Absolutely!"

While the rest of us remained silent observers, the two child psychiatrists, like excited little kids, concocted a plan.

"Let's target the interactional sequence between mother and daughter."

"Fantastic!" cried Gerard.

"At the next interview Hank could tell the family he's realized Tanya is very upset and lonely and needs her mother's support. During the week following the session, Mrs. Jackson should be instructed to keep Tanya home from school and should spend the time with Tanya, even if she has to follow her to the toilet. She must not allow her daughter out of her sight."

Smelder chuckled loudly. "Tell the mother she must avoid all arguments with her daughter, no matter what."

"Yes! Like reversing two magnets, we want them to get so sick of each other that Tanya will be desperate to attend school. When do you see them next, Hank?"

"Next week."

"They're great candidates for the one-way mirror. You should book them in so the rest of your team can observe the family. An interesting case. Any questions?"

Henry's glazed eyes danced to their opposite corners. "I, er, feel funny about giving the paradox. It doesn't seem totally honest."

"The family didn't come for honesty," chided the consultant as he plopped down on his throne. "They're only interested in receiving help. This intervention will give them what they need."

"Remember this is therapy, not a church service," scolded Smelder.

"I... I'm not sure..."

"Listen, Snart. You have to be totally convincing. Otherwise the family won't respond."

"Gerard's right," added Dr. King, smugly. "They'll quickly sense if you're in any way unsure. I'd suggest you rehearse your statements before you interview the family. You want to come across as authentic..."

As Henry reluctantly scribbled down the advice, my mind struggled to understand this absurd technique of reverse psychology. They might as well have suggested that Tanya stuff herself with 10 boxes of chocolate in order to make her sick of gaining weight.

"... Before leaving, I want to check in with our new group member. Have you interviewed any families yet?"

I faced the man in black. "Uh... not yet... I have a soiling family. I mean, I'm supposed to see a family with an encopretic."

"How will you be working with them?"

How the hell did I know? This was only my second day. "I'll conduct an assessment interview... get some family history."

"Don't waste your time with history. Spend the time exploring sequences around the problem–who does what, when, and how. Bring the case back to the next consultation in a fortnight and remember to videotape them."

He glanced at his watch. "I'm late." He made a quick exit with my note pad.

Lunchtime. Couldn't even think of food. A sense of panic surged through my body. Strewth! Never even used a video camera. I fought back tears, remembering my neighborhood motto, "Ashfield boys don't cry."

I meandered into the kitchen cum staff room. Maxine and Violet were seated at the table eating sandwiches.

"Don't let it get you down, kid," said Maxine in a motherly sort of way. "Pull up a chair. Frank King can be a real bastard, especially when he and Gerard perform as tweedle-de-dum and tweedle-de-dee. What sticks in my craw is their interventions, always aimed at the mothers. Why can't they be strategic with fathers? Hell, when my husband left me with three kids 20 years ago, I didn't receive one frigging cent from the bastard."

"You mustn't give this lad the wrong impression," voiced the semi-retired Violet Struthers. She was a small plump woman in her late 60s with strands of gray hair sticking out from under a brown wig.

"What's your name again?" she asked.

"Peter."

Violet sipped her tea. "Well, Potter, some of us are of the old school. Why I've been a psychiatrist for over 30-odd years. I've seen theories come and go. There was a time we only saw individuals and, I daresay, we were a trifle more successful."

Maxine grabbed another sandwich. "Gerard arrived five years ago hell-bent on changing the entire department. When he separated from his third wife, he needed to prove something. God only knows what. Just wish to Christ he would have chosen another department on the rebound. Desperate to make a name for himself, he went with the flavor of the year, this strategic/systemic bullshit. With the continual changeovers in personnel resulting from our battles with Gerard, it became increasingly hard to hire good staff. You replaced Jenny MacDonald. She and ol' Smelder scorched through some ding dongs. Theresa and I are the only ones left pre-Gerard."

"I'm still here," added Violet who was busy sweeping the crumbs off the table. "One-and-a-half days. Tuesdays and Thursdays, I believe. Sometimes a Monday. Right, Maxine?"

"Call for Dr. Struthers," boomed the intercom.

"I'll take that in my room. It was nice meeting you, Potter."

"It's Peter."

"What a lovely name! I once had a client who..."

"Don't forget your phone call."

"Yes. Thank you, Potter."

When she left, the burly nurse confided, "Pathetic. The few clients she has either cancel their appointments or return because they feel sorry for her. Should be put out to pasture. She diagnoses most of her clients with 'Acute Confusional State.' If it weren't for her friends in administration, I doubt she'd still be around. Really gets up my nose. As a part-time medical officer, she earns well over a hundred dollars for every hour she's here, whether she interviews clients or does her knitting. God damn doctors. They take the glory and the money while us real workers get bugger all. I better move it. A client's due in a few minutes."

As Maxine departed, I tried not thinking about our departmental termite mound. I swallowed my slice of carrot cake and gulped the rest of my coffee. It was time to head toward the pediatric ward which was housed in another ancient building adjacent to ours.

Heidi Wentworth occupied one of the seven beds held for our inpatients–the attempted suicides, psycho-somatics, and other urgent cases. I stood in the open ward and gawked at the tiny, thin frame of a 15-year-old girl with short, black hair and pale features, sitting up in bed. Her untouched lunch lingered on the tray in front of her. She reminded me of someone leftover from a concentration camp.

"Hi, I'm your psychologist, Peter Pinowski."

Her hollow eye sockets stared into open space.

"I stopped by to say hi and make an appointment for tomorrow. Will you be free?"

She answered in a monotone whisper. "If I have ta."

"Great! After lunch around two o'clock?"

She shrugged her frail shoulders. "Suppose."

"The nurse will bring you to my office. How are they treating you?"

"I'd rather be home."

"It must be rough," I said, dishing out some empa-thy. "When I'm away from home, I miss my mother's cooking... ugh... not that you would... I mean..."

Spent the next five minutes extracting the other foot from my mouth. She didn't seem to mind, especially when I excused myself off the ward. Thank God, I wasn't videotaped.

WEDNESDAY, JANUARY 12

Counseling room. Clients swarming, pointing video camera. Fish-eye lens distorts my face. I scream. They fasten chains around my waist.To leather couch. Force me to watch video screen. Flashing childhood perversions. I'm tormenting demented Mr. Switzer. Igniting dog dung in paper bag. On his doorstep. Pressing doorbell. I run. Cackling behind bushes. Scenes shift. I peek through key-hole. Sister undressing. Masturbating. Scene shifts again. I steal Pa's precision screwdriver. Bury it near Ma's buttercups...

I woke up from the nightmare with the hammering sound of a kookaburra laughing outside. Cradling my tired head, I rose out of bed.

"Piotr! Piotr!"

Another day, another dollar.

In my tiny cubicle I rearranged the two chairs for my two o'clock appointment. Just as well Heidi wasn't obese, otherwise we'd be in real trouble. I scanned the office one last time. The brown curtains were shut to hide the wire-meshed window; the small desk clock was placed in clear view to keep me focused on the prescribed fifty minutes; and tissues were situated nearby in case of an emotional catharsis.

The secretary's voice boomed over the intercom, "Heidi Wentworth is here."

The digital clock showed 1:49 p.m. I recalled my quick diagnostic tool. Patients who arrive early are overly anxious. Arriving late means they're passive aggressive while coming on time indicates an obsessive compulsive. Better to have an obviously anxious client than a belligerent, resistant adolescent.

Heidi was standing in the waiting area dressed in a pink gown and slippers.

I nodded. "Nice to see you."

Her pallid face stared at the floor.

"Want to follow me?"

She dragged her frail body down the long corridor. My footsteps echoed off the linoleum floor.

"Did you have any difficulty finding our department?"

"A nurse took me."

"That was helpful. I've gotten lost a few times myself."

She didn't laugh.

We said no more until we arrived in my office.

"Have you been watching all the news about the bushfires?"

Heidi shrugged her shoulders.

"Looks like they're forecasting rain by the end of the week. That's good news."

Her eyes never left the floor.

"So, how's the hospital treating you today?" I asked.

She finally spoke. "Wanna go home. Don't need to be here."

"Do you know when you can leave?"

"When I'm 84 pounds."

"How much do you weigh now?"

"Sixty-six." Not much for a five-foot, 15-year-old girl who, according to her file, loves aerobic exercises. Heidi posed an eerie portrait as she slumped in the chair. The darkened eye sockets, matchstick limbs, and black mop hair draped loosely over an emaciated face made me think of my Polish compatriots at Auschwitz. Hard to believe this sort of thing could happen, let alone voluntarily.

"Why do you think you're here?" I asked, reclining in my chair.

"You tole me to come."

"I mean, why are you here in hospital?"

"My parents don't think I'm eatin' much."

"Do you think you're eating enough?"

"Yea."

"You don't have an eating problem?"

She grabbed a Kleenex and began prodding the inside of her mouth. "Don't think I'm too thin like everyone's tellin' me."

"Why don't you eat more?"

"Dunno."

"Don't you like eating?"

The constant probing around her teeth made her gums bleed. She reached for another tissue. "I don't wanna get fat."

"Don't you think you need to gain a little weight?"

"Nope."

"Don't you want to be strong and healthy?"

"Already am."

I gazed incredulously at the ghostly figure. Any thinner and she'd be invisible!

"You don't think you're too thin?"

She shook her head and grabbed a tissue.

I picked up her file. "It says here you were admitted to hospital after signing up for a 40-hour famine appeal to earn money for the starving kids in Ethiopia. That was generous on your part."

No answer.

"Also says, after the famine, you became dizzy and weak and stopped eating altogether. Your parents were forced to seek medical help."

She continued prodding her gums.

An endless silence raised my level of exasperation. Hell, Dr. Smelder was expecting a thorough assessment. My career was on the line! I frantically recalled Dr. Frank King's consultation–sequences; that's it, explore the sequences!

With renewed confidence, I asked, "When you were at home, what happened when you didn't eat?"

Heidi offered a quick glance my way. "Dunno."

"Er... What did your parents do when you didn't eat?"

"They got mad."

"How'd they get mad?"

"They tole me to stuff my face."

"What did you do then?"

"What d'ya mean?"

"What did you do when your parents told you to stuff your face?"

She massaged the base of her teeth with the red stained tissue. "I ate somethin'."

"And... then what!?"

"What'd ya mean?"

Bloody hell! She had to know what I meant. I inhaled another deep, calming breath. "When you ate, did your parents get off your back?"

"Suppose."

Another interminable silence. The little snot wasn't helping at all to establish rapport.

"Do your parents hassle you?"

"What?"

"You know, do they bug you?"

"Yea. Don't like gettin' hassled."

"What do you do when they hassle you?"

"What d'ya mean?"

"You know, when your parents force you to eat. What do you do?"

She glared. "I spew in the toilet."

"You vomit!?"

"I touch the dangling thing in my throat. Wanna see?" She placed a finger in her mouth.

I snatched her hand. "I'll take your word for it."

She surveyed the room. "This your office?"

"Yea."

"Room's pretty small. How long ya been workin' here?"

"Not too long."

"How long exactly?"

I thought of a counseling lecture that dealt with resistant patients. "A client who avoids the therapist's questions and asks her own is showing signs of avoidance. The therapist must gently bring her back to the point of resistance."

"How long ya been workin' here?" she repeated.

"Now where were we?"

"Do ya like the job?"

"What d'ya mean?"

"Ya like talkin' ta people?"

"Yea, guess so."

"Been doin' it long?"

"What's with the questions?" I asked, reaching for the Kleenex. "To tell you the truth, this is my third day on the job." I wiped my forehead. "You're actually my first client, and you're not making it very easy. All I know is that you're stuck in this hospital and I'd like to help you if only you'd let me."

Don't ask me why, how, or when, but her eyes began to water.

Guess if I found out I was my therapist's first client, I would have cried too.

I handed her the tissues. "What's the matter?"

The dam burst. "I don't wanna be here," she sobbed. "My parents got mad 'cause I didn't put on weight... kept saying they'd stick me in hospital, Dad more than Mum... tried eatin' but the food didn't wanna stay down... my parents fought about me... couldn't stand seeing them argue... want everyone ta leave me alone... wanna be normal..."

"How do you know you're not normal?"

"Just know... I look in the mirror... I'm fat and ugly."

"You're not fat," I reassured.

"Yes I am... and ugly too... I'm yucky... I wanna look pretty and I wanna leave this dumb hospital."

"If it's any consolation, after working here only three days I feel like leaving myself."

Heidi wiped her eyes. "You can go if you wanna."

"I guess. But I still have to work somewhere."

"Don't you like it here?" She sniffled.

"Let's just say, I was expecting it to be different. It'll take awhile to become familiar with the staff and the routine. How about you? What don't you like about being here?"

"It's like a prison. Everyone's checkin' on me, doctors, nurses, dietitian. They wanna know what I'm eatin', when I go to the toilet, how much I weigh. I'm sick of it."

I felt my heart warm to this fragile wisp of a girl. "Do you know what you have to do to convince the doctors you're well enough to be discharged?"

"I gotta gain 18 pounds and maintain that for three days before they'll allow me home. That seems forever. I wanna be with my friends at school."

"You know all about the behavioral program?"

She nodded. "The more weight I gain, the more privileges I get."

"How much have you gained since you've been here?"

"Seven ounces in the past four days."

"You've already made progress!" I enthused. "If you hadn't, they wouldn't have allowed you out of bed to come visit my office."

Her scowl told me counseling wasn't a great reward.

"If you keep eating, they'll eventually let you watch TV. In no time you'll be out of here."

She stared hopelessly at the floor.

Before another silence could interrupt our conversation, I asked, "How's the food?"

"Okay."

"It'd be pretty rotten if they expected you to eat crummy stuff. I once went to Boy Scout camp. God was the food revolting. Lost 11 pounds in two weeks."

Heidi smiled. "It's not that bad."

"What's on the menu?"

"For lunch I ordered a salad with cheese and a carton of milk. Was able to finish the cheese."

"Great!"

"I count the calories from my mum's new book. It's called *The California Guide for Diet and Fitness*. Have you read it?"

"No."

She stopped picking her gums. "It's a great read. I can have my mum bring you the book."

"Thanks anyway. I'm on a perpetual seafood diet. Every time I see food, I eat it."

She snickered, "You could lose some weight."

I gazed at my spare tire.

"The book has lots of exercises. You'd enjoy it."

"Oh what the hell, why not." Reading it might just help me understand my client. Who knows, it might even help me with the battle of the bulge.

"You plannin' on stayin' here?"

"Guess I'll be around for awhile."

"I miss my aerobic exercises," She said, relaxing in her seat. "The doctors won't even let me do back bends or leg lifts." She proceeded to discuss her favorite exercise program of hip rolls, squats, and jumping jacks ...

I walked Heidi back to the pediatric ward and deliberated about the frequency of our sessions. Theresa probably would've organized a three-times-a-week schedule while Dr. Smelder would've been content with a weekly interview. I chose the middle ground and arranged to see Heidi on Mondays and Thursdays.

On my return to the department, I bumped into the psychiatric intern, Surjit Bhullar.

"I've finished the ward rounds," he said. "Are you busy?"

"Not especially."

His broad grin revealed gleaming, white teeth. "Do you play table tennis?"

"Is the Pope Polish?"

"May the gods be praised!" he shouted. "At long last, I've found my partner."

The 40-year-old mustached man danced with excitement. "Follow me! I will show you the most important place in the hospital, especially for those trying times when one needs to decathect."

I was about to ask the exact meaning of the clinical word but thought better of it. As the old Polish saying goes, "Silence is the hallmark of a genius."

Tailing behind Surjit's brisk strides, I walked past the swimming pool and into the staff amenities building. In the center of the small gymnasium stood Surjit's pride and glory, a weathered ping-pong table.

He removed his tie and unbuttoned the collar. "I've been seeking an accomplished competitor. When's the last time you played?"

"At the university. Whenever I felt like procrastinating, I played table tennis. I loved to procrastinate!"

We picked up the paddles and volleyed. Our styles were quite different. As a left-handed player, he was more comfortable with topspins and chops, producing a dazzling display of spins and curves. I preferred a power game with plenty of smashes.

"How long you been here?" I asked, whacking the ball over the net.

"Here, meaning Australia or the hospital?"

"Both, I guess."

One of his returns whirled out of my reach. "I migrated four years ago from Punjab where I had a general practice. I grew tired of treating bodies and decided to study psychiatry. It made greater sense to heal minds."

"It pays pretty well," I added.

"Definitely better than India. The opportunities are greater here, especially for my family."

"How many more years before you're officially a psychiatrist?"

"I'm in the third year. After I finish my placement at the Child and Adolescent Department, I'll still have two more years." He winked. "If I can last through Gerard's supervision sessions."

The ball, slicing on my left, nicked the edge of the table. Figured he must be pretty clever. Migrating doctors had to pass a formidable medical exam for re-accreditation designed to keep the overseas competition well under control.

"You play like you procrastinated more than I did."

He laughed. "Table tennis was my saving grace at medical school."

His arm unwound an amazing curveball. My return banged into the net.

"Our fates must be intertwined."

"What do you mean?"

"It's no mere coincidence that has brought us together. We joined the department at approximately the same time. We both love table tennis and are equally adept. I believe our journeys have been linked for some purpose–must be our karma."

His metaphysical mumbo jumbo wasn't going to alter my concentration. I smashed the ball hard and played intensely for half an hour. We each won two games. With the summer heat and the fervid activity, my shirt was sopping. In strange contrast, my opponent showed little indication of a workout. Surjit wiped a few beads of perspiration off his brow. We decided that a rematch was in order and agreed to feed our table tennis addiction by playing during lunch twice a week.

I teased the intern. "It must be our karma."

6:15 p.m. Blackie bounded on top of me, frantically licking my face. It was nice to be welcomed home.

"What's for dinner, Ma?"

"Stuffed pork chops. Take your dog out for a walk. He's been getting under my feet."

I jogged to keep up with Blackie as he sprinted to the park, searching for trees and females. A personality test would've revealed he suffered a compulsive sexual preoccupation. I was continually embarrassed by his indiscriminate humping. Legs of passing pedestrians seemed fair go, especially when the neighborhood dogs were in heat. Such behavior would have Ma impound him on the back verandah, but not for long. His screaming and howling always forced the issue, and he would wind up back in my room. After all, he was one of the family.

The 8:05 at Ashfield Station was packed. Clutching my briefcase and *The Sydney Morning Herald,* I jostled my way past the freshly groomed passengers and the melange of colognes and aftershaves to the lower level of the double-decker carriage and joined the unlucky ones, standing in the aisle, swaying to the undulating motion of the train. My eyes spotted a sensuous young woman five rows ahead. Her silk blouse, a deep blue like lapis lazuli, had its top buttons unfastened. I edged closer. The color of her soft moist lips imitated the reddish stone, carnelian, while a gold necklace dangled a figure of Nefertiti on her sumptuous cleavage. A novel, *Tigress of the Nile,* rested on her lap. I imagined her modern clothes exchanged for those of an Egyptian goddess. She peered down the aisle. Our eyes met. A pulsating charge of electricity surged up my thighs.

As passengers began alighting at Stanmore Station, I inched my way toward the mystery woman. At Macdonaldtown my heart thumped louder–a seat next to her became vacant. Another bloke had the same idea. I acted faster. Ended up tripping over someone's parcel, but victory was mine. The introduction to the goddess, however, wasn't as smooth. When I inadvertently stepped on her high heels, she emitted a painful groan. Before I could enjoy sitting next to her, she collected her book and hastily retreated at Redfern Station. I wondered if we'd ever meet again.

9:30 a.m. Journal Club. I wandered toward the conference room with the article, "Paradoxes, Cognitive Constructions, and Reflexive Loops: An Alternative Theoretical Perspective." Dr. Smelder, with his copy in hand, exited from the toilet.

"Ah, Peter. Did you enjoy the article?"

"I found it most interesting," I lied. "Reflexive loops were on my mind this morning."

Smelder smiled approvingly and led me into the conference room where the rest of the team had already assembled around the large wooden table. We briefly discussed the aftermath of the bushfires which were finally under control.

"The bushfire has taken up enough of our valuable time," announced Gerard impatiently. "Let's discuss this article. I chose it because it clearly elaborates key theoretical concepts," and so he began. "Some degree of reflexivity is necessary in all relationships..."

The balmy summer day and the cockatoos, squawking on the trees outside, reminded me of Ku-ring-gai Chase National Park and our family picnics held on the water's edge at Bobbin Head. I remembered spotting a satin bowerbird as he collected blue bottle tops for his bower in anticipation for the elaborate courting ritual with his emerald green companion.

I thought of the Egyptian goddess and played and re-played the mental tapes over and over again. There were eight carriages on the train. If my memory served me correct, we occupied the fourth. If only she were a creature of habit. I thought of Monday... riding the 8:05... together... talking and laughing... arranging an evening meal...

A black and white currawong pecked on the window and brought me out of my reverie. I glanced around. Nothing but glazed eyes, except for Dr. Smelder who was engrossed in his lecture about cognitive constrictions.

After lunch Henry Snart visited my cubicle. "Do you have a moment?"

"Sure. Have a seat."

The lanky, clean-shaven man entered. Wearing a gray suit, he was the perfect image of a middle-aged preacher.

"I believe colleagues are as important as clients," he said. "This is my first real opportunity to have a chat."

"I've been meaning to ask you, Henry. What exactly does a pastoral care counselor do?"

"Our ministry is to help those less fortunate in the hospital. I left the oncology ward a year ago and joined this department."

"Like going from the grave to the cradle."

He didn't smile. "Where the Lord sendeth, I follow."

I didn't smile either.

"I show the patients there is more to life than just living. I believe in the theology of hope. Counseling may be useful, Peter, but the therapist's attitude engenders hope within the client."

"How do you do that?"

"When I was in the seminary, Emil Brunner's book, *Eternal Hope,* made a tremendous impact on my life. You may be familiar with it."

"Uh... no." Theological books were never high on my priority.

He moved his chair closer and stared intensely, eyes arcing in opposite directions. "Are you a Christian?"

"Uh... Well... I was raised a Catholic."

"But do you believe Jesus is our Savior and our King?"

"Geeze, I guess so."

Henry leaned forward. "Peter, I don't normally talk to clients or staff about my religious views, unless of course they bring it up, but I feel your asking about hope was really a call for spiritual help."

If I could've moved my chair further away, I would've.

"I believe the Holy Spirit works through me, offering guidance to whomever I'm with. I rarely mention God's name, for I know He uses my actions and deeds to spread His word."

"Thanks, but ..."

"The Bible is the best handbook a therapist could possibly have. I keep mine in the top drawer of my desk. It's there anytime you need it."

"I'll keep it in mind. Strewth! Look at the time. There's some phone calls I have to make before our next meeting."

"Remember, provide encouragement and hope, and urge your patients to remain faithful during times of suffering and persecution."

Realizing we had a saint in the unit, I picked up the receiver. "Thanks. I'll remember that when I make these calls."

All I know is that when Henry finally departed, I had given up hope he could be of any help to me.

Shortly after three o'clock, our team sat snugly in the small dark observation room. With Smelder's ample paunch and Maxine built like a beer keg, we had to stagger the six chairs in two rows so all could fit. Gerard, Holy Henry, and Surjit occupied the front, while Maxine,

Theresa, and I settled in the back. Thank God Smelder had enough sense not to light his pipe. We would've suffocated.

Facing us was a large smoky sheet of glass, large as a picture window. While mirrors usually attracted me, I found it quite unsettling viewing into the adjoining room, undetected like foreign spies. Our observation chamber had to be darkened–the only window curtained off with thick black drapes–so that clients would be unable to peer through the mirror and, heaven forbid, observe the observers. As it was, they could only see their reflection on the shiny pane of glass.

The fluorescent light from the interviewing room cast eerie shadows on our faces. Dr. Smelder sat at the command post near the VCR and TV monitor which supplied us with sound from the other side. I still wasn't sure why sessions had to be video-recorded, but who was I to question orders?

Our commander tested the beige phone fastened to the wall. It rang in the other room which indicated the hotline was ready. Strategic mental reinforcements could be transmitted at will to the therapist. All systems were go.

Leela, on the front line, wearing a bright cherry dress–I guess her idea of battle fatigues–ushered the family of four into the stark, white room accented with a poster of Disneyland. A gray, plastic coffee table complete with beige phone and box of Kleenex rested in the center of the sand-colored carpet.

The Stein family settled into the brown plaid chairs and Gerard turned on the video-recorder. A hush fell on our team as Leela began to explain, "Those curtains in front of the mirror are open which means there's a team of colleagues assisting me from behind. They may call from time to time on this phone. Before you leave,

I'll have you sign the release form giving us permission to video."

The 12-year-old boy and girl of 15 glanced around nervously at the shiny glass, the camera fixed in the corner of the room, and the microphone hanging from the ceiling. (St. Ambrose's psychiatric hospital actually placed a person in the room to film therapy sessions. Thank God we were less conspicuous.)

Dressed in a chocolate brown suit, the gray-templed father sat apart from the family and quizzed Leela. "Who exactly is behind the mirror and how many are there?"

Smelder turned toward us with a knowing smirk and whispered, "He's obviously paranoid. A dentist, you know. They're weird. Anyone making a living sticking fingers into mouths and inflicting pain must be a sadist."

Now I knew why Gerard's mouth was badly in need of repair.

In front of me, Surjit pointed toward the boy. A dreadful sight. Angry red eczema covered his entire face while a large, infected boil protruded from his chin like a pink mountain.

I whispered, "This kid's a mess."

"Shhh," hushed Henry, glaring out of the shadows like a stern preacher.

Flanked on either side by her children, Mrs. Stein, a bleached blonde in black skirt with an icy yellow blouse, was agitated. "As I told you on the phone, Ms. Hennessey, when he left us for that other woman three years ago, Johnny became emotionally upset. His asthma worsened and his skin condition deteriorated to the point where he had to be hospitalized three times during the past two years."

Leela turned toward the father. "Do you see your son more often when he's sick?"

"I imagine so," he answered. "Normally Judith won't let me into the house, but when Johnny's sick, she bends her rigid rules. She forgets it was once my home."

"Wally gave that up when he walked out on us!" hissed the 42-year-old mother. "It was *his* decision, not mine!"

"You know damn well we were fighting all the time!" contended the father. "It wasn't good for the kids. I wasn't happy, and if you admitted the truth, you weren't happy either. Rather than stay and ruin our lives, I had the guts to leave."

"That was the easy way out! You dumped the responsibility for the children on me!"

"I was thinking of them. It wasn't healthy seeing us argue every day."

Judith's voice pitched. "Don't give me that crap about being the loving father! You visited your children only when you felt like it. When that other woman wanted an overseas holiday, where was your commitment to your kids then?"

Behind the mirror Henry scratched his head. "I wonder whether they're straying from the subject."

"Quite the contrary," said Dr. Smelder. "This is perfect. We can assess the children's reactions."

Theresa disagreed. "The couple didn't come to discuss their marital conflict. They came to help Johnny with his psychosomatic complaints. Leela should be encouraging the parents to cooperate for the sake of their children."

Maxine readjusted her massive frame. "I wouldn't have involved the father for the first family interview. Throwing him together with his wife was setting the scene for a bloody cock fight. He should've been seen separately."

Our commander turned around. "You're missing the whole point. The father is over-involved in the family. When Johnny gets sick, Mrs. Stein calls her ex-husband rather than deal with the problem herself. Johnny has learned that his symptoms bring Dad back. We needed the father present so we could disengage him from the family."

Maxine's husky voice echoed in the small chamber. "Did you ever think that the father should damn well be involved in looking after his own son rather than leaving it all to the mother?"

Henry stirred to minister the team. "I think we should concentrate our energies on helping this unfortunate family."

"Any suggestions?" shot Gerard.

Surjit offered one. "Can we help the family address the pain of separation?"

Maxine proposed another. "Ask Johnny how he feels about being abandoned by his father."

Not wanting to be left out, I added, "Maybe we should explore the sequences."

Our commander deliberated a few moments before proclaiming, "We'll wait a few minutes and see what develops."

While the couple continued their argument and Johnny scratched his face, Leela queried the daughter.

"Kelly, how do you feel about your parent's separation?"

The 15-year-old girl clasped her hands tightly in the lap of her green-striped school uniform.

"Kelly?"

Still no answer.

"Kelly, how do you feel when your parents argue?"

She finally opened her mouth and revealed shiny braces. "When my parents fight... I feel... like walking out."

"What's it like since they've been separated?"

"Quieter... much quieter at home."

"And how about you, Johnny?" solicited the therapist.

He picked a scab on his cheek. "It's... uh... more peaceful." Then glancing up at his father he hastened to add, "But I miss Dad. He's..."

Brring Brring.

The discussion halted while Leela picked up the receiver.

Our commander fired an instruction. "Ask Mr. Stein what he does when Johnny gets sick." Smelder hung up the phone and declared, "I wanted to track his involvement in the family."

Following her orders, Leela delivered the directive.

"When Johnny has a bad case of asthma or eczema," replied the father, "Judith calls. I usually come over as soon as I can, depending on my patients. Emergencies such as impacted teeth have to be treated fairly promptly."

"Your work always came first," blurted the ex-wife. "When you were living at home, we hardly saw you. Your work and your secretary occupied most of your time."

Leela intervened. "It seems that Mr. Stein comes around more often when his son's sick."

The father fumed. "You didn't mind the money that I earned from the long hours. And you conveniently omitted the fact that you spent weekends establishing that marketing firm. And what about your affair with the janitor?"

"He wasn't the janitor! He was the computer repairman. And he was more of a man than you ever were. At least he wasn't after a new set of teeth like that loony secretary of yours."

Behind the screen Maxine huffed. "That was a ridiculous phone-in. You shouldn't have interrupted the boy. He was talking about the separation. The session's now deteriorated into mud slinging."

"Wh-what the hell you talking about," stammered Gerard. "As a result of the phone-in, we have a clearer picture of the family. If you can't handle the conflict, I suggest you attend to your counter-transference."

She retaliated, "Do you always have to make it personal? Just admit it. You're intervention was a balls up."

My eyes fell on the pane of glass separating the two rooms. A faint reflection of our team danced on the mirror. The heat and tension in the confined space made me claustrophobic. Perspiration clung to my skin. I scratched my arms to relieve the itching and wondered whether I'd have to choose between the family therapists or the analysts. Didn't want to end up like Henry straddling the middle with his eyes perpetually confused. And I doubted Surjit had much choice, what with Dr. Smelder as his supervisor.

The interview progressed or regressed, depending on who viewed it. I was grateful Gerard halted the proceedings to phone Leela with an instruction to join us for a discussion of the battle plan. I overheard Maxine hiss to Theresa, "The wimp needs reinforcements."

The family was left alone in the room without the therapist as referee. I had visions of the Steins erupting into a knock-down, drag-out fight with the husband knocking out his ex-wife's teeth—the ultimate dentist's revenge.

Leela, blinded by the lack of light, stumbled into the observation room. Gerard graciously offered his seat.

"I could hear some of your conversation," she whispered. "Try keeping your voices down."

"Someone became very emotional," said the psychiatrist. "But we won't delve into that now. Congratulations, Leela. The interview's going extremely well. The dynamics are crystal clear. The couple haven't emotionally separated from one another. The boy's symptoms maintain the father's involvement in the family."

Theresa added her interpretation. "Johnny's caught in a loyalty conflict and is unable to talk freely in front of his parents. His internalized anger toward their separation has become somatized, his skin reflecting both the repressed anger and the need to weep over the loss of his father. Johnny would feel less restrained in individual therapy where he'd have an opportunity to open up. I'd like to suggest that a male therapist, possibly Peter, interview him separately while Leela helps the couple work through their separation."

Like a ping-pong ball, I was lobbed onto the table.

Dr. Smelder pounced on her serve. "That would be counter-productive and damn silly. This family must be seen together so they can properly separate. Only when they've clearly established rules about the father's visitations, only then will Johnny realize he can't manipulate his parents to get back together. What are your ideas, Leela?"

She caught the commander's drift. "I agree. After we've helped the couple disengage, then we won't need the father."

"Any further comments?"

I checked the other side of the mirror. The icy glares from the family members could have frosted the glass.

Meanwhile on our side, there was a frigid silence as Gerard handed Leela further instructions. "Assist the parents in convincing their children that the separation is final. There's nothing Johnny can do to bring the father back."

The social worker left, as did Maxine, who excused herself to make an urgent phone call. Probably went to inquire about job vacancies–for psychiatrists!

I tuned out the remainder of the session as the itching spread from my arms to my legs. Scratching offered no relief. I prayed that the interview end quickly.

Not soon enough, as Leela painstakingly carried out Smelder's plan. His periodic phone-ins kept her on target, and she spent the remainder of the session addressing the parents and ignoring the children.

When the family was eventually ushered out, Gerard flicked on the lights. "Good work, team!"

We waited until the family left the building before we surfaced. Don't know why, but Dr. Smelder didn't want patients to see who was behind the screen. He said something about anonymity increasing one's therapeutic power. Apparently, families were supposed to have greater faith in the unknown forces behind the mirror if there were no faces. In our case, ignorance was bliss.

With all that high-powered thinking, most of us needed to visit the toilet. The team sauntered into the unisex loo and occupied the vacant stalls. Our commander-in-chief was allowed first choice. Leela chose the adjoining stall.

As I was pissing into the bowl, I overheard Gerard telling Leela about the interview. In between his grunts and groans (I suspected a cognitive constriction), he was saying the intervention not only shifted the family system but would have a tremendous impact.

I heard a splash and decided I had better things to do than to eavesdrop around the toilet.

With the day finally over, I headed out the door.

"Peter!" called Theresa. "Want a lift to the station?"

It was only a few blocks away, but I figured, what the hell, it had been a long week.

She led me to her little red Honda. "I felt dreadful about that session, the way Johnny was treated. I hope you weren't offended when I suggested your name."

"No worries."

"Gerard seems fond of you, and I thought he would've been more amenable to the suggestion if you were the therapist."

Dr. Smelder liking me? Preposterous. Then again, every now and then I had caught him glancing my way with a funny grin.

She pulled in front of Warrarree Station. "Have you planned a big weekend?" she inquired.

"I'll spend some time with my mates. Thanks for the lift."

She gently patted my shoulder. "See you Monday."

On the train I made a resolution. Staff relationships would not be allowed to interfere with my weekends. Tonight I would celebrate. Ma was cooking one of my favorites–Polish sausage and sauerkraut. However, an electrical fault postponed my meal. The train was stranded 30 minutes underground between Wynyard and Town Hall Stations like a giant caterpillar trapped in a concrete tube. My stomach growled. What a way to start the weekend!

Fr. Czarnecki genuflecting. Near the altar, he pours white burgundy. From silver flask. Into chilled crystal chalice. I kneel at communion rail. Next to voluptuous woman in virginal white. Craving communion. The satin garment vanishes. Revealing soft olive breasts. Her eyes beckon. Our hands touch. Fondle. A blessed ejaculation!

Wet pajamas startled me from the heavenly dream. I nestled my head on the fluffy pillow and replayed the last scene, this time in slow motion.

Didn't get up till noon. Fortunately, I was no longer engaged with Ma in her relentless battle for my soul. She had ceased badgering me about receiving the weekly dose of religion at St. Vincent's. God only knows what she gained from it. She'd perpetually occupy her favorite pew, the very last, finger her rosary beads, and whisper Hail Marys, the cornerstone of her faith.

When I attended university, I finally put my foot down and refused to attend mass. She eventually surrendered. I had become much too old and heavy to be dragged off the mattress. She occasionally sermonized about receiving the sacraments and avoiding hell and damnation. But I figured Christmas and Easter were time enough to keep her and God happy.

Last night I arrived home late. My mate, Florian Bialobrzeski, and I had stepped out for a few beers at Klub Polski. The Harmonics Quartet were playing and a few pairs were dancing on the parquet floor beneath the outstretched wings of the large crowned eagle, our Polish emblem.

When Florian found a partner to polka, I played the poker machines. Even managed to score a few drops. My greed took over as I fed in the winning coins, hoping for a bigger return. Six months ago, I collected a one hundred dollar jackpot. Last night I had no such luck. Could well understand why the Yanks call the pokies one-armed bandits.

"I found us a table near the band," said Florian, with two girls in hand. He introduced me to a young beauty, Katrina, then offered me her friend, Ludmilla. Not anything to write Ma about, but she was Polish and well stacked.

The music switched to the old tunes by the Beatles. My mate grabbed Katrina and left me to fend for myself. Dancing was never my forte. As a kid, I received the distinction of being the first, and only one, to be kicked out of the Polish dancing class. Mrs. Zielinska had to inform my crestfallen mother that my feet were beyond training. I'm sure my sniggering during "The Whirling Skirts Polka," which happened to be followed on the record by "The Busy Fingers Polka," didn't help my cause.

Awkwardness has always been a major problem. Somehow girlfriends never stayed all that long. I'm not sure if it was my warped Catholic indoctrination or the long hours at Sydney University which never allowed enough time for socializing. Whatever it was, I still hadn't found Miss Right.

At Klub Polski, Ludmilla glanced longingly at the dance floor and tapped her feet to the song "Let It Be." I was about to invite her to play the pokies when she asked, "Do you dance?"

"Well, er, not very well."

"I'm game, if you are."

"My foot hurts," I lied. "Stubbed it at work."

"What do you do?"

"I'm a psychologist."

"That must be very interesting."

"Well... I just started this week."

Her head swayed with the music. "I like psychology."

"What a coincidence. I enjoy reading case histories. Do you?"

"I was thinking more about body language."

"Oh... uh... That's not my area of expertise."

She giggled. "We can always learn."

"Er... Are you familiar with Skinner's rats?"

Well, what could I say? What with the women in my family hogging most of the air space, I became skillful at one form of communication, namely, listening. I thought studying psychology would've solved my social clumsiness. No such luck. Girls, somehow, didn't find research studies interesting. Ludmilla was no exception.

Eventually, she excused herself to freshen up. Never did return. I returned to the flashing lights of the pokies which, while not expecting any dancing, merely gobbled the rest of my coins.

WEEK TWO
🦅

MONDAY, JANUARY 17

My third interview with Heidi Wentworth, this time on the pediatric ward. She had lost 14 ounces since our initial session and was confined to bed until her weight once again reached 60 pounds. She wasn't even allowed to walk over to our department for counseling. Since Dr. Smelder was responsible for the family therapy, I figured her weight loss wasn't solely on my shoulders.

The anorexic, dressed in a hospital gown and looking more emaciated than ever, lay whimpering under the sheets. I drew the curtain to separate us from the five other beds in the room.

"What do you want?" she sniffled.

I pulled up a chair. "I hoped you'd be in a better mood."

"I'm not."

"You seem pretty upset."

"Don't wanna talk about it."

"I thought you wanted out of here."

"I do."

"Looks like you're trying to get out of here by fading into thin air. What's going on?"

"Nuthin'."

61

"According to your chart, you now weigh less than when you were first admitted. Didn't have anything to do with our sessions, did it?"

"No one can make me eat."

For a scrawny kid, she sure was bull-headed.

"If you lose much more, they'll put you on a drip. I sure as hell wouldn't want a plastic tube hanging out of my arm."

Heidi dug her head into the pillow.

"Come on, don't do that," I pleaded. "How can I talk to you?"

She curled up into a fetal position.

"What about that book you promised to show me? You know, the diet book?"

A muffled sound groaned into the pillow.

After another futile 10 minutes of coaxing and pleading, I left, a defeated therapist. Little snot! Just had to make it difficult, didn't she. Even after I told her she was my first client. Visions of starting off with a resounding success faded fast. I only hoped the staff wouldn't hold it against me.

At dinner Pa and I sat at the kitchen table decorated with a clear plastic tablecloth patterned with hibiscus flowers. The large kitchen, the heart of our three bedroom brick bungalow, was Ma's domain. She dutifully ladled out servings of potato dumplings and goulash, considering it her prime duty that the family was well-fed. Our bellies were visible testaments.

I wondered if Heidi was having a glucose drip for dinner.

"Have you helped anyone yet, P.P.?" asked Pa as he sopped up the goulash with rye bread. Grease stains were still embedded under his fingernails and in the cracks of his knuckles, the tell-tale evidence of any car mechanic.

Solidly built and well preserved for his 58 years, Jozef, known as Joe to his Aussie mates, kept his white hair and mustache short and trim.

"Still working on it. It takes time."

"Don't know about this psychology stuff. Never had it in my day and most of us turned out okay. Today's generation is too soft. I believe in the old saying, 'A lotta workin' is better than a lotta talkin'. Get your clients busy doing things, then their problems will disappear."

I thought of the anorexic and her aerobic exercises. Pa wouldn't want to understand, even if I explained it. No one could disagree with him, especially if he was wrong.

"The harder you work, the less you have to think. Right ,Marysia?"

Slightly overweight with years of hardship and struggle etched in her wrinkled face, Ma nodded while dishing out the veggies. Gray-haired at 56, she worked tirelessly, never resting for a moment. Even when she found time to watch TV, she kept herself busy, knitting cardigans or crocheting doilies.

"More dumplings?" she asked as she scurried toward the stove.

Her days were a perpetual whirlwind–cooking and cleaning at home, in addition to the part-time money spinners of ironing baskets of clothes, working in the bakery early Saturday mornings, and keeping St. Vincent's church spotless. The word "relax" was not in her vocabulary. I remember catching her one day actually taking a break from the ironing. When she spotted me, she jumped off the couch, grabbed the iron, and heaved it back and forth in a mad frenzy.

She brought another pot to the table. "Piotr, more peas?"

"No thanks. I've had enough."

"There's a coupla spoonfuls left."

"I'm full."

"Are you sure?"

"Yea."

"We can't be wasting them," she persisted. "A growing boy can't have too many veggies."

"Oh, all right."

Heidi popped into my mind again. I wondered how she was faring.

"Who wants to present?" asked Dr. Fiona Crompton, a matronly figure with her red hair pulled back in a bun. Horn-rimmed glasses and a starched white blouse completed the stereotypic picture of an analyst.

Theresa edged forward in her chair. "I want to discuss Joshua Heap."

Our consultant nodded and brought her silver pen to her notebook. If she were taking attendance, she'd notice that Gerard and Leela were noticeably absent. Apparently, Smelder wanted to cancel these consultations because they were individually oriented. Only after intense pressure and lobbying from Theresa and Maxine did he agree to alternate these fortnightly consultations with the family therapy consultant, Dr. King.

"Surjit, Maxine, and Henry are fairly familiar with the case," said Theresa, "but to fill in Peter, this is a six-year-old boy, an only child, who originally presented as uncontrollable, uncooperative and oppositional."

In other words, a real brat.

"The father abandoned Joshua when he was born, and he was being reared by a mother who resented the responsibility. I have been seeing Joshua consistently three times a week. However, I'm concerned about the last session, our 122nd interview."

As the child psychologist elaborated her un-attempt at brief, problem focused therapy, I doodled in my notebook.

"Yesterday Joshua arrived in an agitated, angry state. He started throwing toys around the play room, then filled a dump truck with sand from the tray and poured it over the other toys. He threw the truck against the chair and stomped on the orange koala, his favorite stuffed animal."

Hell, when I was six, my messes had to be stacked, stored, or put in a box or else Ma would've chucked a tantrum. She couldn't stand untidy toys in the house. My wooden blocks spent most of their time stashed in a canvas sack.

"Joshua began drawing pictures on the wall with markers."

"What did he draw?" inquired the pensive Dr. Crompton, her silver pen poised for the crucial notation.

I myself wondered who was responsible for cleaning the wall.

"He drew lots of squiggles merging into one another like a huge ball of spaghetti. What do you make of it, Fiona?"

We waited in respectful silence while our consultant scrunched her brow, squinted her eyes, and tapped her top lip with her right forefinger.

"Probably symbolic of internal confusion."

I glanced at the zigzagging circular spirals on my paper and quickly turned the page.

"What happened next?"

"He picked up the mommy doll and threw it on the floor. I interpreted to Joshua that he seemed pretty angry. He answered back, 'I don't like you.'"

"How did that make you feel?"

"I was upset when he said that," lamented Theresa. "I've invested so much in the relationship. Whenever I get close, he feels vulnerable and pushes me away by attacking. His outbursts seemed more vicious during this last session."

"Persecutory anxiety," reflected the analyst. "Joshua is transferring those same persecutory feelings that he must've felt with his mother onto you, Theresa. Getting close to a mother figure must remind him of his parents' abandonment which then triggers his rage and rejection. He must be experiencing a greater sense of closeness with you and hence feels more vulnerable. He's anticipating your abandonment and is merely acting out his anxiety and anger."

"In our individual therapy I'm helping the boy's mother vent her rage toward her ex-husband," volunteered Maxine cheerfully.

Crompton was momentarily silent while she scribbled some notes. "We're moving into a critical stage. The inner rage is coming to the surface."

Theresa's eyes widened and became transfixed on her mentor. I noted that she fixed her hair in a bun today and wore a matching starched white blouse just like our consultant. Obviously two of the same feather.

"Please continue."

"I asked Joshua why he didn't like me. He said I didn't buy him nice toys."

I drew a cartoon of a kid getting banged on the head with a cricket bat. I sure as hell wouldn't give him any of my toys.

"I offered him another interpretation," added Theresa. "I said he might feel angry with me just like he feels with his mother when she doesn't give him what he wants. He then took a red pencil and poked it through the cardboard box which contained his toys. He kept watching for my reaction as he stabbed the box time and time again."

Fiona and Theresa both stroked their lower jaws and pondered through a long silence.

The analyst finally pronounced. "This is an extraordinarily rich segment. I'm sure you're all aware of the highly sexualized material."

Everyone nodded—except me.

"The destruction of the cardboard box represents the boy's feeling of omnipotence. He believes he has the power to destroy, and symbolically chose the red pencil to thrust into the source of his goodness."

Theresa tapped her top lip with her finger. "I wasn't sure whether to make an interpretation that Joshua was wanting to force his penis into a vagina."

"That would have been premature," offered Dr. Crompton.

I stopped fiddling with my pen and experienced a mental flash-back.

> *Six years old... I spent hours creating a makeshift wooden sword... Spray painted it metallic silver with a canister I stole from the garage... Loved that sword... Used an old towel as a cape and pretended I was one of the Three Musketeers... Thrusting into Ma's wicker basket... She hated it... Threw it in the junk heap... I rescued my trusty blade... Kept it in bed... Ma found it... Snapped it in half...*

"... at the end of the session, Joshua smashed the pencil with a karate blow."

Dr. Crompton jolted me from my stream of consciousness. "Fairly symbolic of castration anxiety."

I felt as if my psyche had been hit with a truncheon. My crossed legs automatically tightened. I quickly scanned the others to see if they had noticed. Thank God, Henry, Surjit, and Maxine were intently listening to Crompton's dialogue with Theresa. I closed my notebook. Didn't want anyone near my doodles.

"Therapy is progressing extremely well," continued Dr. Crompton. "Your work is to be highly commended."

Theresa beamed. "Thanks, Fiona. As usual, your insights have been exceptional."

"Will you be taking on individuals?"

I returned Dr. Crompton's gaze. "Who me?... I suppose."

"Peter's taken on an anorexic girl," mentioned Theresa helpfully.

"Good. You can present her to the group."

I stared in disbelief at my colleague. "Sure."

Dr. Crompton adjusted her spectacles. "You must observe and listen to the anorexic with a third ear. Try and understand what her behavior is telling you. External actions merely reflect the internal world. There is meaning within meaning."

My head bobbed in agreement while my mind pondered, what the hell was she meaning?

"As one beginning in the field of psychotherapy, you're not expected to fully decipher the deeper symbolism, as say our Theresa here."

Like a blushing schoolgirl, Theresa sent an admiring glance toward her teacher.

Crompton expounded further, "The major error of the novice is expecting too much too soon. Initially, I suggest that you merely observe your reactions during the interview, a necessary prerequisite to identify transference or counter-transference. Your anorexic client will redirect her unconscious feelings and desires toward you as the new object in her life and you, in turn, must become aware of your own projections onto her. Hence, developing an awareness of your feelings is paramount to good treatment."

When the conscientious analyst officiously closed her black notebook, indicating our 50 minutes had expired, I felt like a stunned mullet. The growing list of psychiatric terms and conflicting ideas pounded in my skull like resounding tom-toms. I left for an aspirin.

3:37 p.m. Interviewing room. I rehearsed the game plan for my first family interview with the Tortellis. All well and good for the analyst, Dr. Crompton, to caution against accomplishing too much too soon, but the directive from our family therapy consultant, Dr. Frank King, was telling me to produce a significant video-clip. The bloody one-eyed camera, positioned in the corner of the room, stared at me. Not wanting my facial expressions immortalized on the screen, I placed my chair with the back of my brown-checked sport coat facing the camera. I drew the curtains across the one-way mirror to insure there would be no spectators.

3:49 p.m. Studied the genogram once more. Angelo was referred by the family doctor for encopresis. The soiling problem appeared to be non-physical in nature. Guess that meant the psychological plumbing was at fault and the mental spigot needed to be reamed out. I thought of the time Pa opened the clogged drain in the back yard and hauled up raw sewage. Christ, did it stink! Just thinking about it made me nauseous. And my sensitive sniffer wasn't even activated.

3:56 p.m. Evaluated my strategy. The consulting analyst proclaimed, "Observe feelings. Look for your meaning within meaning." The family therapy consultant pronounced, "Explore the sequences–who does what, when, and where, with whom, and why." How I was going to remember all that was beyond me.

4:03 p.m. Phoned the secretary to check on the family. No sign of them. Couldn't be blamed for a "no show" when I haven't even interviewed them. There was an outside chance ol' one eye wouldn't have his turn today.

I surveyed the stark white interviewing room and its solitary poster of Disneyland. Five brown plaid chairs were arranged in a circular fashion. A full box of tissues rested on the gray coffee table. Hoped they wouldn't be needed.

4:16 p.m. Either Mrs. Tortelli didn't understand my English and got the time wrong, or her husband didn't want to come, or maybe the plumbing was miraculously plunged. I experienced a wave of relief. The family interview would be held another time. Hallelujah!

"Your family's arrived," boomed the intercom.

My euphoric mood popped like an overblown balloon. I sneered at the camera which seemed to almost smile at me. Summoning courage to get this over with, I took several deep, relaxing breaths then headed for the waiting room.

I spotted a short and stocky bald-headed man with baggy jowls. I decided against introducing myself as Dr. Pinowski. While lending more status, it still didn't sound right, and I definitely didn't feel like a doctor. Besides, clients would probably relate better on a first name basis.

"Hi. My name's Peter. You can call me Dr. Pinowski."

Dressed in gray trousers and a tan pullover shirt, he greeted me with an outstretched hand. "I'm Mario Tortelli," he said, and pointed to a stocky woman in a black and green dress. "The wife, Angela." Obviously she enjoyed her *fettucine alfredo*. On her plump face a few strands of black hair grew out of a mole just above her lip.

Mario introduced his 10-year-old daughter who was wearing a red and white striped school uniform. She looked like her father.

Mr. Tortelli continued, "My son, Angelo."

Who, on the other hand, took after his mother. His khaki shorts bulged with his flesh.

As we settled into the counseling room, I mentally rehearsed my plan: take it slow and easy; relax the family; begin with general information; there's plenty of time, don't rush into the problem.

I began with the 10-year-old. "What school do you go to, Maria?"

"St. Columbkilles," she answered politely.

"Sounds like a nice school. What grade?"

"Fourth."

"And what about you, Angelo?"

"Yes?"

"What school or grade are you in?"

"Second."

"Mr. Tortelli, what school, I mean, what kind of work do you do?"

"My wife and I own a *ristorante*. Our specialty is *lasagne al forno con salsiccia*."

Brought back memories of the university parties at the local pizzeria. A nip of Chianti right now wouldn't go astray.

"Been in Australia nine years," he added.

I nodded. Having dispensed with the preliminary chit-chat, I was ready to tackle the problem.

"Mrs. Tortelli, can you tell me why you're here?"

With a puzzled expression, she began to reply, "It's..."

"Sorry to interrupt," I blurted, realizing my mortal sin of omission. "But I forgot to mention, you're being video-taped. The camera's in the corner and this is the microphone hanging down from the ceiling. That'll be okay with you, won't it? It's really pretty unobtrusive. You'll hardly notice it."

I could have sworn the camera winked.

Desperate to help little Angelo, they would've agreed to anything. I was supposed to have them sign a release of information form guaranteeing confidentiality but decided to do that later. I was anxious to get on with it.

"So, can you tell me about Angelo's difficulty?"

"Signor dottore," pleaded Mrs.Tortelli. *"Mi può aiutare per favore?"*

"Sorry. I don't speak Italian."

She pointed to her son. "Angelo. Problems *l'intestino.* Every day. *La* home. *La scuola.* Sometimes no go coupla days. Happen again. I not know what to do. *Il dottore* tell me to see you. You fix Angelo."

Strewth! Don't tell me. "Ex-excuse me. I, uh, forgot to turn on the video camera."

I ran out of the room, started the equipment, and rushed back to the family. "So how long have you been having your problem?"

Mrs. Tortelli turned to her husband. *"Di che cosa parla?"*

He shrugged his shoulders. *"Non lo so."*

"Ex-excuse me, but could you speak English?"

Mrs. Tortelli waved her arms. "What you say?"

"Uh... How long has Angelo had problems?"

"Since bambino."

"It says in the file that you've had him checked out physically?"

She shook her head. "No."

"No?"

"Yes. No medical problem. *Il dottore* say," and she tapped on her head, "it's his mind."

"Well, what kind of help do you want from us?" I inadvertently used the plural but was thankful for the mistake. I sure as hell didn't want full responsibility for stopping this kid from shitting.

She jabbed her finger at me. *"Signor Dottore.* Fix *l'intestino.* Make him normal."

Sure I thought, easy as making mud pies in the Gibson desert.

The father turned his chair and gazed out the window. Bloody hell! That would look dreadful on the video replay. Dr. King would crucify me for not involving the father.

"Mr. Tortelli, do you have the same problem with Angelo as your wife?"

"I don't know what's wrong with my boy."

At least his English was better than his wife's.

"He says he can't control himself. When he's at home or school, out it comes. He's embarrassed and kids make fun of him. I tell him, 'Angelo. Watch your bottom. No one likes a smelly boy.' "

"Have you tried anything to get him to stop?"

"I said I'd give him a new bike if he stops. No good. I yell at him. No good. My wife, she asks him all the time if he has to go to the toilet. He says 'no'. Then, a little later, out it comes. He makes the wife sick. She went to the hospital for an operation."

"Sorry to hear that," I sympathized. "What was the operation for?"

"Hemorrhoids."

The thought of Frank King, a real pain in the ass, suddenly popped into my mind. Damn! I still wasn't filming any sequences. I couldn't show this segment either.

Tried pulling myself together: there's plenty of time; take it easy; be calm; relax; just investigate around the problem.

I turned to Angelo. "What does your father do when you... well... take a shit?"

"Hey!" interrupted Mr. Tortelli. "We don't use that type of language with the children!"

"Sorry. I didn't know." I reached for a tissue to mop the stream of perspiration from my forehead, grateful that my back was facing the camera.

"What do you call it when you, uh... have to do a number two?"

The father threw his hands in the air. "We call it 'poodle'."

My deductive reasoning concluded that a number one must be a piddle.

I asked the son, "How do you feel about doing a poodle in your pants?"

He shrugged, "Don't like it."

I could well imagine! "Do you feel embarrassed about it?"

He nodded.

"What do you do when you're embarrassed?"

The eight-year-old squirmed in his tight khaki shorts.

Mrs. Tortelli chimed in. *"Mio figlio.* He tell me. The children at *la scuola* call him names."

I asked Angelo, "What do they call you?"

"Tortesmelli."

"I tell Angelo," joined the father. "The teachers should stop that. They should punish those children."

"Do you have any friends at school?" I asked.

"A few."

"Scusi," interrupted the mother. "No boys ask him to play. I say, 'Angelo, meet some nice boys.'"

Having a hard enough time getting the sequences, let alone talking with Angelo, I asked. "Do you want to make more friends?"

"Guess so."

"Would you like to stop poodling in your pants?"

"Yea."

"What could you do to stop?"

He shrugged, "Just try harder."

"Mio figlio," bellowed Mrs. Tortelli gesticulating with her hands. "He always say, he try harder. Maybe one, maybe two days pass. Clean pants. Then, it comes again. Hard for me to work at *ristorante* and clean pants. Sometimes, I find them under bed. He hides them. His bedroom smell, oh, so bad. I get very upset."

I was upset too, with all the interruptions. Not getting very far with Angelo, I focused on the mother. "What do you do when you're upset?"

She waved her arms frantically in the air. "I yell at my boy. I tell him all the time, 'Angelo. Go to *il gabinetto.'"*

"Who is gabi netto?"

"Same as *la toeletta,"* screamed Mrs. Tortelli.

"The toilet?"

She nodded her head wildly. *"Si!"*

I could only imagine how inept I looked on video. Desperate to tape some noteworthy segment, I asked, "How does your husband help?"

Mrs. Tortelli gestured accusingly at her husband. "He's at *il ristorante.* When he comes home, he ask, 'How's Angelo?' Sometimes I tell him. Sometime no." She pointed to her husband's head. *"Mio sposo* get crazy in *la testa.* He yell at me, 'Do something.' I go to *il dottore.* He tell me. Come here. You fix Angelo."

I wished to Christ she'd quit dumping on me. I threw it back to Angelo.

"Can you tella when you musta go to the toileta?" Strewth! I was speaking Italian.

"Sometimes I do. Sometimes I forget and the poodle sneaks out."

"When do you empty your pants?"

"If I'm at school, I try and wait till I get home."

I'd hate to be one of his classmates. "Who washes your clothes?"

"I wash!" voiced the exasperated mother. "I tell Angelo. Empty poodle. Put it in bucket. Sometimes, he wash pants with poodle in la machine. Bad for la machine."

Could just imagine. I wondered about their brand of detergent as my sniffer detected something foul.

"Dio cane!" swore the enraged father. "Angelo! What did you just do?" He smacked his son on the back of the head.

Angelo blushed deep red. Christ! You'd think he could've held it till he got home. Phew! My nose caught a whiff of the putrid odor. The room reeked. I felt nauseous. Woozy. Had to act fast.

"I think, uh, maybe we should end the interview."

I needed an urgent consultation with or without my video clip. In the meantime, I could put the family off another week and give them a task, something which would make them feel like they're taking positive action.

"I want you to keep a behavioral chart. Make a list of the days in the week and place a check every time he shits, I mean, poodles at home and school. Bring the chart when I see you next week. It will give us a baseline."

Mrs. Tortelli frowned. *"Scusi!* What you say?"

I struggled to make her understand. "Write down how many times each day Angelo poodles in his pants."

She shrieked hysterically, "Already, we know!"

"Yes. Well, I need the chart to check if we're making progress. I can show it to our consultant and give you his, that is, our advice."

The stench became worse. I was close to passing out. I rose from the chair. "Thanks for coming. I'll see all of you a week from tomorrow at four o'clock."

The mother stood up and gestured toward Maria. "You don't need *mia figlia* no more!"

Damn. I should've spent more time talking to the daughter. Dr. King stipulated that all members in the household attend.

"I need her one more time," I pleaded. "There's still a few more questions."

Mrs. Tortelli swept her hand past me while shouting at her husband, *"È un vigliacco!"*

Whatever she said, it didn't sound nice. She angrily pushed Angelo out of the room while Mario and Maria followed.

I opened the windows and allowed the putrid air to escape. The fresh air brought an overwhelming sense of relief that my first family interview was over. Yet there was also an increased burden. Felt sorry for the little boy and guilty about not being able to help. Didn't know what the hell to do. Then I realized that the next family therapy consultation was scheduled a week from today. The tom-toms in my head began thumping once more. I went for another aspirin.

THE WOMEN IN MY LIFE

FRIDAY, JANUARY 21

I spent all week watching for that mysterious Egyptian goddess on the 8:05. Even got off at Redfern Station where she was last spotted scaling the steps. I watched several trains unload. No sign of her.

At the end of the day, Theresa crept into my office and closed the door. "Maxine and I are heading for the pub. Care to join us for a drink?"

"Love to," I lied. "But I'm going out this evening and have to leave straight away."

I dared not be late for my six o'clock appointment.

She sighed, "What a pity."

I started packing my briefcase.

"Do you swim?"

"A little, why?"

She looked at me, her eyes sparkling. "I thought you might join me for a lunchtime swim in the hospital pool, a great way to keep fit and counteract stress."

"I'm more of a dash and splash type."

"I don't mind. We can arrange something next week."

"Yea... sure." I checked my watch. "Hey! Better run. I'll miss my appointment, er, engagement."

As I left the department, the jagged edge of gray clouds merged into darker more ominous ones. A southerly bluster was moving in fast. The dramatic drop in temperature signaled that a downpour was only minutes away. I ran for the station. Too late. It began pissing buckets. Left the damn brolly at home! I shouldn't have refused when Ma yelled, "Take the umbrella!"

The torrential gauntlet saturated my clothes right through to my underwear. While the rain was a welcome sight to relieve the drought plaguing Australia, I wished it could have chosen another time. At least my leather briefcase provided a dry sanctuary for my uneaten sandwich and wallet.

The train was steamy. Small puddles collected around the vinyl seat and dripped onto the sopping floor. A few weary travelers elected to stand in the aisle rather than occupy the other half of my seat. Not that I could blame them.

I disembarked at Central Station and queued for a taxi. While the Counseling Department at Sydney University remained in walking distance, I wasn't prepared to brave another deluge. Neither were the others waiting in the long line.

6:34 p.m. Late for my six o'clock appointment, I fell on the slippery stairs leading to Melody Mill's office. My briefcase snapped open and dumped the sandwich and wallet on the steps. I hurriedly repacked and limped to her room.

Thank God her door was open!

I entered her office and was greeted by concerned words. "I thought you weren't going to make it."

"I'm sorry I'm late. It wasn't my fault. First I got drenched, then I had to wait 45 minutes for the damn taxi. The bloody driver! Almost refused to take me because I wasn't traveling very far..."

"Calm down, Peter," crooned Melody.

My body immediately relaxed in response to her soft, hypnotic voice. The scent of apricot potpourri and the the sight of Melody's full breasts brought back that familiar feeling of being nurtured, cared for. I leaned back into plush cushions and forgot about the puddle on her carpet and my wet bottom soaking the settee. I looked once more at the yellow-winged honeyeater stuffing the gaping mouths of her young brood.

"How's your new job?"

"It's been tough, but I'm slowly settling in."

"I'm very proud of you, Peter. Very, very proud."

Those affirming words, like a psychic healing balm, touched my soul. My eyes watered. I could only sputter, "Thank you, Melody, for all you've done."

She smiled. "I can count you as one of my major successes."

The glow around my body could've easily dried my wet clothes. "I owe it all to you. I've even followed your advice. I've been keeping a journal."

"Wonderful!" She clapped her hands. "Now that *is* progress!"

My beaming moved to high intensity.

"Your continued improvement makes our terminating all that much easier. I thought you might act out your resistance to ending treatment. I've been proven wrong."

I shuffled my feet on the wet carpet. "Well. I did want to talk to you about that. I still don't feel I'm ready. I need more time, lots of time. I'm starting to feel anxious again..."

"Peter, you know we have to end."

"I... I know but I'm really not ready."

She leaned forward in her settee. "Our final session will take place one month from today. You cannot keep resisting that fact."

"But Melody," I protested. "I'm sure to have another panic attack!"

"We've already gone over this. You have the names of private therapists."

"Just a few more sessions?"

She shook her head. "Our last appointment is a month from today."

One month was an eternity! I couldn't bear to give up my Melody. I felt a dead, sickening thud in my heart. A lonely tear dropped on the carpet. "Please?"

She emphatically shook her head and remained resolute. Despite my half-hearted attempts to reason with her, I knew deep down it was over.

I limped out of the abbreviated session dejected and depressed. Outside, a fine drizzle trickled down my face. Thought she'd at least see me for a full 50 minutes. Wasn't my fault I was late. Goddamn rain! There was supposed to be a drought. How would she like it if I abbreviated our final interview and just walked out after 30 minutes. That'd show her. Or not even turn up. Give her a taste of her own medicine! She'd surely miss me. She even said I was one of her major successes. If I didn't show up, she'd wonder where her major success was, how I was doing.

As I plodded past puddles toward Central Station, my anxiety swelled with the growing realization that I'd have to make it on my own. Would my fears return and ravage my mind? Could I survive without Melody's guiding light? I had no other choice. I had to survive—without her. Thank God I had a roof over my head and a job. Yea... after all, I did find a job and I had made some new friends. Theresa Ramadopoulos and her swimming invitation popped into mind. Maybe it was time to let go of Melody and start swimming on my own. Buoyed by the thought of Theresa, I felt warmth return to my chest. It was time to buy some new swim gear. Like an old Gene Kelly movie, I began whistling in the rain.

"Piotr, I told you to take the umbrella!" pierced Ma's strident voice. "Get those wet clothes off before you catch a cold. There's hot ox tail soup on the stove..."

EL BORO SNORO

SATURDAY, JANUARY 22

The hot sun evaporated any moisture from the previous day's downpour. The water level in the dams remained unaffected by the brief interlude with rain. Despite the drought, Ma was hosing the leaves off the driveway.

"Easy on the water!" I yelled.

Her response was to hand me rags and Windex to clean all the windows. Afterwards, she brought out the set of china used at Christmas and Easter. She decided they were dusty and in need of a wash. No wonder Pa ferreted himself away in the garage fixing cars. I tried avoiding Ma's endless list of chores by escaping to my bedroom to tap my thoughts on the computer. Even then I had no peace. Blackie kept pestering me for a run. Eventually let him loose in the back yard.

"Watch your dog!" she cried. "I won't allow dirt into my clean house!"

11:00 a.m. Management meeting. Gerard's room. Maxine officiously passed out an agenda.

Sporting a crimson blouse, Theresa sat opposite me. I flashed a smile. She returned a broad grin. Long, curly black hair crowned a finely chiseled face with dark eyebrows etched in olive skin. For a woman in her 30s, her body was in perfect shape. I never before realized how pretty she was. As a matter of fact, she was downright attractive.

Surjit nudged my arm and winked. He must've caught us exchanging glances. Thank God no one else had noticed. Holy Henry's bobbing eyes were busy focusing on the agenda while Gerard fluttered like an old rooster around Leela, dressed in yet another new outfit, this one a jacaranda blue suit. It was beyond me how she could support such an expensive habit on a social worker's wages.

"We should begin with the kitchen," preempted the burly Maxine Benton who tried to assume command.

"Now you hold on, Maxine," interrupted Gerard. "I have an important memo from the Chief Executive Officer. We're trying to promote the hospital as a community of caring professionals. Therefore, during the next few weeks we're being asked to wear these buttons." He passed out white buttons with red letters announcing, "A Community of Caring."

As I attached the promotional badge of honor, I looked across at Theresa. Our eyes met once more. Her luscious red lips widened.

"Are you finished, Gerard?"

"What is it now, Maxine?"

"I'm tired of raising this topic, but the kitchen clean-up has deteriorated. You'd think we were a bunch of slobs. Without naming names, you men are the worst offenders, expecting the women to wash your dirty dishes."

Sheepishly, I lowered my head. My coffee mug was still in the sink.

"A few dishes hardly seem worth the fuss," said Gerard who made little attempt to hide his disdain.

"It's a gender issue," shot Maxine. "Women are expected to perform kitchen duties, even while at work. That's blatant sexism. I won't be part of it."

"I don't believe in that rubbish, but what do you suggest?"

"I propose a roster. Each of us should be assigned one week to tidy the kitchen. That means clearing the counters, washing the dishes, and throwing out any spoiled food from the refrigerator. This morning I discovered a moldy half-eaten apple. Disgusting!"

I had intended on finishing it following last week's Tortelli interview, but after little Angelo, my appetite never returned.

"It's about time you men took responsibility for the kitchen," demanded Maxine. "One of you can make the roster."

Gerard gazed first at Surjit, then Henry, and finally at me. "Peter, you can volunteer and plan a roster."

I was unanimously proclaimed organizer of the Kitchen Klub. Ma would be proud.

"Let's move onto something really important," beamed Gerard. "Our Leela will now report on the research project."

Leela Hennessey swished her blonde hair out of her face. "After exploring a number of methods to evaluate our clients, Gerard and I favor 'The Family Behavioral Scale' produced by Dr. Rudy James. It consists of 60 statements that a family has to answer, either true or false. The questionnaire will help us evaluate family relationships. I'll pass these examples around."

I scanned the first question. "Dishes are done immediately after eating." Our staff/family definitely scored a false.

"I don't know why the hell we're doing this," objected Maxine. She refused to accept a questionnaire.

"Because we're supposed to be an academic unit," countered our flustered leader. "How else can we prove the validity of what we're doing? Publishing research will insure additional funding."

"Research is a load of bulldust," huffed Maxine. "Before you arrived, Gerard, we tried implementing another behavioral checklist. We copped heaps of flack. I remember one confused mother, when confronted with the silly question, 'Does your son frequently play with his penis?' asked, 'How much is frequently?'"

"For Christ sake," pouted Gerard. "Couldn't you agree, just for once?"

For statement number eight, "We cooperate with each other," we'd score another false.

"What do you hope to achieve?" challenged Maxine.

Gerard patted Leela's shoulder. "Can you satisfy Nurse Benton's question?"

The attractive social worker took her cue. "This scale will help us collect valuable data on the level of cohesion and conflict."

"At least another person around here is committed to research," exclaimed Dr. Smelder. "What do you others think?"

"I see myself as a clinician," responded Theresa, "not a researcher. I don't want my clients subjected to a barrage of forms which merely add to their feelings of depersonalization."

Her soft moist mouth mesmerized me. "What about you, Peter?" she asked.

"Huh?"

"Yes, what's your opinion?" queried Gerard.

I stared at our director, then at my Theresa. "Well... uh... I'm not sure."

Surjit rescued me from my quandary. "Will it help us evaluate the therapist's effectiveness?"

Dr. Smelder frowned. "Possibly, later on. Right now our primary goal is to collect data about our clients."

When Henry raised his hand, Gerard spurned him with a wave. "I don't think any further discussion is necessary. We'll administer the questionnaire next month. Now, where are we on the agenda?"

So much for the last item on the questionnaire. "Each member has an equal say in family decisions."

During the rest of the meeting our commander, with his badge promoting "A Community of Caring" prominently displayed on his lapel, informed us of the following: daily logs were to be instituted to determine how we spent our time; secretarial help was no longer available to type assessments into the computer; and theoretical papers discussed at the Journal Club must be read before, not during, the meeting.

When we were dismissed, Theresa and I grumbled to one another about the extra work resulting from typing our own assessments and maintaining daily logs of all our activities.

"That Gerard makes my blood boil," she fumed. "He acts as if the rest of us have nothing important to say."

"I wonder what he's planning to do with the time sheets."

"I don't know, but I'm sure it's meant to spell trouble. We'll have to make sure to look after our backs."

"Yours looks pretty good to me," I joked.

She flashed a sensuous smile. "They're forecasting hot weather over the next couple of days. Still interested in a swim?"

"Definitely."

"How about Friday during lunch?"

"I'll put it on the calendar."

Her eyes twinkled. "Don't forget your swim gear."

My new apple-green Speedos were already packed in my briefcase.

A DAY OF CRISES

TUESDAY, JANUARY 25

Today confirmed Murphy's Law: "If anything could possibly go wrong, it will." Our ex-Prime Minister, Malcolm Fraser, was probably right when he said, "Life wasn't meant to be easy!"

Around the reception area, there was a hive of activity. Wearing a flashy yellow-and-black outfit with yellow pumps, Leela was chattering to Surjit. "The sight was amazing!" she exclaimed. "Last night that huge 14-year-old girl was admitted on the pediatric ward, paralyzed from the neck down. Couldn't move a muscle. The doctors, more interested in organizing x-rays and tests, should've recognized a classic hysterical conversion disorder. This morning they found her lying spread eagle in her hospital gown near the sprinkler outside the ward. It took four nurses to haul her stiff body onto the trolley. Gerard is presently consulting with the pediatrician." With an air of authority she added, "I assume Gerard and I will conduct the family sessions."

Leela Hennessey and her glossy veneer were getting up my nose. I was sure to hear countless stories about her and Smelder's therapeutic acrobatics.

"There's also a crisis on the Karen Horney Unit," divulged Surjit.

"The adult psychiatric ward?" I asked.

He nodded. "Jules Eaglesham was recently admitted into Riverwood Psychiatric Hospital from an overdose on Tryptonal. Despite several breakdowns during the past three years from manic depressive episodes, he refused to step down from the unit as psychiatrist-in-charge. Apparently hospital administration wished to avoid a public scandal and decided to do nothing." He tapped his button. "So much for our commitment to 'A Community of Caring.' Jules, however, may have overstepped the bounds this time. Before his overdose, he was frenetically organizing a one-day conference entitled, 'Suicide, the Australian Experience'."

I plucked the pink brochure off the bulletin board. "Says that his keynote address is 'To be or not to be, the existential question.' "

"He had scheduled other well-known psychiatrists," added Surjit, "to present a variety of related topics. Unfortunately, he neglected to ask them. His department discovered that people were registering for a non-existent conference. No one knows for sure, but the ensuing investigation may have flipped Jules from his manic phase into a deep depression. His reply was a bottle of Tryptonal."

I tore up the brochure. "Eaglesham sounds like a sandwich short of a picnic."

I left the excitement behind and entered the toilet. When I opened the door, I spotted a mother combing her daughter's hair in front of the mirror. The little girl took one look at me and froze in total horror. She let out a blood-curdling shriek. Panicking, I raised my hands to reassure her, but she screamed again. I staggered backwards blindly and bumped my head on the bloody door. Stupid kid!

Maxine eventually rushed to my aid and consoled the child who, I found out later, had just finished her session. As her therapist, Maxine claimed the girl over-reacted because she had recently been sexually molested in a public latrine. She should've been warned about our unisex loo!

10:06 a.m. Conference room. Family therapy consultation.

Waiting for our expert advisor on treating families, I anxiously scanned the Tortelli file. I desperately needed help for little Angelo. Remembering Henry's appalling experience at our last consultation, I had painstakingly selected a short video segment and had re-written all my notes, now neatly organized on my lap.

"Peter, you're leaking!" cried Theresa.

"What?"

"Your coffee!"

Strewth! My styrofoam cup was trickling coffee through a small hole in the bottom. My notes. Ruined! I grabbed the Kleenex and sopped up the soggy mess. That's what I get for using styrofoam cups to avoid washing mugs.

Considering how the morning was progressing, I thought of another old Polish saying, "After every disaster, anticipate another!"

Our highly paid consultant, Dr. Frank King, finally arrived, late as usual, still dressed in his familiar black shirt and pants.

"We have an emergency on the pediatric ward," launched Leela. "A 14-year-old hysterical conversion disorder."

Frank King's face ignited. "Sounds fascinating! These extraordinary cases provide great material for journal articles."

My soiler needed priority over Leela's converted hysteric. I mustered my courage, knowing that the agony of his criticism would be worth a few good suggestions about handling the Tortellis. "Excuse me, Dr. King, but... I'd like to... well, present my family. I have an eight-year-old encopretic."

Smelder interjected. "Your client's not as urgent as this 14-year-old. At stake is our relationship with the staff on the pediatric ward. They are skeptical about psychiatry. A successful handling of this case will turn the head of pediatrics to our systemic way of thinking."

"Yes, but I need help!"

"I'm sure your case can wait till next time," advised Dr. King.

All well and good for him to say. It wasn't his soiling kid that needed immediate attention. The next consultation was a fortnight away!

Gerard handed Leela the marker. "Can you draw the genogram? Your writing is prettier than mine."

As she sauntered toward the whiteboard, I tuned out. Didn't want to know why or how the hysterical client was converting her bloody emotional problems into bodily complaints. I just wanted to fix Angelo.

While the consultation dragged on, I thought about my appointment with the Tortellis tomorrow. I had promised them a plan. They were depending on me. Canceling their interview wouldn't be very professional, and besides, it would show on the daily log.

"There's an urgent phone call for Surjit," sounded the intercom.

Suddenly I remembered our table tennis engagement over lunch. Surjit and I could bat around a few ideas.

Staff amenities building. Wouldn't you know it, the ball that I brought had a crack. Instead of a crisp ping off the table we played with a dull pong.

My Indian mate plunked the ball over the net. "That phone call was from administration. With Dr. Eaglesham away, the Karen Horney Unit is short-staffed. They've transferred me."

"You're leaving?! When?"

"Next week."

My service crashed into the net. "Next week!"

"They wanted me to start tomorrow. After pleading for the welfare of my clients, I convinced them to postpone my transfer till Monday."

"That was considerate of them. What'll happen to your position here?"

"Apparently they're sending a less experienced psychiatric intern from Drug and Alcohol, Earl Jacobi."

"Why didn't they send him to the adult psychiatric unit?"

"Since I've already completed my placement in adult psychiatry, administration thinks I'm the best person to fill in. In reality, they're employing the domino principle. Reshuffle everyone, create enough confusion, and no one will remember the real crisis. They'll replace Earl with someone from Geriatrics, someone from Geriatrics with an intern from the Crisis Team, and so on and so forth. Don't forget, this is the public service."

Blow the public service, I was upset about losing my mate. "How long will you be gone?"

He batted the ball. "Could be several months. Depends when Jules Eaglesham returns."

"That guy's crazy! Surely they won't send him back."

"Who knows?" shrugged Surjit. "There'll probably be a board of inquiry but since Jules hasn't hurt any patient, there's a good possibility he'll return and head the unit. That is, after some rest and recuperation and a regular dose of lithium. Until then, it looks as if I'll be treating adult patients rather than children and adolescents."

I slammed his top spin and hit him in the head.

"Aren't you pissed off?"

"I'll be sad to leave the department, but everything that happens has a purpose."

"What's that supposed to mean?"

With a backhand slice, he sent the white sphere spinning. "I suppose it's destiny that I return back to adult psychiatry. I must have further lessons to learn there."

My shot careened off the table. "What about here? I need to learn heaps, and now you're leaving."

"We can still meet, in between your swims with Theresa."

"How the hell did you know?"

He winked.

I wanted to ask if anyone else suspected, but my anxiety about the Tortellis resurfaced. And we didn't have much time.

"I need some advice."

"About what?"

While the crack in the ball became more pronounced, I explained last week's interview.

"So you want to know the best way to help Angelo and his family?" he reiterated.

"Of course!"

"You may not like my advice."

"I'm desperate. I'm open to any suggestions."

He served a dazzling curve. "Why don't you try being honest with the family? Tell them you don't have the answers, but you'll work with them and find a solution."

I slapped the ball into the net. "I can't say that! They expect answers."

"There are some benefits of not knowing."

"What are you talking about? I didn't know whether to act as an analyst or a family therapist, and I could hardly understand what the mother was saying! There weren't any benefits from not knowing."

"If you allow yourself the freedom to play the detective, you might discover with the Tortellis what it means to have a child that soils. The answers will eventually come from them, not from books or from me. 'Not knowing' can help you and the family find a creative solution."

"What about Smelder and Dr. King? They'd surely prescribe a therapeutic intervention."

"Techniques can deprive a family the right of discovery."

I slammed the white disc with a forearm smash, breaking the ball in half. "Not only do I not understand you, but there goes our game."

"Can we ever truly decide what is in our clients' best interests?"

"I would hope so. Otherwise I've wasted all those years getting my Ph.D."

Surjit placed the paddle on the table and approached me. "There is a phrase in the Bhagavad Gita, 'All actions take place in time by the interweaving of the forces of nature, but the man lost in selfish delusion thinks that he himself is the actor.' "

"So?"

"Therapists believe that the power to change other people rests with them." He threw his hands in the air like a magician releasing doves. "All an illusion. If clients improve as a result of therapy, it only means they were ready for change. Therapists maintain the delusion that they alone are responsible for solving the problems."

"What are you talking about?"

Surjit picked up the two pieces of the ping-pong ball. "When you smashed this ball, were you the cause of it breaking in half?"

"Of course."

"But it was cracked before we arrived."

"So?"

"The ball had experienced countless whacks over several days, perhaps even weeks, steadily losing its resiliency. Eventually one particular smash created a fracture. Yet even with the crack, the ball didn't shatter. That required further hours of play until it reached a critical threshold where it could no longer remain a unified whole. Your last slam broke it in half, the result, not of one whack, but of hundreds of whacks and bounces."

"So what does all this have to do with my client?"

Surjit flashed his ivory teeth. "Everything and nothing."

"That says a lot!"

"We are all evolving and changing, experiencing the bumps and bounces of life. The therapist only provides one last whack to complete a transformation that has been occurring well before the client ever thought of obtaining help. Lives do not change as the result of one therapeutic encounter. Like the ping-pong ball, a crisis that splits a life wide open has been evolving over a considerable period of time, perhaps generations."

This was getting heavy. All I wanted was a few techniques to hold me over in tomorrow's interview. "What would you do if you were treating the Tortellis?"

He raised his eyebrows and shrugged. "I don't know."

"What do you mean, you don't know? You'd have to do something!"

"If they were my clients, I would ask myself two questions: Why are they coming to see me at this point in time? What could I learn from them?"

I flung my paddle on the table. "They're not coming to teach me! They need guidance!"

"The solutions we offer clients are merely the answers we seek for our own questions. Through them we discover ourselves."

"That's ridiculous!"

He remained calm. "In India I was taught to see harmony in all things. If the planets and stars interact in patterns, just like protons, electrons and neutrons, surely a client and therapist are governed by the same forces. Each acts interdependently and assists in one another's evolution. Therefore, you and the Tortellis have, like magnets, mutually attracted each other.

I returned his mystical logic with a verbal smash. "That sounds like a load of rubbish. I didn't mystically choose my clients. They were assigned to me."

"Let me explain. In Hindu there is a word called 'Maya,' which means we believe there is an external reality apart from us. In actuality, what we perceive on the outside merely reflects our inner thoughts. If we believe our lives are filled with purpose and joy, that is what we will experience. If we think life is a struggle and fraught with hardship, that is what we will create."

"Are you telling me that today is just a figment of my imagination?"

"We are, in effect, participating with this cracked ping-pong ball. Depending on our beliefs, it can be a symbol of catastrophe or a new beginning. The choice is ours."

I grabbed the two halves of what was once a white sphere and threw them in the garbage. "I'd prefer another ball."

"When we are spellbound by Maya and believe we are separate from the rest of the world, we must then attract life experiences to help us achieve a new level of understanding. All events, no matter how wonderful or dreadful, help us to develop a richer inner world. Of course, the impact of our past lives continues to be instrumental in facilitating our evolution."

"Don't tell me you believe in reincarnation?"

Surjit twirled the edges of his black mustache. "Belief in past lives is another way of viewing the world. I believe we are often reincarnated back with the same souls to re-work past issues. A father who mistreated his child in a previous life may need to return as an abused child. I suspect that therapists have had past lives with their clients."

"Sure. I gave the Tortellis a rough time in another life, and now it was their time to give me the shits."

Surjit chuckled. "Some take reincarnation too seriously and become obsessed with the past. It's merely one way to understand the world. I always reserve the right to change my beliefs."

"How can you say that?" I asked angrily. "If you believe something, then it's true."

"Truth is only relative," he answered. "At one time deranged individuals were considered possessed by the devil, a view that now seems barbaric. Today, medication is offered as the alternative cure for the mentally ill. That idea may, in the future, become antiquated. With new information, our perception of the universe is continually altered."

I wasn't sure what to think anymore and, to make matters worse, I wasn't any wiser about handling the Tortellis. "What should I do with my family?"

Surjit's brown eyes twinkled. "Learn from them and discover yourself in the process. You've already learned what it means to feel helpless, just like the family. They're desperately wanting answers, just like you. You are now joined together in this human life drama, each with important roles to play. Become a compassionate detective. But remember: savor each moment. If you rush through a game of table tennis, you can't enjoy the experience—the frustration of missed points or the exhilaration of spectacular returns. The playing is far more important than the final score."

All well and good when you're ahead on points. He departed for a meeting; I left without a ball.

As I wandered back, I became increasingly anxious. I definitely needed a second opinion.

Henry passed in the hallway, and I quickly abandoned hope of receiving his help. Had a hard enough time coping with Surjit's strange ideas. Holy Henry would probably quote some chapter and verse from the Bible like "A voice that cries in the wilderness: make a straight way for the Lord."

Desperate for something concrete, I stumbled into Dr. Smelder's room.

"Excuse me, but could I, well, talk about a case?"

He busily shuffled the files on his desk. "Make it quick. I only have a few minutes."

I explained Angelo's problem yet again.

Smelder peered over his glasses. "I'll have to watch their interactions from behind the one-way mirror."

I panicked, mumbling, "That's okay. I don't want to inconvenience you."

"It should be fun," said Gerard with a mischievous glint in his eye. "Leela can join me."

I gasped. With the dynamic duo watching us, Angelo and I would be shitting bricks.

"When do you see them next?"

"Tomorrow. Four o'clock."

He scanned his open diary. "Can't make it. You'll have to see them on your own."

I breathed a sigh of relief–until he flipped to another page. "Arrange their following appointment for two weeks from Thursday, three o'clock."

"I might have trouble getting them in at that time. The children finish school around three."

"Nonsense. Instruct the parents to remove the children early."

"Are you ready?" asked the perfumed Leela as she barged into Gerard's office.

"If you'll excuse us, Pinowski, Leela and I have an important meeting. Oh, by the way, I'm unable to attend the next clinical computer committee. I'd like you to act as the departmental representative. You don't have to say anything. The meeting's usually very boring and not all that relevant. Just write a memo for my records."

"When is it?"

"Friday. Lunch time."

"Uh... sure." Couldn't really tell him about the pre-arranged poolside date with Theresa, now could I?

I left his office in a dreadful state–with a canceled swim, a delegated non-event, and a future peepshow behind the one-way mirror. And still no strategy for tomorrow's Tortelli interview.

Later that afternoon, Violet Struthers caught me making tea in the staff room.

"Hello, Potter."

"It's Peter, Violet."

"How silly of me. I could never remember those funny sounding foreign names."

With her 30 plus years in psychiatry having taken their toll, Violet seemed as absent-minded as ever. Her misplaced brown wig once again revealed strands of gray hair arching over her right ear.

"Why, just this moment I talked with my son. He's a cardiologist, you know. Must check with him daily. Ever since his father died several years ago, a nasty heart attack, he needs my reassurance. I visit him frequently and counsel him through his depression and loneliness."

"He lives alone?"

"Heaven's no. He has a lovely wife and two beautiful children. But I can tell, he misses Father. Not that they spent much time together. Father wasn't much of a talker. His presence was what counted. Yesterday Father was sitting in his special chair, watching the cricket on the telly. I told him..."

I still wasn't sure how she spent her one-and-a-half days at the department. Talking to her son couldn't occupy all her time.

"Excuse me, Violet. I have some phone calls..."

"Wait. There was something I wanted to tell you." The elderly woman in the orchid floral print scratched her head, tilting the wig further. "What was it?... Oh yes... that soiling child everyone's been talking about."

"Everyone?"

"No, I don't see many of them. But there was this psychologist. She had a colleague who visited Adelaide to learn this technique for encopretics. The therapist was very successful."

"Which therapist?"

"Why the one who taught the course, silly. I was waiting to use this new method myself."

I wondered whether Violet suffered from mental incontinence.

"Potter, I want you to try it."

"What?"

"Let me think."

Her furrowed brow suggested the mental screen was on perpetual horizontal hold. "It was something about externalizing the problem."

"Little Angelo has no problem there. Besides, those phone calls are waiting."

"Wait! It's coming. I remember! Tell Angelo, he's in a race against... what shall we call it?... Frisky Feces."

"Huh?"

"Angelo must practice running to the toilet before Frisky Feces could flop out."

Her body heaved with excitement. "Yes! I have it! Angelo must pretend he's in a basketball competition. Award one basket to Frisky if it comes in his pants. Award another basket to Angelo for dunking Feces into the toilet. The competition would be fun."

She clapped her hands. "How exciting! Reward him with a jelly bean every time he scores... Why, when I was younger, Father took me to the cricket games. We cheered every time the wickets fell. Don Bradman in the crease..."

Never did hear the end of the story. I managed to slip out before the end of the first innings.

AUSTRALIA DAY

WEDNESDAY, JANUARY 26

Interviewing Tortellis in a hot, sweaty cubicle. Angelo, lobbing jumbo blueberries. Through a basketball hoop. Crazy Violet cheers. Tosses her wig. A huge eye peers through window. It's Dr. Smelder, sweating, laughing. I flee into cemetery. Murky and foggy. Frightened, trembling, I spot movement. Behind the stone obelisk, a hand. Surjit's pointing at gravestones. I shudder.

20th Century Tortellis	Alawa Aboriginal Tribe
FATHER Mario MOTHER Angela DAUGHTER Maria SON Angelo PSYCHOTHERAPIST Peter	ELDER Wadjiri-Wadjiri WIFE Nambidjimba BROTHER Wuyaindjimadjinji SISTER Gudjiwa MEDICINE MAN Weari-Wyingga

My name, inscribed on graves. Greek names, Chinese. Playing roles—grandmother, uncle, psycho, therapist, psycho-the-rapist. I run, stumble. A grotesque shadow follows. Thrusts dagger in my back. I shriek.

With a jolt I awoke, covered in a cold sweat. Bloody Nightmare!

POST-AUSTRALIA DAY

THURSDAY, JANUARY 27

Since yesterday's Australia Day was a public holiday, meaning the hospital was short-staffed, a free barbecue for the children and their families was organized by the pediatric ward. It was their effort at promoting "A Community of Caring." Our team cordially accepted an invitation. Smelder, however, stipulated that we circulate among the patients.

The threatening clouds had traveled southward and the sun burst forth in all its glory. It was a magnificent summer day! A scrumptious aroma of sausages and onions sizzling on the griller beckoned me to the barbecue area. I strolled across the lawn past the outdoor aviary where a flock of doves was retained as a calming influence for the children. I yelled at a kid who was banging on the wire cage.

Near the pediatric building, bright streamers decorated the area with the Australian green and yellow colors. A frizzy red-headed clown passed out balloons among the patients. I headed for the lunch queue. Maxine and Surjit joined me.

"How was your interview with the Tortellis?" asked Surjit.

I grabbed a sausage. "The mother... she, uh, canceled. Angelo was sick. I scheduled another appointment."

With Maxine present, I dared not mention that Mrs. Tortelli didn't want another session. I just managed to bring her around by insisting that her son's mental health depended on another visit.

After collecting our sausages and salads, we approached the dessert table. Maxine immediately began shooing the blowflies away from the pavlova. "Where's the plastic wrap?" she demanded as she waved her hands back and forth over the soft-centered meringue. "One of the flies blew on the fruit topping. Baby maggots are crawling everywhere!"

I ran for the plastic wrap. "I'll give dessert a miss."

On my return, Maxine was cheerfully discussing a patient. "That Billy Armstrong over there is in for an operation to correct hypospadias."

"What's that?" I asked.

Surjit volunteered, "He was born with the urethral orifice at the side of his penis."

"In other words," declared Maxine, "he needs an operation to straighten his shooter."

I sniggered, "Thank God he's booked for surgery. Could you imagine Billy-the-Kid aiming his little pistol at the public urinal? At 10 paces he could hit an unsuspecting culprit from the side."

"Fortunately," chuckled Maxine, "he has a sense of humor. When I talked to him earlier, he made fun of our two naval explorers, Bass and Flinders, saying they circumcised Australia in a 12-foot cutter."

We found a table and wolfed down our lunch. Maxine continued to entertain us with stories. "That reminds me," she said, wiping pavlova off her chubby cheeks. "One of my friends in casualty recently admitted a bloke who was sozzled up to his gills, complaining of an obstruction in his swollen organ. On examination, a peanut was discovered lodged in the urethra. When he finally sobered up, the red-faced patient confessed. Apparently, after quite a few drinks he and his girlfriend decided to play zoo. While he begged to feed the mongoose a cobra, she decided to stuff the elephant's trunk with a peanut. Took some prodding and a fair bit of pain to dislodge it. Just as well it wasn't a Brazil nut. I'll bet Mr. Elephant won't be eating for quite some time."

Our raucous laughter caused Drs. Smelder and Towers to face our way and send punitive frowns.

"Watch out for Helen Towers," warned Maxine, nodding toward a short, trim woman eating with Gerard. "Helen's been head of the pediatric ward for the past three years. She can be a downright pain. Doesn't like people. If parents ask her too many medical questions about their child, she labels them 'over involved' and sends them to a social worker for counseling."

When Gerard motioned that we circulate among the patients, I adjourned myself from the revelry. "I'll have a chat with those teenagers in leg casts."

"What's Australia Day all about, anyway?" asked the boy on crutches.

"Dunno," replied his mate in the wheelchair.

"It commemorates the first fleet," I enlightened. "They arrived in Sydney Cove on January 26, 1788."

"With the convicts?" asked the boy.

"Dunno," said his mate.

"Of course," I instructed. "The fleet sailed with 11 ships–two men o'war, three storeships, and six convict transport ships. The Sirius was the flagship. Can you tell me who the captain of the fleet was?"

"What ya talkin' about. This ain't no history lesson."

So much for their patriotism! I left the ignorant bastards and headed back to the department, already late for my interview with Heidi. I spotted Theresa crossing the lawn.

"You missed a good feed."

"I was caught up with a client," she said.

"Listen, we'll have to postpone tomorrow's swim. Smelder delegated one of his boring meetings to yours truly."

"You have to stick up for your rights around here, Peter."

"Yea, well, maybe we can make it another time."

Pointing her finger, she chided. "We'll swim on Monday. Rain or shine."

My two o'clock session began awkwardly. Having arrived late, I greeted Heidi who had been waiting 15 minutes.

"I missed you at the luncheon," I said, trying to break the ice.

She pouted, "Wasn't able to go 'cause I didn't put on enough weight. They said I needed an extra three-and-a-half ounces." She stomped her foot on the floor. "Stupid ward! I'm sick of everyone."

Even though she had gained the 14 ounces she'd lost since arriving at the hospital, the 15-year-old reminded me of Aunt Adele's scrawny old parrot which lost half its feathers. Heidi hid her emaciated body behind a loose-fitting pink robe and fluffy green slippers. At least she maintained her weight near 66 pounds which, according to the behavioral program, provided her the privilege of walking to my office. However, being cooped up in my tiny cubicle could hardly be called a privilege.

A tantalizing whiff of grilled onions wafted through the open window. I missed out on seconds and Maxine's funny stories. The elephant story flashed into mind causing me to chuckle.

"What's so funny?" she sneered.

"It wasn't you. I just thought of a funny story someone told over lunch."

"What was it?"

"It was nothing. Hey, let's look at those books you've brought."

She clutched the books tightly and pursed her lips.

"Come on. Let's have a look."

She remained motionless.

"Is this my punishment for being late? Come on." I reached for a book.

She reluctantly released her grasp. "Mum finally brung 'em."

I opened *The California Guide for Diet and Fitness*. "If you gain the weight that I need to lose, you'll be out of here in no time."

The muscles around her mouth relaxed. A little jocularity went a long way, especially with a perpetual pouter.

"How much do ya weigh?" she asked.

I avoided the question. "This chapter looks interesting. 'Become a Playful Person and Lose Weight.' What does it say?"

"That you should make exercise playful."

"My idea of a fun exercise is walking to the fridge."

She half smiled. "Some exercise could help you lose your tummy."

I didn't laugh. "What's this other book about?"

"Aerobic dancing."

"Do you like to dance?"

"Yea."

"I have two left feet who continually argue about who should lead."

She finally grinned! "I love dancin'. Once thought of becoming a ballet dancer. Ballerinas look so graceful on the telly."

"You've definitely got the figure. Have you ever taken lessons?"

"Used to. Mum wasn't much in favor of it. Said I could go further in gymnastics. She organized daily lessons. She gets excited when I win competitions. Says I have a great future if I specialize in one event. The high bar's my best."

"How does your father feel about your training?"

"He says I practice too much. Keeps tellin' me to take it easy and have fun, but he's always busy himself. Goes out of town on business."

"Has he been able to visit you since you've been in hospital?"

Her face brightened. "He comes a lot. I've seen more of Dad in the past coupla weeks than I have in the past month. He even makes the family sessions."

"How are they going?"

"Don't like 'em. My sister and brother come too."

Knowing that Gerard and Leela conducted a family interview yesterday, I asked, "How are the therapists?"

"The lady doesn't say much, but the fat shrink ignores me and keeps badgering Mum and Dad to make me eat. I keep tellin' em, 'I can handle my own mouth.'"

"What else happens?"

"I can't handle 'em. The fat shrink makes me wanna vomit. He tells Dad he should force me to eat. Then Mum and Dad start arguing. And can ya believe it? A camera's recording everything. I'm not gonna talk anymore in those sessions. If I have anything to say, I'll talk ta you."

Way to go, Heidi! My perseverance was paying off. She trusted me! I've finally established rapport. Wait till everyone hears about our progress. Theresa will be impressed.

"Attention!" I salute female sergeant. She orders,
"Play didgeridoo!" Red-bellied black snake slith-
ers out the Aboriginal tube. Kookaburra, swooping
from tree. Snatches serpent. Cracks its head
against boulder. Tiny thread. Sprouting out my
thumbnail. I tug. It grows fatter. Develops fangs.
The snake strikes. Then escapes into sofa. Be-
tween cushions. Sergeant commands, "Pull it out!"
Help! Anxiety attack!

Bloody dreams! Shouldn't have watched last night's
National Geographic. Showed some exotic reptiles which
activated my snake phobia. I checked under the bed for
creepy crawleys.

Still suffering from a poor night's sleep, I released a
giant yawn as I entered Smelder's musk-scented office,
10 minutes late for the case management meeting. I had
dozed off in my office while studying Heidi's file and,
fortunately, woke up for the meeting.

"I saved a space for you," purred Theresa. She patted the chair beside her.

She looked stunning in a chic burgundy skirt. A sight for tired eyes which couldn't help but notice the unfastened top buttons of her fluffy white blouse.

I whispered, "I brought Heidi Wentworth's file for a progress report."

"I look forward to it," she answered softly. "Did you bring your swimmers?"

My legs quivered. Before nodding, I looked around. Surjit, Henry, Violet, and Maxine seemed preoccupied, but Leela nudged Gerard. He threw a glance our way. "I'll dispense with the administrative matters and move onto the case review. Who needs to present?"

Theresa elbowed my ribs.

I nervously raised my hand, then realized it wasn't necessary. "I, uh... want to present a progress report on Heidi Wentworth."

I heaved a sigh and mentally congratulated myself for volunteering–bound to impress Theresa.

"Make it brief," said Gerard. He winked at his assistant. "Leela and I can report on the last family interview which yielded considerable change."

I scanned my notes. "After six sessions, I'm confident a therapeutic alliance has been established. It's quite apparent that the relationship between Heidi and her mother is intense. The girl is extremely affected by the mother's expectations and is anxious to please her, even to the point of suppressing her own desires. A good example is sacrificing her interest in ballet for gymnastics. I suspect eating may be her way to differentiate from the mother and control one aspect of her life."

I glanced sideways. Theresa was beaming, obviously pleased with my performance. With renewed confidence, I continued, "Our individual sessions have been very productive. She's not only vented pent-up emotions but has also explored the inner conflict with her parents. Just recently she revealed how distressed she was over her parents arguing during the family sessions."

Gerard slapped his thigh. "That definitely proves one thing. Our last intervention was a resounding success. Wouldn't you agree, Leela?"

Her head bobbed wildly in approval, causing her blonde hair to blind her eyes. She delved into her purse and removed a turtleshell brush. "If she was upset enough to tell Peter, our strategy must be working."

"Absolutely!" echoed Gerard. "During the last session, I challenged the parents' enmeshment and overprotection. Both of them, but especially the mother, are afraid to force Heidi to eat. Fearing conflict, which in their eyes means losing their daughter's relationship, the parents back off any demands. I broke the pattern by strategically entering into a coalition with the father, coercing him to join forces with his wife against their stubborn daughter. I told them Heidi was manipulating them and keeping them divided."

"She'll try the same splitting maneuver with the therapists," added the attractive social worker. "I wouldn't be surprised if she told you, Peter, that she preferred individual over family therapy."

I gulped.

Smelder pontificated further. "Be careful, Pinowski. These anorexic girls can be manipulative and downright seductive. She'll try to have you eating out of her hand. Right, Leela?"

She nodded smugly while she brushed her hair.

Feeling like a fool, I bit my tongue and put the rest of my notes away.

Unfortunately, Theresa interjected, "I think you're underestimating Peter's contribution. Individual counseling is helping Heidi disengage from her mother."

Leela revealed her claws. "We realize that, despite his obvious lack of experience, Peter has engaged his client. However, he needs to be cautioned about becoming enmeshed in the relationship. In our family session, Heidi mentioned, among other things, that she was bringing her dieting books to him."

Great! I've a client who's a blabbermouth!

Like a lioness defending her piece of meat, Theresa lashed back. "The fact that Heidi brought Peter her books is merely a sign of positive transference. She trusts him enough to share an important part of her life. The individual therapy has proven to be most valuable in healing her psychic injuries."

Eyes turned toward Leela, who grabbed hold of the bait. Her knuckles, clasped tightly around the brush, turned white. "Any significant change will be the result of systemic shifts that Gerard and I engineer!"

"I disagree! She needs a safe place where she can resolve her inner conflict."

I couldn't help but notice that the king of this jungle was enjoying the clash of the two felines. With a Cheshire grin, he silently puffed on his pipe.

Saint Henry, the peacemaker, eventually intervened. "We mustn't allow this family to split the team. While this discussion has been productive and the issues have been aired, I think we should move on."

This mauled piece of meat could have shouted, "Praise the Lord!"

Violet Struthers, however, had other ideas. She dropped her knitting and prattled, "Potter has an interesting case. Why, I remember this 10-year-old girl I once saw over a period of nine years. She was obsessional about her figure. Became an actress, then started an anonymous group, Over Eaters, I believe. She eventually enrolled me, and by golly, when I lost 10 pounds, my husband..."

"Thank you, Violet," interrupted Gerard sharply. "It's time to press on. But before doing so, I want to emphasize that I wholeheartedly concur with Leela. Pinowski should be extremely careful of future attempts by his client to seduce or manipulate him."

Leela glared triumphantly at Theresa. I hoped neither of them noticed the large wet patch around my armpits. It had dawned on me that my next interview with Heidi was this afternoon. One mauling was more than ample, thank you very much. At least I discovered a thing or two about my client. Not only was she manipulative but, more importantly, she couldn't keep her mouth shut. So much for confidentiality.

Gerard reviewed the new intakes. "We have a 15-year-old suicidal diabetic, a seven-year-old fire setter who burned down his school, a few enuretics, and a nine-year-old boy who compulsively masturbates." The victor was magnanimous in handing out the spoils. "You can handle the enuretics, Pinowski." Bed wetters were my just reward.

Maybe it wouldn't be as bad as it sounded. After all, there was the bell and pad technique. I remembered my university days and the lectures on behavioral conditioning which had proven to be quite effective. I'd merely have to teach the parents about inserting the moisture-sensitive pad under their child's sheets at night. A wet bed would activate a bell, somewhat like Pavlov's dogs, except instead of salivating, the kid would learn to stop peeing. Who knows, I may have inadvertently stumbled on my area of expertise. I would dust off the pads in the storeroom and prove to the team that I could be a capable clinician.

"I'd like to work on a case with Peter," Theresa announced.

"Which one do you want?"

She faced me. "Why don't we take the compulsive masturbator. It could be an interesting case."

Desperate to redeem myself in the eyes of my colleagues, I jested, "We should use a paradoxical intervention and instruct the boy to masturbate more frequently."

Thank God, everyone laughed–except Gerard. "That's an excellent idea," he deadpanned. "I'd be interested to learn how that turns out."

Trust Dr. Smelder!

Theresa touched my arm lightly and winked, "We can discuss the case over lunch."

During our brisk stroll toward the staff amenities complex, Theresa boiled. "That Leela infuriates me. The little weasel, hiding behind Gerard. She couldn't even acknowledge all that you've done for Heidi."

"I felt rather foolish this morning. Especially when she mentioned the diet books."

"There's no need to be ashamed. Heidi was confiding in you."

"I don't know what to think."

"Now don't get down on yourself. You showed courage by sharing the case in front of the group, knowing full well that Gerard and Leela were involved with the family."

Theresa sure knew how to make me feel special.

"It's important to know I can bank on your support," she continued. "Those two narcissists must realize they don't have a monopoly on therapeutic wisdom. Christ, they infuriate me."

We passed through a metal gate and stopped near the pool. Theresa tested the water. "Perfect! A strenuous physical workout will prevent the frustration from becoming noxious."

With the sun's golden rays pouring from the heavens, Theresa's black hair fluttered in the warm breeze. "Sorry about not swimming last Friday," I said.

"Be careful of Smelder. He would delegate sleeping if he could get away with it. I don't want your enthusiasm and freshness destroyed by the system. I'm glad you've joined our department."

I blushed. "Gee, thanks."

She gently grabbed my arm and led me toward the change rooms in the red brick building. "You're sweet, Peter. Let's forget the others."

She left me floating, euphoric. Was this love? My swelling chest affirmed the answer.

I emerged wearing my apple green Speedos and waited for Theresa. Scantily clad sunbathers, baking on the pebble pavement, surrounded the pool.

"I thought you'd be swimming by now."

My eyes bulged at her magnificent athletic frame. She sported a black satin one-piece surrounded by cherry trim lace. Her bare back revealed broad bronze shoulders that were formidable. And all this time I thought her blouses had extra padding!

Her perfect physique made me self-conscious of my flabby middle. Heidi was right. I did need to lose weight.

"Let's swim," she beckoned and dove into the clear blue water. She created a rippling wake as her pumping legs and windmilling arms gyrated in total rhythm. She completed her first lap then started another.

I stopped gawking, placed my glasses on the edge of the pool, and plunged into the cool water. Attempting to swim seriously next to Theresa was like running the marathon with an Olympic gold medalist. I didn't last very long. Huffing and puffing, I stopped for a rest–a good excuse to stare and admire such beauty.

Switching to the breast stroke, arms sweeping in wide
arcs, she glided her way effortlessly through the water.
My Aphrodite.

I renewed my attempt at swimming and accidentally
strayed into her lane. We collided. Or rather, her thrusting physique rammed into my floating frame. I gasped
for air.

She reached into the water and lifted my head. "Are
you okay?"

Coughing, spluttering, "S-s-sorry. Lost my direction.
Better rest."

I hauled my body onto the hot tiny pebbles and
closed my eyes. The sun penetrated my aching muscles.

Twenty minutes later, Theresa was toweling her wet
hair. "That felt fantastic. Let's finish off with a sauna."

"My body's already well-done."

"Come on, Peter. It'll do wonders for you."

She led me down a small flight of stairs to the
sauna–unisex, of course. We entered a dimly lit cedar
room, large enough for six bodies, with wooden plat-
forms on two adjoining walls.

"We're in luck," she whispered. "There's no one
here."

"The other swimmers may be more sensible, roasting outside."

Facing a scorching stove, we each leaned against a
separate wall and rested our feet on the lower platform.
Theresa filled a ladle from a plastic bucket and slowly
poured the water on the blistering coals. A cloud of mist
hissed. My pores swelled from the searing heat and
moisture sprinkled my skin. I had to remove my foggy
glasses.

"A splendid way to end a workout."

I crossed my arms around my flabby middle. "You
sure look fit."

"I have to, for the competitions."

"Competitions?"

"Didn't you know? I train most evenings as a body-builder."

"My God, you're a lady wrestler?"

"Oh, don't act so surprised," she said as she poured water on the glowing coals. "I've been lifting weights for the past several years. Originally, I merely wanted to lose weight, but then I got hooked. You're looking at someone who recently came in third at the East Coast Body Building Championship."

Beads of perspiration poured off my brow. Compared to Theresa who was seven years older, I was a physical wreck. "I'm afraid I'm out of shape."

She pushed her finger into my soft belly. "Baby fat," she chuckled. "Easy to burn off. Regular exercise will tighten your abdominal muscles and increase your stamina. Let's check your muscle tone."

She kneaded my thighs and legs which went all wobbly. "You have potential. A good workout with me would do you the world of good. Wouldn't want you to become one of those tough, macho types, though. I prefer men soft and tender."

The softness between my legs was disappearing. Little Freddie was stirring. My face flushed beetroot red.

"I'm roasting."

"You're probably not used to the heat. Take a cold shower and cool off. I'll wait for you."

Emerging into the cool air brought immediate relief. Freezing water, acting like shock therapy, sent Freddie plummeting. When I re-entered the sauna, my lungs choked on the fiery air.

"Feel better?"

"It's cooler outside."

"The temperature here is perfect." She combed the black hair with her long fingers, squeezing the drenched curly locks. Two tiny streams created waterfalls plunging down her broad shoulders over the two protruding peaks and disappearing into the valley.

"It'll be fun working on that case together, Peter."

The thought of the newly referred client–the masturbating boy–sprang to mind. I gazed hypnotically at her physical paradise, the firm breasts bulging beneath the swimmers, her olive thighs.

"With all your experience you've probably learned heaps of techniques."

"I'll enjoy showing them to you," she purred.

I stared at her pointed nipples stretching the satin fabric. She reached for the ladle and splashed more water on the sputtering red rocks. Another rising cloud of scalding vapors hissed.

"A-h-h-h-h." She readjusted her back against the wall and spread her legs wider. Without my glasses, I wasn't sure, but I could've sworn a lone pubic hair had escaped the confines of the cherry trim lace.

An uncomfortable bulge grew between my legs. Desperate to hide big Freddie, I laid my hands on my lap.

"How will you handle the masturbating?"

I blushed. Oh my God! She noticed. No! She was talking about the boy... The masturbator...

"I... I don't know. I was counting on you."

Through the rising steam a drop of moisture fell from Theresa's nose onto her partly opened lower lip. Perspiration streamed down the nape of her neck, seeking refuge in the cleavage. Her legs seemed to widen further. She dropped her hands to her lap. Not sure what was occurring. The temperature. Felt light-headed.

Queasy. Thought I saw her fingers delicately stroke the inside of her thighs.

The heat was unbearable. Sweat and steam poured from my face as Freddie struggled to emerge from the Speedos. I crossed my legs and hunched forward to prevent his appearance.

Her wet lips parted. "I'll go easy with you since it is our first experience together."

I stared at her biceps and triceps. Wasn't so sure. A wave of anxiety cascaded through my body. A tremor slowly crept up my legs. They began shaking uncontrollably. Felt dizzy. Faint.

"A-h-h-h," she cooed. "My body feels so re-l-a-a-a-x-xed.

My eyes strained. More movement. This couldn't be! Her right hand, edging closer to her pubic area. One of her fingers. Sliding under the black satin. Near the lone strand of hair.

My legs twitched more visibly. Freddie, signaling, wanted to expel an espresso.

"Have to leave," I blurted. "Any hotter and I'll explode."

I rushed out of the sauna into the cool breeze. Too late.

Back in the men's locker room I had another cold shower. Took my time though, to get over my embarrassment.

Outside the building Theresa's face radiated contentment. "I thoroughly enjoyed myself, Peter. Hope you had as good a time as I."

I meekly nodded.

"We must do it again!"

My confused head, still spinning, mumbled, "Yea... Sure." It was all happening too fast. "I better hurry or I'll be late for Heidi's appointment."

Lunch had taken longer than I ever imagined. And I didn't even get a chance to eat!

Arriving a few minutes before two, with the sauna etched on my mind, I darted off to the loo. As nature would have it, Heidi had similar intentions. We practically bumped into each other making our grand entrance. If the damn hospital had only installed staff toilets, we would've avoided the red faces.

We both exchanged an uncomfortable "Hi" and entered.

She selected a stall nearest the door while I chose one at the far end. This client/counselor relationship was getting ridiculous. Behind the cubicle I waited patiently, hoping she'd quickly depart. No such luck. Only the sounds of silence.

After what seemed an interminably long time, my bladder could wait no longer. Realizing that pissing in the noiseless chamber echoed like a deluge over Ayers Rock, I pressed the flush button and simultaneously released a torrent of amber liquid gurgling noisily down the bowl. She'd never know the difference.

I rushed out of the toilet and prepared my office for our next encounter.

Recalling Gerard's warning, I cautioned myself to be on guard. Wasn't going to allow this skinny 15-year-old to even think of manipulating or seducing me. And she had a big mouth.

Heidi seemed surprisingly pleasant and cheerful as she entered my room. "I've put on some weight," she said enthusiastically, plopping herself on the chair and adjusting the pink robe over her lap.

I scanned her bony face. "How much?"

"One-and-a-half pounds over the weekend. Thought you'd be pleased."

"Hmm. How do you feel about it?"

"I'm allowed to watch the telly now. If I gain a little more, they'll let me walk around the grounds."

"You seem pretty pleased about that."

"Wouldn't you? I wanna put on weight as fast as I can."

"Why's that?"

"I wanna go home. Don't like it here. The doctors keep..."

My mind flashed back to the steaming sauna with Theresa's sensual body gyrating in slow motion. The movie unreeled frame by frame. Her black curly hair resting against the cedar panels... the sleek, sweating physique reclining on the wooden bench... erect nipples yearning to escape... muscular legs spreading slowly... her moist lips widening...

"Sorry I made it hard on ya," she rambled.

Perspiration trickled down my forehead

"... didn't wanna talk to anyone when I first came here. Wanted to be left alone. I feel much better now..."

Another scenario danced in my mind. Theresa, naked... I had shed the extra kilos around my middle... My body looked smashing.

"I've told Mum talking to you has helped me put some weight back on. Didn't you hear me?"

"Huh?"

"Didn't you hear?"

"Yeah. Of course." Plagued by a wave of guilt, I splashed cold water on the sauna, dissolving the film strip–for the time being. Determined to stay on track, I displayed bold words on my mental screen. *Concentrate. Focus. Heidi. Be careful.*

"Somethin' wrong?"

"Just thinking. How's it going with your mother and father?"

"We're gettin' on okay."

I leaned forward. "Can you be more specific?"

"What d'ya mean?"

"Last session you mentioned that you were interested in ballet while your mother preferred gymnastics. Did you talk to her about it?"

"Not really. Just been talkin' about being here in hospital. About wantin' to go home."

"What else has been happening between you and your mother?"

"Nuthin' much."

"Hmm. So why are you so desperate to go home?"

Her pursed pout returned. "How'd ya like being imprisoned in some hospital?"

"We're not talking about me, we're talking about you."

"You seem different today. Did ya have a hard day or somethin'?"

Her question set off alarm bells. Resistance. Avoidance. Smelder was right. She wants me to dance her tune.

"Never mind about me. We're here to help you."

She reached for the Kleenex and dabbed at her gums. "What for?"

"To get you better."

"How many times have I been seein' ya?"

"Don't get off the subject. This is our seventh session. And you haven't said much today about your mother."

"You're actin' strange. Did ya have a fight with your boss or somethin'?"

"It's not your concern."

"Did I do anythin' wrong?"

"Not really."

Her eyes teared. "If I did I'm sorry 'cause I've been tryin' real hard to gain weight. Been stuffin' myself. Even though I hate it. Thought you'd be pleased."

Like swirling marbles in a tin can, confusion tumbled around my head. One side of my brain felt sadness. She genuinely wanted to get better. The left side thought otherwise. She was consciously evoking sympathy to seduce my emotions and gain control of the interview. I heard Gerard and Leela shouting, "Don't be manipulated." Damn! If only Heidi had kept her mouth shut.

"I'm tryin' to be honest," she whimpered. "It's not all that easy. But you're actin' different. Not like before. How come?"

Conflicting views twirled inside my mind like some jumbled mess. Seduction. Trust. Manipulation. Honesty. And adding to the muddle, three dimensional pictures of Theresa kept resurfacing.

"What's the matter?" spoke the agitated voice.

My mental torture continued. Get a grip on it! No time for lengthy deliberations. Find direction. Surjit appeared in my mind with an instruction: "Be honest!"

"Uh... listen, Heidi... I, ugh, got into trouble with Dr. Smelder. When you mentioned in the family session about bringing me your diet books, I received a rap over the knuckles."

"How come?"

I shrugged. "They said you were controlling therapy."

Her face grimaced. "Sorry. Just thought you'd wanna look. Didn't mean to get ya into trouble."

"Forget it. But I was wondering if you could... like ... keep our sessions to yourself. They *are* supposed to be confidential."

She nodded. "I better not tell Mum. She blabs everything."

I offered her my hand. "If you'll be straight with me, I'll be honest with you."

"A deal."

We shook hands enthusiastically and secured our pledge of secrecy. If the smile on Heidi's face was any indication, we had moved a step further in our relationship. We both agreed to be cautious about what we said, and to whom, about our sessions. Neither of us wanted to be manipulated further by the system.

"Now let's put our heads together and see how you can get out of here as fast as possible..."

ANOTHER PEEP SHOW

FRIDAY, FEBRUARY 4

Sitting behind the one-way mirror in the tiny, dark observation room, our team listened to Henry's benevolent voice. "The Jacksons are presenting for their fourth family interview. You may recall, I showed a videotaped segment of their first session at Dr. King's consultation on January 11th. At that time, hopelessness pervaded. The parents stumbled through a valley of darkness, despairing over Tanya, their overweight nine-year-old daughter. A chronic bed wetter prone to temper tantrums, she defiantly refused to attend school. The mother felt overburdened and extremely troubled by her wayward daughter..."

Gerard impatiently interjected, "Tell us what happened during the last session so we can move onto today's interview."

As if on a pulpit, Henry sermonized further. "I last saw the unfortunate family two weeks ago and offered them Dr. King's advice. Using his paradoxical technique, I instructed Mrs. Jackson to keep Tanya at home and prevent her from attending school. She was to keep her daughter in sight at all times while attempting to understand Tanya's affliction. As Dr. King postulated, the objective was to create an unbearable intensity of closeness between the mother and daughter. We wanted Tanya to get so sick of her mother's shadow that she would view the prospect of returning to school a far better proposition than staying at home."

"We've got the picture," said our director. He switched on the video recorder. "Bring them in."

Henry closed the door behind him, encasing the rest of us in the stuffy enclosure, more like a small church vestry. The luminescence of the interviewing room filtered through the smoky pane of glass separating the two worlds, one with harsh fluorescent lights, the other with gray shadows.

Leela sat next to Gerard who occupied the front seat near the phone. Maxine, Theresa, and I sat in the back. Surjit, now working with adult psychiatric patients, was sorely missed.

A somber Jackson family followed Henry into the interviewing room. Like Jack Spratt and his wife, the lean 39-year-old Reginald was joined by Veronica, his 35-year-old obese partner, who promptly plopped on a creaking, plaid chair. Sylvia, aged 12, and her 11-year-old brother, Felix, sat in between the parents. Tanya's chair was conspicuously vacant.

"Where's Tanya?" inquired Henry.

Mrs. Jackson's lips quivered. "We did exactly as you told us. All last week I kept Tanya home from school. I tried talking to her. Just like you said. In the TV room, the kitchen, even followed her to the bedroom when she didn't want to talk no more."

Obviously everywhere that Tanya went, Mrs. Jackson was sure to follow.

"We took your advice about praying together. That's when she turned real bad. Swearing, cursing. You never heard such language! I couldn't believe she was my own daughter. Whenever I approached her, it was like... she became possessed. Using filthy words..."

"What happened?"

Tears streamed from her eyes. "On Monday she turned into that other person, yelling and screaming. In the afternoon she ran away. Didn't pack anything. I followed her down the street, but with my legs, I couldn't keep up."

Henry passed the Kleenex.

"Tanya was missing two whole days. Reggy left work to help me find her. We kept Sylvia and Felix home. Couldn't allow them to attend school, what with my Tanya missing. I called the police. They couldn't find her. Then came this nasty woman, Mrs. Chittick, from child welfare. They had placed Tanya in a foster home. Mrs. Chittick blamed me, called me grossly negligent for allowing Tanya to wander the streets..."

The streams turned into deep sobs. The distressed woman grabbed more tissues, then passed the box to her children. Her husband sat motionless and stared at the floor.

"... It wasn't my fault she slept in the park where the man grabbed her. God forbid, he could've forced sex. Thank God for Tanya's loud voice. Her screaming saved her. Brought the police..."

She blew her nose. "Tanya told them I was making her crazy, harassing and abusing her. Can you believe it? Me? Abusing my own daughter? I haven't laid a hand on any of my children. Reggy will tell you. How could they say such a thing? I only did what you said."

An agitated Henry rearranged his spindly legs. "You may have gone overboard with what I said."

"No, Reverend Snart," protested the father whose strawberry birthmark actively twitched on the left cheek. "Me wife did exactly what you told her. She believed in you. You said you'd help us straighten out me daughter. You have to talk to Mrs. Chittick and explain what happened."

"Yes, of course. I'm very sorry. I'll talk with the appropriate authorities."

Behind the one-way mirror, Smelder's voice crackled, "Henry shouldn't have backed down. It's the parents' responsibility to deal with the welfare department, not ours."

"Couldn't Henry just contact them?" I asked. "And explain what he was doing?" I mean fair was fair, and the family did follow his instructions.

Leela offered a curt reply. "This family wants to relinquish its responsibility and place it on Henry. He has to teach them about facing their own problems."

On the other side of the screen Henry was seeking forgiveness from the weeping mother. "I'm so sorry. Your burden is heavy. I'll do whatever I can to assist you."

"Damn it," cursed Gerard. "Henry's being sucked right into the family's pathology. He should know better!"

"He needs a phone-in," suggested Leela. "Remember, he responds better when the message is laced with a few words of encouragement. God only knows he needs them."

Brring, brring.

Henry fumbled with the beige receiver.

"You're doing very well," spoke Gerard in as supportive a voice as he could muster. "But you must get the parents involved in deciding what *they're* going to do. Not what they're wanting *you* to do."

The therapist nodded and meekly hung up the phone.

The back row rumbled as Maxine's voice thundered. "Your whippo twango technique backfired! These people are worse off."

"It hasn't backfired!" countered Gerard. "Our strategy was to separate an enmeshed mother and daughter.

And separate them we did. The crisis pried the two apart. We've achieved a hell of a lot in such short a time."

"At what cost?" challenged Theresa. "The girl's in a foster home, probably feeling rejected and suffering untold emotional damage."

Leela hissed, "As Gerard said, this crisis was necessary. Look at the parents. They're finally cooperating together. That's an achievement in itself."

Theresa retaliated. "What about Tanya? Isn't anyone interested in what happens to her?"

"How is Tanya?" inquired Henry. His question merely prompted an uncontrollable flood of tears. The Kleenex was in great demand.

"Me Tanya won't talk to us," sniffled the father.

"She says she hates me," sobbed the mother. "Doesn't want to live with us no more."

The display of emotions even moved Gerard. "This mother's histrionics are hindering her daughter's development. She's blubbering on like a baby. Henry has to take charge."

He yanked his communicator off the hook.

Brring, brring.

"For Christ's sake," he barked. "Quit messing around with their emotions. Help the parents develop a plan of action. They must make a decision about taking the next step. Get on with it!"

Henry's shaking hand attempted to replace the phone on the table but dropped it on the floor.

Behind the mirror, Maxine's burly figure rose, reflecting a menacing shadow off the smoky glass. "I've had it with these goddamn Peeping Tom sessions. There's no clause in my contract that says I have to sit behind a mirror. You can shove these sessions you know where."

Her huge frame jostled the chairs as she made a hasty exit.

Maxine's walkout must've jarred our director because he shot a cold stare at Theresa and me which
warned, "Don't dare move a muscle." No way was I
budging.

The family's weeping eventually brought Gerard
back to the interview. He placed another call. Henry's
receiver didn't ring. Gerard tried again. Still no response.

He frantically searched the wires attached to the wall.
"What the hell's wrong with this bloody phone!"

Leela spotted the problem. "The red light on Henry's
phone is flashing. He must've pressed the Do Not Disturb button. "

"Bloody Hell! The idiot."

"Before the session deteriorates further," offered
Leela smugly, "we should remove him for a consultation."

Gerard concurred. "Peter, knock on the door and
tell Henry to come here."

Before I could clamp my mouth, the words popped
out. "Do you think that's a good idea?"

"Listen kid. I've been in this game a lot longer than
you. Go and get Henry."

Well, I was closest to the door, and he was The Director.

Like a hall monitor sent to pull a student out of class,
I feebly knocked on the door. No answer, except the
muffled sounds of sobbing. With a gnawing ache in my
gut, I pounded louder. The door cracked open slightly
to reveal one of Henry's roving eyes. You'd think he
was getting busted. I waved him out. His eye returned a
puzzled stare.

"The phone," I whispered. "It's not working. Dr.
Smelder wants to see you."

He excused himself from the family and joined me
behind the mirror.

"What the hell happened?!" cursed Gerard.

Henry stumbled in the dark room. "I... don't know."

"You bumbling idiot. You pressed the Do Not Disturb button and cut me off!"

"I'm sorry. It was an accident."

"Don't ever do that again! And what do you think you were doing with your clients?"

Henry scanned the darkness. "I, uh, was empathizing with their terrible plight. They're distressed..."

"Of course they're distressed. Any fool could see that. The family has you caught up in sympathy. Not much good with that. Go back and organize the parents. Stop their whining. I can't stand whining parents. Have them take charge of their lives and develop a concrete plan."

Leela provided her idea of an encouraging word. "The therapist's job is to hold the lantern while the family chops the wood."

She might as well have added, "You dumb shit."

Wearing his crown of thorns, Henry turned to leave.

I nudged his arm. "Psst. Don't forget to release the Do Not Disturb button."

It was the first thing he corrected when he returned to the family.

"Sorry for that interruption... We'll spend the rest of the time planning what we can do."

Brring, brring.

"It's not what *we* can do, for Christ's sake. It's what *they* can do!"

Scrupulously checking the DND button, in case it had been accidentally pressed, Henry reiterated Gerard's directive. "What can you do about your situation?"

The strawberry birthmark on Mr. Jackson's left cheek twitched again. "That's why we're here, Reverend. You told us you could help me daughter."

"Yes, I understand. But you must realize, I can't make decisions for your family. You must devise your own plan."

The father scratched his head. "But we did exactly what you said."

"Yes I know. I was merely trying..."

Brring, brring.

"You don't have to defend yourself! They're getting you off track!"

Now I knew what happened to peacemakers. I imagined the gap widening between Henry's floating eyes—one focusing on Gerard's directives, the other on the family's plea for help.

Ever vigilant about avoiding the DND button, Henry stumbled through the rest of the session, assisted by Gerard's frequent phone-ins—"Damn it! Make them face their responsibility."

The Jacksons eventually did make one decision—to continue with family therapy. Whoever believed "The meek shall inherit the earth"?

The afternoon's drama finished just past five. I followed an irate Theresa into her office. She fumed, "They become cruel and incompetent hiding behind that mirror! I need some fresh air."

"I myself could use a drink." Then mustering my courage, I asked, "Would you, uh, care to join me?"

"I can only stop for a quick one. I'm scheduled to work out at the gym. Today I need an intense catharsis."

We found a quiet little corner at the Turramurra Hotel. Huddled around a small wooden table, we nursed our Riesling.

"Smelder's such an ass!" she seethed. "I don't trust that creep. He's power mad. You'll never catch him watching any of my interviews."

"I'm not so lucky. When I asked for help with the Tortellis, Gerard informed me that Leela would assist him behind the one-way screen. After their performance today, I'm sure to have a panic attack!"

She placed her warm hands over mine. "Don't let it get you down. I'll provide moral support."

The Riesling, her moist hands, and consoling words created an ambience of simmering passion. Dr. Smelder wasn't nearly so overwhelming what with the ray of hope beside me, fueling my confidence and courage. I wanted more time with her. But would she be interested? She did come out for a drink. But maybe she wanted the relationship kept professional.

I gulped the rest of the white wine. "Theresa... uh... would you like to... uh... go out sometime?"

"What did you have in mind?"

"Oh. I was just wondering... I mean... you don't have to if you don't want to, but I thought that you, I mean, we... Tarongo Zoo?"

"I'd love to!"

"You would?! Fantastic!"

She squeezed my hand tightly. "The zoo brings out my animal."

The wine and I giggled.

"Did you have a specific time in mind?"

"Not exactly. What suits you?"

"I can't make it this weekend. Friends are visiting from Melbourne. The weekend after is free. We can take the ferry to the zoo and have a picnic at Bradley's head."

"Sounds terrific!" I couldn't believe it. She accepted!

"I have to leave. The gym closes at eight o'clock. I'll see you Monday and look forward to the following weekend."

She kissed me on the cheek and left.

What a way to end the week! I was falling in love with Aphrodite. With a light head I floated toward the train station. A radiant Theresa, emblazoned in my psyche, accompanied me on the ride home.

"You're late!" chastised Ma. "The *barszcz* has gone cold..."

THE MIDNIGHT EXPRESS

WEDNESDAY, FEBRUARY 9

Couldn't fall asleep. Theresa was sensuously flirting with my mind. Since our time in the sauna, her nightly visitations were becoming regular. Her delicious naked body danced. Black fluffy hair, luscious crimson lips, erect pink nipples, succulent olive thighs... I was obsessed with my Greek goddess. Her seductive physique tormented my brain. Fiery passion seared my loins. I tossed and turned, tortured by frustration. Recalled Father Blaszczynski's edict–self-denial, mind over matter. Since I never went blind, my mind attended to the matter at hand... Theresa erotically gyrating in the sauna... A welcome release heralded a night of peace.

THE ZOO

SATURDAY, FEBRUARY 12

9:10 a.m. Circular Quay. Having anticipated this day
all week, I anxiously scanned the sea of faces. The 9:15
ferry was loading. I'm sure she said to meet at Taronga
Zoo wharf.

"Sorry I'm late," she panted. "I ran from the Domain Parking where I left the car."

The sight of Theresa stole my breath. At five feet,
eight inches, she sported black body-fit shorts with iri-
descent pink stripes down each side and a white T-shirt
with the picture of a flamingo nestling against her chest.
She raised a wicker basket. "I brought a box lunch for
our picnic."

"Looks heavy."

She purred, "Lots of yummy food."

"Can hardly wait. We better hurry or we'll miss the
ferry. I bought the tickets."

We hopped on the *Fishburn* as the pulsating noise
erupted from its engine. We hurried to the open deck
already packed with passengers basking in the sun.

"Check out the rainbow spinnaker," pointed
Theresa. Her hair flew wildly in the warm breeze. "It's
glorious!"

"A bonzer day. Hope it doesn't get too hot."

She pulled out the sunscreen. "I'm prepared. Want some?"

"Just a little."

She gently rubbed coconut scented lotion on my arms and face, then applied the cream over her smooth legs.

A steady hum vibrated through the ship, pressing its hull against the waves. The engine opened up full throttle. It throbbed its way into the harbor, leaving a lather of foam trailing in its wake. Flanked on either side by soaring seagulls, the *Fishburn* slipped effortlessly through the bluish-green water and passed the naval ships anchored near Bradley's Head. As we approached Taronga Zoo, the engines fired in reverse and churned the water into an egg-white froth. Bumping and scraping against the giant wooden pylons, the ferry floated to a halt.

While the boat was secured, I waited impatiently like an excited child. The zoo, built down the face of a hilly escarpment, provided spectacular views of Sydney Harbour.

"What'll we see first?" I babbled.

"Let's take the bus to the upper entrance and work our way down to the lower exit."

I collected the tickets while Theresa scanned the map. "We should visit the reptile house first. It's on the way to the koalas."

I didn't want to spoil the moment by discussing my snake phobia. I braced myself and took a deep breath, then scampered down the long, dark corridor. I felt my way along the cylindrical rail, avoiding any glimpse of the slimy beasts. The light at the end was none too soon, and the open air brought immediate relief.

Exiting much later, Theresa chuckled. "That was quick. I thought we were supposed to enjoy ourselves?"

"Yea... well... it's too nice a day to be indoors."

She linked arms. "Okay cuddly, let's find the koalas."

We spotted the little gray fur balls slumbering on outstretched tree limbs.

"Joshua, my six-year-old, is making tremendous progress," said Theresa. "During our last session he slept much of the time, quite a sharp contrast from his normally disruptive behavior."

"What did you do?"

"I've consistently provided him with a contained therapeutic environment. This has enabled him to regress to an infantile state in order to discover a sense of security he never had as a child."

"How many sessions have you had?"

"Thus far, 132. He'll still need at least another year."

As we walked arm-in-arm, I found Theresa's vast experience and knowledge comforting. She was opening up another world.

Listening to her case analyses was a sheer delight! We laughed at the frolicking and splashing antics of the fairy penguins.

"I remember treating an unusual case of aquaphobia where this small girl was so frightened of water she couldn't even wash her face..."

We meandered toward the primates and stopped at the spider monkeys. An isolated male was sitting in the corner playing with himself. Theresa remarked, "I thought we worked particularly well together with little Terry and his family. His compulsive masturbating is clearly a reaction to the extreme puritanism of his parents. Staunch Catholics have a difficult time even uttering the word 'sex'."

Along the railing a mother stood with her young daughter reading a plaque on the fence. The small girl asked, "Mummy, what's a pen... is?"

The blushing woman replied, "It's nothing. Let's go and find the kangaroos."

Theresa and I examined the inscription on the plaque:

1. Spider monkeys do not have thumbs. They'd get in the way when they swing around.

2. Tails are used like a third hand.

3. The clitoris of the female is very large and looks very much like a male penis. The male penis is seldom visible.

4. The females always look pregnant, even when they're not.

5. So, if you see a pregnant-looking spider monkey with what looks like a penis, no thumb, and three arms, it's a female.

"That's a pretty explicit sign, especially with children all about."

"Don't be such a prude, Peter. It's all perfectly natural–good sex education."

"When I was a young boy we never used technical words."

"What did you call your genitals?"

My face flushed. "Uh... Freddie."

"Freddie? Where did it come from?"

"Think my ma invented it from my middle name, Frederic. "

She poked me in the ribs. "Freddie, how cute."

"Hey, stop it. I'm ticklish. Where to now?"

"This animal is famished. Let's catch the seal show, then exit at the lower entrance and find a picnic spot."

"We can give the baboons a miss," I jested. "We see more than enough of Gerard and Leela."

Clowning along the way, I felt liberated with Theresa at my side. While her intellect impressed me, her lack of inhibition both excited and distressed me. I didn't care. I was being released from my sheltered cocoon.

We left the zoo and walked along the winding asphalt road toward Bradley's Head which jutted into the harbor like a small finger. A fifteen-minute stroll brought us to a sign that said, "Sydney Harbour National Park."

At the top of the escarpment we gawked at Sydney's majestic skyline sprawled out like some giant canvas. The Opera House and its white tiles sparkled in the sun; Centrepoint Tower created a stark silhouette in the sky; and the Harbour Bridge extended over the blue-green water like an enormous coat hanger. Seconds ticked into minutes.

Theresa clutched my arm. "Let's climb down and pick a spot near the water."

We followed a well-worn path which descended to a series of sandstone steps.

I stumbled. "These were no doubt built by convicts."

A stone's throw from the water's edge, Theresa claimed a green patch of grass from among the many picnickers. "Hope you like Greek food."

"If you brought it, I'll eat it. What have you got?"

She spread out spinach pie, stuffed capsicum, feta cheese, garden salad with black olives, and a bottle of red claret. My mouth salivated.

We indulged in the feast while our eyes reveled in the spectacle of billowing sails promenading up and down the gleaming harbor. A few fishermen were catching flathead on a pier while two pelicans greedily flapped their wings.

"This is paradise," I proclaimed. "A fantastic setting, sumptuous food, beautiful wine, and marvelous company. Cheers!"

We clinked our plastic cups and sipped the claret.

Theresa snuggled closer. "You're not like those macho men who have to put on an act and get it their way. You're much gentler. Softer. Yummier."

She kissed me sensuously on the lips. My legs quivered.

A couple of children, encamped several feet away, began to stare. "There's other people around," I whispered.

She breathed into my ear. "Forget about them. Pretend we're the only ones here."

I couldn't relax, not while watching for voyeurs.

Theresa sensed my anxiety. "Drink up. I'll take you to a magical place nearby. You'll love it."

I swilled the rest of the claret then helped Theresa pack up. I grabbed the basket and clutched her arm. We stumbled up the stone stairs, climbing back to the road where we crossed to the other side.

With a mischievous smile she pointed. "This is it!"

Three huge steel cannons stood idle on top of a small knoll commemorating a time when they protected the harbor.

"Wow! When were they installed?"

"The etching on the wall over there says 1871. Let's explore."

The three mammoth guns spaced in a large semicircle were interconnected with a network of open, stone-faced trenches about five feet deep. Like two little children, we climbed one of the canons mounted on a wooden turret. Theresa looked into the barrel while I straddled the empty metal tube.

"Is that a cannon you're sitting on, or are you just glad to see me?"

Must've been the red wine. We were hilariously giddy.

"Come here!" she called, descending into the concrete maze.

I followed her through the trench which, surrounded by sandstone blocks, converged into another maze.

"One of these leads into a tunnel under the hill. I think this is the one. Yes!"

We proceeded slowly, allowing our eyes to adjust to the dim light. The dark musty tunnel separated into two. One led into an adjacent chamber while another trailed off into total darkness.

"Let's explore this room," she whispered. "They must've stored the explosives here."

We clung to one another's arms and entered a concrete bunker the size of a bedroom. Across the stone face, love notes and hearts had been scrawled with colored markers.

"This is the magical place I promised."

I fumbled among the dark shadows. "It's kinda spooky."

Theresa's arms drew me nearer. I could smell a slight trace of coconut mingling with the claret on her breath. Her breathing became deeper, fuller. She placed her hands on either side of my face and drew her lips next to mine. We kissed. Then kissed again–she, more passionately. Our arms were locked in a tight embrace.

My knees trembled. She pressed my body tightly against the stone wall. Her fingers began roaming, pawing at my clothes.

She unbuttoned my shirt. "I want you!"

I wanted her too, but she was moving too fast. My legs wobbled uncontrollably. My breathing became erratic.

She fondled my bare chest. "I want you! Do you want me?"

The wine answered. "Y-y-yes."

I kissed the nape of her neck.

"Lower, lower," she pleaded.

As I kissed above her breasts, Freddie awakened. But so did my fears! I didn't bring any protection. Wasn't ready for fatherhood, and I definitely didn't want to catch a nasty disease.

Theresa's groping hands weren't all that concerned.

Neither was Freddie, desperate to make an appearance and enter the tunnel.

It was all happening too fast! How did one stop a speeding locomotive?

"In here, Niki. Bet you can't find me!"

"Yes I can, Stevie. Ready or not here I come!"

Children. From outside. Rushing into the tunnel. I pulled the emergency cord. The locomotive screeched to a halt. We frantically covered ourselves before being spotted.

I staggered out the entrance and inhaled a lungful of air, thankful to be back in daylight.

Theresa wasn't as relieved. "Let's go to my place. We won't be interrupted."

"It's getting late. Maybe we should call it a day."

"We have plenty of time. And we won't be disturbed."

"I've told my parents I wouldn't be too late. Besides, we have to catch the ferry and pick up your car."

"So let's start walking."

"Listen, Theresa. I think we might be moving a bit fast."

She stroked my arm. "You could at least stop by for a cuppa tea. I can show you my psychotherapy books," she enticed.

She knew how to make an offer I could hardly refuse.

Shortly after six o'clock we arrived at 44 Hercules Street, a three-story block of units in Chatswood. On the top floor, Theresa pushed open her door. "I purchased this two bedroom apartment four years ago at a very good price. I'll lead the grand tour."

One of the bedrooms was converted into a study-cum-exercise room. A white laminated desk piled high with books occupied one corner while a black padded bench, surrounded by weights of varying sizes and shapes, sat in the middle of the floor.

"Two of my passions. Training and psychotherapy."

I picked up Carl Jung's book, *Memories, Dreams and Reflections.*

"I'm currently digesting his works," offered Theresa. "My analyst and I have been discussing key concepts."

"Which ones?"

"Jung's archetypes, particularly the animus and anima. Brilliant stuff! He encouraged patients to explore their polarities, especially the repressed side of their psyche. You men must discover the anima, your soft feminine side, while we women must explore our masculine force, the animus."

"Your weight training should assist you there."

She prodded my ribs. "With only part of it. How about a drink?"

"Just a quick glass of wine. Don't want to stay long. I have to grab a train home."

"Come into the living room. I'll fetch some wine."

I sat on her black leather lounge facing a wall paneled in silver-flecked square mirrors which helped create the illusion of a much larger room. Stereo equipment and bookcases occupied another wall.

She shouted from the kitchen, "Have a look around. White burgundy okay?"

"Sure."

I went to inspect the weird assortment of wood carvings on her shelves.

"Like those?" She asked, handing me a wine goblet.

"What are they?"

She picked up a male figurine with a large elongated penis pointing downward. "Wood carvings. From Rarotonga, one of the Cook Islands. I picked them up while on holiday last year. Now that's what you'd call a huge Freddie!"

"What does it represent?"

She chuckled, "Don't you know?"

"Yea, well, I mean, the figurines."

"They're images of the fisherman's god. The sign of a good yield."

I sipped the wine. "Aren't you joining me?"

"Had more than I should at lunch. With my weight training, I have to watch my caloric intake." She pulled out a record and placed it on a turntable.

"Don't see too many of those around anymore."

"I still haven't purchased a compact disc player. I enjoy the sounds of my old records. Do you like Carl Orff?"

"Never heard of him."

She sat next to me on the leather couch. "His *Carmina Burana*–a scenic cantata in Latin–is one of my favorites. I love the tension, the accelerating pace, the crashing cymbals."

"What's it about?"

She snuggled closer. "It's about the primeval forces becoming aroused, rejoicing in earthly pleasures and the intoxicating effect of love."

After the claret at the zoo and my white burgundy, I was experiencing a different type of intoxication. I glanced at the mirror and the reflection of Theresa's darting tongue wetting her lips.

She rubbed her spandex shorts enticingly against my side. "Last night I had a dream about us."

"Oh?"

"Care to hear about it?"

"As long as I don't have to analyze it."

"I dreamt you were spending the night here. I was showing you my equipment. Your back was on the training bench and you wanted to press my weights."

Her hand slid to my knee. "Want me to show you how to do it?"

I tried swallowing. My throat wouldn't function. And my damn knees! They began their familiar shake. I tried steadying them with my hands but the trembling became more visible.

"I'm burning inside. Let's do it."

The old fears resurrected. I had no protection! I was out of my depth with this lioness in heat.

"It's starting to ache. Touch me."

She grabbed my hand and pressed it between her legs. She groaned sensuously.

"Are you nervous?" she whispered.

"No, well, yes, I..."

"In *Carmina Burana* the virgin succumbs to her passion. *Dulcissime, totam tibi subdo me!* Sweetest boy, I give my all to you!"

Theresa kissed me hard. "Give me your tongue!"

I complied. Like a vacuum cleaner her salty mouth consumed my tongue, extending it completely. She sucked harder. I gagged.

"Take off my shirt and bra," she commanded.

Woozy from the wine, I surrendered. With her moans spurning me on, my fears and inhibitions faded. I removed her shirt. She ripped off mine. Her breathing erupted, quicker, more erratic. I struggled with the bra. The damn snaps wouldn't budge.

"Take off my shorts and panties," she groaned before launching into my mouth yet again.

One of my hands continued struggling with her bra while the other attended to her shorts. Her breathing and moans grew louder, more frantic. Her black hair flailed in the air. The cymbals crashed in *Carmina Burana.* She plied my tongue and ripped off my pants with one hand, pinching my nipples with her other.

When I removed her black panties, she grabbed my hand. "Yes! More vigorous. Yes! Faster!"

With a wisp of coconut wafting in the air, I concentrated on that last snap. Jammed. Whatever happened to velcro? The more I struggled, the more my legs shook, the hotter Theresa got.

Then came those damn thoughts yet again.

"What about protection?" I whispered.

She frantically grabbed her purse and removed a foil packet. "Here. Use this," she moaned.

I fiddled with the Trojan condom, the lubricated ribbed variety. My anxieties resurfaced. I muttered, "You don't have any diseases, do you?"

"Ugh... It's okay!"

What did she mean, "It's okay"?

"It's okay, Peter!" she half yelled, half groaned. "I want to get on top. Hurry. Hurry!"

I took her literally. Flushed with excitement, I sheathed Freddie then attacked the last snap of her bra. It broke, releasing small tight breasts peaked with cherry brown nipples. Oh my God! The sight was too much. I exploded. Theresa pushed me on the floor and mounted. I felt like Carmina getting burana'd on the turntable. The cymbals crashed once more as she unleashed a gigantic scream.

We collapsed in one another's arms–exhausted animus and anima.

We made love once more that night in her waterbed. I wasn't as nervous and almost came inside of her.

Brring. Brring. The phone. Ringing. Ringing.

Theresa slurred, "Who can that be?"

I massaged my groggy head. Christ! It was after two in the morning.

"Hello?... Yes... Who?... Yes... He's here... Peter, it's for you."

"Me? Who is it?"

She giggled and handed me the phone.

"Hello?... Ma! Whatya calling here for?... Yea, I'm okay... I gave you this number in case of an emergency... I told you I may be late... lost track of time... We were talking about clients, professional stuff... Of course, there's lots of people here... Yea, well, I didn't realize it was so late... No, probably best to spend the night here. There's a spare room... Of course the others are staying... I know I should've called... Sorry... What?... The phone was in the other room... Couldn't hear it with everyone talking... I'll be home tomorrow morning... Talk to you then. *Dobra noc.* Good night."

IN THE DOG HOUSE

SUNDAY, FEBRUARY 13

"Psiakrew Piotr!"

Whenever Ma called me "dog's blood," she was bloody angry.

"It's 11 o'clock! Where were you?"

"I told you I ended up staying the night. There were other people sleeping over."

She wiped her hands on the dishtowel. "Why didn't you call last night? Pa and I weren't able to sleep. I waited up for you."

"I was having a good time. I forgot."

"You forgot? You never stay out that late without calling. What were you doing?"

"Talking psychology."

"You should've phoned!"

"Yea, I know. Sorry."

"What's wrong with your neck?"

"It's stiff. Must've slept the wrong way." Damn water bed! I bobbed up and down every time Theresa moved. And Christ did she move! My neck hurt like hell. Tilting my head to the side was the only way I could ease the muscle spasm.

Folding his newspaper, Pa walked into the conversation. "You made Ma very upset. You should've called. You know she doesn't sleep when you stay out late."

Ma pounced again. "How many were there?"

I ignored the inquisition and went into the kitchen. They followed.

"Were there others sleeping in that woman's flat?"

I stopped in my tracks and yelled, "I'll be 29 this Wednesday! I don't have to tell you everything I do, who I see, where I go, what I do. And yes, lots of people were sleeping over."

"You've worried her sick!" yelled my father who, with his short white hair and mustache, often acted and sounded like the Gestapo. "Kept Ma up all night! You should've called!"

"I have my own life to live!"

He waved the paper in my face. "Not when you live with us! It's our house! I worked bloody hard for it. You either live by our rules or get out. Find another place!"

"No, Piotr!" she shrieked. "You don't have to do that! He doesn't mean what he's saying."

She faced Pa and screamed in Polish. He roared back, *"Ty idiotko!"* then bolted toward the garage.

She shook her hands angrily after his retreat. After Ma calmed down, she said, "Don't mind him. He sees how worried I get when you don't call. Something could happen."

"Well nothing happened!"

"Let me cook you some eggs."

I felt like a prisoner of war. Receive the daily ration of food and check in by curfew, or else the bloodhound will be out searching.

"Piotr, be a good boy. Next time call."

I sat down at the table and nursed my sore neck. "Just leave me alone."

"Now be honest. Who was there?"

"Please leave me alone!" I stormed into my room and slammed the door, leaving the grand inquisitor standing in the hallway.

VALENTINE'S DAY

MONDAY, FEBRUARY 14

Theresa was back on the pill. That alleviated my fear of pregnancy, however, my anxiety about catching a disease continually haunted my mind. Though I had to coax her, Theresa and I had blood tests in order to confirm we were not HIV positive. Since both of us had not been sexually active for the past four months (for me, it was immeasurably longer), a negative test would formally stamp a seal of approval on our commitment to be sexually active.

"We won't receive the results of the test for another two weeks," said Theresa as we left the doctor's office. "I know we're both safe. I donate blood regularly to the Red Cross and the tests have always been negative. And since you haven't had sex in the past year..."

"Actually, it's really been a year and a half, well, maybe two years. I went to my doctor twice during the past year to have tests, just to be sure. They all came out negative."

"Peter, you're paranoid about it all. You don't need to be continually tested."

"I know, but they say the HIV virus may not show in the system for up to three months after the last sexual exposure. You can never be too sure. Who knows, I may be a special case."

She kissed me passionately. "Don't worry. Trust me. You're safe with me."

Later in the day we exchanged Valentine gifts. I gave her the book by Harville Hendrix, *Keeping the Love You Find*. She presented me with a set of hand grips.

Love is bliss!

HAPPY 29TH BIRTHDAY!

WEDNESDAY FEBRUARY 16

Another stinking hot summer day. I dashed to the observation room behind the one-way mirror. Gerard and Leela were there sipping coffee and eating jam rolls while waiting to watch my three o'clock Tortelli interview. With my armpits saturated, my heart racing, and stomach cramping, I struggled to suppress my overwhelming anxiety. What a way to celebrate my birthday!

"We haven't much time," declared Smelder. "Brief us on the family."

I cleared my throat. "The Tortelli family consists of the parents, Mario and Angela, and their two children. Maria is 10 years old and Angelo is eight. He's the presenting problem, encopresis."

Leela munched on a jam roll. "When did you last see them?"

"A month ago. January 18 to be exact. This is actually their second appointment. They canceled again last week."

Gerard scooped a tad of cream off Leela's upper lip and licked his finger. "You may have lost them, Pinowski. They may not show."

If only!

"Peter, your clients have arrived," resonated the voice on the intercom.

Gerard sipped his coffee. "Let's not waste any more time. Have you checked the microphone and video camera?"

Trust my luck. "They're working."

"Bring them in."

Combating the panic, I walked slowly toward the waiting room. Thought I'd have a giant spasm attack before the counseling even commenced. Never in my life had I been watched while doing it.

Near the reception desk I found the stocky Mrs. Tortelli in a floral-patterned black dress sitting with her plump son bulging out of his khaki school shorts.

"Where's Mr. Tortelli?" I asked, scanning the area.

She tugged on a black hair growing from the mole above her lip. "He no come. At *ristorante.*"

"And Maria?"

"No need. Just Angelo."

I was in deep trouble! My legs shook as I led them into the interviewing room. I then stopped in total horror. Strewth! I forgot to mention.

"Uh... I have some colleagues assisting me behind that mirror over there."

"What you say?"

I pointed. "Behind that mirror, there's people helping you."

"What you say?"

Brring, brring.

I answered the phone.

"Where's the father and daughter?" interrogated Gerard.

I muttered, "They weren't able to make it."

"Who talk?" questioned the mother.

Smelder responded, "We're wasting our time seeing the two of them. Send them home. Tell her to bring her husband and daughter to the next session."

Perspiration rolled down my cheeks. I took a deep breath. "Mrs. Tortelli, we... uh... have to finish this interview. My colleagues inform me that we need your husband."

Brring, brring.

"Don't forget the daughter!"

"We also need Maria."

"What you talk?"

"We need Mr. Tortelli and your daughter to come with you and Angelo."

Her hands gestured wildly as she bellowed, "I'm here! You're here! Angelo here! All here!"

"Yes, I know, but..."

"Angelo. Still no good. Poodle comes. You fix."

"I'd really like to help, but we can't fix the problem until the whole family is here."

She shook her bewildered head. *"Non capisco!"*

The phone reverberated once again.

"She's controlling the interview," berated Gerard. "You're wasting our time. Send her home."

My clothes were saturated. "I'll make another appointment so your husband and Maria can join us."

Wearing a savage scowl, the mother abused her son in Italian.

"Calm down, Mrs. Tortelli..."

I asked Angelo, "What's she saying?"

He shrugged his shoulders. "Me mum's mad 'cause she took time off from the restaurant to take me out of school for this appointment. She's blaming me."

"Calm down, Mrs. Tortelli..."

Brring, brring.

Leela's composed voice startled me. "Peter, it's very important you end the interview. Her histrionics are preventing you from terminating. She must understand that you're in control of therapy. Get out of the chair and open the door so she clearly gets the message that it's time to leave. Arrange another appointment at the receptionist."

I stood up. "We have to finish. I'll make another appointment on the way out."

The only thing that moved was Mrs. Tortelli's mouth which cursed, *"Dio cane!..."*

Thank God I didn't understand Italian.

I opened the door and motioned that we leave.

She wouldn't budge. Her finger wagged in my direction while her shrieking voice pierced my skull. "Angelo need help!"

"Please, Mrs. Tortelli..."

I glanced desperately at the mirror.

Leela rang again. "Leave. She'll eventually calm down. Wait for her in reception."

I did just that. Five minutes later, Angela Tortelli huffed past, dragging poor little Angelo. I wasn't game to ask about setting another appointment.

Back behind the one-way screen, Leela was rewinding the videotape.

"Where's Gerard?"

"Since the other family members didn't show, and nothing much was happening, he said it wasn't necessary for the two of us to remain. He put me in charge. Did you schedule an appointment?"

"No. She left in a rage."

"Give her a call in a couple of days. She'll cool down. Her son will still be soiling. That should provide the motivation to force her back with the entire family."

I had my doubts. Mrs. Tortelli left in a very shitty mood. I knew exactly how she felt.

4:50 p.m. I was resting my weary head on my desk. Suddenly, I was grabbed from behind.

"Bloody Hell! You startled me."

Surjit chuckled. "Glad I caught you napping. It's a sign you're settling in."

"You must've been a cat burglar in a past life."

"I brought you something." He handed me a present wrapped in gold and silver foil.

"How'd you know it was my birthday?"

"I have my ways. Open it!"

Like an impetuous child, I ripped through the wrapping. I uncovered a book, *One Flew Over the Cuckoo's Nest*.

Surjit beamed. "Ken Kesey is one of my favorite authors."

"The old movie with Jack Nicholson was fantastic. But I never read the book. Thanks."

"It seemed appropriate. At our hospital, it's not the patients but rather the staff that create the cuckoo's nest."

I recalled my recent experience in front of the mirror. "You can say that again!"

"Are you doing anything special for your birthday?"

"There's a small family gathering later this evening. The big party is Friday night. Theresa's taking me out."

He winked. "Don't do anything I wouldn't do. How about some table tennis next week?"

"I wouldn't say no."

He patted me on the shoulder. "Happy birthday!"

This must've been the year for books. Earlier, Henry had presented me with an embossed edition of the Bible.

"Hurry, hurry!" Ma shouted. She frantically wiped the protective plastic which covered the sofa. "There's plenty of work before your party. Get busy! Uncle Janek and Aunt Adele will be here at eight. We're doing all this for you!"

Tension still crackled in the air. The party was a peace offering. Ma was still upset about my staying overnight at Theresa's. She persistently badgered me, claiming I wasn't telling her everything. No person in his right mind would.

"Quit dawdling! Clean off the pictures in the dining room."

I feather dusted Our Lady of Czestochowa, the Black Madonna with a scar on her right cheek. Ma loved regaling her version of the picture displayed prominently on our wall. She said that the soldier who slashed the Byzantine painting with his bayonet promptly fell to his knees and became a convert the instant he saw blood oozing from Our Lady's face. Sounded more like a miracle bred of ignorance. Yet Ma was a true believer.

Having been raised an obedient Catholic, she was obsessed with sexual purity. Thought everyone should be like the Virgin Mary, or in my case, like an asexual Saint Joseph who happened to be edged out by the Holy Spirit.

Couldn't possibly imagine my parents ever romping in bed. At 56 and 58, with 37 years of marriage behind them, my mother and father had produced Stella and myself plus the several miscarriages in between. According to Father Blaszczynski, they would have been past their sexual quota. After all, he preached sex was strictly for procreation.

"Hurry up! Piotr!"

I frantically pushed the duster around the bookshelf, past the neatly arranged memorabilia of Poland: a burnished wooden plate; Chopin's monument in Lazienki

Park portrayed on pressed wheat; a couple of dolls dressed in the traditional costume of red, white, and black; a book of poetry by Adam Mickiewicz; and Professor Oscar Halecki's classic, *History of Poland,* sitting next to Pope John Paul II. All were reminders to keep the fires of tradition burning.

"They're here!" she cried.

With all the excitement, you'd think the Pope had just arrived.

I forced a grin and greeted our guests.

"Happy birthday, Piotr!" screamed an ebullient Aunt Adele–not exactly a Polish pin-up. Fifty pounds overweight with false teeth, she sported a face that looked as if it was continually run over by a group of Gdansk soccer players.

Couldn't imagine my father's older brother, Janek, mustering any passion. Maybe that's why they never had children. To be fair, Janek was no spring chicken either, with a shiny bowling ball head and a smile graced with two darkened front teeth. As a child, I used to believe they had turned black from axle grease.

We gathered around the walnut veneer dining table while Ma brought out the pork roast. She placed it among the mashed potatoes, the chopped cucumbers in cream, a tomato and onion salad, and the baby peas.

Sharpening the carving knife, Pa looked like a sheared sheep with his snow white hair and mustache clipped to a stubbly fuzz, the result of yesterday's haircut by the fastidious Mr. Marszalek.

"Ojciec nasz..." began my mother in a solemn prayer of thanksgiving. A simple acknowledgement would've done–rub a dub dub, thanks for the grub, yeah God.

"... Amen." We raised our heads and reached for the food. Blackie, sitting patiently under the table, chewed at my shoes while waiting for the scraps.

Pa solemnly lifted the glass of vodka. *"Na zdrowie!* Good health!"

We returned his salute and devoured our meal. The brothers discussed the garage while the two women talked shop. "Are these crystal glasses the ones you bought on sale?" asked my Aunt.

"I picked them up last year with a coupon from the Sydney Herald. By the way, they had a special at Woolworths on sauerkraut, 20 cents off each tin. I bought two cases."

"You have a great eye for discounts."

"Take a dozen cans when you leave," said Ma.

"Dziekuje bardzo. Thank you very much."

"Prosze bardzo. You're welcome. I always say, buy food in season and clothes out of season. Check for the sale and use a coupon. I've saved lots of money over the years."

I ate in silence, remembering the time we sat in a restaurant and Ma filled her purse with the extra sachets of ketchup, mustard, and sugar. She would've taken the salt and pepper shakers had I not stopped her.

"... happy birthday dear Piotr, happy birthday to you!"

With a giant puff I extinguished all 29 candles. I then sliced Ma's walnut and carrot cake.

"It's hard to believe how quickly you've grown up," said Adele with a fork poised near her mouth. "I remember when you were thinking of becoming a priest."

"It wasn't me. It was Ma."

Her mouth crunched on the walnuts. "You would have made your mother proud."

"My Piotr would have made a very good priest. He had the vocation, I could tell. I loved watching him as an altar boy dressed in his red cassock. I would iron his white surplice extra special and even sewed his birth date on the collar so he could tell which was his."

I recalled the times in the sacristy. Used to sip wine with the other boys and devour communion wafers.

"He should've joined the seminary. I took him for guidance to Father Blaszczynski, God rest his soul."

"He was a drunk," I contended. "He would scream at us for pouring too much water into his wine. The nuns kept it all hushed up that he drank himself to death."

She rapped my knuckles. "Don't you talk that way! He baptized you and gave you first communion. He was a holy man!"

"Ma, you know the stories that were going around."

"I won't hear it!"

My aunt reached into her purse and removed a white envelope. "Piotr, open up your presents! This one's from us."

With Blackie nuzzling at my hands, I opened the sealed flap and found a Hallmark birthday card with a 10 dollar note.

I kissed her cheek. *"Dziekuje."* Generosity was never a trademark of my relatives. Even after working many years for my uncle, my father still hadn't been offered a partnership in the garage.

Slightly pickled on his vodka, Pa slurred, "This one's from me and your ma." He passed a huge box covered in blue tissue paper. Unable to contain his laughter, he gagged, "Go ahead... Open it."

I cautiously unpeeled the tissue. A large brown box revealed the inscription Tide Laundry Detergent. Pa, the perpetual joker, must've wrapped one of Ma's bargains.

She was already cleaning up. "Put the paper in this garbage bag."

I pulled open the cardboard flaps, and Pa erupted into guffaws. It was my Macintosh! He had wrapped up my computer!

He chortled, "I told you it was a combined present for graduation, Christmas, and birthday."

Everyone giggled. Except me. I was busy checking all the connections. Thank God it wasn't damaged.

"Your sister sent you this." Ma handed me a small package. "It arrived yesterday in the post."

Although she lived in Melbourne with her husband, Stanley, and their two children, Stella always remembered birthdays.

I tore past the layer of brown postal wrapping, through the gaily colored green and gold, and pulled out a shiny black cardboard container, half the size of a shoe box. I removed the lid and pulled out a heavy object.

"Who's that?" asked my Aunt.

"Freud." Or more precisely, an imitation bronze plaster bust of a bearded Sigmund wearing spectacles. I immediately dubbed it "Siggy," a perfect desktop companion for my computer.

"Don't believe in that psycho stuff," chided Uncle Janek. "When I came here after the war, no one mollycoddled me. Didn't speak much English and still got a job. Better off for it. Right, Jozef?"

My father tottered on his chair. "The more you give, the more people want. You have to stand on your own two feet."

"Look at me," pointed my uncle. "I own a service station and the garage is always booked weeks ahead. Your pa and I have more cars than we can fix. We never needed psychology."

"Leave the boy alone," defended Adele. "I'm sure he's doing a good job, whatever it is."

Pa reached for the sliwowica and small crystal glasses. "One final toast for the night!"

By this time, the two brothers were the only ones imbibing the plum liquor.

"Na zdrowie!" saluted one.

"Na zdrowie!" echoed the other.

I cheered that today's celebration was finally over.

A monstrous pelican. Beckons to its widening mouth. I float forward. Through the tunneled throat. Past doors. Opening. Closing. Into black emptiness. An energizing power. Compels me onward, inward. Speeding out of control. I can't resist. Distant light. Pierces the darkness. Brilliant gold oval door. My fingers tremble. Reach out. Grasp golden ring. The door groans, creaks. White heat. Streams through archway. Hot winds. Blowing, whistling. Blister my body. I shed my skin. Freedom! Into fiery light, I walk. Re-born!

I wiped my eyes and woke, bathed in love, as if immersed in a warm, sensuous pool that nurtured, comforted, healed. The flame of love blazed in my heart. Theresa was my sanctuary. As Olivia Newton-John once sang it, "I'm hopelessly devoted to you." Tonight we will embrace once more and be one.

8:03 p.m. Newtown. I paid the taxi and waited outside Taverna Stekki where Theresa had decided to christen my birthday. Compared with Wednesday night's aborted attempt, this evening's celebration was destined to be a joyous occasion.

I planned on spending the night at Theresa's so I decided against borrowing Pa's Holden. Too much anxiety. His paranoia about someone scratching the shiny finish would allow him no rest, and Ma would be worrying all night whether I had an accident. Theresa wanted to pick me up. I wasn't quite ready for her introduction into the family.

I spotted her red Honda turning the corner. A few minutes later she approached me with a sumptuous kiss.

I gasped, "Stunning as usual!"

Her white translucent dress revealed a faint outline of tight scant panties and breasts that were free of constraints. A large gold hoop encircling a shiny black stone dangled from each of her earlobes.

She slid her hands over my blue silk shirt. "You feel lovely."

"I bought it especially for tonight."

She unfastened several buttons to reveal my chest. "Now you're dressed for Greek passion."

Since getting to know Theresa, I had witnessed plenty. "Lead the way!"

She opened the door to Taverna Stekki where a bustling, boisterous room greeted us. A three-piece band electrified the crowd with guitar, mandolin, and bouzouki. Tables were filled with chattering, festive people and a Mediterranean sea of dark-haired bodies swayed their drinks in the air, toasting the celebration of life.

Theresa shouted at the man in a black suit.

"Table for two. Ramadopoulos."

"Right this way." He escorted us near the small stage where a white starched tablecloth awaited us.

"Just as well you made reservations," I said.

She put her hand near her ear. "What?" The music was deafening.

I yelled, "Just as well you made reservations!"

She nodded. "Without them, we'd never get in on a Friday night!"

Our white-jacketed waiter passed out menus. "What will you be drinking?"

"Bottle of retsina," answered her loud voice.

While the nuns at St. Vincents taught us to never raise our voice in public, this was the night to break traditions. I bellowed, "What food would you recommend?"

"Let me order. No weight training diet tonight. We're here to celebrate!"

My heart burst with joy. I wanted to proclaim to the world, *"I'm in love!"* Floating on a cloud of euphoria, I basked in her aura and surrendered to Aphrodite.

The dry white wine arrived and she ordered our meal—taramasalata, tzatziki and fried calamari as appetizers, mousaka and octopus for the main course.

The wine flowed and the appetizers appeared. Tearing into a fresh loaf of bread, we feasted on a pink creamy fish roe, garlic and dill yogurt, and fried squid, while clinking our glasses of retzina along the way. We sampled from each other's plates, sharing the sumptuous meal.

I swayed with the exhilarating music and proclaimed myself another Zorba, shouting, *"I love you!"*

My Greek goddess gently, lovingly stroked my face then reached for my hands. She dipped my forefinger into the fish roe and placed it in her mouth which playfully sucked and nibbled. Ecstasy! I lost all sense of time as the night whirled from one sensation to another, hands caressing, mouths munching, kissing...

When the band stopped for a rest, our voices once again returned to a normal decibel.

"This is positively the best birthday present I've ever received. You've made me so happy!"

"Wait till tonight. We will be even happier!"

"What would you like for dessert?" interrupted the waiter.

"Two *galaktoboureko,*" ordered Theresa.

"What's that?"

Theresa licked her lips. "Creamy custard, sandwiched between sheets of flaky pastry, dripping in a sweet gooey liquid. Yummy!"

"Sounds decadent."

She lifted her wine glass and clinked my retsina. "Here's to decadence!"

"How did you become so liberated?"

"Freedom arrived when I left home. Even though it's been nearly 30 years since they left Greece, my parents still keep the old traditions alive in Ulladulla. Dad fishes his trawler along the south coast with my three younger brothers. I love my heritage, but we're in a new country. I won't be chained by the old traditions."

"How old were you when your parents migrated?"

"My parents left the Peloponnese in 1965. I was seven. Those early years were painful. Dad worked long hours fishing. I rarely saw him. Just as well, he's a real chauvinist. He insists that women be subservient to men. As his only daughter, in addition to being the eldest, I was expected to learn English quickly and become the family interpreter. When I wasn't helping my mother, I had to cater after my three younger brothers. Even made their beds. Liberation arrived when I attended Sydney University. A huge weight fell from my shoulders, and I decided that my life would take precedence over everything else. I had sacrificed enough for my family. I will never be subservient again."

The waiter arrived and set our dessert on the table. "Your *galaktoboureko.*"

Before he left, Theresa placed another order. "Two glasses of ouzo!" She smiled coyly. "Have you tasted anise liqueur?"

"No, but I'll give it a go."

She combed her fingers through her curly black hair. "It's exhilarating to be free. No shoulds, nots, or expectations."

"I'm not as liberated. My mother still depends on me emotionally and has been like that ever since I was a kid."

"Another product of migrants."

"Except my parents migrated twice. They left Poland in 1957 and met each other shortly after arriving in America. They got married and had my sister, Stella, nine months later. They lived on Milwaukee Avenue in Chicago for 14 years. During that time I was born. When my father made the momentous decision to join his brother and sister in Australia, Ma wasn't at all happy about the thought of migrating yet again. Having lost her relatives during the war, the newfound friends in the Polish neighborhood served as her substitute family. Pa argued that his blood relatives came first. He wanted to work with my Uncle Janek in Sydney. He could then visit my Aunt Elzbieta in Melbourne more frequently than he could staying in America.

"I was six when we arrived in 1971. I'll never forget it. My mother became very depressed. At the age of 13, Stella was lumbered with the extra chores while I took on the job of cheering Ma up."

"Speaking of your mother, how does she feel about our date tonight?"

"She can be very bigoted. Ma doesn't like women who aren't Polish or Catholic, and you don't exactly fit the bill on either account. I didn't want to spoil tonight's celebration so I told her I was going out with some mates from school."

Theresa's eyes became wild. "I don't want another late night call!"

"Not to worry. I said I was spending the night with my mate, Florian."

"What if she calls him?"

"He'll cover for me and make an excuse why I couldn't come to the phone. Then he'd call your number."

"Great! Instead of your mother, we'll get a wake-up call from your mate."

"Don't worry. It'll work out."

I felt a cool draft across the table. "Peter, you can't spend your life avoiding confrontations with your mother. Sooner or later, you'll have to stand up to her."

"I know. I just wanted tonight to be special, without any hassles. After all, we are celebrating my birthday!"

"Promise you'll tell your mother about me."

"I promise!"

"What will you say?"

"That I've met this amazing Greek woman—intelligent, beautiful, and passionate."

"What else?"

"Bold, spirited, fantastic in every possible way."

"Right answer!"

The ouzo arrived and the band re-emerged to transform the mood. A waiter in the distant corner yelled, *"Opaa!"*

I sipped the anise liqueur. "Christ! This is strong stuff!"

She laughed. "As Zorba says, 'Here's to life!' "

We clinked our glasses.

"Opaa!" came the roar from another table.

With a devilish glint she squeezed my knee under the table and gleamed, "You may not realize what's in store for you!"

I downed my ouzo. "I'm ready!" And ordered another round. The pulsating music and laughter caused my head to bob and sway. When the band played *Zorba,* my inhibitions dissolved.

My partner yanked me from my chair to join hands with the frenzied merrymakers snaking their way around the small restaurant. With the occasional kick in the air, Theresa twisted and turned to the intensifying rhythm while her jiggling breasts struggled to be liberated from the white translucent dress. We danced and we hugged and we danced some more.

Then waiters moved tables and brought out piles of plates. For a mere 25 dollars, one could hurl an arsenal of ceramic platters against the brick wall. What an offer! I quickly joined the queue and purchased two stacks to share with Theresa.

I heaved the first dish. "This one's for Gerard Smelder!"

"Opaa!"

Theresa smashed one of hers. "Take this, Leela Hennessey!"

"Opaa!"

"To Ma's intrusiveness!"

"Opaa!"

We both crashed ours at the same time. "Freedom!"

"Opaa!"

Plates splattered everywhere. One for my third grade teacher, Sister Francesca, who continually slapped my knuckles with her ruler. Another for Pa's practical jokes. I even remembered my ex-therapist, Melody Mill, and our final session which was supposed to be this evening. Who needed it! I found my own catharsis! *"Opaa!"*

What a night! There must've been a thousand discs shattered near the wall. As the waiters swept up, Theresa and I danced some more, laughed a lot, and ordered more ouzo. Amid the resounding *"Opaa!"*

It was after two in the morning when we arrived at her apartment. How she managed to drive home, I'll never know. With my head swirling and spinning, I stumbled through the door and collapsed on the black leather lounge. I just wanted to nestle quietly and intimately with my lover and caress her soft skin.

Theresa turned on the stereo and blared an old favorite by Olivia Newton-John, "Physical." She began miming Olivia as she gyrated rhythmically to the music, beckoning me to get physical. "Come here!" she announced. "I want to dance!"

I could only gaze dreamily at her luscious body. My mind instructed both legs to move. Only one responded. She came to my assistance and lifted me off the lounge. She pressed me tightly against her pelvis while her open mouth came down hard on mine, feverishly kissing, probing, and sharing the taste of anise. She tossed my glasses to the floor, then reached inside the back of my pants and squeezed my bottom with her talons. When she pulled my underpants tight into the crack, I protested. "Ouch!"

"Let's do it in another room," she rasped.

Pawing my pants along the way, she guided me into her study where she cleared the padded bench, scattering weights and Winnicott's book, *Playing and Reality*. She guided me downward, singing along with Olivia about wanting to hear my body talk.

With my back on the vinyl bench, my body could barely move, let alone speak. My anticipation grew into excitement. I wanted to cry out, but her insatiable mouth kissed wildly, preventing me from uttering a word. Her probing tongue then wandered to my ear and hungrily explored each crevice. My legs erupted into their familiar quake, prompting her mouth to suck hard on my neck.

"Slower!" I pleaded.

"I want you!"

Her hands clawed at my silk shirt and ripped it open. The buttons popped across the floor. I gasped. There went 45 dollars. "You're moving too fast!" I cried.

My words merely acted as an aphrodisiac. Her chest heaved and she moaned, "I love to see you tremble!"

Like a ravenous animal, she flung her dress and panties off and frantically tore at my underpants. Freddie was already standing at attention. I was caught in her whirlwind of unquenchable emotions. Her appetite was frightening yet exciting. My mouth struggled to adhere to her wiggling breasts.

My distress escalated when she grunted like an animal. Her powerful arms pinned me to the bench while her roaming mouth began nibbling my earlobes, nostrils, neck, then shoulders. I squirmed with a breathless protest.

With my quivering body acting as her stimulant, her passion became unbridled. "Tell me you want it!"

My breathing quickened and the muscles tensed as the pressure intensified around my loins. My mind screamed with delight. "I do!"

Then her nibbling turned into biting–my chest, stomach... When she moved below my waist, I panicked. Freddie came just in time!

She rushed to mount, but Freddie wasn't cooperative. Her breathing became frantic, her moans more audible. She straddled my face with a command, "Eat me!"

I burped on the *galaktoboureko* and gagged for air.

Theresa gyrated faster. "Eat me!" she demanded, then grabbing my hands directed them to her erect nipples. "Play!"

Locked between those muscular thighs, I had little choice. Her fingers clutched my legs for support while her mouth released sensual groans whenever I moved.

"Y-e-s-s-s!!" The more she groaned, the more her rippled thighs tightened their vise-like grip. The smell of musk became overwhelming.

"O-h-h-h!" I moaned.

The quickest way to save my skull was to work fast! I knew there was a clitoris somewhere around there, but had never met one face to face. I probed deeper, praying she would climax soon. In my search for the right spot, her passion rocketed, propelling her hands and thighs to squeeze even tighter. My head felt dizzy. And on top of that, a strand of pubic hair was caught between my teeth. At that point, I would have welcomed a phone call from Ma!

With my cranium on the verge of collapse, her body released a series of violent tremors. We both screamed. She relaxed her hold, allowing the blood to surge back to my head. We both toppled on the floor, much too exhausted to utter the sound, *"Opaa!"*

THE DOG HOUSE REVISITED

SATURDAY, FEBRUARY 19

It was late in the afternoon when Theresa dropped me off. Wasn't game to invite her in, not with my buttonless shirt flapping in the wind. Tried sneaking into the house, but Blackie's barking revealed my presence.

"Piotr!"

Avoiding Ma's screech, I rushed into my bedroom and slammed the door behind.

"Piotr! Przydz tutaj!"

I grabbed a clean shirt. *"Czekaj!* Wait! I'll be out in a minute."

"Where were you?" she roared.

My silence didn't stop her interrogation.

"Were you with that woman from work?"

I opened the door and faced the firing squad.

She pointed at Theresa's love bites plastered across my neck and shrieked, *"O Jej! A co to jest!?* What is that!?"

Christ! I should've worn a turtleneck.

"What are those?"

Despite the summer heat, I buttoned my collar. "It's nothing."

"You lied! You told me you were staying with Florian. I called his mother this morning, and she said you weren't there last night. Where were you? And look at your disgusting neck!"

"I have to take Blackie out for a walk."

"Psiakrew!" she swore. "Don't leave until I get an answer. I can't trust you anymore. Where were you? And don't tell me you were with some other boys because I called your friends."

"Jesus! Why don't you phone all of Sydney?"

"If you tell the truth, I don't have to call no one."

I headed for the fridge with Ma hot on my heels.

"Did you spend the night with that woman?"

"Okay already. I was with Theresa. I didn't tell you because I knew you'd get upset."

The veins bulged on her neck. She swung at my shoulder and connected.

"Ouch!"

"I don't want my boy sleeping around with some whore!"

"She's not a whore! I love her!"

"How can you say that? She's not one of us!"

"Just because she's not Polish doesn't mean I can't love her."

"It won't work. She wouldn't fit in with the rest of us."

"I love her and that's the only thing that's important. She makes me happy."

"She'll use you, Piotr. That type of woman only wants one thing. That's all they're after."

"How can you say that? You've never even met her!"

"I don't have to. I know her type. Look at your neck. It's wrong what you do. A good woman would never let you sleep in her house."

"We love each other!"

"Agh!" she growled and stormed out of the kitchen, leaving me alone at last. The peace was short-lived. She promptly returned armed with a plastic bottle.

"Hey!"

She spritzed my face once more.

"Cut it out!"

Again she pumped the nozzle.

"For Christ sake, that damn holy water won't change my mind!"

"Don't you swear in my house!"

"Then leave me alone."

"That woman has you under her spell. You need a nice Polish girl, like Jadwiga Niedzwiedzka."

"She's ugly and stays home all day weeding her parents' garden."

"So?"

"Theresa's educated. We work together. We're interested in the same things. I love her. Can't you see that?"

"Because you have marks on your neck means you're in love? Your father and I are together 37 years. I knew he was a decent man. Before we were married, he never wanted to do those things. That showed respect. And respect is love."

I stared at my mother. She'd never understand.

"Please, Piotr. Give her up. She only brings trouble. Look how she makes us fight."

I shook my head and whistled for Blackie. We both needed a walk.

14TH SESSION WITH HEIDI WENTWORTH.

THURSDAY, FEBRUARY 24

"... been arguing with Mum lately."

"What about?" I asked.

"'Bout everythin', I guess. She's not happy unless she's runnin' my life. She still hassles me about eatin', even when I put on the stupid weight."

Rounder cheeks confirmed that Heidi had, indeed, gained close to nine pounds since being admitted six weeks ago.

"What do you tell your mother when she hassles you?"

"Dunno. Just get cranky. Feel like walkin' out, which isn't very easy on the hospital ward."

"Why don't you tell her exactly how you feel?"

"I try doin' that in those family sessions with the fat shrink. He says I act like a brat. My parents listen to his garbage then treat me like a baby. I just wanna get outa here as fast as I can. I'm stuffin' myself silly."

"Let's stay with one issue, Heidi. I think it's central. What do you fight with your mom about?"

"She always asks questions. Wants to know what I'm thinkin' all the time. As if she wants to get inside my head and run the controls."

I leaned forward to punctuate my advice. "Asserting yourself is part of growing up. Our mothers have to eventually let go. The only way they'll learn is when we stand up for ourselves. It's important to live your own life..."

The results of the HIV test proved negative. I breathed a sigh of relief, especially since we had stopped practicing safe sex. Theresa had continually reassured me during the past two weeks that we were safe and there was nothing to worry about. The test results certainly eased my anxiety. The likelihood of the laboratory making an error was minuscule. My mind was at peace and easily dispelled the occasional lingering doubt.

LUNCH WITH SURJIT

🦃

THURSDAY, MARCH 3, 1994

Surjit joined me in the cafeteria queue. "We haven't shared a meal in quite a while."

"I've been flat out, what with cases and everything."

I wasn't ready to launch into a discussion about my love life. Spending time with Theresa caused the past two weeks to whiz right by, like a roller coaster spilling in perpetual motion. I was still recovering from the bruises sustained while roller skating last weekend, not to mention the physical workouts at her apartment. I was far too exhausted to even record my journal entries.

Surjit filled his tray with tuna salad and a carton of juice. "How are your cases going?" he inquired.

"Still having problems keeping families in therapy," I said. "My best results have been with the b.w.'s–the bed wetters."

"What's your secret?"

"The bell and pad technique. I just instruct the parents to place the electrode-embedded pad under the child's bed sheets. As you know, b.w.'s are notoriously deep sleepers. When they wet the bed, the bell brings them to their senses."

"Much success?"

"Clients take to it like a duck in water. I've monitored the development of five families with a behavioral chart recording their progress. After a couple of weeks of improvement, I have the b.w. drink a large glass of water before bedtime to extend the bladder and insure that sufficient control has been developed."

I lifted my tray which contained a chicken casserole, salad, piece of cake, and two cans of Coke. I followed Surjit to a table with a window view–overlooking the parked cars.

"Most cases are doing extremely well," I added. "There's only been one incident of symptom replacement. Little Bernie became so frightened when the alarm bell sounded that he now refuses to sleep in his own bed. Win some, lose some."

"I almost lost one this week," sighed the psychiatrist. He placed his navy blue suitcoat on back of the chair. "I went on a home visit Monday to hospitalize a paranoid schizophrenic who had been threatening the neighbors. I didn't realize he had a history of using firearms until the tactical squad arrived, which wasn't until I had already knocked on the front door. I waited in the archway while the police scampered for position. When the door creaked open, the police lifted their rifles."

"What did you do?!"

"Quite honestly, I wanted to flee, but when I saw the man's agitated face, the words tumbled out of my mouth. 'I have a serious problem,' I said. 'The police could shoot us if we don't go to hospital. Could you help me?' "

"What happened?!"

"He nervously eyed the firearms, then meekly surrendered. I could have hugged him."

"Way to go!"

"Unfortunately, he was out in three days. When his case was presented for committal, the magistrate said there was insufficient cause to detain him since he hadn't yet harmed himself nor hurt anyone. On a positive note, our investigation discovered that his mother's house, where he had been living, was being used as an emergency placement for foster children. Realizing their error, the welfare department promptly removed the children. You never know what he could've done."

"Strewth! I'll stick to my bed wetters, thank you very much."

"So it hasn't been an easy week," said Surjit munching on the tuna salad.

I pointed to his black mustache. "There's tuna above your lip."

He gave a wipe with his napkin. "By the way, whatever happened to that paralyzed 14-year-old girl?"

I stabbed my last morsel of chicken. "You mean the hysterical conversion disorder? What a joke! Gerard used a strategic paradox. He informed the confused girl that her physical paralysis served an important function for the family. He warned her about getting better, saying that any improvement would precipitate a crisis–either her mother might leave, the father might start drinking again, or one of her sisters could become an addict. She became furious with Smelder's constant badgering and demanded that her mother remove her from hospital. She left uncured in a wheelchair. We heard later that she attended a Pentecostal church and, after receiving the Holy Spirit, was instantly healed. Of course, when Gerard heard about it, he credited his therapeutic wizardry. He intends to present a paper about his miracle cure at the next psychiatric conference. He'll take credit for any success and blame the failures on the patients or staff deficiencies."

We finished our meal and poured ourselves some tea at the large communal urn. We returned to our table where Surjit shared another recent case. "An Asian man was admitted on the ward and began running around the floor holding onto his penis. He kept on screaming, 'I'm losing it'. Turned out to be a rare symptom, called Koro, where the patient believes his penis is retreating into the body. In actual fact, his mind does cause it to retract. We decided against offering the traditional Asian treatment, which meant fastening a string between the legs to prevent his shrinking member from disappearing while a week long vigil, with family members taking turns holding onto the string, convinced the patient that his penis was secure."

I nudged Surjit. "The poor guy probably became frantic because you admitted him on the ward with no strings attached."

He laughed. "By the way, how's everything with Theresa?"

I shuffled uneasily in my chair. "Good as gold. We've been seeing quite a lot of one another."

I didn't want to mention that the gold was tarnished and our workouts weren't always working out. I was particularly upset with Freddie's trigger-happy response. And my research on premature ejaculation didn't solve the problem. I already knew I was overly anxious. Prescribing sensate focus techniques to retard ejaculation was all well and good, but between Freddie's low tolerance for frustration and Theresa's ravenous passion, I never came inside of her. Not that it stopped Theresa. She always managed to discharge multiple sets of orgasms.

To make matters worse, Ma was forever haranguing me about coming home late. In spite of her harassment, I was determined to remain on the roller coaster. I was often hanging on by the seat of my pants, but riding with Theresa had become the greatest thrill of my life. I wouldn't be derailed–not by my mother or a complex Oedipus.

I stared at my friend sipping from the white porcelain cup. I desperately wanted to ask for help, yet couldn't bring myself to expose my fears and anxieties, not to another bloke. Hell, no one ever heard of James Bond talking with his friend about relationship problems or a hair trigger.

Surjit tapped my shoulder. "Peter, there's a purpose for everything in life."

"What are you getting at?" I asked, still consumed with my mental morass.

His gaze was piercing. "Inner conflict provides fertile soil for creative solutions."

I nervously fidgeted with my cup while wondering if he had direct access to my mind.

Surjit continued, "Unpleasant experiences present opportunities to develop courage and wisdom."

Was it his turn to play "Let's get metaphysical"? I didn't need unpleasant experiences. I just wanted to get it off with Theresa, without any problems.

He relaxed his gaze and leaned back in his chair. "Have you read *One Flew Over the Cuckoo's Nest?*"

"Haven't had time, what with Theresa and everything."

"Read it and think of this," he said. "Life is like a book. A story must unfold in its unique way with its particular pace and purpose. We wouldn't enjoy a book if the protagonist arrived one day and left the next. His relationship with himself and others develops as a result of fermenting tension."

"So?"

"The reader always knows that the main character is in the perfect space at the right time, no matter what is happening. The protagonist, however, isn't privy to such information. He is shaped by a variety of experiences, many of which become crises. Yet each crisis pushes him further into the story. Conflict and pain generate movement and growth. They provide opportunities to taste defeat and achieve victory, important lessons for any worthwhile character."

"Well, as yet I haven't read the novel," I said, steering the conversation into something more concrete.

Surjit's face lightened. "Would you care to join me for an interesting episode about life? I play table tennis with some clients every Wednesday afternoon." He winked. "For therapeutic purposes, of course."

What the hell. At the very least, I'd have another opportunity to play ping-pong.

PING-PONG THERAPY

𝕏

WEDNESDAY, MARCH 9

I entered the Karen Horney Adult Psychiatric Department and strolled into the recreation room. A pervasive antiseptic scent hovered over the black and white checkered floor tiles. In the center of the barren chalk white room, four older-looking adolescents huddled around a ping-pong table.

"Excuse me, is Dr. Bhullar around?"

A grossly overweight patient of some 18 years with bright orange curly hair and a gray tracksuit bounced the small ball on the table. "You mean the Sooj?"

"Dr. Surjit Bhullar was supposed to meet me here at three o'clock."

"He hasn't come."

"Whadda ya want 'im for?" interjected a character straight out of the Rocky Horror Picture Show. This peroxide blonde punk with jelled hair spiked into three points swaggered menacingly toward me with paddle in hand. "You mental or something?"

"Me? No! I'm Dr. Pinowski. I was supposed to join Dr. Bhullar for your group session."

He tugged at his leather jacket. "What kinda name is Pissowski?"

I stared at the punk's dangling razor blade earrings then at the prominent scar of a Maltese cross over his third eye. "It's Pinowski and I'm Polish."

"You some shrink?"

The other three left the table and were gathering around. Strewth! Where the hell was Surjit? I backed toward the wall and cautioned myself: don't panic; play it cool. "Actually, I'm a psychologist. Dr. Bhullar... the Sooj... said you play table tennis on Wednesdays."

The patient with spiked blonde hair flicked the razor blade under his right ear. "What's it to you?"

My voice cracked. "The Sooj... asked me to join you for table tennis."

The punk lifted his paddle in the air. "We don't like table tennis. That's for fairies. Ain't I right?"

The others stared, waiting for a response. Wasn't game to wipe the sweat creeping down my face, lest it be interpreted as fear. I scanned the hall. No sight of Surjit! I turned to the more friendly, obese patient with orange curly hair.

"Don't you play table tennis today?"

Before he could answer, the peroxide punk, still clutching the paddle, moved closer. "I said, me mates and me don't play no table tennis. That's what fairies do."

"Surjit said..."

The punk's Maltese cross glared menacingly. "The Sooj ain't here, is he?"

I said nothing.

"Whadda ya say?"

Blocked by the four inmates, I eased myself across the wall. The trickle of perspiration down my cheeks turned into a torrent. "Well... what do you do here... at three o'clock... in the group?"

"Whadda ya mean?" he sneered. His yellow spikes made him appear much taller than his actual size.

"You know... how do you spend your time... with Surjit?"

He glanced at the others, then smirked. "We play ping-pong."

"Huh? Isn't that the..."

"Haw... Haw..." The jiggling razor blades led the others in a chorus of guffaws.

The bastard! "Good joke. Didn't quite catch your name."

He sniggered, "That's 'cause I didn't throw it to ya. Haw... Haw..."

I forced a smile through clenched teeth and plotted my revenge.

"A baldheaded youth in blue denims broke the tension. "I'm Jono." He was probably around 19, but without any hair, looked well over 30.

"I'm a skyzofreenik," he volunteered. "The doc back home in Wagga Wagga says my thoughts about UFO's result from skyzofreenee. I keep telling him, the aliens from Orion kidnap me in the middle of the night and insert probes in my brain..."

"Ya got 20 cents?" interrupted the belligerent punk.

I placed my hand in the pocket to prevent the silver from rattling. "No."

"Then have ya got a 50 cent piece in your pants? Haw... Haw..."

The others joined in like raving kookaburras. If it wasn't for that damn Surjit, I wouldn't be standing in this cuckoo's nest getting batted around by a group led by Rocky Horror himself.

"Da ya know how ta make a Maltese cross?"

I glared warily at the scar on his forehead.

"No."

"Ya poke his eye with a burnt stick. Haw... Haw... Ta show ya there's no bad feelings, ya can meet me mates."

He pointed the paddle at the obese patient with orange hair.

"This here's our Irishman, Vince Faherty. He's here 'cause he keeps rippin' off girls' knickers from clothes lines. The judge says he's a pervert."

"I'm not a pervert!" Vince defended angrily.

"Don't get your knickers in a knot. I'm not askin' what kinda undies you're wearin' today."

Vince blushed. "Knock it off!"

"Touchy, touchy, ain't we."

The punk then tapped the shoulder of a young man in tattered jeans. "This blabbermouth is Norm Comensoli. We call 'im Talkin' Norman."

Thinner than a pasta noodle, Norman slouched as if half-cooked. A baggy brown beret slumped over the front of his head and secluded part of his face. His eyes were shaded with Polaroid sunglasses which, with the glare from the fluorescent tubes, created an eerie impression of silver-plated eyes. The thongs on his feet revealed each toe branded with a tattoo of a star in sky blue ink. I wondered if he and Jono had met the same aliens.

I reached out and shook his sweaty palm. "Glad to meet you." Then gagged on the revolting stench from his armpits.

Norman offered an innocuous smile.

I choked, "Why are you in hospital?"

The punk answered, "He's not much of a talker, our Norman. Never heard 'im wag his tongue. He's bent between the ears. Floats 'round with that silly grin."

Norman widened his smile.

"And you've met me space cadet, Jono."

I nodded to the self-pronounced schizophrenic from Wagga Wagga, then turned and faced the Maltese cross. "What's your name?"

"Doc Murray. You can call me Doc."

I asked the wise ass, "What's the Doc in hospital for?"

"Nuthin'." The punk adjusted his leather jacket where the end of a crepe bandage trailed from his left sleeve.

"He tried to waste himself," volunteered Vince Faherty.

"At least I'm no pervert! Ya wouldn't catch me sniffin' no knickers."

Vince adjusted his gray tracksuit. "I never tried to waste myself!"

"Shut your mouth, ya fat queer."

"I'm no queer..."

"Sssh," hissed Jono as the fluorescent lights reflected off his shiny skull. "The aliens... They're searching... Picking me up on their sensors."

Doc gave Vince a shove. The huge patient stood firmer than a mound of concrete. The punk lifted his paddle. "I'll shove this up your ass..."

"Rack off..." shouted Vince.

"The bulging eyes," whispered Jono. "Sssh... The aliens..."

Only Norman stood smiling. Hell, I only came for a friendly game of ping-pong.

"Settle down!" I said.

Doc and Vince paid no attention and kept jostling one another, exchanging curses.

"Fuckin' fairy!..."

"Fuckin' psycho!..."

In a panic, I turned to fetch the nurses.

"I see everyone's met my friend, Peter."

We all stopped and stared at Surjit calmly strolling toward us. I glared daggers. How dare he abandon me to these feral misfits!

He patted my shoulder. "I hope you've showed your manners to my guest."

Doc grabbed hold of the razor blade dancing below his right ear. "Been killin' some time till ya came. Where ya been, Sooj?"

"I was held up in the emergency ward with a patient who overdosed."

"No worries," said the punk. "We're waitin' ta play ping-pong."

Surjit picked up the ball and threw it to Doc. "The four of you can start. Doc and Jono, why don't you play Vincent and Norman? Peter and I will keep score for the first game."

Vince waddled toward the table and whined, "Norman's too slow."

"Haw! Excuses," taunted Doc. "'Cause you can't beat me and me space cadet, Jono."

"We'll be switching sides after the first game," mediated Surjit.

I watched as the suicidal punk and the bald schizophrenic challenged the knicker swiper and his mute partner. Between Vince's huge bulk jarring the table and the half-awakened Norman peering through his Polaroids, Doc and Jono easily wiped them off the table.

The punk pampered his bristled yellow hair. "Ya scumbags! Me 'n Jono need some men to give us a go."

I wanted to beat him so bad I could taste it. "I'll have a go. Care to join me, Surjit?"

"Not this game. We wouldn't want it to be too unequal. Play with Vincent."

"Haw!" sniped Doc. "What a team! A Pole and a pervert!"

The arrogant bastard was going to eat ping-pong balls. With my adrenalin pumping, I picked up the red paddle. "Are you with me, Vince?"

Somewhat dejected, he asked, "You any good?"

I winked smugly, then whispered, "Doc's left side is his major weakness. Hit all the balls there."

"Huh?"

"Just follow me," I instructed then turned toward my opponents. "You can have the first service."

"Right, Jono. You serve to the Pole. No mistakes. We're gonna kick ass."

Standing diagonally opposite me, Jono hit the first of his five serves. I smacked it hard past the punk.

Jono served again. Another slam bounced on the left.

Doc cursed, "Watch how you're servin'. We ain't up in no spaceship."

We were soon up five nil. It was now my turn to toy with the cretin. "I'll go easy on you."

The patient tugged at his earring. "I can handle me self."

I sent him the dipsy doodle. The ball hit his paddle and careened wildly off his nose.

"Lucky shot," he taunted.

I hit more of the same. He swatted the balls everywhere, except on the table.

"This paddle ain't no good!" he cried. "Jono, gimme yours."

Two more dipsy doodles and we were up 10 nil.

"Fuckin' paddle!" screamed the outraged patient who slammed the paddle on the floor. The handle split in two.

"Look who's the scumbag!" heckled Vince who hadn't even served, let alone returned the ball. "One more point and we have a whitewash."

"Fuck off! Don't wanna play no more."

Vince baited, "Who's the fairy now?"

"Fuck off, pervert. I ain't playin'."

"You can't quit," called Surjit, acting as referee.

"Whaddaya mean? I just did!"

"You have to finish the game."

Doc stormed from the table. "Don't have ta do nuthin'."

The psychiatrist stepped toward his patient. "Here in hospital you have to do something, and quitting isn't one of them."

"I don't give a shit!"

"I do!" shouted Surjit stunning us all into submission. "Your life's far too important."

"Hmph."

"I won't let you drop out of the game just because it was tough going. You don't realize it yet, but your life is the most precious thing you own."

Doc placed his hand over the left wrist where the crepe bandage had unraveled. "It's nuthin' but a game."

"Sure, it's a game. But the reason you're here is to learn how to play it differently. If you quit every time you miss difficult shots, you're cheating yourself. When Peter hit those balls to your left, he was offering you a chance to improve your backhand."

I looked at my mentor rather sheepishly.

"Quitting is not the way to master the game," continued Surjit. "If you only play opponents that serve easy volleys, you'll never learn about courage or perseverance." His voice softened. "No one can ever fault you for trying. We're here to help each other. Go back and fight for your life."

The patient in black leather rubbed his Maltese cross and blustered, "Aw, fuck it. Give me another paddle."

Surjit patted Doc's shoulder and escorted him back to the table. He picked up a green paddle and served to Vince, who promptly netted the ball.

"Haw! Ya drongo!" cried Doc.

With his mammoth hulk continually crashing into the table, Vince made a valiant effort and returned one out of five serves. His service didn't prove much better. Nevertheless, we still held the lead, 12 to eight.

"We're catchin' up, ya scumbags! Me ploy to get ya over-confident worked!"

As a result of Surjit's speech, I had resolved to play less competitively, however, after Doc's repeated blustering, I reversed my decision. "It's Jono's service," I jeered.

While Jono served, he muttered about the aliens. I slammed four of his five serves past Doc, who managed to return one. Vince easily muffed it into the net. I finished the game by serving my razz-ma-tazz spins.

"Twenty-one to nine. We creamed you!" cheered Vince, smacking my paddle to punctuate victory.

"The sides were none too even," pouted Doc. "Next time I'll take the Sooj. We'd whip ya." He headed for the toilet. "I have ta siphon the python."

My partner's bravado went into high gear. "We'll take on any challengers!"

"Norman and I will play," announced Surjit.

With his baggy brown beret tilted slightly over his scrawny head, Norman, handicapped by thongs, shuffled toward the table. Just grasping the paddle seemed effort enough for the smiling zombie whose reeking body odor could be smelled from across the table.

Surjit removed the Polaroids. "You need to see the ball, Norman."

He squinted and blinked as he adjusted to the light.

"Now I want you to concentrate," coached the psychiatrist. "We want to make a contest of this game, don't we?"

Talkin' Norman merely grinned.

Surjit tossed me the ball. "Serve to me."

The odds were definitely in our favor. Surjit and I were competitively matched. However, the overweight Vince, though not much of a player himself, could easily outplay a lethargic Norman who probably didn't have a clue what game he was playing.

Surjit played like a demon. His left-handed curve whirled and spun across the table. God only knows how, but with a few encouraging words and the gentle pat on the back, he managed to coax a few hits out of Norman.

Behind 18 to 17, I urged the Irishman on. "Take it easy, Vince. Over the net... No!... Not so hard! Try again... You have to get the ball onto their side of the table!" We lost 21 to 19.

Surjit bellowed, "You did it, Norman! We won!"

Could have sworn the weedy patient grunted a response, but I was too angry to notice. We could've won if Vince had served the goddamn balls over the net. The vanquished now had to sit out the next game.

Surjit bounced the ball on his paddle. "Jono and Doc, you're next."

"We're gonna lose," said the punk.

"That's the spirit," chided the psychiatrist. "Throw in the towel before you work up a sweat."

"All right, Sooj. You're askin' for it. Jono, we're gonna whip ass."

Since Vince and I destroyed the challengers, I figured Surjit would make easy meat of them, but then again, the man from India was full of surprises. The game that wasn't a contest suddenly turned into one.

"Good on ya, Jono!" Doc screamed after his partner scored a decisive point. I couldn't understand it. Surjit was playing with intense concentration, not like he was throwing the game. Hell, Vince and I slaughtered Doc and Jono. I scrutinized my friend more closely, then finally twigged. The left-handed bastard was using his other hand!

When Jono slapped the ball past Norman, Doc roared, "We beat the Sooj! Haw! We beat the Sooj!"

The psychiatrist offered congratulations. "Nice game. I'll need to practice before our next session."

"The Doc'll be ready. Right, Jono? I haven't even used me secret plan."

Surjit patted Doc's shoulder. "You men can continue playing, but that's it for me. Let's thank Peter for joining us. Maybe he'll consider coming back in the future."

My mouth gaped. No more of these group sessions, thank you very much.

While the patients resumed their ping-pong, Surjit accompanied me out of the building.

I scowled. "How come you let them win?"

"I didn't."

"Like hell! You were playing right-handed."

"I wanted to equalize the sides and make the game challenging for everyone, including myself."

I recalled my easy victory over Doc and Jono. Hell, they deserved to be creamed.

"If you had played many games with them," said Surjit, "you would have become bored at the lack of competition."

I hated it when he acted as if he could read my mind. I sneered, "Why didn't you just spot them points?"

"Not as much fun. I wanted to become more proficient with my right hand."

"But you can only hold the paddle with one hand!"

"Who says it always has to be the same one?"

"What?!"

"My clients help me improve an aspect of my game while I help them advance theirs. Our interactions become mutually beneficial. Together, we learn."

I could only shake my confused head.

"Did you enjoy the group?"

"Not when you weren't there," I chided. "They mucked around. Don't you think they need more intensive therapy than playing table tennis?"

"I coach them individually. The group offers them a valuable opportunity to gain confidence by improving a concrete skill and, more importantly, by learning to relate."

"Twenty years wouldn't be enough time."

"You should have met them four weeks ago. They could only abuse each other, and they rarely finished a game. Now they're starting to have fun."

"Fun! They abused me something fierce when you weren't there."

He laughed. "Part of their ritual."

"Those rituals I don't need."

The psychiatrist turned to leave. "I have to see another patient."

"When are you coming back to our unit?"

"Not for some time. At least not until after the changes."

"What changes?"

In his mystical voice, Surjit pronounced, "Many changes are in the wind. Don't worry, they are all necessary."

Don't worry, he says! "What are you talking about?!"

As he entered the building, his voice trailed, "Whatever happens will happen..."

JOURNAL CLUB

🦅

FRIDAY, MARCH 11

"I hope everyone has read their copy of 'The Clinical Syndrome of Child Sexual Abuse,'" voiced the burly Maxine Benton. Today she was playing the role of teacher. She stood at the head of the large square table in the conference room while the rest of us took our seats. I placed my unfinished reading assignment on the varnished wooden surface.

At the other end of the table, sitting directly opposite Maxine, Gerard impatiently adjusted his brown tweed jacket. "Yes, yes, I'm sure we've all read it. Let's get on with it."

The instructress straightened her starched white uniform. "This article should be mandatory reading by all staff, especially since our sexual abuse cases are steadily increasing. During the past 10 years, child sexual abuse has erupted into the public's consciousness..."

My attention span wandered as Theresa, sitting opposite me, toyed casually with the buttons of her ivory lace blouse. She sensuously licked her upper lip and playfully nudged my thigh with her shoe.

I caught sight of the austere Henry, to the left of Theresa. His dancing, protruding eyes sent a punitive glare. I averted my eyes from the gray-suited figure and buried my face in the article.

"I've lost my place." announced our geriatric psychiatrist, Violet Struthers. She occupied the chair on my right. Working only part-time, she forgot to show up yesterday, one of her regular days, not that anyone missed her. This morning she arrived a day late. Confusion followed her everywhere. Still wearing her tilting brown wig, she dithered, "Which page are we on?"

Maxine rolled her eyes. "We're on the first page."

"Where?"

"At the beginning where it says, 'The perception still persists of nubile adolescents playing seductive games...'"

"Sorry I'm late," announced Leela. She sauntered into the room with a tantalizing low-cut lemon yellow dress. Gerard, ogling lustfully at her cleavage, tripped over the chair in his rush to seat her on the throne next to his.

Undeterred, Maxine continued, "The article points out that the overwhelming majority of child sexual abuse cases establish that the victims were, more often than not, less than eight years old at the time of the molestation." Our teacher tapped the table to emphasize her next message. "It clearly states that any disbelief by adults in positions of authority will further the victim's feelings of helplessness, self-blame, and isolation. When survivors look back on their lives, they are often more angry and resentful toward those who rejected their cries for help than toward the perpetrators."

She shook her head. "It's hard to believe that, despite all the publicity, most adults who hear about any accusation still fault the child. I can't for the life of me understand how anyone could disbelieve a child's story about abuse."

"There have been situations when children have been known to lie," offered Gerard who leaned back in his chair.

His antagonist sneered. "How can you say that?"

"I once assessed an adolescent girl who reportedly was raped. Upon investigation and, I might add, some clever questioning, the girl finally admitted she fabricated the whole story. She thought it would prevent her from getting into trouble for staying out till three in the morning."

Upon hearing this, Maxine sizzled. She stabbed her finger at the article. "It says right here that healing the survivor is dependent on an attitude of acceptance and validation by others. "

"That may be so," frowned our director, "but I still reserve the right to clinically assess and judge the validity of any story. No sense going off half-cocked."

"Christ! I don't believe I'm hearing this! The research clearly demonstrates that few children exaggerate or invent claims of sexual molestation."

"Everyone knows statistics can be manipulated by the researcher," challenged Gerard. "And what about the current controversy about the False Memory Syndrome? Clients who claimed they were abused are now recanting their statement."

"That's a dangerous backlash to the crucial work around retrieving repressed memories."

Gerard pulled out his pipe. "My countless years of clinical experience have taught me one thing: keep an open mind about collecting evidence before pronouncing someone innocent or guilty."

The nurse threw her hands in the air. "For Christ sake! It's a fact, most perpetrators are either a trusted member of the family or someone in a position of authority. It's a fact, the vast majority of perpetrators are male. The statistics back it up."

"I've already told you what I think about statistics which, I suspect, have been manipulated by hysterical radical feminists."

Maxine huffed, "With an attitude like that, you shouldn't be treating any survivors of sexual abuse."

"You have no right to tell me who I can and who I can't treat around here!"

With Theresa and Leela about to join the foray, and Violet fast asleep, Henry Snart intervened. "Perhaps we've strayed off the topic."

"How can you say that?!" demanded the nurse. "The critical issue here has to do with believing a victim who is powerless. All this bull about false memories puts the client back in the old position of being victimized as the suspect."

Henry's eyes wobbled, one toward Gerard, the other toward Maxine. "I thought it might be more productive if we focused primarily on the article."

Gerard angrily shuffled his papers. "If you had more experience, Henry, you'd realize the literature doesn't provide all the answers."

"I realize that, but..."

"Personal experience is always the best teacher."

"Yes, but..."

The instructress's husky voice bellowed, "The victim's story must be accepted and validated!"

"Maxine?" boomed the intercom.

"Yes?"

"Sorry to interrupt," apologized the secretary, "but a parcel from America has just arrived. The courier won't accept my signature."

"I'll be right out." Before leaving, our teacher gave us further instructions. "When I come back, we'll discuss some typical reactions of sexually abused children. You can share the responsibility for summarizing them."

"Peter and I can discuss the notion of 'Secrecy,' " volunteered Theresa.

Henry cleared his throat. "I'll present 'Hopelessness.'"

Maxine looked at Leela. "You can summarize 'Entrapment.'" She then glared at Gerard. "Why don't you present 'Retraction.'"

Violet, her head nodding in deep slumber, was given a reprieve.

When she returned, Maxine's dour expression had been transformed into one of jubilation. She carried a large brown parcel, the size of a small television, stamped with overseas stickers.

"They've finally arrived!" she exclaimed, forgetting all about the article. "I've been waiting for these over six months."

Making like Christmas in March, she plonked the carton on the table and excitedly unwrapped the package. The rest of us looked on curiously.

"Fantastic!" She lifted a large floppy female doll dressed in a floral garment with black woolen hair. "This is the new set of anatomical dolls designed for treating children who have been sexually abused."

"Show us!" enthused Theresa.

Maxine removed three more cotton figures–a large male wearing dark navy trousers and matching shirt, a little girl in pink stripes, and a boy dressed in powder blue clothes.

Her face glowed. "They're perfect. Much better than the old dolls I've been using."

"Look at the pretty dollies!" blurted Violet, awakened by the excitement.

Theresa held up the small male. "Could you give us an update on their use with clients?"

"I'd have to give a proper demonstration," said Maxine.

Showing the doll to Smelder, Theresa solicited, "Surely you wouldn't mind if we were given a brief update."

Our director sucked on his pipe and eyed the cotton figures. "This time has been set aside for reviewing journal articles."

Leela, obviously intrigued, uncharacteristically added her support to the proposal by coyly batting her eyes. "They are cute, Gerard. And they could help us with today's theme."

He lecherously gazed at her cleavage. "All right. Let's have a look at them."

The burly nurse enthusiastically obliged. "As you know, these dolls are made with all of the anatomically correct parts, complete with breasts and genitalia."

She took hold of the large male, stripped the outer clothes, and revealed white cotton briefs. "All undergarments are fitted with easy-to-use Velcro." Which she promptly unfastened to expose a fuller-than-life stuffed penis complete with testes and black woolen pubic hair.

I thought the manufacturer was stretching it a bit. I mean, how many blokes walk around with a constantly erect penis.

"Is this really necessary?" coughed the blushing pastoral counselor.

"Look, Henry," Maxine scolded. "If we're inhibited about dealing with these imitations, our clients will sense that and become hesitant themselves. We have to develop a comfort level ourselves so clients can feel safe using them with us."

He fidgeted in his chair and said no more.

Maxine passed the dolls around. I was handed the large female, a cuddly figure with softly padded parts.

Theresa held onto the little boy while Gerard and Leela shared the girl dressed in pink stripes.

"I want a dolly too!" giggled Violet. The delighted psychiatrist received the undressed adult male. Her eyes bulged.

"When we're seeing the child individually," explained Maxine, "it's important to go slow in order to create a climate of openness. We don't want to lead the child on, do we?"

We all shook our heads.

"During the interview, the victim will show us exactly what happened to her body in a less threatening way. Introduce the dolls one at a time as pretend people. When the victim becomes more comfortable, ask her to select a particular figure. Then calmly ask the child to describe a non-threatening anatomical body part, like the eyes, with a question, 'What are these?' After the child says, 'Eyes,' follow up with another question, 'What are eyes used for?'

"Repeat this procedure with the anatomy that's visible, then nonchalantly ask the child to disrobe the doll. Maintain a non-judgmental manner and ask the client to again describe what she sees. Following it with the same 'What is it used for?' question will elicit important clinical information. Remember, the victim should name and discuss the genitalia. Before going any further, however, I'd like to suggest that you take some time and familiarize yourselves with these new dolls. See what they look like under the clothes."

We followed her instructions and began disrobing our pretend people.

I removed the adult female's dress and released her bra. As I recalled my awkward experience with Theresa's snaps, I realized the Velcro was a damn good idea. The large boobs were aptly padded. Beneath the panties, a mound of curly black fuzz encircled a pink hole.

A wave of guilt and embarrassment cascaded through my body as I stared at the undressed figure. I nervously glanced to my right where Leela was holding the little girl while the chuckling Smelder undressed her. Across the table, Theresa's little boy stood naked. Our eyes met. Theresa responded with a seductive wink then gently flicked the little doll's erect penis.

My face couldn't have turned any redder.

"You'll notice," Maxine instructed, "the manufacturer realistically created holes for all the orifices–mouth, vagina, and anus."

I imagined all the mischief Barbie and Ken could get into.

"After you've explored one, pass it along," said the nurse.

Henry twitched in his chair. "I don't particularly want to get involved with these dolls."

Maxine huffed, "I need one of you men to work with me. Incest and molestation cases are arriving daily. I can't handle them all by myself."

The irony of it all. Ma used to chastise me whenever I played with Stella's dolls. Now, as an adult, I would get paid to not only play with them, but also take off their clothes. "I'll volunteer."

"That's not a good idea, Pinowski," interjected Dr. Smelder. "You're much too inexperienced." He turned toward Henry and issued a directive. "I know you'd prefer not to, but I'm afraid you'll have to get involved with the sexually abused cases. Maxine needs a man, and I'm over-committed. Since you have more clinical experience than Pinowski, you're the logical choice."

Henry shuffled his long legs. "I, ugh, don't feel comfortable with this type of therapy."

"Nonsense!" blustered Gerard. "You must expand your professional field of interest. Besides, we'll see how your idealistic Christian values hold true under the grizzly facts of life."

"It's... just that... I don't..."

"All you need is experience," gloated the psychiatrist. "That, my boy, will only come with plenty of practice."

"I don't think I can be all that effective."

Smelder pointed his pipe. "We all have to get our hands dirty some time or another."

Leela handed Henry the little girl, already undressed.

He hesitated, then reluctantly accepted the doll.

"Remember," added Maxine. "You must create a permissive environment. The client must trust the therapist before she will feel free to show exactly what happened. Most victims are overwhelmed by guilt and believe they were somehow responsible for the abuse."

Our director leaned back on his chair and puffed on the ebony stem. "I've known some pretty seductive pubescent girls who enjoyed the power of seducing their fathers."

"That's what you men like to think," bristled Maxine. "Those girls become so traumatized it affects them the rest of their lives."

He scowled, "I don't want to get into that right now. It's time you finish the demonstration."

That afternoon I stopped for a cuppa tea in the staff room. Henry was sitting alone at the table. "Can I have a word with you?"

"Sure," I said. "What's up?"

"I have a dreadful feeling about this morning's meeting. Those dolls are sinful and perverted."

I grabbed for a doughnut. "It did seem weird undressing dolls in public. But don't hassle yourself. Maxine will show you how to use them properly. After awhile, you'll think nothing of it."

"You don't understand. Jesus died on the cross for our sins, and those that continue to sin will be dealt with harshly. As Paul said to the Romans, Chapter 1, Verse 18, 'The anger of God is being revealed from heaven against all the impiety and depravity of men who keep truth imprisoned in their wickedness.'"

I stopped eating.

"In Verse 24, Paul continues to warn, 'God left the wicked to their filthy enjoyments and practices with which they dishonor their own bodies.'"

A hot flash ran down my spine. Did Henry know about me and Theresa?

"They have given up divine truth for a lie and have worshiped and served creatures instead of our Creator."

Strewth! He must've discovered. No wonder he was making with the sermon.

"Sorry, Henry. I have to make an important phone call." One small lie was better than a long explanation.

As I slovenly pedaled the exercise bike, I watched Theresa endure yet another workout at the Chatswood Fitness Center. She had entered another body-building competition and hoped to capture a silver medal next month. Weight training had moved into hyper-drive as her rigid schedule included six straight days of intensive workouts–an hour of aerobics in the morning, a 30 minute swim at lunch, and three hours of weight lifting in the evening.

Keeping up with her training was bad enough, but the change in her eating habits had become unbearable. Her special low fat, high protein diet consisted of minuscule portions of lean white meat, fruits, and veggies. Two days before the competition, she "carbed up" by eating stacks of carbohydrates, rice, potatoes, bread, and pasta. Not exactly my way to enjoy food.

I slowed down on the exercise bike and admired Theresa's athletic body. The rigors of training and diet had paid off. She sported a sleek, muscled V-shape physique. Sweat dripped from arms that powered the weights over her shoulders.

I peered down at my waist where the once multi-layered middle had shrunk two sizes. If it wasn't for love, there'd be no way I'd be spending Sunday afternoon at a glorified gym. What the hell, she needed my support during training, and besides, the workout released energy that might otherwise have been expended on me. Not that our love-making was any less physical, just less frequent. My only objection was being hoisted like some dumbbell.

Freddie's short fuse was still a cause for consternation; however, my efforts at mental relaxation were starting to pay dividends. Last night I actually penetrated before emission. Unfortunately, with Theresa frantically shouting, "Hurry! Hurry!" Freddie couldn't last very long. Having discovered my vulnerability, Theresa took it in stride.

"How's it going?" she asked as she toweled her wet face.

I sat motionless on the bike. "Taking a break."

She put her arms around my waist, squeezed my tummy, then bit my earlobe. "You've been slacking off again."

"After all, it is the end of the week."

She moved her hands up my chest and pinched my nipples. "How about a relaxing sauna?"

"There's too many people around." Besides, I wasn't in the mood to get Freddie all stirred up.

Her mouth began sucking on my neck. The stares from perspiring exercisers propelled me into action. I quickly slid off the bike to avoid capture in one of her strangleholds. Groping in public was never my idea of fun.

"Let's shower," I suggested. "And head for a cappuccino. I told Ma I'd be home for dinner."

She reacted as if splashed with cold water. "You don't have to leave so early."

"It's been awhile since I've been home for Sunday dinner."

"I thought we'd have a sauna then go back to my flat for a light workout."

"We already had one last night. Since I'm still living at home, I have to make the occasional appearance. At the moment, I'm not on very good speaking terms with my mother."

"Then bring over some of your clothes. We could spend more nights together."

"I'm not ready for that. Why spoil a good thing?"

My lover pouted. "Peter, you're 29! Your emotional development demands more independence."

"Let's not get into that again."

"You're avoiding the issue. Your mother has you wrapped tightly in her web. You have to cut the cord sooner or later and experience freedom."

"It's all happening too quickly."

"You wouldn't be so uptight and anxious if you stayed over more frequently. Your guilt feelings about being disloyal to your mother are preventing you from relaxing sexually. Once you resolve your attachment issues, your performance will improve."

She stroked my chest sensuously. "So, what will it be? Stay at home and seek intensive therapy to work on separation, or spend more nights with me for some free analysis?"

I collected my towel. "I don't know."

"You could help me train at home."

"How about that cappuccino?"

"You can't change the topic that easily, Peter."

"Why not?"

"Avoidance is no way to solve the problem."

"I'd just like to drop it for now."

"Then drop it!" she ranted. "I'm having a sauna!" With towel in hand, she stormed off in a huff.

Strewth! What's a bloke to do?

"Theresa..."

DR. FIONA CROMPTON'S CONSULTATION

🦃

TUESDAY, MARCH 15

"To date, I've had a total of 19 sessions with the 15-year-old girl, Heidi Wentworth. As you know, she was hospitalized in early January for anorexia nervosa and weighed under 66 pounds. Over her three month period of hospitalization, she has managed to gain 17½ pounds, thus qualifying for discharge. While experiencing several relapses, she has stabilized her weight at just under 86 pounds. She should be released within a week or two."

"Hmm," mouthed the consulting analyst, Fiona Crompton. She jotted some remarks in her black notebook.

"I've continued to see Heidi twice a week."

The analyst's large bosoms heaved. "Hmmm."

"Her weight gain seems indicative that, with the help of my therapeutic alliance, she has resolved a number of issues."

Dr. Crompton, her red hair set back in that familiar bun, peered over her horn-rimmed glasses. "How does she feel about leaving hospital?"

"I think it's safe to say she's fairly ambivalent. Last month she maintained the target weight for two of the three required days. Then she regressed and lost two pounds."

"Hmm."

"I'd like some advice on the best way to handle her discharge. I want to continue therapy on an out-patient basis."

"Oh, yes! You must continue with psychotherapy. You're entering a critical phase. For our patient, leaving hospital means withdrawing from a caring, nurturing environment, and especially from you, Peter. She has developed a strong transference relationship. Any departure from on-going therapy at this point would be counter-productive and would reinforce the fear that growing up results in abandonment."

Theresa, Maxine, Henry, and I nodded our heads.

"This anorexic has grown up with a perception that her body has been developing separately while the person, trapped inside, has been diminishing. Her situation has been one of oral helplessness, creating the sensation that her physical and sexual being is fraught with danger."

I stopped nodding. What the hell was she talking about?

"I could only postulate. Pressure must have been exerted to behave according to the mother's pathological needs. If, as an infant, Heidi did not comply, her mother probably responded in a manner which conveyed to the child that she did not exist. In other words, 'If you are not what I want and expect you to be, you do not exist for me.' "

Theresa added, "Shakespeare would have aptly put the girl's dilemma, 'To be or not to be.'"

"Exactly!" said Dr. Crompton who sat forward in a rare moment of exhilaration. "We understand Heidi's existential question: either act in accordance with her mother's pathological wishes, or face emotional annihilation."

Strewth! I never realized it was that serious.

"Her possessive mother, unable to differentiate between herself and her daughter, has treated our patient as an appendage. Consequently, the client has found it difficult to separate and develop her own feelings."

"Heidi has often told me she doesn't like displeasing her mother."

The consultant rested a hand on her chin and reviewed her notebook. "Hmmm." Silence loomed like an ominous cloud while she gazed toward the ceiling. She finally shared her reflections. "Her phrase may be symbolic. An indication she is transferring her fear of displeasing on to the therapist. Considering her impending discharge, she is expressing concern about losing her attachment to you, her new mother figure."

"Hmmm," I muttered.

"Treatment must help her discover and restore herself as a fully integrated whole. A strong therapeutic alliance will enable her to test limits so she can develop her individual personality. She needs to realize she will not be rejected by the therapist. As her confidence and trust in the relationship grows, her inner sense of security will blossom like a newborn child."

Newborn confusion swirled around my brain. "What specifically should I do in the sessions?"

The analyst paused before speaking. "It's paramount that the patient become actively involved in the treatment process. She must become a co-discoverer of her own inner reality."

"Hmm?"

"Keep the sessions unstructured. Respond to whatever she presents."

"They're still having family sessions aren't they, Peter?" asked Theresa.

"Yes. Gerard and Leela conduct family therapy weekly."

"Gerard is rigidly hostile and resistant to individual psychotherapy," vented Theresa in a cathartic release. "He wanted to terminate these consultations with you, Fiona, until Maxine and I threatened to bring the matter before the hospital board. He's blinded by that family system's paradigm."

Fiona Crompton closed her eyes, shook her head wearily, and heaved her heavy breasts. "This girl must be free from the noxious interactions of the family. Individual therapy is the only way she can develop a separate identity away from her mother. For the child's sake, Peter, you must continue to see her individually. She will probably need several more years of intense psychotherapy."

Theresa, Henry and Maxine nodded.

I could only reply with another, "Hmmm."

FAMILY THERAPY CONSULTATION

TUESDAY, MARCH 22

Gerard nibbled on a hot cross bun while he addressed the eminent consultant, Dr. Frank King, and the rest of the team. "Leela and I have been achieving great progress with our anorexic patients and their families. I brought one of the earlier videotapes of the Wentworth family to contrast with our last session. It will show how incredibly effective our approach has been."

Surprisingly, Theresa and Maxine said nothing. They just rolled their eyes and shook their heads while Henry politely asked Violet Struthers, who was sitting on his right, to stop muttering to him. Next to Gerard, Leela smiled coyly at the muscular Dr. King, who was gaping at her black silk stockings.

"We should have a look at the tape," proposed the consultant.

Leela, wearing a short lime-green dress today, followed his suggestion. She tossed her golden hair to the side of her face and strolled toward the video trolley. Dr. King brushed flakes of dandruff off his black pullover while his gaze followed the social worker's shapely legs.

"Leela, fast forward to that crucial segment in the second session," instructed our elated director. He placed his half-eaten hot cross bun on the table. "You'll love this earlier session, Frank. There's plenty of action. We really hammered it home with the parents. I unbalanced the system by aligning with the father and undercutting his conflict avoidance pattern with the daughter. Leela and I eventually forced both parents to collaborate against this dominating child."

Leela pushed "play" on the VCR; the screen flickered.

We watched an emaciated Heidi dab at her gums with a Kleenex while an animated Gerard spoke to Mr. Wentworth. "How can you let your spoiled child treat you and your wife like this?"

"She's not really spoiled," defended the bewildered father.

"You're telling me your 15-year-old daughter, who's refusing to eat, is not spoiled?"

Mr. Wentworth straightened his black business suit and smiled at Heidi. "She's really a nice person."

Dr. Smelder challenged him. "How can you call her nice when she's killing herself?"

"She has emotional problems."

"Her problem," chastised Gerard, "is that she's challenging your manhood, saying you can't make her eat. She's prepared to die to prove she's right. Do you want your daughter to be right and dead? Or do you want to be right?"

"I do, of course."

Heidi's older brother and sister watched her scream, "I wanna leave! Don't let him say those things!"

"There, there," comforted the distraught mother.

"How can you mollycoddle her?!" challenged Dr. Smelder. "Your daughter's having a tantrum, and you're mollycoddling her!"

"We never believed in physical punishment," she defended.

"If I had a child who was killing herself by refusing to eat, I'd make sure she was eating."

"We've tried," said the father. "We really have tried."

Gerard picked up a plate of food and handed it to him. "Your daughter's making you impotent. It's about time you claim back your potency. Get your child to eat some of this."

He meekly picked up a sausage roll. "Come on, honey. Have this, so you can get better."

Heidi was defiant. "I'm not eatin' nothin'."

"Make her eat!" commanded Smelder. "It's eat or die!"

"The Doctor wants you to eat."

"Come on, Heidi," soothed the mother.

"Don't help her. Help your husband. If your daughter doesn't eat, she'll die!"

The helpless parents stared at each other.

"Make her eat something!" roared the child psychiatrist.

The couple sprang to life.

"Have some of this," offered the father.

"It'll make you strong," countered the mother

"I don't have ta!"

The exasperated Mr. Wentworth shrugged and faced the psychiatrist whose loud voice bellowed, "Tell her!"

Reluctantly, he raised his voice. "Eat this."

Heidi was defiant. "No."

Her father's face turned red. "Eat this!"

"No!"

"Eat this!"

"No!"

The father grabbed Heidi's shoulders and shouted, "Now eat!!"

"No!!"

"If you don't eat, we'll force it down your throat!"

"Ya wouldn't!"

"She's challenging your potency." harangued Smelder.

"Hold her!" yelled the father.

His wife restrained her while he tried jamming the sausage roll into the clenched mouth. With what little strength she could muster, Heidi resisted both parents and gagged on the food.

When they released her, she spat the mashed sausage roll at her mother, who promptly slapped her daughter across the face. "Don't you dare do that again!"

"You hit me!" screeched Heidi. Her voice soon dissolved into heaving sobs.

"I'll have to hit you again unless you start eating," sobbed the mother. "I don't want you to die."

"Stop the video," interrupted Gerard. "What do you think, Frank?"

Dr. King showed his thumbs up. "Nice piece of tape. Whatever you do, don't erase it. Great material for a book."

Smelder beamed. "During that interview, I broke up the cozy coalition between mother and daughter and finally forced the parents to face their child's problem together. The anorexic realized it was a no-win situation, especially with Leela and myself present."

"I'm impressed," said our consultant. He looked dreamily at Leela's black nylons. She returned a seductive grin.

"Considering the initial resistance," continued Gerard, "we've engineered a major structural shift in the family. This is evident by the anorexic's weight gain. The girl currently looks healthy and is ready to be discharged this week. Leela, show everyone a short snippet from the latest interview which is our 11th session."

She inserted another video. "Fortunately, Gerard and I have taped every session. We plan on editing them later for future presentations."

Frank King winked, "Great material."

The TV flickered once more. Gerard and Leela were again facing the parents. A placid, yet healthier Heidi, sat near her older brother and sister.

"I think we all deserve some credit for helping Heidi grow up," said the psychiatrist magnanimously. "She looks hardier and happier. Wouldn't you agree, Leela?"

"Definitely!"

The father patted his daughter on the knee. "I want to thank you, Dr. Smelder. Without you, we wouldn't have known how to manage her. I just hope we can maintain the same progress at home."

"I'm confident you will," said Gerard. He turned toward Heidi. "If you start losing weight again, it would mean another hospitalization. The next time would probably be longer."

"I think Heidi has learned her lesson," the mother cajoled. "Right, dear?"

She shrugged. "I guess."

Smelder offered further instructions to the father. "Remember, you're the boss. Make the rules and stick to them. I won't tolerate any impotence. But in case there is a setback, the hospital is here to assist you. We'll monitor your progress during the follow-up sessions."

Mr. Wentworth shook Dr. Smelder's hand. "How can I thank you?"

"That's what I'm here for."

I tuned out the rest of the consultation and the further gratuitous remarks. Bloody hell! They acted as if I wasn't even involved in the case. I've seen the girl twice a week over the past three months. Surely I deserved some credit!

THE 22ND SESSION

🦃

THURSDAY, MARCH 24

"I can't wait till tomorrow," she chirped.

"You're looking better than I've ever seen you."

Heidi reminded me of a shriveled flower brought back to life. Wearing a warm yellow dress, she sprouted full rosy cheeks. Even the dark shadows around her eyes had disappeared.

I commented on her transformation. "You even seem taller."

"Just edged past five feet."

"I'm proud of you, Heidi. You've become one of my great success stories."

Actually, if you took away the bed wetters victoriously ringing the bell, my scorecard would be abysmal.

"Thanks."

"I was wondering. Which helped more, the individual sessions or the family interviews?"

She contorted her face and pretended to vomit. "I hated that fat shrink."

"Dr. Smelder can be a real pain when he wants to."

"Had my parents around his little finger," she spewed. "He acted like I wasn't there."

"It must've been comforting to know that you could talk with a therapist separately."

"Yea. Thanks. Can't wait till I get home."

"How's your relationship with your mother these days?"

"We're gettin' on okay. As long as I'm eatin', she's off my back."

"Remember, there's other ways to stand up for yourself other than starving to death."

She sneered, "You won't be catching me back here. The past three months was awful."

"I'll be sad to see you go, Heidi. We've become good friends, haven't we?"

My chest expanded with a growing sense of satisfaction. In such a short period of time we had developed a strong bond of trust. I couldn't contain myself. "I've really enjoyed our time together."

"Yea."

"I'm pleased we'll still be able to keep up our contact."

Her face lit up. "You'll have ta come and visit me. I'll bake you a German chocolate cake."

One of my favorites. However, I doubted the analyst, Fiona Crompton, would approve of home visits.

"I've arranged to continue seeing you Mondays and Thursdays."

"Yea... well... what with all my school work... I have stacks of catchin' up. Could we like make it once a week?"

"Once a week? If you think I've helped you thus far, wait till we really get going. Now's when the fun begins."

Her rosy cheeks faded. "Yea...You've been great, Peter. But... I don't wanna miss out on any more school or my friends. I've been gone too long."

"But you've done so well. I'd hate to lose our momentum."

She frowned. "I'm already better. I'm eatin' and feel happy. Once a week should be plenty time to say hello."

Dr. Crompton had warned me that I would be tested. According to Fiona, Heidi would unconsciously want to know if I cared enough to remain committed to the relationship. I poured on the reassurance. "Heidi, I care about you. I only want to see you get healthier."

"I am healthy. The doctors say I can go home. That means I'm all better."

The analyst was emphatic. My client needed long term psychotherapy. I leaned forward and softened my voice. "I wonder if you're ready to tackle it on your own. We still have work to do."

"Like what?"

"Like... discovering your identity... who you are... what you want."

"I know who I am and I wanna leave this dumb hospital."

"But you're always trying to please others, especially your mother."

She prodded the base of the front tooth with her finger. "So what."

"You can't go around trying to make other people happy."

"I'm happy now. I'm eatin'. Everyone's off my back."

"If everyone's off your back, then what?"

She scratched her head. "What do ya mean?"

"You see. You don't know. That's what we can find out together."

"I don't need help anymore." she pouted. "I don't ever wanna come back to this hospital!"

I slumped back in my chair. I wasn't ready to say goodbye. The grimace on her face dissolved. She edged forward and lowered her voice. "Ya helped me heaps, Peter. I just wanna do it on my own. It's not that I don't like ya. I wanna do it myself."

"Hmm."

"You really have helped."

I couldn't let her stop therapy. We've only had 22 sessions and there was so much more to accomplish. Besides, what would I tell Dr. Crompton?

"I'd like to see this problem through to the end," I said. "It would please me no end to help you stand up for yourself."

"I'm already doin' it."

"Yea, but if we continue working as a team, we can achieve twice as much."

"I dunno."

"Don't pull out now. Give it another go. Just another year of therapy."

She shook her head. "Naw. I need to catch up on school work."

"All right. I'll compromise. Twice a week for six months. And I won't take 'no' for an answer. Besides, your parents have already agreed to it."

She slouched and released a huge sigh. "If I have ta."

Granted, she wasn't jumping with excitement, but at least she consented. Who knows, after six months, she may even want to extend therapy another year.

INTERDEPARTMENTAL MEETING

MONDAY, MARCH 28

Theresa whizzed her little red Honda through traffic, traveling toward the Department of Family and Children Services in Hornsby. Large silver earrings, dangling above her shoulders, accentuated the black-and-white checked pantsuit. Australis perfume permeated the enclosed vehicle. As I inhaled the sweet scent, my olfactories went all tingly.

Usually, afternoon interdepartmental conferences with the local district officers were far from stimulating. Today, however, was to prove the exception.

Theresa slid her hand to my thigh.

"Don't want an accident today," I said, returning her paw to the steering wheel. "Keep your mind on the road."

Her moist mouth cooed, "Let's pretend I have a stick shift." She thrust her hand between my legs and reached for the zipper.

My engines revved into second gear. I clutched her arm. "Theresa! We'll be at the meeting in a few minutes." With my prematurity, I didn't want the checkered flag to signal Freddie into accelerating further.

"I just want a quick feel, Peter. Don't be such a prude."

"These tan pants will show any wet spots."

Her eyes twinkled. "No one would notice."

"I would!"

"Where's your sense of adventure? Take a few risks."

"All well for you to say, but last week we were almost caught with my pants down when the cleaners came to empty the trash in your office. If I hadn't put the chair against the door..."

"We had plenty of time to recover."

"Barely! And what about Maxine? She saw you fondling me in the kitchen. God, was I embarrassed. What if a client saw us making out? Then what?"

Oblivious to what I was saying, her left paw struggled with my hands and the zipper while her other hand steered through passing traffic.

The car swerved and I grabbed for the wheel. "Not now!"

She might have persisted if it weren't for the silver Volvo blasting its horn. The near miss finally convinced her to keep her mind on the road and out of my pants.

We arrived without any further incident and joined Gerard, Maxine, and Henry in the reception area at the Department of Family and Children Services. The district manager, a haggard-looking, thin woman named Norma Piper eventually appeared. After the perfunctory greeting, she ushered us into a gray carpeted conference room with a large mahogany table. Chrome chairs with gray padding surrounded the table. Two district officers were chatting around the cafe bar in the corner.

Norma introduced a tall, portly woman who reminded me of an oversized adolescent with dark glasses and pigtails. "This is Connie Larder. She handles the teenagers who run away or are out of control and need temporary accommodation."

Norma then turned her attention to a young, dazzling brunette who reminded me of a model, wearing heavy make-up and an enchanting mandarin dress with matching silk scarf. "This is Geraldine Spencer who deals with our neglected children."

As I wondered how deprived clients would enjoy dealing with such a flashy dresser, a bearded man with moppish red hair walked into the conference room.

"This is Bruce Kunkel," said Norma. "He works with the physical and sexual abuse cases."

After I shook his clammy hand, Gerard reciprocated by introducing his team. The summit was about to commence. We helped ourselves to tea and coffee and moved toward the large mahogany table. Our team gathered on one side of the table, with Theresa and me at the far end, while the district officers presided over the other side.

Dr. Smelder didn't have much respect for district officers and believed they were incompetent and insufficiently trained. I dare say, the lack of reverence was mutual. They continually complained that therapists were never available when needed. Gerard often pontificated, "Clients that live in crisis merely expect others to respond to their crisis. The duty of the therapist is to contain anxiety and teach self-discipline through arranged appointments."

I only knew that I sure as hell wouldn't want their job, especially being paged late at night for cases involving abuse or neglect. I quite enjoyed uninterrupted sleep, thank you very much.

Norma called the interagency meeting to order. "Bruce, could you present the first case?"

The bearded man with moppish red hair opened a four-inch-thick file. "I have a sexual abuse situation that needs an urgent referral for counseling. The family's name is Timms. The seven-year-old boy, Tommy, has been assaulted by his 17-year-old step-sister who has since been removed from the house and is currently living with a relative. The parents have agreed to bring the boy for therapy and have signed the consent form."

"Can you tell us the nature of the offense?" queried Dr. Smelder.

Stroking his red beard, Bruce replied, "When I interviewed Tommy on his own, he didn't say much. He only nodded his head up and down for a 'yes' and sideways for a 'no'. Through a long series of questions, I discovered that whenever his parents went to the pub for a drink, the step-sister would play with Tommy. Seemed to be going on for several years."

"You have to be more specific," chided Gerard. "What exactly did the girl do?"

The district officer cleared his throat. "Apparently, the step-sister would fondle Tommy's penis until erect, then attempt penetration."

"Was the boy hurt?"

"When I asked him how it felt, he didn't answer."

"With proper interviewing techniques," lectured the child psychiatrist, "you could have gathered critical information."

"We use anatomical dolls in our interviews," beamed Maxine.

Norma Piper, looking even more haggard, intervened. "Can we please allow Bruce to proceed?"

He nervously tugged at his beard. "Even though Tommy was uncooperative and refused the doctor's attempt to procure an anal swab, there appears to have been no anal interference. This was confirmed during the disclosure sessions where Tommy was asked to repeat the details in the series of individual interviews. The first occurred with a police officer, then with a female juvenile officer. The next two interviews were conducted by a hospital social worker, then a sexual assault worker. When I was assigned the case, I thought it urgent that the boy undergo psychological tests before receiving therapy."

"We'll determine that when we interview the family," informed our director as he casually sipped on his tea.

Bruce flicked through the file. "Considering the number of helpers who have been involved thus far, I don't want the boy to get mucked around."

"Who reported the abuse?" asked Maxine.

"The parents came home early one night. The father went off his rocker when he spotted the step-daughter masturbating Tommy and called the police. Mind you, the father was full of grog at the time. Not sure what he would have done if he was sober."

Smelder swirled his tea in the plastic cup. "I wonder about the father's sexual feelings toward the step-daughter. He might have been reacting to his own sexual arousal. Who knows, he could've been fantasizing about the girl himself. How would you describe the step-daughter? Is she attractive?"

"She's nice looking," answered Bruce. "She's 17 with blonde hair."

"Is she well-developed physically?"

The district officer continued fidgeting with his facial hair. "When I saw her, she wore a large tank top. I couldn't see much, but I gathered she was developing."

"This father may have sexualized the step-daughter and, consciously or unconsciously, wished to be masturbated. She may have acted out the father's projected fantasies."

Upon hearing this, the district officers, some with raised eyebrows, murmured to one another. I doubted they were sharing praiseworthy comments.

Gerard didn't notice. He was caught up in his own reverie. "This girl would be a very interesting subject to work with," he mused. "Let's see if we can attempt to understand her sexualized nature..."

While Smelder rambled on, oblivious to the others tuning him out, I scrawled the picture of a blowhard on a notepad. Suddenly, I flinched in my chair. Roaming under the table was Theresa's right paw! I glanced around at the glazed eyes slowly being hypnotized by Gerard's pontificating.

"Not here!" I whispered punitively.

She returned a wink and moved her chair flush against mine which was at the end of the table. No one noticed, or seemed to care. Discreet fingers worked slowly and deliberately around my crotch. My left hand moved to battle Theresa's right paw. I dared not make too much of a scuffle lest it draw attention my way. I hoped my nonverbal glares would force her to cease and desist. She pushed her pad closer to me. On it was written, "You feel delicious. My panties are soaking."

I couldn't believe this was happening. She knew Freddie was trigger happy. I scrawled, "NOT HERE."

"... and the treatment of such offenders," continued Smelder's hypnotic voice which had already caused one district officer to nod off, "needs trained professionals who..."

Theresa's hand persisted under the table. I began to lose the battle as her erotic manual massage slowly brought Freddie to her side. I gasped and closed my eyes in horror. I couldn't stop Freddie from exploding.

I fell into a state of shock. The evidence! What about the evidence on my tan pants?! My senses brought me back with a jolt as Theresa's cup of tea crashed onto my lap.

"I'm terribly sorry, Peter," she apologized. "I must have knocked it over with my elbow."

No matter what Ma says, Theresa's one hell of a creative woman. Her tissues materialized as if from nowhere, and we swiftly mopped up the mess. I was so embarrassed, I could hardly look around the room which suddenly had been brought back to life. I peeked to my left where Theresa flashed a broad Cheshire grin. I wasn't smiling. I excused myself to go clean up. As far as I was concerned, the meeting was over.

LUNCHTIME STROLL

HOLY THURSDAY, MARCH 31

"You promised."

"I know, Theresa, but I've always been with my family for Easter."

"But we arranged to be with my family down the South Coast. They want to meet you."

"Ma was really upset when I told her we'd be spending the Easter Holidays together. Actually, she flew into a rage..."

Theresa swatted at an overhanging branch. "You promised! We planned on driving down to Ulladulla on Saturday."

"I know. I'm really sorry. But..."

"Your mother has manipulated you again!"

"I didn't realize she had invited my sister and her family from Melbourne. They're flying up tomorrow, and my aunt and uncle will be joining us on Easter. I couldn't let the family down."

Theresa halted near a tall eucalyptus tree. She blazed, "What about me? Didn't you consider my feelings?"

"Of course! You know how much I care about you."

"It doesn't show!"

"Don't say that. I don't ever want to lose you."

"Hmph! You said you'd spend more nights at my apartment. That hasn't happened."

"Right now isn't the best time."

She ripped a handful of leaves off a branch. "You're 29 years old! You can't be forever pleasing your mother. Stand up for yourself and resolve your Oedipal issues!"

I recoiled from her burning remark and tried quelling the flames.

"Honestly, I want to meet your folks. If Ulladulla wasn't so far... "

"It's only a five hour drive."

"Let's not argue. We could make it another weekend."

"You'll find another excuse," she seethed. "What are you frightened of?"

"Nothing. Ma just goes off the wall. One moment she's hyper-hysterical with her blood pressure pole-vaulting to the ceiling. The next moment, she's super-depressed. She's having a hard enough time coping with our relationship. Whenever I stay the night with you, she either gives me the silent treatment or blows a vesuvius. I thought I'd make Easter a bit easier for her. After all, I am her only son."

Theresa grasped my arm. "Can't you see it? You're codependent. You're obsessed with pleasing your mother. She's crippling you emotionally. She's using her manic depression to manipulate you, to make you guilty and maintain the symbiotic relationship. Every time you talk of leaving, you suffer separation anxiety. Face it. The little boy doesn't want to leave his mother's bosom!"

"Could you just leave her breasts out of this! Christ, lay off the analysis you!"

Her olive green eyes softened. "Then come with me. It'll be fun. You could help my dad fish off the trawler."

"I'm sure we'd have a fantastic time. But I promised to be home on Easter."

Her fury raged. She slapped at the tree. "Have it your mother's way. I'll visit my parents, with or without you. I thought you were ready for an intimate relationship. Stay home with your mommy!"

"How can you be like that?"

"I'm not waiting around while you resolve your codependency or your identity crisis."

"What are lovers for? I need you."

My incensed lover stormed brusquely across the road, then whirled around and thundered, "I'm not sure what you need!"

Her voice disturbed a flock of rainbow lorikeets perched high in the trees.

"Wait!..."

No use. She disappeared behind a row of hedges. I watched the colored birds soar toward the open sky.

EASTER SUNDAY

🐦

APRIL 3

Pa dutifully carved the Easter ham while Ma brought out the food. Creamed spinach, sweet potatoes, and sauerkraut were placed around the centerpiece–a large wicker basket overflowing with blessed hard-boiled eggs, caraway cheese, rye bread, and homemade Polish sausage. I was spared the task this year of taking the basket to St. Vincent's for the ritual blessing on Holy Saturday. Ma didn't want to hassle me further, considering I was still stewing about staying home. Damn! I should've taken up Theresa's offer to be with her family.

"*Obiad Gotowy!* Dinner's ready!" called the cook.

With Blackie scrambling under our feet, we gathered around the decorated table. Pa occupied the patriarchal head and was flanked on his right by the men–Uncle Janek, my brother-in-law, Stanley Lesniowski, and me. Aunt Adele, my sister Stella and her two children, Danka and Krystyna, faced the men. Nearest the kitchen, at the foot of the table, Ma meticulously rearranged her cutlery which had been jostled from its symmetrical pattern.

She had worked feverishly preparing for this Easter. In addition to stuffing hog casings with her seasoned sausage mixture, Ma spent countless evenings painting the "Pisanki," eggs which she had painstakingly hollowed by blowing out the innards through tiny pinholes at each end. Then, having concocted an onion skin dye, she had encircled each egg with intricately painted Christian symbols—triangles, elaborate crosses, and decorative fish. I faced my elaborately adorned egg perched on a mound of green plastic grass while Ma began the Lord's prayer. *"Ojciec nasz, ktorys jest w niebie..."*

The smell of the baked cloves clinging to the glazed ham made my stomach grumble. Under the table, Blackie growled.

"Amen." I grabbed for the ham.

"Piotr!" she shrieked. "First the *oplatek.*"

A lover of tradition, Ma carried the Christmas Polish custom over to the Easter meal. She passed each of us a white rectangular wafer of unleavened bread. Mine was stamped with a picture of the crucifixion. I wasn't in the mood for yet another ritual. Breaking bread and wishing good luck was furthest from my mind as I thought of linking arms with Theresa and toasting homemade wine.

My mother gave a wish, *"Wesolych Swiat,"* and tore the first portion from my *oplatek.*

I jerked a piece off her wafer and muttered, "Happy Easter to you, too." Instead of eating cardboard dough, I should've been feasting with my lover.

"Wesolych Swiat." wished Aunt Adele. "Hope you find a nice Polish girl."

I tore a segment from her wafer. "Happy Easter," I muttered, and secretly hoped the cloves on the ham would break one of her false teeth.

"Even if you don't have a proper job," said Pa, "I hope you keep it a long time."

I reached for the wafer in Pa's outstretched hand. Car grease permanently embedded the crevices around his knuckles. He could never appreciate what I did for a living, believing that if a man didn't work up a sweat, he wasn't really a man.

I exchanged bread. "Don't work too hard."

I wished Stella and Stanley Happy Easter and sent their nine-year-old daughter, Krystyna, a filthy look when she grabbed an extra large chunk of my *oplatek* and stuffed it in her mouth. Spoiled brat! Younger than her sister, Danka, she would always have a tantrum whenever she didn't get her way.

When she stole my last portion, I kicked her under the table.

"Waaa... Uncle Peter kicked me."

"Did I? Sorry, Krystyna."

I offered her an Easter wish. "I hope you get what you deserve." And snatched her *oplatek*.

"Waaa... he stole my..."

"Piotr! Stop!"

I tossed the wafer back in her face. Damn brat!

"Piotr!" hissed Ma. She wanted order before passing the basket of blessed food.

Finally the best ritual commenced. Conversation all but stopped as we began eating. The few words that were used signaled a voracious need to satisfy hunger. Bending arms and moving mouths worked in unison amid the noisy symphony of forks and knives.

After his first helping, Uncle Janek breathed a contented sigh. With one hand wiping his shiny bald head, the other reached for the sauerkraut. "Who are you helping now, Piotr?"

I stabbed another slice of ham. "People."

"What type of people?"

I stared at the large man stuffing his mouth. "An interesting case was admitted last week. A 17-year-old boy actually believed he was wearing a crown of thorns and predicted he would be crucified."

"A real weirdo," said Pa as he wiped the mashed potatoes off his mustache.

My uncle's fork poised mid-air. "I can't understand these young people."

"They have it too easy," added my father. "They're after the dole. They act crazy so they don't have to work."

"Bludgers!" echoed Janek.

"There are still a few communists around who want to change the country."

I tuned out as Pa raved on. If it wasn't the commies or Jews, it was the Aborigines or Asians.

Aunt Adele smudged her lips with a napkin and caught my gaze. "I understand you're going out with a girl."

"Someone from work."

"Your mother tells me she's not Polish. Is that wise?"

I shrugged.

She reached for the sweet potatoes. "They say marriage lasts longer when two people have the same nationality and religion. Me and your uncle are a perfect example. We've been married 36 years."

I glanced at the childless couple devouring food as if there was no tomorrow.

"You have to consider these things when you go out with someone. They always say..."

"Peter," rescued my sister, "do you remember how we'd offer up our lollies for Lent?"

Sweet Theresa immediately sprang to mind.

"Ma would place the licorice whips and lollipops from Uncle and Aunty in a glass jar," continued Stella. "We'd check the container every day and drool."

I longed for our tight embrace, Theresa's delicious lips, her cherry brown nipples. "Ma would slap our hands whenever we snuck any," I added. "We shouldn't have to give up what we really want."

"A small sacrifice for Our Lord," retorted my mother.

"I didn't ask him to get strung up for me."

"Don't talk like that!"

"All we ever do around here is sacrifice."

Ma raised her fork. "We scrimped and saved to give you a better life, a better education, so you wouldn't have it as hard. Remember the encyclopedias?"

"How could I forget? You're forever bringing them up."

She faced my Aunt. "I needed a new iron then, but I made do with the old one until we paid off the books. This is how my son gives thanks for all that I've done."

"If you would have sacrificed less, I would've heard less."

She slammed her fork on the plate. "Enough, Piotr! It's Easter. We don't need that."

"Hey, I didn't even want to be here!" I tossed my knife on the table for good measure. It pierced Ma's pisanki.

Her horrified look at the broken egg shell–her masterpiece–could've broken a thousand eggs. She flung her napkin on the table and huffed out of the room.

I avoided everyone's gaze and stared at my plate, only to be interrupted by a smack on the head.

"What's that for?" I said, rubbing my forehead.

Pa retaliated, "For having a smart mouth!"

Felt like telling the ol' man off, but I was in enough trouble already. Bloody stupid egg! I just wanted to be in Ulladulla with my Easter bunny.

WEDNESDAY, APRIL 13

Ma still hasn't forgiven Easter and Humpty Dumpty's demise. Neither has Theresa. She's refused to go out with me for the past two weeks. Not much to write about, as I've spent my evenings in the bedroom sulking. If it weren't for our joint case together, Theresa and I would hardly be communicating. Our interview with Terry and his family was painfully strained, but at least we chalked up a success story. After nearly three months of therapy, the nine-year-old boy finally stopped his compulsive masturbating. We'll check the family in a month's time, and if the sexual activity has ceased, Theresa and I will close the case.

ANZAC DAY DREAM

MONDAY, APRIL 25, 1994

Sister Bridget enters classroom. Waving tall pointer. I crouch behind desk. Shoot arrow. Wounding her shoulder. She winces. I aim another. Thud! The heart. She claws at black habit. Stumbling over desks. I must be free. Another arrow. Zing! Strikes its mark. She tumbles, clutching wooden shaft. Robes ripping. Blood oozing, down naked chest. She lunges forward. Strangling my throat. I reach for quiver. Empty! Talons sink deeper. I gasp. No air. Hands, squeezing tighter. Choking. I scream. No... NO!... NO!!

"What is it?"

"Who's there?!"

"It's me!"

"Ma! What are you doing?"

"I heard you shouting."

"Christ... It's three in the morning... And put that holy water away! You spritzed my face!"

"It will heal your mind. You were having a nightmare."

"Yeah, well, I'm all right now."

"Jezus, Maria..."

"Say your prayers in your own room! I need some sleep."

The 1915 Aussie massacre on Gallipoli by the Turks was never a good reason to celebrate, but who would knock a day off work. I stayed in bed most of Anzac day.

POLISH CONSTITUTION DAY

Today commemorated Poland's first constitution in 1791. Its theme should have reminded me of liberation. Instead, my emotions were shackled by a tortuous set of invisible tentacles. On some days my chest heaved in an attempt to stop the steel band from tightening its vice-like grip. I continued to struggle with the pain of emotional withdrawal from my relationship with Theresa who persisted in giving me the cold shoulder. I desperately missed her. Without her, my life seemed meaningless. My brooding continued, leaving little time for my journal writing.

FRIDAY THE 13TH

"You have a phone call, Peter," announced the intercom.

"This is Dr. Pinowski."

A soft voice resonated in the receiver. "This is Sarah Reingold. I'm a social worker at the Child Guidance Clinic in Hornsby. I recently conducted an assessment interview with Mrs. Tortelli, who was seeking help for her son. Did you receive my fax of her signed 'Release of Information Form'?"

"Yes, I did."

"I understand she received counseling from you."

"Uh... that's right. I had two sessions with the family. Hold on, I'll get the file."

I retrieved a manila folder from the filing cabinet. "I saw them the first time on January 18, and then on February 16. Mrs. Tortelli was extremely resistant and wanted to control the therapy. The chief child psychiatrist and I decided that we needed the entire family in order to be effective. The mother, however, never followed through."

"Angelo still has a soiling problem," Sarah informed me. "When I asked Mrs. Tortelli about the counseling with you, she became very agitated and almost incoherent."

"Her English isn't very good the best of times."

"I had difficulty understanding her but eventually unraveled that when she received help at your department, she found the therapy very disturbing."

I wasn't about to cop the blame. "As I said, she was extremely resistant to any of our suggestions. The clinical team questioned her motivation for help. She must be receiving some secondary gains from maintaining her son's soiling."

After a brief pause, the soft voice responded, "Mrs. Tortelli is most likely a major factor in Angelo's encopresis."

I released a sigh of vindication. "I wholeheartedly concur."

"Her attempt to control therapy may be similar to her control issues with Angelo. Soiling may be a passive-aggressive response."

"That's exactly how I assessed the situation!"

"If that's the case, it may be counter-productive to change therapists."

"Come again?"

"It's probably better if I refer them back to you."

"I'm not so..."

Her voice firmed. "Mrs. Tortelli must confront her resistance and her overwhelming need to control. If I provided counseling, it would reinforce her avoidance. After a few sessions, she'd probably resort to her established pattern of therapist hopping."

"Yes, but..."

"You've convinced me that family therapy should continue at your department. I'll inform the mother that she should recontact you for another appointment."

"On the other hand," I said. "Mrs. Tortelli may relate better with a female counselor, and you have developed a rapport with her."

Sarah's voice was resolute. "It's quite evident that you have a handle on the case. You've described a family that's prone to shifting therapists to avoid facing issues. Their pattern needs to be confronted at the onset. We must prevent them from seeking therapy elsewhere. I think we both agree, the logical solution is that the Tortellis return back to you."

"But surely, you can't force her to contact us."

"I'll tell her it's our policy not to provide counseling when clients have begun therapy at another agency. As Angelo's soiling worsens, she'll have no other choice but to make another appointment."

I could hardly wait!

THE MIRROR

🐦

WEDNESDAY, MAY 18

3:58 p.m. Panic-stricken, I went to the toilet to compose myself. On a 10-point scale, my stress level had skyrocketed past 30. Gerard had scheduled a new family for me to interview in front of the one-way screen. He and Leela were to provide back-up behind the mirror. Just because I was losing some cases, especially the acting-out adolescents who refused to behave themselves. Hell, Gerard could've at least acknowledged the success I was having with the bed wetters.

To make matters worse, Smelder had recently decided to give up smoking. His nicotine withdrawal had produced a Mr. Hyde who belched black ferocious barks. He roared every time I made a mistake. I was becoming edgy and tense. The added stress from working with Theresa on the staff and the ongoing hassles with my mother didn't help my concentration.

I entered the loo and found Leela in front of the mirror. She was painstakingly applying fresh maroon lipstick. God, I hated unisex toilets! I splashed cold water on my face and combed my hair, then mentioned to Leela that the family had arrived.

My nerves played hopscotch under my skin as I went to collect the Dickensons. This family had not one, but three adolescents, the eldest of whom was sexually act-ing-out. I had no idea what the hell to do with her. I tried counting each step as a form of relaxation. Bloody useless. Just made me more anxious. I entered the wait-ing room and stared at what must have been five of the most hostile people I ever saw. The broad-shouldered father with a trim gray beard greeted me with cold, pierc-ing blue eyes.

I nervously offered my hand. "I'm Dr. Peter Pinowski."

The casually dressed man rose from the chair and warily scanned my body from the top of my brown hair down to my tan loafers. With a crushing handshake, he replied, "I'm Barry Dickenson."

I introduced myself to the frail mother sitting with a mustard cardigan decked across her shoulder. She frowned and nodded a weary head. I then turned to-ward the tallest of the children who was standing near the entrance. I extended my hand to the identified pa-tient. "You must be Ruth."

The 17-year-old stout girl returned a defiant scowl and folded her arms around her short, tight red dress. She made me feel like a bloody fool as my outstretched hand remained empty. I refrained from repeating the gesture with the other two children. Annie, a 16-year-old girl wearing jeans and a sloppy pullover, grunted when I acknowledged her, while her 14-year-old brother, George, said nothing. He just stared at his black shoes.

Bloody hell! I was in deep trouble.

I ushered them into the interviewing room where, today, the Disneyland poster seemed especially ludi-crous. Ruth sat opposite her father while her mother, sister, and brother filled in the gaps. I sat between Ruth and Mr. Dickenson with my back facing the one-way mirror. I prepared for a turbulent ride by fastening a mental seat belt.

Before I could mention the video, Ruth eyeballed the camera mounted in the corner. "I don't wanna be on the bloody telly."

"Is that really necessary?" challenged Mr. Dickenson.

"Well... uh... not really."

Brring, brring.

Already?! I picked the phone off the gray coffee table.

"Hello?"

"Don't say hello!" barked Gerard. "Just listen. Tell the father we video all sessions in order to review them later."

He hung up abruptly.

"We need to, uh, video the session so we can review it and decide how to help you... If that's okay with you."

"I don't want any perverts watching me!" bellowed Ruth. Her outstretched legs revealed crimson panties that matched her snug dress. "I don't wanna be here!"

"We're getting help for you once and for all," shouted her father. "I'm tired of you staying out all hours of the night worrying your mother sick, coming home with alcohol on your breath. God only knows what you're doing!"

Brring, brring.

"You have to tell them that you have consultants behind the one-way mirror."

I gulped. "Uh, before we get..."

"Oh sure, Dad," she hollered. "Tell the man the names you're always calling me. Tart, slut, whore, fuckin' bitch. Tell 'im what you say."

Brring, brring.

My armpits sprung a leak as I lifted the receiver once more.

"You must take control of this session, Pinowski! Don't let them interrupt you all the time. No wonder you're having problems. Tell them to stop talking until you've explained the videotaping and the one-way mirror. Don't ask permission. Tell them this is how we work!"

I replaced the phone on the table. "I need to explain a few things, if I may."

"Hold on," announced the father. "The doctor wants to say something." He nodded for me to continue, then lit a cigarette.

I took a deep breath, anxious to get it over with. "I just wanted to mention that we're videotaping the session, and there are two consultants helping me behind the mirror who may be phoning in from time to time, and if that's okay with you, can you tell me about some of your problems?"

Ruth gawked at her reflection. "No one told me people'd be pervin' at us."

"Excuse me," I said while I reached for the ringing phone.

"The father's smoking."

"Huh?"

"The father's smoking!" shouted Gerard. "He's not allowed to smoke!"

Christ! That was never a problem when Smelder was a nicotine addict.

"Excuse me, Mr. Dickenson, but... you're not allowed to smoke. Hospital rules. Sorry."

He angrily extinguished his cigarette on the side of the packet.

"Can you tell me about your problems?"

The father glowered. "My children have their own TV's, bikes, even telephones. Doesn't seem to matter. When I was brought up in Wallangra, we had respect. My daughter, Ruth, has none whatsoever. She wants to visit the beaches and shops at Manly and prowl for boys. God only knows what she does. Last Saturday she came home at four in the morning."

Ruth stamped her feet. "I'm almost 18! What do ya expect me to do? Hang around the house all day?"

"Tell the man what you were doing Saturday night!" growled the father.

Brring, brring.

"Ask Ruth why she thinks her father's so worried."

The father didn't sound worried. He was more like pissed off. I wasn't about to argue with the director.

"The consultants want to know..."

Brring, brring.

"Don't tell them the message is from us! Act as if it was your own idea."

Wasn't sure about any of my ideas, not with my nerves running the marathon.

I turned to my left. "Ruth, why is..."

"I was out with friends," the 17-year-old defended. "You're always sayin' I'm sleepin' around with boys. You're the one with the smutty mind."

"Ruth, why is..."

Brring, brring. Not again!

"Aren't you paying attention? She's already told you! Now ask the father why he doesn't trust his daughter?"

I blinked at the receiver. "Mr. Dickenson, could you tell us..."

"You know damn well stacks of boys have been calling the house. I overheard one of them on the extension. Said you were hot in bed."

"How could you?" shrieked Ruth hysterically. She swiveled toward me and screamed, "Could you ever live with someone like that?"

I pictured my own mother and said, "It must be pretty tough."

"You're damn straight it is!"

At last, I was establishing rapport.

Brring, brring.

"Be careful, Pinowski," warned Gerard. "She's seducing you to side against the father. Empathize with him."

I faced Mr. Dickenson. "It must be pretty tough for you too."

His voice boomed. "Do you have any kids?"

"Not really."

"If you had girls, you would worry yourself sick about them."

"I guess... er... most parents would."

"Kids are like cowcakes," grumbled the bearded man. "If you leave them alone, they're okay. When they're disturbed, they create a horrible smell."

"Oh, Barry," implored his embarrassed wife.

"It's true, Syl. If Ruth doesn't like what we say, she storms out of the house with the shits. Annie and George aren't as bad yet. But give them time. I'm sure you know what I'm talking about, Doctor."

Anticipating another phone-in, I looked at the silent receiver. No call. I tried to remember the last message. Did Gerard say, "Empathize with the father"?

"It must be pretty tough, Mr. Dickenson."

"It hasn't been easy," he said. "Especially knowing my daughter's screwing a score of other blokes."

"Get fucked!" Ruth screeched. "You're not Mr. Innocent!"

The frail mother began shaking. The father raised his fist. "Watch your mouth! I won't be having a daughter of mine talking to me like that."

"You tellin' us you never had some on the side? What about those weekend boating trips? What were you catching?"

"You slut!"

Unsure where to proceed, I desperately glanced at the unusually silent communicator. I checked the Do Not Disturb button. It hadn't been pressed. Why wasn't Smelder calling? Maybe he thought the interview was going well. Or wanted to give more rein. I decided to take control.

"We should try and calm down..."

"How can you let Dad talk to me like that?" cried Ruth, eyeballing her mother.

The helpless mom pleaded, "Settle down, dear. Listen to the doctor."

"It must be pretty tough for you too, Mrs. Dickenson."

"She's an ol' cow," Ruth blurted. "Doesn't do anything, except what Dad tells her."

"You little shit! How dare you call your mother a cow?"

"Come off it, Dad. Since when have you really cared for her? You treat her like scum. We know about the affairs."

Smelder should've phoned by now! I wasn't sure whether to involve the other two children sullenly staring at the carpet or to bite the bullet and tackle the squabbling father and daughter. I chose the latter. "What do you want changed?"

"I want my daughter to stop sleeping around with every other bloke..."

"Fuck off! You might as well call me a whore. I don't have to take this shit! I hate you!"

Ruth bolted from the room.

Didn't know whether to send the parents to fetch her or go after her myself. I needed assistance.

"Excuse me. I better consult with my colleagues."

I quickly exited the counseling room and opened the door to the adjoining darkened viewing room. My eyes stared into blackness. At first I thought the room was empty. No. Could hear sounds of scuffling. Shapes became clearer. I rubbed my eyes. More movement. What was Leela doing?

Smelder rose to his feet holding onto his pants.

"Pinowski!" he howled. "Get back in that room and help that family!"

"What's been happening here? There hasn't been any phone-ins."

"Never you mind about that," thundered Gerard. "March! The family needs you."

"But..."

"Don't argue, Pinowski! Get in there! Now!"

"But..."

"You heard me! Move it!"

I entered the interviewing room again, unsure what to say or do, plagued by thoughts of the darkened room.

POST MORTEM DISCUSSION

🐦

THURSDAY, MAY 19

Gerard and Leela left immediately after yesterday's interview. Hardly said a word. I was called into Smelder's office for this 10 o'clock meeting. His golden-haired social worker sat next to him as he adjusted his glasses.

"As you were aware, Pinowski, I stopped the phone-ins during the Dickenson interview. You became confused and disoriented when I offered assistance. You began to see things that weren't there."

I pictured the two alone in the dark observation room. "I thought I saw you..."

"It was obvious, Pinowski, your perceptions were clouded. However, you can't blame yourself entirely. That chaotic family overwhelmed you. It happens all the time with inexperienced therapists."

The lecherous bastard glanced at Leela who smiled coyly. He continued, "After conferring with Leela this morning, I've come to the conclusion that your family therapy skills are very inadequate. Your thinking is not at all systemic. As a result, your projections are distorting your perceptions. It's no wonder the Dickenson family decided not to return for further sessions."

"But I thought I saw..."

"We can't have you projecting your own inadequacies and hangups onto other people."

"I don't understand."

He gave a fatherly smile. "I have decided to send you to the next Family Therapy Conference which will be held in Canberra this July. Our Capital City isn't so bad during winter. Just take some warm clothes. You can use the time away from the department to learn additional skills. You're a smart lad, Pinowski."

"But..."

Gerard put up his hand. "Don't you worry, the department will pay for the conference."

I spotted the picture hanging on his wall. Ducks in V-formation were flying through gray clouds while a hunter, sheltered in a wooden boat, aimed his shotgun. The ominous grin on his face told me to forget everything.

1ST DAY OF WINTER

FRIDAY, JUNE 3

At the end of the day, I caught up with Theresa when she left her office. "How about going out for a drink?"

She returned an icy stare. "No thanks."

"Can't we forget the past and make a fresh start?"

"I have a bodybuilding class this evening."

"Come on. Just one drink?"

"There's an upcoming competition. I can't gain any weight."

I scanned her physique which rippled with muscle. "Then how about a mineral water?" I pleaded. "Please? The vibes are bad enough here with Gerard and Leela. But it's become unbearable since you've iced me out of your life. The rest of the team must feel the tension. Can't we at least clear the air?"

She glanced at her watch. "Just a quick one. My class starts at six-thirty."

She drove me to the Turramurra Hotel. In silence. My mind whirred like a computer, yet I was unable to think of the right words to say. She parked the red Honda, and I stepped into the cold wind chafing at my face.

When we entered the pub, I suggested, "The table near the heater?"

"I prefer this one near the door."

She grabbed a chair facing the entrance. I sat opposite her with my back to the wooden door. Each time it swung open, a frosty draft swept across my shoulders and neck. I huddled into my coat.

We ordered and Theresa sipped her Perrier. I gulped my stout. "I'm sorry about what happened to us. I thought we had a good thing going."

"How's your mother?" asked Theresa caustically.

"She's been off my back lately."

"I wonder why?!"

"Let's not bring her into this. Can't we just stick with what's happened between us?"

"I don't think there can be an *us* when you're so codependent on your mother."

"What do you want me to do? Leave just like that?"

"I don't expect you to do anything. I thought you were man enough to spend time with me rather than with your mummy!"

"I want to be with you! Why do you think I asked you here?"

"Maybe you can't handle the tension in the department. Maybe you want me to kiss your boo-boo and make it all better."

"What do I have to do, crawl? We had something special, Theresa. I don't want it to go down the drain."

"You rarely entered it, if you catch the drift."

A cold blast from the swinging door chilled my bones.

"What are you talking about?"

"Are you dense?"

"Is that it? My coming too soon. Is that what's bothering you? Hey, that's easily fixed. No worries."

Theresa checked her watch. "I'm not interested in any further involvement. You need time to mature."

"Don't worry about my prematurity. I've been studying the therapy manuals."

She downed her Perrier. "According to Freud, a premature ejaculator has repressed sadistic feelings toward women and wants to deprive them of pleasure. I no longer want to be the mother figure who becomes the recipient of your unconscious resentment. As long as you fail to address these issues, you'll always be codependent and unconsciously resentful." She collected her bag. "Sorry, Peter. I have to run."

"Wait a minute. I don't want to deprive you of pleasure! I want to be with you. I won't let my ma manipulate me. What do I have to do? I'll move in with you."

"It's too late."

"Theresa!" I pleaded, desperately clutching her arm. "We can work this out. You're the only woman I've ever loved. Don't walk out on me! I don't know what I might do. Without you, my life's not worth living."

Using her arms of steel, she forcibly pried my hands away from her body. "Don't threaten me with emotional blackmail. It's over. We had fun, but now that's finished. We can talk at work, but as far as I'm concerned, it's strictly professional. 'Bye."

"Wait. Not yet." I followed her out of the pub into the freezing night air. "One more chance! I won't flub it this time."

The only response was a howling wind.

"Theresa, I need you. Please! Don't go."

She disappeared into the darkness.

I stood numb on the pavement. My wildest dream had been swept away with the frosty wind. Surely, I wasn't that bad. She even admitted that we did have some fun. I could've provided more good times. If only she would've let me. Hell, the least she could've done was drive me to the train station. Bloody woman!

The icy breeze pushed me onward. If only Ma hadn't hassled me, everything would've been fine. She really blew it for me this time. Bloody woman!

The train roared through the underground tunnel, screeching and squealing around each bend. The face of Heidi Wentworth flashed on the sooty window. Hell, she didn't show up for today's interview. Didn't even bother calling. Pictures of Theresa and my mother joined Heidi's image flickering on the glass. Bloody women!

QUEEN'S BIRTHDAY

🦃

MONDAY, JUNE 13

Normally, I would've been more than happy to have wished Elizabeth birthday greetings in exchange for the day off, but there didn't seem much to celebrate. Theresa's absence from my life still left an unfillable black hole. The long weekend dragged on tortuously, and my brooding deepened.

To make matters worse, Ma had organized a barbecue this afternoon with Uncle Janek and Aunt Adele. She was already flustered and kept nagging about chores that were never done to her satisfaction.

I snuck out the back door with Blackie and spotted our neighbor's nosy beak poking over the fence, searching for evidence. Fortunately, I had wrapped the small carcass in a plastic bag and stashed it in the trash. Mrs. Trineckova vehemently hated Blackie, especially his late night barking. If she ever found out that one of her precious brandy chooks had escaped from the cage and crawled through our fence, she would have flown into another hysterical tirade, especially if she discovered that the small chicken was crushed by Blackie's powerful jaws. I could see her now, flapping her arms and squawking incessantly, "Get rid of the mongrel!"

This was not a time to face Mrs. Trineckova, another family function, nor my mother, for that matter. Blackie and I jumped into Pa's Holden and headed for Lane Cove Park. It was the best solution for dog and master.

A RAY OF LIGHT

WINTER SOLSTICE, TUESDAY, JUNE 21

During the morning break, I sat alone on the hospital bench in the cold crisp wind. I sipped my Earl Gray tea.

"May I join you?"

"Surjit! I thought you had de-materialized from the hospital. Whenever I visited your department, you were either out or unavailable."

He joined me on the wooden seat. "I've been very busy since Jules Eaglesham returned to head our unit."

"What about his manic depression?"

"Stabilized, as long as he takes his lithium. He convinced the hospital brass that he was capable of resuming not only his psychiatric duties but his administrative ones as well." With a wink he added, "They must owe him a few favors."

"Couldn't he make another suicide attempt?"

"The staff and I have been watching Jules very closely. Thus far he's coping."

"Who's in charge of whom?"

"I ask myself the same question." Surjit blew into his cupped hands. "Isn't it rather cold sitting out here on the bench? There's not much sun."

"I needed the fresh air."

Surjit peered into my eyes. "The problems of the world must be sitting on your shoulder."

"It's been one of those months."

"Want to talk about it?"

"Thanks, but it won't resolve the hassles at home, Theresa's deep freeze, or the shabby treatment I get from Smelder. I doubt whether I'm even helping any of my clients."

He touched my shoulder lightly. "Those are too many burdens to carry alone. When you're struggling to remain on the road, it's difficult to see where the path is heading."

I stared at his dark face and recalled the enjoyable times we had over table tennis. Listening to his philosophizing often left me confused, yet, in a strange way, it calmed my spirit.

"How can you be so peaceful?" I asked.

He rubbed his hands together for warmth. "Peace doesn't come easy. The seeker must travel a formidable journey."

"What journey?"

His eyes sparkled. "Through illusion, past the veil of forgetfulness. Only then can you truly see."

"See what?"

"How can you see what you cannot see?"

"I don't get it."

"We've been taught to search for happiness outside ourselves in something we can see and touch. Experiencing pain in the world often forces us to look within. Lasting peace comes only when our eyes have turned inward and pierced through the darkness."

"I still don't understand."

"You have forgotten who you really are."

I scratched my head. "I know who I am."

"Then who are you?"

I glared at the psychiatrist. "You know who I am."

"So tell me, who are you?"

"Your long lost ping-pong partner," I added smartly.

"Who are you really?"

"You know... a psychologist."

"You're more than what you do. Who are you?"

"What is this, 20 questions?"

"When you remove your roles, who are you?"

"Just me."

He tapped my chest. "Your special journey within will reveal who you are."

"Where's my path heading?"

"We each must find our own way."

I declared, "A few sign posts wouldn't go astray."

"Ultimately, our search through the experiences of life will lead us back home."

I raised my eyebrows. "Home?"

"To our very essence, our True Self."

I nestled my hands around the warm cup of tea. "I need something concrete. How do you find this essence?"

Surjit reclined against the bench. "There's a story about a wise sage called Jayadratha. He agreed to teach the ancient wisdom to Sathana, a new disciple. One summer morning, Jayadratha walked a beaten path along a winding river which carved its way through the countryside. His student followed. 'Master,' he spoke 'how do I discover my True Self?' Jayadratha walked on in silence. They arrived at a place where the water was shallow and still. Succulent figs dangled from trees on the opposite banks. 'Great Master,' repeated Sathana, 'how do I find my True Self?' Again the great sage said nothing. Seeking the ripened fruit, Jayadratha began wading through the river. The young man followed and spoke once more. 'Master, how can I discover my True Self?' Jayadratha stopped midstream and suddenly seized the student by the scruff of the neck. He pushed the struggling head underwater. Many seconds ticked by until Sathana was finally released, gagging and gasping for air. 'Why did you do this?!' sputtered the irate disciple. His master finally spoke. 'When your desire to find Truth is as great as your desire to breathe, only then will your answers come, and then in an instant.' "

I heaved a mighty sigh. "Isn't there an easy way?"

The psychiatrist stood up. "If there is, I haven't found it. Come. Let's stretch our legs."

We strolled across the hospital grounds and paused near a liquid amber which, next to the green eucalyptus trees, seemed out of place. The bare branches of the deciduous tree still clutched a few remaining reddish brown leaves.

Surjit plucked one. "We're like this tree in winter. Our roots are waiting to bathe in the spring of life to awaken once more. The light of understanding will bring the realization that we are not bodies, but merely spirits interconnected with the Divine Mind."

I followed as he walked on. "We have a choice," he said. "We can continue on the mandala, the wheel of life, in a dream-like state or walk the path toward Self Realization."

I tripped on a stone. "Be more specific!"

The man from India stopped. He stared intensely at my face. "Peter, surrender totally to the essence of your being. Realize that you and Divine Essence exist as one. There is no other reality. United in this awareness, your mind will direct your life toward your destined purpose."

"If you know all this, why are you working with Dr. Eaglesham?"

He shook his head. "As yet, I don't fully know. I thought my calling was to work with children. I resisted my return to the Adult Psychiatric Unit. That only created more internal struggle. Once I accepted the decision, my life flowed more harmoniously. It soon became clear that I had much to learn from the adult patients."

"What? How to go crazy?"

"It's been over four years since I migrated from India. During that time, I have periodically experienced deep despair. My heart pined for my relatives back in Punjab. As life would have it, many of my clients are migrants who also experience difficulty adjusting to the new culture. As they tell me their woes, I listen with a third ear, not just for their hidden messages, but also for mine. I have learned that a client will inadvertently speak about the therapist's very own issue. And of course, the therapist will often reflect back what he most needs to hear."

"I still can't believe that helping clients is another way to further myself."

"Just like a magnet, the forces of life draw together parallel experiences which appear to the uninitiated as coincidences. There is a relationship between the world within and the world without. The client and therapist, in effect, follow this universal law by mirroring different facets of each other."

"That doesn't compute."

"When the time is right, it'll become clearer."

"That sounds like a cop-out."

Surjit patted my back. "You may be right. What I do know is that you mustn't let your burdens weigh you down. A healthy dose of play therapy should relieve the tension. Tomorrow, table tennis over lunch. Doctor's orders."

June 21

On the shortest day of the year, the sun finally made its appearance.

THE 43RD INTERVIEW

THURSDAY, JUNE 23

Heidi Wentworth handed me a small paper bag.

"What do we have here?" I asked, peering into the brown sack.

"Cupcakes. Made 'em last night."

"What kind?"

"Chocolate pecan."

"My favorite! I'll have one now, if you don't mind." My teeth crunched a pecan. "Yumm. You bake a mean cupcake."

When she was discharged two months ago, which also meant access to the family kitchen, she appointed me her official taster.

"Do you want the recipe?"

I licked chocolate icing off my finger. "I much prefer eating over cooking. So tell me, what's been happening?"

"Mum's enrolled me in a ballet class, and I'm now 92 pounds."

"Congratulations! You have come a long way."

My mind flashed to our first meeting back in January when I had faced an emaciated 15-year-old girl who weighed less than 66 pounds. Within five months, I had witnessed a physical transformation. Previously sallow cheeks had puffed to a rosy complexion, and bones, once concealed by a loose blanket of skin, now were padded by flesh. Though still thin-looking, she had stabilized her weight and presented like a normal adolescent in her 10th year at Hornsby Girls High School. Her navy blue skirt and matching jumper remained neatly pressed, even after a day at school.

"How's your classes?" I asked.

"Gawd, I missed out on heaps when I was stuck in hospital. I still have stacks of catchin' up."

"You'll pick it up in no time. You've certainly proven you have will power. With your mind, you could achieve practically anything."

"Would you say I'm cured?"

I nodded enthusiastically. "Definitely on the road to recovery."

She smiled. "Have another cupcake."

I reached for another tasty treat.

"Ya still livin' at home?"

"For the moment."

"Aren't ya kinda old to be livin' with your mum?"

"I'll be moving out one of these days."

"Why haven't ya left?"

"Why the interrogation?"

"I dunno. Curious."

"As a mate of mine says, when it's meant to happen, it'll happen. Anyway, we're here to talk about you. I daresay, I'm proud of what you've accomplished."

Heidi chewed at her fingertips. "I kinda wonder... when I don't have ta come."

"You're not thinking of stopping therapy?"

Her teeth snapped a fingernail. "You even said I'm cured."

"Hold on. I said you're on the road to recovery. You have a way to go."

"I really wanna do it myself."

"We've been over this a hundred times, Heidi. You've been missing appointments lately, and that shows you're resisting therapy. Believe me, you're not ready to go it alone. My consultant, Dr. Crompton, has indicated you still need quite a bit more counseling."

She started nibbling the nails on her other hand.

"Look on the bright side. See how much progress you're making."

She nodded meekly.

"The fact that you now weigh 92 pounds is another milestone!"

"Yea."

"Besides. You're becoming a fantastic cook."

She gave a half-smile. "Have another cupcake."

I reached into the brown bag and thought of Surjit. What lesson was I supposed to learn from my modern day Lazarus? Maybe she was here to show me I could really help someone, that therapy does work, that I can be a success. I swelled with renewed confidence. At this moment, I felt as if I was in the right place at the right time.

MANAGEMENT MEETING

🦃

MONDAY, JULY 4

In Gerard's office. I took the chair furthest from Theresa who responded with an icy stare. We were hardly speaking to each other since we concluded our one and only joint case–the 11-year-old compulsive masturbator. My frequent attempts to bridge the gap had little effect. She continued to pout like a spoiled child. I decided that since she wasn't talking to me, I wouldn't talk to her. She had to make the next move.

Maxine arrived with the agenda, took the chair next to Theresa, and directed a frosty glare toward me. Women, as usual, sticking together. Didn't have to talk to her, either.

I sat among the men, flanked by Henry on my right and Earl Jacobi, the long-awaited intern, on my left. Earl had finally arrived last week as Surjit's replacement. His bronze hair, fresh face, and good looks, plus an affable personality, made him an easy addition to the team. His smooth manner, however, smacked of a used car salesman–not necessarily a negative characteristic for a psychiatrist. Having been transferred from the Drug and Alcohol Unit, Earl was now serving the second of his five years of psychiatric training.

He and I quickly became mates. Not that we had much in common, but we were about the same age, and, more importantly, we had to survive this wacky department. I had to endure his strange notions about therapy and the perpetual cloud of his cigarette smoke, but I needed a friend, especially in this cuckoo's nest.

Tension crackled in Smelder's room between the men and the women. An aloof Leela uncharacteristically sat among the women, reading the agenda. Gerard took a seat next to Henry and nervously cleaned his spectacles.

"It's past 11 o'clock," announced Maxine, compulsively obsessed with punctuality.

Smelder replaced his glasses. "Let's begin. The first item is the literature meeting. Who's responsible for the next article?"

I cleared my throat. "The paper I chose explores different ways to enhance a professional team. Here's photocopies for each of you."

As I passed them around, I quoted from the text. "To work effectively, members of a therapeutic team must communicate and cooperate." I peered at Theresa and pointed to the article.

She scowled. "The author would surely agree that a productive member must have some expertise."

She wasn't that hot of a therapist herself. Hell, interviewing clients twice a week for umpteen sessions didn't prove anything.

"When you read..."

"No need to get into that now, Pinowski," interrupted Smelder. "You can summarize the article next Friday. Our next item involves a circular from administration advising us that all departments continue to enforce the smoke-free policy. Apparently, some of the hospital staff have been slacking off. As a former smoker, I wholeheartedly support the hospital policy. Those needing help with their nicotine addiction can attend seminars at the Drug and Alcohol Unit."

Earl elbowed my ribs. "I used to teach those classes." He showed me his brown-stained fingers. "I'll need a supply of air freshener for my office."

"The next item," continued Gerard, "involves my upcoming brief sabbatical. I recently received approval to attend The International Child Psychiatry Conference which will be held in Venice next month. While in Italy, I will be spending time in Rome, Florence, and a few other cities to visit family therapy programs. I will be away six weeks starting the beginning of August."

"That's next month," said an acerbic Maxine.

"I know it's short notice," Gerard defended, "but I was awaiting final authorization from the finance committee."

She huffed, "Hospital covering your expenses? Sounds more like a paid holiday."

"Not that it's any of your concern, but my contract allows a teaching sabbatical every second year. But don't you worry. I'll bring back plenty of new ideas. The Italians have some exciting concepts on family therapy."

Maxine glanced at Leela. "Aren't you going?"

"No!" she pouted.

Our director mopped his forehead and offered Leela an indirect apology. "I submitted a request for another staff member to accompany me. Unfortunately, I was informed that since Peter had already been approved to attend The Australian and New Zealand Family Therapy Conference at the end of this month, the finance committee couldn't afford any more funds, nor allow further leave of staff."

Leela's heavy make-up cracked as her face grimaced in anger.

"Who will be in charge while you're away?" asked Theresa.

Our commander addressed his troops. "Since I was unable to secure a temporary replacement, I've therefore asked Dr. Jules Eaglesham to provide psychiatric backup."

Groans echoed throughout the room. "He's just returned back to active duty after his recent suicide attempt," voiced Maxine.

"I know it's not the perfect arrangement, but I'll only be gone six weeks. During that time, Maxine, as the senior member of staff, will be responsible for the day-to-day running of the department. Any medical emergencies can be handled by Earl. Of course, if you have any pressing family therapy problems, our Leela will have the answers."

I glanced at *our* Leela. Her sneer showed that she wasn't a happy camper.

"If it's any consolation," offered Gerard whose mouth stretched into a glowing smile, "I'll return from Italy with a bag full of intellectual goodies for everyone."

I could hardly wait for Santa Smelder to leave. Stuff the goodies. I'll take the six weeks without his intimidating presence. Lady Luck was finally turning my way. And in just three-and-a-half weeks I was off to the conference in Canberra. Hallelujah!

"Let's move to the next agenda item, which is Frank King's family therapy consultations. Leela and I seem to be the only ones discussing our families during his visits. I want someone else to present a case. Any volunteers?"

Arms remained motionless, mouths remained shut.

"Jacobi, you can present one of yours."

All eyes turned to the new boy on the block.

"That's an excellent idea," Earl crowed. "I don't, however, have any difficult cases. I wonder if we could discuss principles of strategic systemic family therapy. I understand you and Dr. King are experts in the field."

Gerard hesitated, then answered, "All right. Since you're new in the field, we'll use Frank's next consultation to review some of the key concepts. I'll present a video of my most recent success. You can bring a case to the following consultation."

Maxine shifted her bulk uneasily in the chair. "Can we move on? We must discuss the Jenson/Murray family."

Gerard removed his glasses and rubbed his eyes. "Fill us in on the details."

She opened the folder. "The children's solicitor informed me that the court hearing will proceed in several months. We must document any relevant material on behalf of the children, Conrad and Richard."

"I don't want my staff appearing at court like a bunch of galahs," rebuked Smelder. "Has anyone read the pediatrician's report?"

"I've talked with Helen Towers," said Maxine. "Her physical examination proved positive. The anus of both boys showed signs of severe traumatization. Helen will corroborate that they were abused sexually."

"Good! That's what the court likes to hear. What other professionals have been involved?"

The nurse scanned the notes. "Initially, the mother notified the police who, along with the juvenile officer, talked with the young boys. They were referred to the sexual assault worker who, after conducting an investigative interview, sent them to Dr. Martin for the initial medical. He referred them to Dr. Towers in pediatrics. Following her examination, Helen Towers sent the boys to us for therapy."

Gerard turned to Henry. "How are your assessments going?"

As if like a puppet, Henry bounced to life. "I've seen the boys three times. Conrad is four years old and Richard Jr. is eight. While it appears that they have been sexually abused, they can't, or won't, reveal the perpetrator."

Maxine jostled her chair. "What exactly did the boys say?"

With each eye simultaneously exploring different ends of the room, Henry stammered, "Both, uh, say that a man in the park, uh, stuck his, uh... wee-wee in their bum."

"They're protecting the father," Maxine decreed. "I've been counseling the mother individually, and she believes Conrad and Richard Jr. must've been warned by the father that if they said anything, he would go to jail. The bastard deserves to be put behind bars! Let the inmates give him what he deserves."

"We don't know for sure it was Mr. Jenson," defended Henry.

"Come off it," berated Maxine. "The evidence clearly points toward him. Research shows that the majority of offenders are known and trusted by the victims."

"Have you recorded the sessions on videotape?" asked Gerard.

Henry hesitated. "Uh, no. I thought it might inhibit the boys."

"For Christ sake, they won't know the difference. You can use the transcripts of the tapes for evidence."

"I'm not so sure about the video," protested Henry and his wobbling eyes. "I... uh... feel self-conscious with the camera. It might also make the boys reticent."

"Cut the crap, Snart! There's no better way to record any disclosures. After you've established trust, they will be ready to open up. Use the dolls and get them to show you what happened."

"But..."

"No buts!" stormed the psychiatrist. "Videotape the sessions. Remember, you may be cross-examined by the father's attorney."

"The bastard!" fumed Maxine.

"Calm down. We don't have conclusive evidence yet. Mr. Jenson counter-claims that the mother's boyfriend was the culprit."

"Bullshit, Gerard. You've interviewed the father. You know he's a slimy lawyer who's protecting himself. The boys admitted they were molested by a man in the park across the street from where the father lives. The mother swears it was him."

"But she's seeking custody. She may be using this to sway the court in her favor."

Maxine's rage almost toppled her chair. "You know damn well the bastard's guilty as hell! I'm prepared to help Gayle Murray protect her children at all costs."

"She's a drug addict!" Gerard challenged.

"Gayle was hooked on Valium, the result of male oppression. The relationship she had with Richard Jenson practically killed her. Now that she's no longer living with him, she's drug-free. But that has nothing to do with the fact that these boys were sexually abused by a man, namely the father. Even the boys' drawings indicate funny business with him. Wake up, Gerard! Quit protecting the man."

"This, uh, may be getting us off track," mediated Holy Henry.

"Oh, shut up!" shouted the agitated nurse. "You men are all alike! No wonder you're not producing the evidence. These boys must be protected."

"My department doesn't need someone going off half-cocked," stormed Gerard. "I won't take this bullshit. My reputation is at stake. Try and remember, you're professionals."

Maxine puffed her cheeks. "Hmmph."

"Sooner or later we'll uncover the perpetrator. I've scheduled a few more interviews with Mr. Jenson. He's agreed to be videotaped."

"I reviewed his last videotape," she scowled. "He must've rehearsed every one of his answers, just as if he was in the courtroom, pretending to be the concerned father. Even when he admitted drawing on the boys' naked bodies, he covered himself, saying he used colored soap markers as a game to prevent the boys arguing about taking a bath. He's a cunning bastard."

Henry added his own words of consolation. "As he sows, so shall he reap."

Smelder quickly countered, "God doesn't provide assessments, Snart. You do. Concentrate on your interview and pray that those boys identify a perpetrator."

"I still remember the case of Mr. Hop-a-long," seethed Maxine. "The bastard owned a preschool and had been playing sexual games with a few of the children, telling them to pull down their pants so he could play leap frog over their bottoms. He was acquitted because of insufficient evidence. The arsehole even received financial compensation because his so-called reputation was destroyed. I don't want the same thing happening here."

"Give yourself another six sessions," Gerard advised Henry. "As soon as you develop the boys' trust, you'll discover the true story."

Maxine tossed the folder on the table. "The court report for the custody dispute is due in two months, and the father has hired one of the best barristers in the state. If he wins, the bastard could be awarded custody. The welfare of these boys lies in your lap, Henry. Don't screw them up."

Smelder picked up the file. "Taking into consideration the transcripts, assessments, and psychological tests, I wouldn't put a wager on the report being less than 80 pages."

Just as well I wasn't involved in this seedy episode. I despised assessments. Besides, this case had the potential of slithering through the valley of darkness. I wouldn't want to be in Henry's shoes, not for all the potatoes in Poland.

When the meeting was adjourned, Henry seemed visibly shaken. He leaned next to me and whispered, "I feel Satan's work is among us. Pray with me, Peter. Psalm 59. 'Rescue me from my enemies, oh God.... '"

I poked my head into Earl Jacobi's cluttered office. "Could you spare a few minutes?"

"Sure, mate. Anything to get out of work." The bronze-haired psychiatric intern shoved a pile of files off a chair. "Grab a seat."

"I'm having trouble completing an assessment. It's been hanging around like a bad smell, and the parents keep phoning for the results."

"No worries," he said. He closed the door then reached into the top drawer of his desk. He removed a pouch of Drum tobacco, along with a packet of cigarette papers, and began the ritual of rolling his own. He shredded tobacco over a wafer-thin paper, then created an impacted cylinder. Using his tongue, he stamped a seal of approval. After he struck a match, he nodded. "Go ahead."

"This 13-year-old girl, Michelle, was referred for poor school performance–underachieving. She's the only child of two university professors who believe their daughter should be performing top marks. The parents requested a psychological profile and insisted upon a battery of psychologicals so they could help their daughter improve her grades. I questioned the need for such extensive testing, but the pushy parents put the screws on. Said that unless I met their request, they would take it to the director. Considering my relationship with Smelder, I had no choice. It was then up to Michelle, who completed the Wechsler Intelligence Scale for Children, the Lateral Dominance Examination, the Finger Tapping Test, the Purdue Pegboard, and the Speech-Sound Perception Test. I added the Rorshach, the Bender-Gestalt, Benton's Visual Retention Test, the Thematic Apperception Technique, and the Achenbach Child Behavior Checklist."

"So what did you find out?"

"I learned Michelle was right-handed, liked sports, especially swimming and netball, had an average I.Q., wasn't very good in spelling, had some difficulty in solving complex problems, and worried excessively because of her parents' expectations.. I don't know what to do. The parents aren't going to be happy. They were expecting more pathology."

He exhaled a cloud of smoke. "You're taking this much too seriously, Pete. If you want to be successful, you'll have to learn the Jacobi method of writing assessments, the fastest way to crank out a report."

Earl sucked hard on his Drum, then blew toward the stained ceiling. "First of all, develop a template, a concise report that can be used as a guide for future assessments. I have a few."

"Thanks, but it's probably better if I develop my own."

"Suit yourself, mate. But whatever you do, use heaps of therapeutic jargon. You know, the client suffers from low self-esteem, insecurity, anxiety, depression, emotional deprivation, poor bonding, that sort of thing. Add an impressive diagnosis from the International Classification of Diseases, especially the Psychiatric Disorders specific to Childhood and Adolescence. Once completed, that assessment can be modified and changed to suit any new case merely by altering the names and some of the facts."

"You pulling my leg?"

"Hell, I'm dead serious. I reckon everyone classifies clients differently anyway, depending on their orientation."

"That's not very scientific."

He puffed on the cigarette. "Assessments aren't that important. After they're done, who reads them? The hospital and the clients just want to know that someone has diagnosed the problem. A few labels can go a long way to relieving everyone's anxiety. That's what we're paid for. However, just in case, C.Y.A."

"C.Y.A.?"

"Cover your ass. Never use definitive statements in your report. Always use ambiguous words such as, 'it appears', 'it seems', or 'possibly'. If you're ever discovered to be wrong, which is most unlikely, you've given yourself an escape hatch."

"But what about the diagnosis?"

He chuckled. "That's easy. Stick with something standard. I diagnose most boys who act out as Conduct Disorders–a great category because everyone knows Conduct Disorders are untreatable. If you don't help them, it's not your fault, and if by chance you cure them, you're a goddamn miracle worker."

He smashed the butt in a metal ashtray. "For girls, I use Neurotic Disorder. It covers phobias, depression, anxiety, you name it. And if you have any doubts about diagnosis, use a generic category like Disturbance of Emotions Specific to Childhood or Adolescence. I reckon all kids have disturbed emotions. It's rather simple once you get the hang of it."

"What about professional ethics?"

"They're nothing more than a bunch of rules that keep changing depending on which bimbo is making them up."

"I think I'll stick to my old method. It seems... well... more honest."

He rolled another fag. "Listen, mate. You've got a major problem."

"What's that?"

"Your attitude. I reckon you take this job too seriously. You'll end up like everyone else here, uptight and burnt-out. It was a hell of a lot better working at Drug and Alcohol."

I could well imagine.

"You'll have to visit me on the weekend. Meet the wife and kid. I'll teach you how to unwind."

The intern moved closer and sheepishly scanned the room as if to make sure no one was listening. I glanced around, halfway expecting to find someone. Then I realized the door was shut.

"Sssh," he whispered. "I have a stash of el primo dopo, courtesy of Drug and Alcohol. A concerned mother brought in some hash she discovered under her son's bed. She wanted to dispose of it rather than see her son tempted." He winked. "I commended her for placing it in the right hands. Great stuff, too. You smoke, don't you?"

"Not really."

"Don't give me that bull," he said. "Everyone's had a bit on the side."

"Tried it once," I confided, "as a participant in a university research project. They were testing the effects of marijuana on students. We were even paid money, but I kept choking whenever I inhaled."

"Well, mate. We can do our own research at my place. My Kristy bakes a magic brownie that'll blow your head off. What do you say?"

"Well... uh... "

He slapped my arm. "C'mon Pete, loosen up. It'll be a blast."

Getting my head blown off didn't sound like much fun. On the other hand, he was one of the few people in the department that didn't have the shits with me. Without Earl, I'd be stuck with Holy Henry, reading passages from the Bible.

"I appreciate the invitation, but I'm off to Canberra in a couple of weeks. Maybe when I come back."

"No worries." He opened the pouch of his Drum tobacco. "We'll celebrate when you return from the conference."

"Uh... sure."

"We're in a gold mine, Pete. Want to make some easy money?"

My body stiffened. "What did you have in mind?"

"The hospital's always looking for human guinea pigs to test new medications, submit to experiments, donate sperm, blood, and God knows what else. Mind you, it pays pretty well. I pick up an extra two hundred dollars every month. You should get in on the free cash. On public service time." He snickered, "I reckon it's all in the name of science."

In the two-and-a-half weeks since Earl had joined our department, I had learned plenty, not exactly the stuff Surjit had been teaching.

THE 46TH SESSION

MONDAY, JULY 18

Through the wire mesh embedded in the glass window, I watched the steady rain. A giant Norfolk Pine swayed with the wind and sprayed water across the grass. Heidi was 20 minutes late for her four o'clock appointment.

When the receptionist announced her arrival, I collected a drenched girl. She deposited her soaked umbrella on the floor tile and sulked. There were no baked treats today.

"You canceled the last two weeks. What's going on?"

She stared at her soggy black shoes. "Had stacks of homework."

"That's what you said every time I called you at home. You missed the last four sessions because of homework?"

"I had ta do it, didn't I?"

"I've talked to your school principal. He says you're doing very well. What's really bothering you?"

She kicked at the puddle on the floor. "I don't need to come no more. I'm eatin' okay and Mum's off my back. I wanna leave hospital for good."

"Not that again!"

"How would you like seeing a shrink twice a week?"

"I'm a psychologist."

"Same thing. Besides, the family sessions with the fat shrink have ended. I don't need our meetings no more."

"But look how far you've progressed."

"Then why do I still have ta come? Even when I'm all better. That's not fair!"

"Therapy is like getting coached, as if you were learning the game of table tennis. You have definitely improved your game, but you still need to serve better and develop a backhand. I can coach you on the finer points."

"I don't like table tennis."

"Yea, well, let's say if you did, you wouldn't want to quit when you could be competing up there with the pros."

She swished her feet in the water. "I don't wanna compete. I'm happy the way I am. I don't wanna come no more."

I sat forward. "Heidi, if you leave now, you might one day wish you could have had more sessions."

She stared out the window.

"Therapy provides a sense of security knowing you can talk to someone about your problems."

She stamped on the floor. "I don't have problems. I wanna catch up on school and leave this dumb ol' hospital."

I couldn't allow her to end therapy. Heidi still needed me. Besides, I had just boasted to the analyst, Fiona Crompton, about her continued improvement. The consultant stipulated that therapy should continue for at least another year. I couldn't conclude my most successful case, not without a struggle.

"We've come a long way together. I'd like to see this through to the end."

"I dunno. If I say yes, I might not come back. I really wanna say goodbye today. You helped me heaps. I wanna end as friends. Okay?"

"But you need more coaching."

"Others need more help than me."

"But no one bakes cupcakes as well as you."

She didn't even smile.

"What do your parents have to say about this?"

"They tole me I don't have ta come as long as I eat and stay outa trouble."

"Maybe I should talk to them."

"No matter," she said defiantly. "My mind's made up."

I sat in silence, disturbed only by the gentle patter of rain rhythmically tapping against the tile roof. Wasn't sure what to do. I could insist, but more likely than not, she'd cancel out like she's done the previous four sessions.

"Okay. Let's compromise. Instead of twice a week, you can attend counseling once a week."

"Naw. I'm better. You said so yourself."

"You mean you want to stop completely? Right now? Today is our last session?"

Her right shoe danced in the puddle. "Yea."

"You have to give me some time to get used to the idea. How about if we have a limited number of sessions?"

"Naw."

I stamped my fist on the desk. "Listen, I've compromised. Don't be so bullheaded. Can't you give a little?"

Our blue eyes met.

"How many?" she asked.

"Let's say... eight more sessions."

"Too many. I wanna end now."

"All right. Make it five. I'm a long goodbye person. What do you say? Five more sessions. For me. For our friendship."

Heidi sighed unenthusiastically. "If I have ta." Then added, "Five more and that's it."

"No cancellations!"

She hesitated. "I guess."

"Remember. The next five Mondays. Four o'clock, sharp."

With great reluctance, she nodded.

"After that, I'll leave the door open in case you ever decide to come back."

I doubted she would. For quite some time she had been sending strong signals. I didn't want to acknowledge them. Working with her made me feel I had accomplished something. My success with bed wetters had more to do with an electronic pad. With Heidi, it was different. We had a relationship where she had grown healthier and stronger. Maybe she really didn't need me anymore.

I stared outside at the weeping Norfolk Pine.

FAMILY THERAPY CONFERENCE

WEDNESDAY, JULY 27

"Piotr! Piotr!"

"Huh?... What time is it?

"Czwarta!"

"Four o'clock? Christ, Ma! I told you that I set the alarm for five."

"I don't want you to be late."

"The goddamn plane doesn't leave till 7:15!"

"Don't you swear!"

"Yea! Yea!" What a way to start a conference.

8:25 a.m. I arrived at the Australian National University in Canberra. The theme for the Australian and New Zealand Family Therapy Conference was "Getting It Together." I desperately needed time to get my life together, away from intrusive parents, away from the tension brewing within the department–from Theresa and Maxine's colluding silence, from Gerard and Leela's lovers' quarrel, and from Holy Henry's religious crusade. As for Violet Struther's mental confusion and Earl Jacobi's bizarre ethics, I needed time away from them too. Since the hospital was prepared to foot the bill, I wasn't about to quibble.

297

After serving six months at Prince Andrew's Hospital, I was suffering early signs of burn-out. In addition to irritability, nervousness, and emotional exhaustion, I felt mildly depressed, dejected, and demoralized. An urgent respite was needed. I mentally prepared myself to be optimistic about the next four days. I had to "Get It Together."

My room at the university didn't exactly lift my spirits. Smaller than my office, it was furnished with a single bed propped against a red brick wall and a wooden desk and chair. The only decoration was a large fading poster of the smiling Aussie comic, Norman Gunston, sporting tiny pieces of red-blotched toilet paper plastered on his chin to cover razor nicks. A small sink with a mirror occupied a corner while a tiny electric heater, fastened on the wall, inefficiently supplied the heat. Canberra's winters were notoriously frigid; this was no exception. I was already freezing. I doubted whether Smelder's accommodations in sunny Italy would be as Spartan. I unpacked my bags in the tiny built-in wardrobe and left for the nearest toilet block.

Occupying the middle stall, I thought of the early morning rush, or more appropriately, flush, what with everyone dashing off to seminars. Under the bottom gap in the stall to my left, I spotted a handbag. Strewth! It was accompanied by pair of high heels. Must've been in the wrong toilet! I quickly scurried out, not before bumping into a young woman who wasn't all that fussed about my presence. Finally twigged. Unisex toilets struck again. All well and good for the university to stamp out sexism, but there were special occasions when a bloke needed privacy.

Registration occurred in the foyer of the A. D. Hope Building. I scanned the participants gathered around the tables. Not a single familiar face. I collected my plastic folder and busied myself sorting through the paraphernalia–maps, Qantus Airlines notebook paper, descriptions of the workshops, places of interest, even a pen.

With half an hour to go before the 9:30 start, I still couldn't recognize anyone. Nervous in crowds at the best of times, I felt awkward approaching strangers. Was always more comfortable with listening than talking. After all, the world did need spectators.

Waiting for the blasted conference to commence, I checked my plastic folder once more. I scanned the brochure advertising a coach tour: "Visit our Capital City–the National Gallery, Parliament House, the War Memorial..." A furtive glance around the foyer confirmed my fears. More participants arriving, none familiar.

I reviewed the conference itinerary yet again. A few plenary sessions were scheduled for all participants. However, the bulk of the four days consisted of a smorgasbord of seminars and workshops run concurrently. I was overwhelmed by the list of theories and techniques, such as "Integrative Family Therapy for Children with Tourette's and Attention Deficit Hyperactivity Disorder," and "Eye Movement Desensitization and Reprocessing for Traumatized Vietnamese Families."

I was struck by some of the presenters' names which must have influenced their choice of expertise. Roxanne Schnapps was demonstrating her work with alcoholic families, Max Sugar was showing his research on obesity, and Brandon Whippler was presenting a multi-disciplinary approach to counseling teenage boys.

After reviewing the various selections, I decided to enroll in the full-day workshops which were limited to 20 participants. I figured that a small group setting would provide a safe structure to meet people. Discussing theories would be a great icebreaker. At least I'd have something to talk about with the others. For tomorrow,

I signed up for "Gestalt Techniques for the Family."
Friday's fare was to be "Treatment of Couples with
Sexual Dysfunctions." Free advice on my own problem
wouldn't go astray.

Today I planned on taking it easy. My eyes searched
the room bustling with clusters of participants talking
and laughing. I remained with the ranks of others standing alone reading timetables, waiting to get it together.

During the morning plenary, Dr. Kenneth Simshank,
imported from New York, opened the conference. Like
most Yanks, he knew bugger about Australia and expressed his disappointment that koalas and kangaroos
weren't scampering everywhere.

"That reminds me of the story about the four family
therapists," continued Dr. Simshank. "Each espoused
their own theoretical model. The structuralist advocated
a reorganizing of the family structure, while the strategic therapist stressed the need to explore sequences–who
was involved in the problem and when it began. The
third, a communication theorist, argued that the family
should be assisted to talk with one another, while the
experiential therapist believed in creating a new experience. To help resolve their debate, they enlisted the aid
of Mrs. O'Connor, a single parent with five children.

"The Irish woman listened to each of their theories
and was then invited to select the method that would
prove most useful for her situation," said Dr. Simshank.
"Mrs. O'Connor seemed most amused and replied,
'When me kids cause me trouble, I use them all. If they
start bashing each other, the first thing I do is organize
them to sit on the couch. The second thing I do is find
out who did what and when. Then, I give each of me
children a good talking to. And the last thing I do is give
them an experience they'll never forget!' "

From then on his lecture was all downhill. El boro
snoro. I checked around the sea of faces, all unknown.

At least I was able to catch up on the few winks that I lost early this morning.

Before lunch, I attended two short seminars which only increased my boredom, tiredness, and loneliness. Like being at a sales convention, the presenters zealously hawked their particular brand of therapy. One punctuated her words by stamping her foot. "Discover the cybernetic way through Temper Tramping," she raved. "You too can cure 100% of clients with behavioral problems." The other gesticulated wildly at his videotaped segment entitled *Vomit Victories*. "Watch this satisfied family deconstruct their unworkable reality and help their child overcome psychogenic vomiting." The bus tour around Canberra was beginning to sound attractive.

I persevered through lunch and ate with a group of psychologists. They were interested in debating endogenous versus exogenous depression. I left before dessert, having had more than my fill of depression.

Afternoon's fare wasn't much better. I watched a videotape of a counselor helping a family cope with grief and loss. Their one-year-old child recently died after choking on a life saver. As I witnessed the intensely sad drama unfold, I wondered how the clients would feel having their most intimate moments viewed by hundreds of professional voyeurs.

I avoided the late afternoon seminars, figuring I had received more than an ample share of depression for the day. Instead, I circulated around the foyer and checked out the stands selling books and promoting courses.

"Vote for Moshe Rosen," said the bearded man behind a desk.

"Never heard of him."

"He's a social worker at the Men's Cooperative in Melbourne. He's running for president of the Family

Therapy Association of Australia. The election's on Saturday."

"Why should I vote for him?" I asked.

"Because he's a Newmanist."

"A what?"

"A Newmanist," preached the bearded one. "One who belongs to the movement of liberated new men. One who acknowledges that men are oppressed by society. Moshe advocates that therapists empower clients to actively challenge traditional roles and values. We must free ourselves from the shackles of gender. It's time for new men: men who take time for relationships; men who are sensitive, loving, and nurturing; men who cooperate rather than compete; men who reverse roles to stay home and rear their children; men who... "

"What about women?"

"Women expect men to act like the fathers they wished they had. They treat us like success objects. They want us to financially support them, make decisions for them, and protect them. Moshe reckons we don't have to do any of that. He calls for an end to penis waving."

"Huh?"

"We don't need to flaunt our sexuality to prove our masculinity. The macho mystique is coming to an end. We're using our warrior energy to trailblaze a new destiny for men's relationships. A new age for the Newmanist Movement."

I eyed this new man suspiciously. "I'll think about it."

The bearded one squeezed my arm. "Don't forget. The election's on Saturday morning. We need your vote, brother."

I extricated myself and sauntered over to the opposition who were also eager to give me attention. At any rate, it beat the hell out of talking to myself.

"Can I help you?" asked a young woman cuddling her baby.

"Just finding out about your candidate."

Suspended above her, a larger-than-life picture of a white-haired matronly woman smiled at me. The caption read, "Dr. Pamela Crouch, renowned child psychiatrist from Queensland, represents traditional family values and Christian morality."

The woman handed me a position paper, adding, "Dr. Crouch believes we've lost sight of family life. Society encourages family breakdown by supporting the notion that both parents should work. Women must realize that mothering is a God-given role and must be treasured. It's a woman's right to stay at home and care for her children."

The disciple then turned her attention to her baby and began cooing, "Isn't that right, sweetie? You'll be a mommy one day too..."

My cue to leave. Besides, it was getting towards dinner time, and my stomach was gurgling. I ate alone and retired for an early night's rest. I couldn't hack the convivium. A social gathering over wine and cheese sounded fine, but not with a group of strangers, and the evening video festival, *Treating the Lonely Adolescent,* didn't look like much fun. I prepared for an uncomfortable night in my cold, brick cell as I nestled with Ken Kesey's novel, *One Flew Over the Cuckoo's Nest.*

DAY TWO
FAMILY THERAPY CONFERENCE

THURSDAY, JULY 28

A mighty yawn announced my entrance into the gold-carpeted room where the full-day workshop, "Gestalt Techniques for the Family," was about to commence. I joined the other 19 participants already seated in circular fashion. That spelled trouble—we were meant to participate. I wasn't in the mood, not after a sleepless night in a lumpy bed and a freezing room.

"I have an exciting day planned," enthused our facilitator, the tall, spindly Trevor Ravenscroft. Garbed in a white flowing caftan, the bald psychologist stood in the center of the circle and fingered a string of turquoise beads dangling around his neck.

"Fritz Perls, the founder of Gestalt therapy, encouraged us to live in the here and now. We'll be spending a full day learning to do just that. I'll save the theoretical discussion till the end of the day so the bulk of our time can be spent experiencing Gestalt techniques."

My eyes frantically located the exit in case I needed a quick escape.

"We'll start with warm-up exercises," called the psychologist. "Everyone stand up and mill around the room... Make eye contact with one another... Don't use any words, merely greet each other with your eyes."

I walked around like a stupid zombie attempting his eye-balling technique, but, with every new set of eyes– didn't matter if they were blue, brown, or green–I turned yellow. I slowly headed toward the exit.

"Stop where you are!" announced Trevor.

I froze in my tracks.

"Find a partner with whom you feel comfortable."

The bloke next to me extended his hand. "How ya goin', mate?"

"We might as well pair off," I said.

"Orright. Me name's Clinton."

"I'm Peter."

"Sit across from your partner," instructed Ravenscroft. "Then repeat the phrase, 'Now I see...' then fill in the blank. I want the partner to respond with the same phrase and then add what he or she sees. Take turns back and forth, repeating the exercise."

I arranged my chair opposite Clinton and volunteered, "You go first."

He scanned my face. "Now I see your glasses."

I replied, "Now I see your nose." It was a god awful big one at that.

"Now I see blue eyes and curly brown hair."

"Now I see a receding forehead." Not to mention an ugly, greasy blackhead.

"Now I see a blue-striped shirt."

And on and on it went, ad nauseum.

"Let's stop and process that experience," said the Gestalt therapist.

His idea of processing meant that everyone was supposed to share feelings. Strewth! This was quickly turning into an encounter group. After completing more "Get-

ting to Know You" mind games with a score of participants, I positioned myself nearer the door.

Trevor rubbed his turquoise beads. "We'll now explore the use of fantasy which, in a safe environment,
can be a potent tool in revealing aspects of our internal
world that might otherwise be unavailable. This is a rich
exercise filled with delicious opportunities." He placed
a cassette in the recorder, dimmed the lights, and instructed us to lie on the floor and close our eyes. I peeped
around to check that no one else was looking at me.

With the sound of flutes in the background, our
guide's melodious voice lulled us into our inner journey. "Allow yourself to become comfortable... As your
body relaxes, follow my instructions... Create this scene
in your mind. Imagine yourself back home with your
parents... Go back to the time when you left home for
good."

As if reading my mind, he added, "If you haven't
left home yet, then imagine the time when you will
leave... Take time to paint the characters in the scene...
Hear the conversations... feel the atmosphere... inhale
the fragrances... Now have a conversation with the
people in your mind... Allow the scene to develop. Do
that now. I will wait for you."

Like an old movie projector, my mind began flickering images on a blank screen. In the garage, Pa was
sprawled under the Holden, changing the oil. Ma, standing in the kitchen, was stirring oxtail soup. An odor of
rancid vegetables permeated through the house, past a
portrait of Stella with her husband and two girls, and
through my open doorway where I sat at my desk, typing a journal entry on the computer. Blackie was asleep,
snugged next to my feet.

Ma enters. "What are you doing?" she asks.

I quickly switch off the computer. "Nothing. Just playing a computer game."

"Dinner's almost ready. Hurry down to the shops and buy a fresh loaf of rye bread."

Trevor's soft voice wafted into the scene. "Let the fantasy evolve... Imagine yourself leaving home... saying goodbye to your parents."

I handed Ma the rye bread as she ladled the soup at the table. "I have to leave. It's time to say goodbye."

"No!" she screams. "You can't! You must stay with us. We need you."

I turn to leave. She tightly grabs hold of my arm.

"Trevor Ravenscroft says I have to leave. Don't worry. I'll be back."

"How do you feel about leaving?" asks the psychologist.

Bloody awful! I see her crumpled, devastated face. I move to reassure her, to take away the pain.

"Now think of an object," coaches the voice. "Something to remember, that you'd like to take with you. What is it?"

"I must leave, Ma. I need something to remind me of home."

Ever so reluctantly, she hands me a cup brimming with steaming oxtail soup. "It'll keep you warm," she says.

The cup spills, scalding my hands.

"Let's stop there," said Trevor abruptly.

With my hands still burning, the rancid liquid languished in my nostrils.

The dimmed lights were brought back to life. Dazed, I rubbed my eyes, my nose, my scalp to purge myself of the reverie. I sucked in a lung full of air. My awareness slowly drifted back into the room, back to the participants, back to tears streaming down numerous faces.

"Let's process that experience," oozed the empathic instructor.

I stared at the gold carpet hoping someone else would speak. There was no way I was going to bear my soul in front of these strangers.

The silence was broken when a young woman called Belinda wiped her eyes with a hanky. "My father died three years ago... I felt... so sad... I could see his smiling face standing next to my mother... When I left home, I wanted his picture... Mum wouldn't give it to me... I desperately wanted it. I loved him so much... but never took the time to tell him."

Trevor moved closer to the bereft woman. "What would you want to say to him?"

Belinda sniffled. "I wanted... to tell him..."

Her sobs drowned out the remaining words.

"Go ahead," he prodded. "Say them."

She dabbed at her eyes. "Daddy... I love you... I miss you, Daddy. God, I miss you!... It hurts... so much..." She weeped uncontrollably while the rest of us watched in silence.

Trevor eventually helped the woman to her feet, wrapped his long arms around her body, and gave a gentle squeeze which triggered a further gush of tears squirting down the blushed cheeks. Some of the other participants moved closer to touch and console her. With every new hand lending support, the distraught woman wailed louder. Others began to weep. I was freaking out. Didn't come for group therapy. I merely wanted to learn a few extra techniques. I resolved to bolt during the lunch break.

The Gestalt therapist moved to other participants and asked them about their inner journeys. I avoided his gaze.

"All relationships and objects symbolize aspects of our internal selves," he declared.

Wasn't sure of the meaning of my cup with hot soup, but I wasn't game to ask. Those who revealed their fantasies were given the opportunity to either bawl their eyes out or experience an angry catharsis. These techniques were definitely not for me.

"We have time to experiment with another Gestalt method before we break for lunch. 'The Empty Chair' can be an invaluable tool to externalize conflictual parts of our life."

Desperate to avoid another 'feeling' exercise, I raised my hand to try and steer him toward a theoretical discussion. "Could you describe how effective these techniques are with resistant clients?"

"Come up here; I will show you."

"Uh... that's okay. I was..."

He strolled toward me with his outstretched hand. "Join me in the center of the group."

"Ugh... I'd rather not."

"Just what I wanted to hear," said the psychologist. "You're already resistant. You can help me demonstrate that clients don't have to be motivated to reap the benefits of Gestalt therapy."

"I'd, ugh, really prefer to watch." My bum sank deeper into the carpet.

"Nonsense. It'll be fun."

My heart palpitated louder than African drumbeats. Everyone was staring. I thought I'd have an anxiety attack right there in the room.

"Now don't worry," he comforted. "What's your name?"

"Huh?... Oh... Peter Pinowski."

"Just relax, Peter. I'll work with you right where you are."

He brought over two chairs. The other participants edged themselves closer.

"I don't think..."

Trevor placed his hand under my shoulder and coaxed me off the floor. "We'll do a very simple exercise. Okay?"

I nodded nervously. "Something very, very simple."

"Just relax in one of these chairs," he said. "How old are you?"

I sank in the cushioned seat and stared at the standing Gestaltist. "Twenty-nine."

"I'd like you to tell me the age of the other members of your immediate family."

"My father's about 58, my mother's 56, and I have an older sister, Stella, who's 36."

"What nationality are your parents?"

"Polish."

"When did they migrate?"

"They left Poland around 1957."

"To come to Sydney?"

"No. They initially settled in Chicago. They were there 14 years, then moved to Sydney in 1971."

"Why did they migrate?"

"I guess they came to America for a better life. Then my father decided to join his brother and sister who lived in Australia. My uncle owned a business in Sydney and offered him a job."

I avoided mentioning that Pa constantly complained about the blacks and wanted to move to a white country.

"How did your mother feel about migrating?"

"Fine," I lied. She hated leaving America. She had fallen in love with the U.S.A. and was most upset about leaving her friends and way of life. She argued bitterly with Pa about the decision.

"How old were you when you arrived in Sydney?"

"About six."

Ravenscroft patted my shoulder. "Now I want you to remember the time when you first attended school here in Australia. Pretend your mother is sitting opposite you in this empty chair. I want you to tell her how you feel about going to school."

I glared up incredulously. "Just talk to the chair?"

"That's right. Just talk to the chair. Pretend she's facing you. Then, I'll have you switch seats so you can respond as your mother would. Don't worry, I'll be coaching you."

I suspiciously eyed the willowy psychologist as he played with his turquoise beads. The bastard was blocking my exit. There was no turning back. I faced the empty chair where my imaginary mother was supposed to be.

"I start school tomorrow. I'm ready for the big day."

Having completed the bloody task, I looked up at Trevor.

"Now switch chairs," he beckoned. "Become your mother and respond as she would."

I plopped myself down in my mother's seat and answered smartly, "He's a good boy."

The others in the room laughed.

"Remember, you're Mrs. Pinowski," interrupted the psychologist. "Talk directly to Peter."

Playing my mother, I smiled, "I'll have sandwiches ready for you when you come home."

"Switch chairs again and tell your mother how you feel."

I sat in my own seat. "I feel okay, ready for school."

"You're six years old," said Trevor. "Do you feel nervous?"

"Not really."

"Remember, you're the new kid from America. You even talk differently. Aren't you a little nervous?"

"Just a little," I said. "Some of the kids make fun of me because I'm a Yank."

He pointed to the other chair. "Switch places. Respond as your mother."

I lowered myself into her chair. A crushing weight fell on my shoulder. I was immobilized.

"Tell Peter how you feel," he instructed.

"I... I'm sad you're going to school... I'll miss you."

"Why, Mrs. Pinowski?" asked Trevor.

"My son has been my companion. We would spend lots of time playing games."

"Tell Peter about moving to Australia."

As my mother, I faced myself. "When we came here, you were there for me... Your pa was never around, always working."

That early scene flashed in my mind. My despondent mother hated the move. She despised Pa for uprooting her from her adopted country and her newfound friends. She became deeply depressed and stayed in bed all day. I hated Pa for destroying my active, attentive mother. She was transformed into a sick, lifeless shell who cried much of the time. I desperately wanted to reach out, to make her happy, to return her to her former self.

"Sit in your own chair," directed Ravenscroft. "Tell your mother what you're feeling."

I changed places. "I can't stand it when you're sad, Ma. I hate seeing you cry. I feel so guilty when I leave... My jokes don't even cheer you up. You're always so miserable... staying home, crying... Go out. Have a good time. Don't be unhappy. Please, Ma..."

"Change chairs," guided the soft voice. "Become your mother."

My shoulders drooped from her burdens. "I'm so alone. Stella's older... spends time with her friends. Pa's at the garage. You keep me company. But now you're leaving... going to school. Don't leave, Piotr. Please don't leave. I can't bear to be alone... Don't go..."

One small tear fell from my mother's eyes. I choked down our feelings welling up inside.

"Change chairs."

I couldn't bear her misery. I swallowed the sadness. "Don't cry, Ma. Please. Everything will be fine... Please don't be sad... I'm sorry if I hurt you. I didn't mean to... Don't get depressed... I'll be back..."

My nose was running; eyes were watering. During those early years, her lifeless body lay motionless in bed. Pa eventually sought help for her depression. She was hospitalized several weeks. I felt abandoned as a little boy, lost in my new country. When she returned, she was less despondent, but I still worried if she would fully recover. Desperate, I shouldered the task to keep her out of hospital, doing whatever it took—listening to her complaints, telling jokes, cheering her up, anything to make her happy.

The therapist touched my shoulder. "Let's stop there. We don't want to go any further."

I faced him, tears streaming down my face. "I didn't want her to leave."

"You have some important work to do with your mother, Peter. I don't think it's appropriate right now to delve any deeper."

What was he talking about? I was having a conversation with my mother about the past as if she were here in the present, and he tells me it's not appropriate to delve any deeper! I removed my handkerchief to wipe my eyes and blow my nose.

"Beneath your sadness lies a volcano of anger. At the moment, those emotions might be too difficult for you to handle. It was sufficient to raise the issue to a level of awareness. How do you feel?"

I glanced around the room. People were staring. Waiting for me to speak. A large woman dabbed her eyes with a pink hanky. I didn't even know these people! My heart and soul had just been publicly laundered. For what? To demonstrate a bloody technique? How did I feel?

"Okay... I guess." I couldn't bear processing any more of my emotions.

"I want to finish with a hug," glowed the psychologist. "I feel your anguish."

My legs wobbled as I stood up to endure Trevor's all-consuming embrace. Why was I hugging this man? Was this part of the demonstration? My body became numb; my mind began to swirl. Try as I might, I could never make Ma truly happy. I remembered acting sick in school so they would send me home. She needed looking after.

Ravenscroft removed the empty chair. "Thank's for volunteering, Peter."

The big, blubbering woman with the pink hanky gave me a crushing bear hug. In the process, she broke the pen in my shirt pocket. Others crowded around touching me for support. I'm sure they would've offered hugs, but the dark blue stain was expanding noticeably around my pocket. I removed the pen. It only made matters worse. Ink leaked over my hands and pants, forcing the crowd to disperse.

I continued the clean-up operation with my handkerchief while Trevor offered his summary. "As you have just observed, 'The Empty Chair' is an extremely powerful technique for bringing out hidden conflicts. Even a resistant client could involve himself..."

When we broke for lunch, I dashed to my room and faced the mirror. What a mess! Ink was smudged everywhere–hands, clothes, even my face. As I scrubbed off the ink, I discarded the idea of missing the second half of the workshop. My absence would be too conspicuous. The tongues would start wagging. I had to show them a Pinowski could handle personal issues. I put on a clean outfit and headed for the cafeteria.

"I'm Ursula Puckeridge," volunteered the large, tall woman standing outside the lunch room.

I turned to face the participant from the Gestalt workshop, the one with the crushing hug which broke my pen. Sporting dull brown hair, she was housed in jeans and a scarlet jumper.

"I was looking for you, Peter. Have you had lunch?"

"Not really."

"I've already eaten, but I'll join you."

Bloody Hell! When I needed a friend, I couldn't buy one. Now that I wanted to be on my own, suddenly I've inherited a companion.

"Your agony reminded me so much of my son," continued the non-stop mouth of the hefty woman. "When Gerry was born, I told my second husband to bugger off, the blithering idiot. I became super depressed. Gerry was my only salvation. If it weren't for him, I would've chucked it in. My little boy gave me the will to live. I had let others down but not my Gerry. I loved him. We became mates and did everything together. When he started school, it all came to an abrupt halt. I couldn't handle it. It was as if a huge chunk got carved out of my belly..."

My empty stomach growled. I collected chicken Parmesan, green salad, two slices of garlic bread, custard pudding, and some jam tarts. Ursula collected tea and pavlova with strawberry topping. Her perpetual chattering provided background to my meal.

"... I went back to school into social work. Yet I worried about Gerry constantly, especially when he kept vomiting at school. I took him to specialists. They said there was nothing wrong physically. I didn't want to muck around. We sought counseling. We each saw a therapist three times a week for three years. Gerry missed a fair bit of school, but I didn't care. We needed to straighten out our emotional problems. I didn't want him screwed up like me. The best thing I could offer my son was the opportunity to grow up normal..."

The garlic bread gave me indigestion.

"... Social work helped fill the void. I finished my degree and began working with disturbed children. Gerry's now in high school. He still doesn't have many friends, but he's a born whiz on computers. He's designed programs to handle our household expenses, income tax, even statistics on my clients. He's real clever that way..."

A glance at my watch interrupted her life's saga. "We'd better head back to the workshop."

Her mouth kept running. "We love traveling together. We like to go hostelling. We've been to..."

At any rate, she had taken my mind off this morning's painful encounter with Gestalt techniques.

We arrived late. At least that was better than the six participants who failed to return. They may have been wiser than the 14 of us masochists who came back for more.

Trevor Ravenscroft reappeared in his flowing white caftan. "I want you to experience another delicious opportunity–dreamwork. With this technique, the gestaltist's goal is to help the dreamer re-own and then integrate individual fragments of the self. Would someone like to share a recent dream?"

After what happened this morning, I wouldn't even share a happy dream, not that I've had any recently.

Ursula, however, was primed. She raised her hand.

"Bring your chair to the front," instructed the psychologist.

Her mouth revved before she plopped on the cushioned seat. "Last week I experienced a horrific dream. I was visiting an ancient Scottish castle. There weren't any doors, only tiny windows on the stone face. Someone inside was howling and screaming for help. I rushed to save her and climbed a wooden ladder. The windows were too small. An axe materialized and I hacked at the stones. With one massive swing, I crashed through and plummeted down a bottomless hole. I plunged into the mouth of a gargantuan monster. I shrieked, 'Save me!' No one answered. I woke up sobbing."

Trevor's eyes widened. As if handed a sumptuous meal, he proceeded to gestalt Ursula. "I want you to become the different parts of your dream. Speak as if you're actually the castle. Describe how it feels. Then become the person inside screaming for help. How does she feel? Become the axe, then the bottomless hole, and then the dragon."

Another intense emotional scene followed, with Ursula catharting all over the place. Isolation and despair predominated. Every time she spoke, her empty, lonely feelings rumbled to the surface. Her weeping became uncontrollable. Torrents of tears blended with slimy mucous oozing from her red nose. The pink handkerchief could hold no more. Trevor spent the good part of the afternoon mopping up, and appeared overwhelmed by the large woman's constant demand for hugs. Every time he embraced her, she sobbed. With every sob came a renewed plea for a hug. Her hunger was insatiable. The front of Trevor's caftan was drenched from sweat, tears, and nose drippings.

I definitely wasn't cut out for this gestalting. I was relieved when the workshop, after the odd smattering of tearful awakenings, angry outbursts, and of course, hugs, finally drew to an end.

Our group leader mopped his brow. "Before concluding with a group cuddle, I want you to remember my rendition of the Gestalt prayer: Do your own thing and live up to your own expectations. You're not here to please others."

Now he tells me! If I would've known that, the "Empty Chair" would have well and truly been kept empty.

That evening Ursula persuaded me to attend the convivium for wine and cheese. At that point, anything would've been better than reading alone in a freezing room on a lumpy bed. Besides, after that gut-wrenching workshop, I needed to unwind. I downed two quick glasses of Riesling.

Talk and laughter resounded throughout the foyer as the wine flowed liberally. The impending election of the president of the Family Therapy Association of Australia became the burning topic for the night.

"Can we count on your vote for Moshe Rosen and the Newmanist Movement?" asked a mustached chap wearing a gold stud in his left ear.

"Not sure," I said, sipping another Riesling.

He pulled me to one side. "Brothers must support one another. If Pamela Crouch wins, we might as well get our balls cut off. She's power-mad and a castrating shrink-bitch to boot. She wants the Association to promote right-wing Christian values."

"Thanks for sharing that with me," I slurred.

"Watch out for her roving band of Delilahs. They'll try and seduce you. Don't vote with your dick, vote with your head."

Wasn't sure what he meant, but after he left, my head and my dick were both spinning. Must've been the Riesling. Didn't care. I was talking to people, lots of them. In fact, everyone seemed to be talking. Some were even hugging, the result of the insistent Ursula. The theme of the conference was indeed happening. We were "Getting It Together."

"Are you voting for Dr. Pamela Crouch?" asked a spunky-looking woman.

"Sure," I said, reaching for more wine. "I'll vote for anyone."

"Dr. Crouch will bring a sense of morality to the Family Therapy Association. Radical feminism has inflicted untold damage towards the breakdown of the family. We're for truth and justice..."

"And the Australian way!" I saluted.

"This is serious," she chastised. "There's a rumor going around. Moshe Rosen is gay. We don't want homosexual values among Australian families, now do we?"

"I'm not sure." The Riesling was affecting my comprehension.

I watched her march off toward another victim. That evening I was visited by more people politicking. They didn't stay very long when I asked loudly if they were homosexuals. The rest of the night became a blur. Don't know how, but I managed to stagger back to my cell. I was oblivious to the fact that my bed was lumpy and the room was freezing. The only thing I could do was crash.

DAY THREE
FAMILY THERAPY CONFERENCE
FRIDAY, JULY 29

A kookaburra's laughter woke me at first sunlight. My head throbbed like a tom-tom. Further attempts to reclaim lost sleep were quickly abandoned. I clawed my way out of bed and made for the showers where I managed to grab an empty stall ahead of a scurrying, robed contender. The steaming hot spray splashed new life into my exhausted body. Could've stayed there forever, until a bloody woman banged on the door. "Hurry up," she yelled.

"Hang on," I shouted, then leisurely toweled myself dry. When I opened the door, I recognized the face. Dr. Pamela Crouch and her beady eyes glared angrily below her floral shower cap–a sharp contrast to her poster. I pulled the terrycloth robe tight around my body and nicked off. If she won the election tomorrow, it wouldn't surprise me if nonsexist showers were banned at future conferences.

I ate breakfast with Ursula Puckeridge and suffered another cacophony of personal revelations. If it wasn't last night's dream, then it was the all-consuming relationship with her son, Gerry. Her non-stop chatter split my headache in two. I excused myself early and swallowed four aspirin.

Having signed up for the full-day workshop, "Treatment of Couples with Sexual Dysfunctions," I arrived with my notepad 15 minutes early. I breathed a sigh of relief when I noticed that the chairs were organized lecture style. The aftershocks of Ravenscroft's gestalt circle were still reverberating underground.

When Dr. Olga Finegold appeared, there was standing room only. More than 100 participants, some together with spouses, gathered in the large red-carpeted room containing only 20 chairs. She announced that the group was far too large and was limited to the 20 participants who had previously registered. She culled the numbers by reading the roll call. A few of the rejected professionals, with partners in tow, complained bitterly on their way out, most upset about losing an opportunity to learn more about sex.

"There has been an increasing number of clients with sexual dysfunctions," began the attractive Dr. Finegold, an impeccably dressed gynecologist in her mid-30s. If ever a bloke needed sex therapy, this shapely brunette was the person to see. A wedding ring was noticeably absent.

"Today we will discuss several common sexual problems. Before proceeding, however, let's quickly find out where your interests lie. Can each of you mention the type of clientele you're currently working with?"

"I'm Father Rodger," commenced the first. "I counsel couples at St. Paul's Cathedral in Brisbane. Many of my clients have difficulty handling their guilt about sexual feelings. I'm interested in hearing ways to help them feel better about their own sexuality."

"Thank you, Father," said Olga. "Sexual problems often stem from ignorance or faulty information. Re-education is an essential tool with any form of sex counseling. Most of us were brought up with puritanical ideas about our bodies..."

I flashed back to my high school days with the Christian Brothers at St. Pat's in Strathfield. One pathetic lecture on sex education was offered during my entire stay. That noteworthy session was delivered by the ancient Brother Sturgess who, upon his arrival, nervously pulled down the blinds for fear that the neighbors might peer through the window. He then proceeded to hang male and female anatomical pictures on the blackboard which appeared more like slabs of meat than real people. Brother Sturgess had great difficulty looking at the naked illustrations. Probably thought he'd be led into temptation. He used the pointer thrust over his left shoulder to identify the important parts. Didn't even bother turning around. When he referred to the testicle, he mistakenly pointed at the armpit. However, when he mentioned vagina, the pointer zoomed right on target. Just as well he didn't teach in a coed school.

"And what about you?" asked Dr. Finegold, staring in my direction.

"Oh... my clients?... They're premature ejaculators. I'm interested in learning techniques to assist their performance."

She nodded. "Sexuality is often perceived in terms of performance rather than enjoyment. The premature ejaculator is caught up in this obsession to perform. He fears failure and rejection by his partner and is frightened, not only of his own sexuality, but also of losing control. We'll cover the treatment later in the day."

While intimidated by her list of fears, I focused on the word "treatment." That would provide me with the road to recovery. My depressed mood lifted slightly and I relaxed in my seat.

Others continued to reveal their clientele and sexual concerns. One sullen woman with the face of a prune treated frigid women and anticipated new methods for becoming orgasmic. A husband and wife team were fascinated with the use of erotic fantasy to improve a couple's sexual relationship.

"I'll discuss visualization shortly," responded the gynecologist.

Other interests covered the A to Z of sexual habits–from anal sex to zoophilia. The major consensus, however, was to focus on the three biggies–impotence, premature ejaculation, and female orgasmic dysfunction.

Olga Finegold flipped on the overhead projector and read from her transparency. "Creating the right climate for treatment is essential for the therapist. In order to counteract the negative conditioning of experiencing sex as anxiety producing, clients should never be pressured to perform..."

Her recitation of the technical theory became ponderous, too slow for my liking. I was anxious to hear her remedy for prematurity. My tired eyes drifted from the overhead and surveyed the participants. A tempting blonde in black leather gear sat several seats to my left. She caught my starry-eyed stare and returned a smile that ignited my loins.

"... but before describing techniques, we must first talk about language. In our professional capacity we must continually refer to genitalia. Words like vagina, labia majora, penis, testicles, etc. sound commonplace to us. However, some clients find the language too technical. If that's the case, we must discover a terminology with which they feel comfortable. Take the word penis, for example. What other descriptions have you heard clients use?"

The sex therapist placed a new transparency on the overhead and recorded the participants' responses. "Dick... love cobra... banger... jolly giant... cock... shaft... sausage... gherkin... dumbo's trunk..." With a smattering of chuckles and smirks, the list went on and on. I still preferred "Freddie."

After employing the same exercise for clitoris, breasts, masturbation, and intercourse, Olga moved to the first technique. At last!

"Visualization is a potent tool with most sexual dysfunctions. By creating an imaginary, stimulating sexual situation in a relaxed, non-pressurized environment, the therapist can mentally shift the client from spectatoring, that is, genital watching. This would allow the client's body to respond more naturally."

My mind strayed to the alluring young woman wearing tight, black leather pants. Ash blonde hair flowed seductively across the shoulders of the matching leather jacket.

"This first technique can be used to help the client focus on an erotic situation while, at the same time, diminish the anxiety associated with sexual arousal. To demonstrate this, I would like you to choose a partner, preferably one of the opposite sex."

There was a mad scramble. I barely beat out the priest who leapt across several chairs. Father Rodger sneered my way, having been forced to pair off with the prune-faced woman. As the victor, I introduced myself to the youngest looking participant, Karen Stone. The snug leather gear revealed a sexy, svelte figure. Lady luck was turning my way.

"Briefly become acquainted," instructed Dr. Finegold.

I stared into Karen's hazel eyes. "Where do you work?"

"At a clinic for sexual disorders in Perth. I'm a clinical psychologist."

"We have something in common," I drooled. "I'm also a psychologist. What type of clients do you work with?"

"Well actually," she confessed. "I deal primarily with men suffering from erectile dysfunction."

"Impotence? Do you have much success?"

"I've only worked at the clinic less than a year. I'm still developing my repertoire of skills, but I like the exercises developed by Masters and Johnson, particularly the ones on sensate focus."

I thought of the times I practiced them on myself, without much success. "Have you had any luck?"

Her moist lips widened. "Men quickly become frustrated if they haven't achieved a full erection after their first exercise. I try and keep their morale from plummeting. I hope Dr. Finegold will address that issue."

"That's a hard one," I added sympathetically.

The gynecologist gave further instructions. "In your pairs, choose a role, either as the therapist or the patient. Later, you will reverse roles, so it doesn't matter which part you play first. The patient should then choose some sexual dysfunction as the presenting problem."

"You can be the patient," offered Karen. "I want to practice this technique on an impotent client of mine."

"I'm not sure I like that role."

She batted her eyes seductively. "It's only a role-play, Peter."

My encounter with fantasy, guided by the gestaltist, Trevor Ravenscroft, still reverberated deep within. Wasn't prepared for another mental dive, at least not without a safety net. My mind was made up. "I really prefer to be the therapist."

"We'll each have an opportunity to be the client," she protested. "Why can't you go first?"

"I'd rather not."

"That's being childish."

"Remember," announced Olga. "We are profession-als and need to bear in mind the highest code of conduct during these simulations."

"Well, I want to be the therapist," she demanded. "I need the experience."

"Let's flip for it."

"Okay!" she huffed. "I don't want to argue."

The coin tossed tails. I won.

Karen's face turned sour. "Hmmph. Then I'll be a frigid client."

Finegold provided more directions. "Spread your-selves around the room. There's plenty of space. Make sure you're not too close to other pairs. For those of you who are the therapist, you will be conducting a guided imagery exercise. Have your patient take a comfortable position, either sitting in a chair or lying down on the carpet."

"I want to sit on the chair," announced my client emphatically.

"First of all, I want the therapist to relax the patient. Proceed slowly and create a sensual scene that your cli-ent might relate to. He or she may prefer soft lights, romantic music, and a candle-lit dinner with a partner. Or the client may favor an incense-filled room while receiving a massage. Create a mood where your patient can become sensually aroused. Don't, however, move into any imaginary sexual activity. Take 20 minutes for this exercise."

I surveyed the ash blonde sitting stiffly in the chair. My voice quivered, "Get nice and relaxed."

She responded by pursing her lips and folding her arms tightly. Bloody hell! She didn't have to play the role so seriously!

"Just relax," I repeated. "Close your eyes and relax... Now imagine a scene with your partner... You've
eaten a nice meal and have just arrived back at his house
where he lights the fireplace... He cracks open a bottle
of claret while you light a few candles... He burns strawberry incense... You choose a compact disc... Soft music
plays in the background... You both feel romantic... He
offers to massage your shoulders... You then recipro-
cate... You feel warm and loving."

I checked my watch. There was still 15 minutes! What
else could I do without getting her sexually involved
with her partner? I scanned her tense and rigid body—
the clenched teeth, the taut arms around her chest. I
should've let her play the therapist.

The minutes ticked by agonizingly. I added phrases
that should've relaxed her. "The tension in your body
eases... You let go of the tension... You let go... Your body
feels relaxed... The massage is relaxing... You're feeling
sensual... very, very sensual..." They had no affect. Her
body remained a block of ice.

"Time's up," signaled Olga. "Spend the next five
minutes sharing feedback. What was effective, what
wasn't."

Karen Stone sprang to life. "You didn't relax me
properly. I felt rushed. I couldn't relate to a fireplace.
Perth has a warm climate, you know. The smell of incense repulses me, and I can't stand the taste of claret.
Massage oil makes me itchy. I found your phrases at the
end repetitive and unimaginative. You could have paced
yourself with periods of silence, and besides, I don't have
a partner. We recently broke up."

"Fair go!" I defended. "I've never done anything like
this."

Dr. Finegold interrupted. "I'm hearing feedback that
the therapist moved too fast and wasn't on the same track
as the patient. This is a common therapeutic error."

Karen nodded smugly. The bitch!

"Reverse roles. Before you start, ask the patient to construct a situation that would be sensual. As you've discovered, if therapists impose imaginary scenes in which clients are unable to relate, they're setting themselves up for failure. I would like the therapists to now briefly explore with your patient his or her idea of a sensual scene."

"I liked the massage and the fireplace," I declared. "And besides, you didn't exactly cooperate in the role-play. You made it bloody difficult. See how well you perform, now that you're the therapist."

"I'm sorry," she conceded. "It was the role-play. I over-identified with the part. I'm not normally like that."

"You want an impotent client? I'll give you one you'll never forget!"

She touched my hand. "I didn't realize you were so sensitive."

I peered into her hazel eyes. "My imaginary scene would've worked for me."

She brushed my hand lightly. "Let's work together this time."

Her gentle stroke softened my anger.

The gynecologist instructed us once more. "Take the extra time and relax your patient. During your guided imagery, employ as many senses as you can while you paint a three-dimensional picture. Remember, do not guide the patient into sexual activity. You have another 20 minutes. Begin."

"I'll sit in the chair."

"I found it extremely stiff," she counseled. "The carpet would be more comfortable, Peter."

I sprawled out with my back resting on the soft, red fibers. Karen knelt at my side.

"It would make it easier if you closed your eyes."

I hesitated.

"Relax... Close your eyes..."

When I turned out the lights of the outside world, my anxiety soared.

"Take a few deep breaths," she soothed. "Just let out all the tension when you exhale... That's good!... Breathe out all your tension. Take another deep breath and exhale any discomfort... You feel more and more relaxed... More and more calm. Good!... Allow your body to really let go... You're becoming very relaxed... Let all your muscles get soft... Breathe nice and easy... Good!... Re-l-a-a-x-x-x... Yes... Re-l-a-a-x-x-x... Now, I want you to imagine a scene with your partner."

"I don't have one," I whispered.

There was a short pause. "Then imagine a former partner whom you still love."

Despite all our hassles, I did care for Theresa–my one true love.

"All is forgiven," adds Karen. "It's raining... You've arrived at your lovers's place... You've just had dinner at a wonderful restaurant... having enjoyed a sumptuous meal... She's wearing an attractive outfit... one that has always pleased your eyes... Picture her in your mind..."

My muscles soften. I relax. Theresa, dressed in a short lavender skirt and a transparent silk blouse, walks into my mind. Silver bangle earrings sparkle beneath her curly raven hair.

"You ignite the logs in the fireplace... The wood crackles and sizzles... Flames flicker against the walls... Shadows playfully dance on your partner's face... She smiles..."

Theresa displays her playful mischievous look. All is forgiven. She brings out a bottle of claret and pours two glasses.

"She plays her favorite song..."

Nana Mouskouri echoes a Greek love song in the background.

"You feel a warm glow... a strong attraction... She feels the same..."

Yes. She wants me. I want her. Freddie wants her. He wanted her now! My right eye peeped at Karen. She was mesmerized, like a snake charmer, playing to a rising cobra. She caught me peeking.

"Keep your eyes closed," she pleaded. "Stay with the scene. Relax... Re-l-a-a-x-x-x... Yes... Re-l-a-a-x-x-x..."

My mind sinks back into trance.

"Your partner offers some claret..."

Theresa sips from my glass then kisses me liberally, dribbling red wine over my lips. She takes another drink and opens my mouth with her probing tongue. Claret trickles down my throat.

"She has a vial of wild strawberry scented oil... She wants to massage you... She lays a blanket close to the fireplace... Slowly, she undresses you."

Yes! Yes! She tears off my clothes then removes her own, tossing them across the floor. The scent of strawberry fills the room, making her wild. She kisses then bites my neck, shoulder... The flames dance and shimmer to another Greek melody.

"Her hands are oily, slippery..."

She empties the vial on my stomach. Her hands massage all over. She climbs on top, gliding up and down, smearing oil from my body to her olive skin. Her firm breasts glisten. Her moist lips suck on her middle finger lubricated with the wild strawberry.

I hear the words, "Desire me!" Not sure whose voice–Karen's or Theresa's.

My excitement grows, becomes intense. She smears oil on my left leg and mounts it, sliding up and down. I watch the flames' shadows flicker on her heaving breasts, expanding and contracting in rapid succession. Drops of sweat and oil tumble down her body. Freddie, tall and strong, sways. Her thrusting increases. She heaves and moans. My body quivers. I desire her. Yes! I want her! Desperately. My wild eyes plead for release. Her hands grasp Freddie. Not yet, Freddie! NO!!

I opened my eyes. Karen was smiling like the charmer who had tamed the spitting cobra. I quickly placed my hands over my crotch and mumbled something apologetic. I prayed that no one else, particularly Olga Finegold, had noticed.

"Don't be embarrassed," comforted Karen. "You've shown me that my imagery technique can be very effective. I can hardly wait to practice it on my impotent men."

She kissed me on the cheek. "Thanks, Peter. You've increased my flagging self-confidence."

Hell, boosting her confidence only increased my prematurity.

"I feel like celebrating tonight!" she exclaimed. "Will you join me for dinner?

I rose deliberately to my chair and placed my notepad on my lap. "I guess so."

Karen Stone sat opposite me in Telecom Tower's revolving restaurant on Black Mountain. Perched on top of the world, we peered down at Canberra's wintry night. The twinkling lights below created a magical fairyland illuminating the surrounding edge of Lake Burley Griffin, which looked like a black hole in the center of the city.

"Let's order champagne," she proposed, still decked out in her black leather outfit. "We'll celebrate a stimulating workshop and our final night at the conference."

The waiter arrived with a bottle of Great Western and poured the bubbly.

She brushed back her thick blonde hair. "I found Olga Finegold an excellent presenter, the best thus far."

"The visualization techniques were good," I added, "but I was expecting more discussion about the premature ejaculator. One of my clients desperately needs help."

Karen buttered her roll. "I personally prefer to use the 'Squeeze Technique'. Are you familiar with it?"

"I've read about it, but never tried it myself."

"It's fairly simple. After the client has been properly aroused and stimulated, the woman takes hold of the erect penis and, with her forefinger and thumb, squeezes firmly under the head. Let me show you."

She grabbed my left thumb and squeezed tightly above the knuckle. "This reduces the client's erection and his urge to ejaculate. By repeating this several times, he becomes conditioned to last longer before ejaculating."

"Ouch!" I cried as I removed my thumb.

"The penis can handle the pressure."

Anyone squeezing Freddie that hard would freak him out. I soothed my thumb with a rub. "What's it like, talking to clients about sex all the time?"

Undeterred by the presence of our waiter pouring more champagne, she answered casually, "Initially, I was uptight and nervous, but after the first few clients, I became desensitized. Penis and vagina became part of my vocabulary. Sexual problems now seem an everyday occurrence. I do worry, however, whether I sound too clinical. That's why I was relieved that the imagery exercise was so effective this morning."

She did have to raise that again. "I'm sorry."

"Don't apologize, Peter. I arrived at the conference with my confidence slipping. A number of my clients had dropped out of therapy. I was demoralized, even questioned whether I should leave sexual counseling altogether. That broke me up. I knew there was a need. Impotence affects one out of every 100 males under the age of 35, and it rises to one in every four males after they're 70 years old. You restored my confidence this morning. Now I know I can help those men."

Karen moved closer and whispered, "I'm glad you were my partner." She planted a sensuous wet kiss on my lips.

I was no longer sorry for my premature awakening.

Our meal arrived. Duck à l'orange for Karen while I received the Trout Almondine. We consumed more champagne, savored our meal, and relished the view, a fitting way to end a conference. I recognized a few other faces cozily dining in pairs. Must've been that time to celebrate newfound relationships and "Get It Together."

We finished eating and sat quietly while we admired the twinkling fairyland below. I felt warm, contented, but exhausted. The champagne plus my lack of sleep over the past two nights, not to mention the emotional trauma of the workshops, were all catching up with me. I stifled a huge yawn.

"Why don't we leave," she suggested.

We paid the bill and organized a taxi back to the university.

I walked her to her tiny room.

"How about a nightcap," she tempted. "I have a bottle of Tia Maria."

I yawned again. "I'm pretty tired. Maybe another time."

"There isn't going to be another time, Peter. I leave for Perth tomorrow night. Just a quick one." Her moist lips touched mine.

We entered the barren cubicle where she promptly turned on the electric heater fastened to the brick wall. The coils began glowing fiery red. She organized some glasses and poured the Tia Maria.

"This will warm us up," she cooed.

We sat on the creaking single bed. Karen snuggled closer. "The true mark of a professional is to practice the techniques before teaching them to clients. I never ask a patient to do anything I'm not prepared to carry out myself."

She placed her hand on my knee. My weary body wasn't in the mood. I was already bushed, and the nightcap was providing the knock-out punch. It had been a long, arduous three days. I could only think of sleep.

She removed my spectacles. "Do you want me to show you the 'Squeeze Technique'?"

"I... uh... think it's late. I really am very tired."

"Nonsense. Experimenting with this technique will revitalize you."

She nestled closer; the bed squeaked. Her open mouth offered a sensuous kiss.

If only I had more energy.

She breathed into my ear, "Let's take off our clothes and practice the homework. Who knows where it will lead?"

Groaning, piercing cries suddenly resounded in the room next door. Karen giggled. "They must be practicing some of the techniques. Their grunting last night kept me awake. Tonight, we can join them with animal noises of our own." She began peeling off her gear.

"Wait," I said. "I don't have any protection."

She fiddled through her purse and found a Sheik condom. I figured, what the hell, might as well have a quickie and enjoy the last night. The thought of a sedated sleep spurred me on. I definitely needed a good night's rest.

I was still removing my shirt when Karen's svelte naked body crawled toward me. The springs beneath us creaked and moaned. She tore open the packaged Sheik and pulled out the rubber sheath. Her tongue flicked my ear. "Now let's have a look at that penis of yours."

"Uh... wait a moment." The bloody zipper was jammed.

"You're really exciting me," she cooed. "Show me your erection, and I'll show you the 'Squeeze Technique'".

I finally removed my pants. I gave Freddie a nudge and a shake. He was sound asleep.

"What's wrong, Peter?"

"Nothing... just need a bit of time."

Our nude bodies embraced. She glanced at Freddie, then at me.

"It'll be all right." I may be premature, but Freddie always managed an erection. He hasn't failed me yet.

The single bed squealed under our weight. Karen held onto the limp condom.

"I'm... not ready yet... give me a few moments."

She kissed me on the neck and face, then checked Freddie's response.

"Do you need manual stimulation?" solicited the distressed voice.

"I'm... not sure."

Damn it! Wake up, Freddie! I conjured a picture on my mental screen. Saw Freddie smiling between my legs.

We had to talk. I remembered Trevor Ravencroft's "Empty Chair" technique and yelled in my mind, *What's wrong with you?!*

Freddie sat limply on a chair and faced me. The tiny hole on the top of his head spoke. *"I'm tired."*

Tired? This is no time to be tired.

"I hardly know this girl."

Neither do I, but that's no reason to fall asleep. When you spring into action, I'll know her better.

"I don't want to."

You have to! I'm in charge here. I command you to get up!

He turned away in his chair. *"No. I won't!"*

You have to!

"Try and make me," he answered defiantly.

Karen interrupted my mental conversation. "What's wrong, Peter? What's the problem?"

"Just a moment!"

Freddie, you're embarrassing me. Please cooperate, just this once.

The tiny hole mouthed, *"I feel anxious. And guilty."*

So do I. But I'd feel a hell of a lot less anxious if you'd only stand up and be counted.

"I can't."

Why not?

"Too much pressure."

Karen, still holding the condom, began tugging at Freddie. "Is there anything I can do to make it more erotic?"

"I'll have another drink."

While she reached for the Tia Maria, I continued my mental conversation with Freddie. *How can I ease the pressure?*

He yawned. *"How about resting awhile?"*

No. Not yet. You'll sleep after you've done your duty. Until then, no rest.
"Goodnight, Peter."
Freddie! Wake up!! Freddie!!!
No use. He was sound asleep. I felt crushed. Karen looked devastated. I eventually left her room with Freddie snoring between my legs.

FINAL CONFERENCE DAY

🦗

SATURDAY, JULY 30

11:15 a.m. My bags were already packed. Even though I was thoroughly exhausted last night, I didn't sleep. Was still furious with Freddie for conking out on me. In the past, I couldn't stop him. Now, I felt powerless, unable to make him rise for the occasion.

I avoided today's seminars and the closing plenary. Had originally planned on visiting the National Art Gallery with Karen this afternoon, but now it was out of the question. Couldn't face her, not after last night.

Feeling lower than a slug's navel, I handed in my keys and waited for a taxi in the freezing wind. An irate supporter of Moshe Rosen passed by.

"We bloody well lost the election to Pamela Crouch!" he raved. "The bitch's scare tactics worked. The Newmanist Movement has taken a beating."

I clutched my jacket and nodded sympathetically. "We sure have."

POST CONFERENCE BLUES

THURSDAY, AUGUST 11

3:23 p.m. The lightning crackled in the distant sky; the thunder rumbled overhead. Huddled next to the heater in my office, watching the clouds release a torrent, I grabbed a tissue and blew my nose. Couldn't shake the bloody cold I caught at the conference. I was still haunted by memories from Canberra. Two weeks had elapsed since that dreadful night–with Karen frustrated, Freddie snoring, and me helpless. What did women expect anyway. Pull the magic lever and presto erecto? Press the orgasmic knob, push the ejaculation button?

The rain pelted against the tile roof. Gutters gushed with rapidly flowing rivulets. A waste bin overflowed outside. I recalled the Gestalt workshop and reflected on the throbbing internal pain. Shouldn't have dredged those childhood experiences about Ma recovering from depression. I always hankered to be more adventurous, but when she was sick, I couldn't stop myself from hanging around the house and worrying about her health. Then she started worrying about me. That only caused me to worry more about her. I became a prisoner in my own home. I hated being responsible for her happiness. What could I do? Hell, stewing on the rubbish from the past only made matters worse.

Earl Jacobi strolled into my office puffing his rolled cigarette. "Hey, matey," called the bronze-haired psychiatric intern. "Join me and the others for a few drinks at the pub."

"No thanks. I don't want anyone catching my cold." Couldn't get enthused about joining the others, especially with Theresa there. I'd suffered enough humiliation for awhile.

"Lighten up, Pete. Remember, Smelder's off in Italy. When the warden's away, it's time to break out of the cell."

"I'll give it a miss today. I'm behind on my paperwork."

He blew a puff of smoke my way. "Listen, mate, forget your reports. Enjoy the party with the rest of us. I reckon if you have one boot in the past and the other in the future, you'll end up pissing on the present."

"Not to change the subject, but who's the therapist for the one-way screen tomorrow?"

Earl flaunted a boyish grin. "I was. My phone call, informing the family that I had to attend a crisis, may have helped with their decision to cancel. We're commiserating the loss of our one-way mirror opportunity at the pub. Come on, join us."

I pulled out my handkerchief and blew. "Thanks, but I'll go home early and hit the sack. I have to get rid of this God-awful cold."

"I have some great medication at home. You doing anything Saturday night?"

"Not really."

"Why not come around to the house for dinner? You've never met my Kristy and the little squirter, Josh. Last week he turned one."

"I'm not really in the mood for company."

"I won't take no for an answer," Earl stated emphatically. "You promised before you left for the conference. Besides, I reckon you haven't been your old self since you've returned. With Smelder away, we're home on a pig's back. Here's my address. See you Saturday night, seven o'clock. Don't wear the tux."

"All right," I sniffled.

"Good on ya, mate! We'll have a blast."

Ma stopped hassling me about going out in the rain when I mentioned Earl Jacobi was a doctor and would administer some medication for my cold. Actually, driving Pa's Holden in a deluge wasn't exactly my idea of a fun night. Would've preferred staying in bed under my *pierzyna*. Thought of my old poem:

You beckon me on a cold wintry night.

You unselfishly soothe and release my fright.

You impart a warm and tender embrace.

You share my bed and caress my face.

– My *pierzyna*.

With the cozy eiderdown on my mind, I arrived at 69 Darling Street, where Earl's renovated terrace house matched the other trendy homes in Balmain. I closed my brolly, popped a Fisherman's Friend throat lozenge, and knocked on the door.

He appeared in scruffy jeans and a red and black striped cardigan. "Come on in, mate. Take off your wet shoes. Here, give me the umbrella. I'll show you around."

The grand tour included a view of two small bedrooms, a quaint living room with a burning fireplace, and a rustic dining room. Earl's ubiquitous tobacco smoke permeated everywhere. We entered the tiny kitchen where his wife, Kristy, was feeding their one-year-old son, Josh.

"Luv, I want you to meet my mate, Pete."

Holding a small plastic spoon, Kristy looked up. "I'm glad you were able to make it," said the petite blonde.

Her warm smile made me feel welcome. Dressed between trendy and bohemian, Kristy's golden ratted hair hung like a bush over her purple knitted jumper. Black slacks accentuated violet eye shadow, lavender lipstick, and magenta fingernail polish. Amethyst crystals dangling beneath her earlobes brought me to the conclusion that she had a fetish for purple. I wondered if her undies were lilac or plain plum.

"Get something for Pete to drink," said Kristy. "Hope you like vegetarian lasagna. I'm a vegetarian."

"My mother cooks veggies all the time."

After being handed a glass of rosé, I sat on a stool and watched Kristy shovel another mouthful of mashed food into Josh's mouth. The kid promptly spat half of it out again, then rubbed the gooey mass into his flaxen hair. I realized I was far from ready to raise an ankle-biter.

I sipped my wine. "Bet he keeps you busy."

Earl nodded. "You can say that again. He's sleeping much better now, but he used to wake Kristy every night. I reckon I could sleep through a hurricane."

"You could say that again," offered his wife.

"I've been tracking Josh's developmental stages. He was sitting up by himself at seven months. Yesterday he took his first step."

"Earl's forever preoccupied," added Kristy, "whether Josh is performing like a normal child. I keep telling him, psychiatry won't keep our child healthy. I'm more concerned with nutrition. We are what we eat. I recently completed an eight-week course, "The Vegetarian Way of Life." You'd be amazed how the different enzymes work in our digestive system. Unbelievable! Next month I'm studying macrobiotic cooking. Thus far, I've kept Josh away from sweets and feed him mainly fruits and vegetables, and of course, breast milk."

No sooner had the words been uttered, when she picked up her son, plumped him on her lap, pulled out one of her boobs and pointed it at his face. Both Josh and I opened our mouths wide. Spellbound, I watched the little tike attack the teat with great gusto, sucking noisily.

"I intend to breast feed as long as possible," she said, obviously quite comfortable about exposing herself. "As soon as he's fed, I'll put him down to sleep. Then we can settle down to our own meal."

Feeling rather embarrassed about observing the suckling, I turned toward Earl and asked for another glass of rosé.

When he refilled my glass, he suggested, "While we're waiting for dinner, why don't we light up. It'll stimulate our appetite. You'd share a joint with us, wouldn't you, Pete?"

"Geez... I don't think so."

"Our stash is homegrown. Grew it out in the shed. The plucked leaves were too damp for smoking so we used a little ingenuity. Kristy stuffed them into a little bag she had sewn and put them in the clothes dryer for 10 minutes. Pretty damn effective, eh luv?"

She laughed and continued feeding the boy. "We do have a few vices. If you live life too purely, you become unbalanced."

My eyes veered toward Josh gurgling away with his lips attached like a limpet. Earl fetched the paraphernalia for his own oral stimulation and began rolling a joint.

"Don't think I should, what with my cold and everything. Besides, I have to drive home tonight."

Earl slapped my back. "Relax, mate. No worries. That's why we're smoking early in the evening. There'll be ample time to get straight before you leave. If you're still stoned, you can use the extra mattress in Josh's room. He won't mind."

I coughed. "Smoking irritates my lungs. And with my cold, I don't want to take any chances." Besides, sucking on someone else's cigarette never turned me on. Who knows what I could catch.

"No worries," added Earl, dragging hard on the homegrown. He filled his lungs to bursting point and passed the joint to Kristy.

She inhaled slowly, held her breath, then exhaled a billowy cloud. "You boys move into the living room while I put Josh to bed. I don't want him inhaling too much of this."

Earl grabbed the dope and led the way. I plopped down on the easy chair while he sprawled on the lounge in front of the fireplace. He finished the joint and rolled another. White clouds floated hypnotically above our heads. Wispy spirals danced playfully around the room, unfolding and enfolding.

My host emitted another smoke ring. "You know, Pete, I thoroughly enjoy psychiatry. I earn a good quid and... Wow!... Those colors... shining on the stained glass lamp shade... Far out!... Check out the ruby red... You don't know what you're missing, mate... Wow!..."

"I'm back," rejoined Kristy. Her husband, babbling about the emerald greens and sapphire blues, was too stoned to take notice.

She handed me a thick brownie. "Take a bite."

I bit into the moist confection and chomped on tiny pieces of grit. "It's crunchy."

"One of my special macadamia squares made only with natural ingredients–whole grain flour, macadamia nuts, raw sugar, carob, plus our added herb-superb. I keep them on hand for you non-smokers. If you finish it now, you should be buzzing when the food arrives."

Feeling light-headed and woozy from the surrounding dense clouds, I decided that, having taken my first bite, I might as well go full hog and party hardy. I gnawed at the carob treat. "What are the tiny bits?"

She poured the magic herb onto a thin white paper and laughed. "It's either the macadamia nuts or the dope."

She shared the new joint with Earl as I slowly ingested the brownie.

"Good on ya, mate," he encouraged. "Check out the colors... Wow!..."

White puffy windmills circled around my face, creeping up my nostrils. An electric shock suddenly jolted every muscle. My skin tingled; my head spun. The light in the room pulsated. Now I could see it–a purplish haze streaming through the stained glass... Fantastic!... Dazzling colors, flickering on the ceiling... A laser display while the stereo played eerie music by Kitaro. Fantastic!...

"Better heat dinner before I get too stoned," said Kristy, whose lovely face glowed a soft rose complexion. "Your taste buds are about to experience some superb sensations."

Her smile turned into a giggle. The giggle burst into laughter, or rather a high-pitched cackle. Her amethyst earrings dangled and swayed with every snort of air. I thought of a large purple budgerigar and convulsed on the floor holding my gut. Everything seemed utterly ridiculous, even when Kristy and her chortling departed toward the kitchen.

I was still rolling on the floor, crying with laughter, when Earl's face turned pensive. "Mate, do you ever think of clients?"

"Sure," I giggled.

"I mean do you ever fantasize about them?"

"Sometimes they appear in my dreams."

His eyes bulged wide. "What kind of dreams?"

My head buzzed like a thousand bumble bees. "Nightmares, lately... Don't like remembering them... Let's just say clients aren't very nice when I'm asleep."

"I have sexy dreams," he confessed. "Especially about this 16-year-old girl, Cindy, who looks more like she's 22. God, is she stacked. A real looker, if you know what I mean. She could easily be a model. Has creamy legs, luscious lips, a curvaceous body... During our sessions she lets her short skirt creep up to expose her panties. She wants me to see them... I know she has the hots for me."

"How can you tell?"

"By the way she talks and licks her lips. You can see it yourself. She's on video."

"She lets you tape the sessions?"

"Never asked. She'd be too self-conscious. I tell her the camera's not recording. Have a great segment showing Cindy with her skirt raised. Great stuff! She's wearing apricot panties. Want a peek?"

"You have it here?"

He picked up a videotape lying on the VCR in the corner. "I review my interviews at home. Kristy's interested in my work so we watch the sessions together. Sure beats the rubbish on the telly. Want me to wack it in?"

"I'll give it a miss... Don't feel like seeing clients right now."

"You'd enjoy it... During this session she tells me how the boys tease her about having large breasts. God, are they sumptuous! She's uncomfortable about her body developing... Doesn't know what to do about the strange feelings. I reckon I'd know what I'd do about them!"

My mind swirled as I watched Earl greedily smack his lips.

"It'd be bloody easy getting it off with her. She'd only need a little encouragement... I'd open her up by discussing those juicy feelings... Like ripening a tomato... She wants to be plucked. I can feel it... I reckon it'd be so easy, right there in the interviewing room... Counseling her on the art of loving... Delicious!... Of course, I'd cover my ass... The case notes would indicate her obsession with sexual fantasies about her therapist... That she continually wanted, no, pleaded that the therapist make love to her... If she ever made a report, my case assessment would merely indicate she was delusional."

With horror and disbelief, I peered into his glazed eyes.

Earl slapped my leg. "Wouldn't do anything like that," he laughed. "If I ever got caught, my career in psychiatry would be ruined."

Was he joking or serious? The dope was making me paranoid. I saw flames leaping in the fireplace. A demonic shadow shrouded his frame.

"I plan on learning hypnosis," he sniggered. "No telling what kind of fun I could have practicing on patients." The ominous shadow rose. "Let's check on dinner. If I know Kristy, she'll be pigging out."

With my legs somewhat wobbly and my head definitely fuzzy, I cautiously followed my host to the dining room. The table was already decked out with food and candles. Kristy was munching out of a large wooden salad bowl. "Unbelievable!" she exclaimed, licking her fingers. "This garlic dressing is unbelievable! Try some."

She fed me a lettuce leaf spread with gooey dressing. I gagged. Bloody hell! She must've used the whole

348

goddamn garlic. I coughed and spluttered, "Water!" And staggered to the kitchen frantically looking for a glass.

"Don't you like garlic?" she cackled. "Did you see Pete run? You would've thought his mouth was on fire. Here luv, try some."

I returned with my water and found Kristy stuffing the salad in her husband's mouth. In between serves, she kissed his lips liberally.

"Ahem... Can I do anything?"

Earl slurped, "We're all set, mate. Sit down and dig in."

Dig in is what we, or rather, they did.

"Unbelievable lasagna!" cried Kristy. "Ohhh!... Unbelievable!... Ohhhh... The sauce... Ohhhhh... Taste this zucchini... Unbelievable!..."

My eyes were hypnotized by their bizarre sounds and behavior. Earl purred as he sucked on the tomatoes while Kristy, eating the lasagna with her hands, screamed, "U-n-b-e-l-i-e-v-a-b-l-e!"

Strewth! We never ate like this at home.

Another thunderbolt, this one a hundred times stronger than the first, struck home. The macadamia brownie kicked in, sending its herbs pulsating through my veins like a live electrical current. My body throbbed; my mind swirled. I shut my eyes and rested my head on the table before it fell off. Everything twirled like on a ferris wheel spinning backwards... Time passed forever... God knows for how long... When I opened my eyes, Earl and Kristy were staring, smiling.

She giggled, "Look's like he got a rush, luv."

"I reckon those macadamia squares pack a mean punch," he laughed. "How're you feeling, matey?"

"Woozy. The room's gyrating."

"No worries," he consoled. "Enjoy it. Watch the candles. Can you see them dancing?"

I focused my eyes on the flickering flames. "Everything's glowing brighter, like Christmas lights... I feel another rush coming... The ferris wheel's whirling... Ohhhhh!..."

"You're ready for the lasagna," Kristy cackled. She passed the casserole dish. "It's unbelievable!"

My hands struggled to grasp the food and fill my plate. I don't know how, but the lasagna found my mouth. Mmmmm! Different herbs signaled their presence. First basil, then oregano. I met parsley, sage, but not rosemary. My taste buds cried out for more ecstasy. Green olives screamed indescribably. Red capsicum exploded with sweetness. Baked potato joined the sour cream in a scrumptious holy union. Burgundy jelly, wiggling and wobbling, slithered around my tongue with orgiastic delight... It was *unbelievable!*

My hostess sliced a mango into two large wedges, then cut the orange flesh into a checkerboard. She folded back the skin, forcing luscious miniature squares to emerge. She sucked heartily, dribbling juice down her chin, punctuating each groan. "Ugh... U-n-b-e-l-i-e-v-a-b-l-e!"

Earl moved closer and licked the sweet droplets off her face. She offered me the other wedge of mango. Securing the slippery morsel, I devoured the orange pulp and drooled over the slithery skin as it caressed my lips. I closed my eyes and savored the sweet nectar lingering in my mouth. I echoed another of Kristy's "Unbelievable!"

Mango fiber, lodged annoyingly between my teeth, brought me out of my reverie. When I opened my eyes, my hosts were sharing the enormous seed, each sucking on half. Their lips touched as teeth and tongues munched and slurped. Saliva oozed down the sides of their mouths.

When Kristy surfaced, she peeled another piece of fruit–a Queensland banana. She mouthed off the top and moaned, "Ohhhh... unbelievable!" She erotically pointed the ripe fruit toward her husband's lips. He took a bite, then she another. Their oral feasting was interspersed with sensuous groans until Earl paused. "Don't be rude, luv. Offer a piece to our guest."

The half-eaten fruit made its way toward me. I roared, "That's one way to make a banana split!" and erupted into a wave of hysterical laughter. I was having dinner with a couple of fruits. I fell off my chair laughing, tears streaming down my face. Kristy released another cackle as I struggled back onto the chair. Tried sipping wine and chuckling at the same time. A fiasco. Rosé trickled out my nose while I coughed and spluttered and spilled wine on the carpet.

Wasn't sure when we finished dinner, but somehow I found myself on an easy chair by the fire, listening to more Kitaro. My hosts were on the lounge sharing a joint and creating another thick fog. I was still spaced out on the brownie.

Earl exhaled. "Do you like flowers, mate?"

"Huh?... They're okay."

"Show him the new plant, luv."

She arrived back with a potted plant sprouting a vibrant red, waxy heart-shaped leaf. She told me the name–anthem, a thum, ant's thumb. Or was it anthurynum?

"I love this yellow stamen," said Kristy, gently stroking a prominently tapered finger protruding from the red heart. "It's rough at the base but is unbelievably smooth at the tip. Feel this, Pete."

Never thought much of fondling plants but figured, what the hell. I went over for a quick feel.

"Doesn't it look like a prick?" asked Earl.

"Don't be so crude," mocked Kristy.

Crude or not, I quickly removed my hand.

He released another cloud. "Just joking, luv."

Joking? I feel woozy again. The fog keeps rolling in... My head is floating. Another jolt... The ferris wheel spins faster... Blood rushes through my body... I mentally fasten a seat belt... Everything's amplifying. Kitaro's eerie synthesizers envelop the room. Kristy, stroking the stamen, moistening her lips... She peers into my eyes... Is she leading me on?... Earl, watching... Am I hallucinating?...

He places another log on the fire. "Strokin' that thing's making me horny."

She cackles, "Everything makes you horny."

He tickles her ribs. "You want to turn us on? I know how hot you get after smoking dope."

She turns to me and coos, "Does stroking this plant make you excited?"

"Geez... I don't know."

"Listen, mate. I reckon any guy would be turned on watching my Kristy feeling up that plant. If you were in my shoes, wouldn't you get horny sitting next to her?"

I become a ball caught between their ping-pong communication... Not sure which part I'm supposed to play. Kristy's dark hypnotic eyes capture my gaze.

"Yea... guess so."

He whispers in her ear... She looks at my crotch... She smiles. Bloody hell! Freddie's awake... Her eyes move from my pants to my face. Her smile widens. I smile back... She giggles. I giggle. We both laugh... Earl isn't laughing. Or is he smirking? Don't know. Don't care... Another rush...

I stare at Kristy–her purple sweater, nipples protruding, leaking, leaving two wet spots... She describes an Egyptian necklace she once owned... Outlines the shape with her fingers tracing over her sumptuous nipples... The leaping flames from the burning log cast shadows on her face... Can't take my eyes off her. I know I should. I can't... My body quivers. Freddie stretches... The intensity... Unbearable... My eyes touch her cheek, her lavender lips. They open slightly... The tip of her tongue flits in and out. I want a taste... The bulge in my pants grows hard... The scent of musk permeates the air... I follow her widening eyes to my groin. She flushes with excitement... Turns toward Earl. Her twinkling eyes send a signal. The message is clear.

As if in slow motion, he leads her to the floor... He eats her probing tongue. I can taste the wine on her breath... He chews her lips. She cries an unbelievable groan... Their hands and mouths explore each other's faces, sharing another meal of love... Wet fingers slide in and out of gaping mouths gurgling, "Ahhhh!" and "Ohhhh!"... His tongue slithers in her ear... He reaches under her sweater and plays with lactating nipples. My eyes plead, Yes! Play with her nipples! Yes! Remove her clothes... She senses my participation, loves it. She flashes a smile my way, then closes her eyes and disappears to her unbelievable sounds and sensations...

I watch as if mesmerized by some hypnotic trance. I should leave. Must leave. I try moving out of my chair. My mental seat belt holds firm. Too dizzy... I stay.

The fire crackles; the temperature rises. He peals off the purple jumper, then her bra. Her beautiful engorged breasts send droplets of cream cascading past her navel. Like one of Pavlov's dogs, my mouth drools. He sucks one nipple; my eyes covet the other. Oozing sweet, creamy liquid... Oh, so lovely...

They remove their remaining clothes—shirt, pants, indigo panties... They pant heavily, pawing each other's bodies... Freddie is hard and firm. He spots Earl's big one and becomes self-conscious.

Positions change, then change again...They kiss... probe... touch... sweat... moan... His tongue finds the mauve polish, glistening on her toenails. She howls, "Unbelievable!" yet again... They become intertwined. He mounts. Their grunting and groaning increase. Kitaro's bells chime... Yes! Faster!! Faster!!!... They scream, shudder, then collapse, exhausted.

They lie still in front of the fire. Dark shadows flicker over their sweating bodies. I become self-conscious and turn my gaze to the burning log, not knowing what to say, except, "It's time to go home."

Earl stirs to life. "God, that felt wonderful. Getting stoned always makes us horny."

His naked wife moves to the couch. "That was unbelievably decadent. I could do this all night. Unbelievable! Since Josh was born, our free time has been limited so we take any moment we can get."

"Hmmm," I murmur.

They burst into laughter and stare at me. I become uneasy, edgy. Earl moves next to Kristy and touches her breasts. She whispers in his ear. He faces me. "It's your turn, mate. Let's see what you got."

I freeze, then panic! "Huh? Oh my God!... You don't want me to do it with your wife?... No!... I can't... Oh my God!"

Kristy fondles one of her nipples, causing the milky droplets to flow into a stream. She glares at my crotch. "It'll be an unbelievable experience."

Freddie bounds to life and urges me forward as if to say, "Come on, mate. Give it a go!" He was stoned out of his head!

"Join the fun," she entices. Her ring finger plays with her pubic hair then waves seductively. "I like the bashful type."

Freddie struggles to leap out of my pants. He doesn't know what he's doing! I can't make love to a married woman. I don't even know her. And not in front of her husband. Christ! I work with him. And their kid's in the next room.

She beckons. "We're ready. We're both getting unbelievably horny."

What does she mean, "We're ready"? I look at Earl who's stroking his thighs. Is this one of those troy mages, trois manages, *ménage à trois,* whatever they're called? This is way over my head. Don't even know where the hell my twirling head is, was.

Kristy lifts her breasts. "Would you like to suck on one of these?"

"Oh my God! Gotta go... It's late... Seen too much..."

Don't ask how, but I rip off my mental seat belt, grab hold of Freddie, pick up my shoes, and bolt for the door. Don't want to give them any time to restrain me. They might force me to do unbelievable things. As I stumble out of their house, their voices ring into the darkness.

I managed to get home by two in the morning–just barely. Might've driven through a couple of red lights. Couldn't really tell. All a blur. Not much traffic. Was lucky to arrive home in one piece. Pa's Holden wasn't so fortunate. It was too tight a squeeze parking in the garage, especially in my condition. I swiped the door and knocked off the side mirror. Thank God, I didn't touch his pride and joy, the new Commodore.

"Piotr?"

Strewth! Ma was waiting up, watching the telly.

"Piotr?"

"Yea," I grumbled.

"Jak sie masz? How are you?"

"Dobrze. Fine."

"Piotr?"

I rushed into my bedroom and slammed the door. I breathed a sigh of relief. She would have spotted my glazed eyes for sure. Weary, exhausted, and woozy, I collapsed onto the bed and fell fast asleep snuggled against the warm, welcome bosom of my eiderdown *pierzyna*.

MANAGEMENT MEETING
🦃

MONDAY, AUGUST 22

Maxine occupied Gerard's plush leather chair and commandeered the meeting. With Smelder away in Italy, our department was undergoing a radical transformation.

I was becoming more disconnected from the team, especially after that bizarre night at Earl's. I had since avoided him, thinking he was some sort of pervert. Earl sensed my anxiety and discomfort and stopped pressuring me to associate with him. He increasingly closeted himself in his smoke-filled room. For all I knew, he might've been using the homegrown. When not in his office, Earl was happily counseling his burgeoning caseload of pubescent girls. Whatever he was doing, I could count on him covering his ass.

With Gerard away, Earl wasn't the only one enjoying himself. Maxine had moved into the director's office and was flaunting her newfound power through daily memos. Theresa expanded her caseload of psychotherapy patients, most of whom were being seen three times per week. This was a sharp contrast to the fortunate few that Gerard used to allocate for intensive therapy. At least Theresa seemed happier focusing on her counseling, which eased the tension between us—but only slightly. The great wall of China separating us still held firm.

As for Holy Henry, he began taking his pastoral counseling more seriously, proselytizing that judgment day was close at hand. Ironically, he was now the only one I really conversed with. Just had to put up with with his periodic raving, "Resist Satan's temptation and receive salvation through Jesus."

Leela suffered the most from Smelder's absence. She was the only one interviewing families, and the team sessions behind the one-way mirror were completely abandoned. So much for the department's commitment to family therapy. Without Gerard's protection, Leela's status as social worker/family therapist had been relegated lower than the cleaning lady. The increased strain was beginning to show. Her once stylish wardrobe was now replaced by casual jeans and sloppy pullovers, and she developed a horrible case of cold sores which mushroomed around her lips. I noticed her making overtures to Earl, but he didn't seem interested, not with his commitment to pubescent patients.

And as for Violet Struthers, well, let's just say she had become even more erratic. No one ever knew for sure when she would grace us with her presence. When she did happen to arrive, she might appear with a wig in the morning, but by the afternoon her hairpiece would have mysteriously vanished.

"Let's have an update on the Jenson/Murray family," directed Maxine as she rested pompously in the executive's seat. "Henry, what's the status of your assessments on the children?"

He opened the file. "I've interviewed the four-year-old boy, Conrad, and his eight-year-old brother, Richard Jr., nine times. I have alternated the sessions–one week seeing them individually, the next week counseling them together. We're still establishing a trusting relationship."

"But have they disclosed that the father has been molesting them?" interrupted Maxine's husky voice.

Henry shifted his gangling legs. "Not yet, but I've introduced the anatomical dolls. Conrad's more open and curious about playing with them. Richard Jr., on the other hand, is more defensive and needs time and encouragement before he can more freely express himself."

"Christ, you can't take all year," frothed Maxine. "The court hearing is coming up next month. Haven't you read my memo?"

Henry meekly nodded.

"If I read that slimy bastard correctly, the father will try and postpone the proceedings. As a lawyer, he'll use every trick of the trade to gain custody. Arrogant pig! During his last session with Gerard, he knew we were watching behind the one-way mirror and smugly answered the questions as if he were performing in a courtroom. That sincere father act didn't fool me. Guilt oozed from his face when he made the charge that Gayle Murray made up the allegations in order to gain custody. What a load of bulldust! My client would never do such a thing."

Leela hesitantly raised her hand. "Excuse me, but Gerard wasn't totally convinced the father was the perpetrator. We could replay the videotape of Mr. Jenson's last interview. It still contains the team's post-session discussion."

"I'm sure we know what we said. Your memory may be fading, but I recall stating emphatically that the father was guilty as hell."

"I was merely suggesting that Gerard..."

"You must be missing him terribly," derided Maxine. "Bit lonely in bed?"

"Let's not get personal," counseled Henry. "Conflict will only promote hate. Hatred's not good for the team nor our souls."

The psychiatric nurse moved to the edge of the chair. "You better collect more evidence," said Maxine, "or your soul will receive heaps from me. I don't want you buggering up the case. Those boys' emotional and mental well-being are at stake."

His eyes floated uneasily. "I can only do my best."

"You'll have to do better than that! The boys said they were molested in the park across from where the father lives. Have them show you on the dolls what actually happened. They might just let it slip and disclose the father as the perpetrator. The bastard even confessed he used colored markers on the boys' naked bodies."

"They were colored soap crayons in the bath," said Henry.

Maxine bellowed, "Christ Almighty! Whatever they were, have them show you what he did! Maybe I should watch you behind the one-way mirror."

"N-n-no," stammered Henry. "It would ruin the trust that I've developed. The boys are very sensitive to any form of voyeurism. I told them we wouldn't be watched."

"Use the dolls, drawings, whatever. Remember your report will carry a lot of weight. We don't want those boys to be sexually abused ever again."

Theresa shook her head enthusiastically. "They will need long-term psychotherapy to save them from further psychological damage. Have you taught them protective behaviors, Henry?"

"I've... uh... concentrated purely on assessment."

Theresa turned toward Maxine. "Once the court hearing is completed, the boys should be instructed how to protect themselves by learning to say "no" to any possible sexual advance."

"I've already organized Henry to attend a seminar on protective behaviors," stated Maxine. "He can then teach his clients all about protecting themselves."

Theresa smiled in agreement.

"We're developing a damn good reputation for treating the sexually abused," puffed Maxine. "With increased public awareness, there will be even more disclosures. That means a swelling caseload of patients who have been traumatized by sexual abuse. We better be prepared."

HEIDI WENTWORTH'S
51ST INTERVIEW

MONDAY, AUGUST 29

You're losing weight, aren't you?"

"Yea, I guess."

"How much?"

"Don't know."

"You don't look so good."

"I'm okay, Heidi. Don't worry about it." Bloody hell! I wasn't feeling all that great, but being reminded of it didn't make me feel any better. Wasn't sure what was happening. I had lost my appetite and the weight was literally dropping off. Mornings were becoming a battleground as I literally struggled to force myself out of bed.

"You all right?"

"Yea, sure," I said, snapping out of my reverie. "So you made it this week?"

Her eyes dropped to the floor. "Sorry about last week. I planned on makin' it, but my friend had a birthday party. Couldn't miss that, now could I?"

"I had my doubts whether you'd keep your side of the bargain and complete the five sessions."

Her rosy cheeks broadened. "I had ta come and say goodbye, now didn't I?"

August 29

"I'm glad you made the final session. You've done really well."

Her school uniform, a navy skirt and jumper, was filling out widthwise and lengthwise. No sign of anorexia there.

"When do you turn 16?"

"Next month, September 25th. I'm a Libran. Wanna come to my birthday party?"

"I don't know. Depends on my work around here. How's things with your mother?"

"We're gettin' on okay," she said cheerfully. "No fights."

"Are you sure you can handle it on your own?"

She shook her head defiantly. "I'm not coming back, if that's what you're askin'."

"I wouldn't dare. You'd bite off my head."

She smoothed out the wrinkles in her skirt and relaxed into the chair. "You helped me heaps, but this is the last time I'm comin' to hospital."

Even if I had forced the issue, she wouldn't have come back. The analyst, Dr. Fiona Crompton, was royally pissed off because I had allowed a person with Heidi's degree of pathology to terminate. I peered at the thriving adolescent sitting across from me. A wave of sadness lapped across my face. "I'll miss you, Heidi. We've become good mates. I'm sorry this is the end."

"I can always drop by. Just to say hello."

I doubted whether I'd ever see her again. Within eight months she had won a major victory over anorexia. There were bound to be setbacks, but her fierce determination should keep her out of hospital. While admiring her success, I felt somewhat ashamed. She had managed to conquer her eating disorder, leave the hospital, and rebuild her life. Meanwhile, I was wearily trudging a deepening treadmill in the department.

363

"Almost forgot," she added, opening her school case. "Here's a cupcake and a card."

I wasn't very hungry, but the thought in itself brought a warm, fuzzy feeling. I opened the envelope. The cover of the card showed a picture of Van Gogh with a bandage around his head. Inside was the inscription, "Thanks for lending me an ear. Love Heidi."

"Thanks, I needed that. Hey, I've an idea. Why not finish on a high? Let's nick off to the cafeteria and buy some soft drinks and chips. My treat."

Her eyes lit up. "Excellent!"

As we strolled out of the department, I put my arm around her shoulder and gave a gentle squeeze. "You don't know how much I'll miss you."

She blushed. So did I. I promptly removed my arm. "So... Do you want a Coke or a Pepsi?"

Didn't care what Fiona Crompton would say about my last session with Heidi. She'd probably interpret soft drinks and chips as avoiding the issue of termination. What the hell. It was a nice way to say goodbye.

SPRING CLEANING

🦃

SATURDAY MORNING, SEPTEMBER 3

Pink camelias and yellow wattle were blooming in the back garden, and humming bees were collecting nectar among the red bottlebrush. The flowers sent a sweet fragrance drifting in the breeze.

"Piotr!" called Ma. "Here's the bucket. The kitchen ceiling needs a wash."

I tossed the rubber ball to Blackie. "In a minute." It was too magnificent a day for chores, and Blackie and I needed the fresh air.

"Piotr!" she fumed. She had organized the annual spring cleaning which meant an endless list of jobs—washing windows, clearing out the garage, dumping rubbish at the tip, and of course, cleaning the kitchen ceiling.

"I'll be there in minute. What's the rush?"

"Psiakrew!" she swore, and stormed into the garage to collect the ladder. When she made up her mind that something had to be cleaned, it had to be done right then and there. I went to help her with the ladder, but she pushed me aside. "I'll do it myself!"

Wasn't about to argue with her. I tossed Blackie the ball and soaked up the sun.

Several minutes later, I heard a loud scream, then a crash. I bolted towards the kitchen.

"Ma! What happened?!!"

Her still body was sprawled on the wet, soapy floor next to the fallen ladder and overturned pail. Blood oozed down the side of her head. My heart raced. I rushed to her side. Please God, don't let her die! Not from a stupid accident!

I checked for signs of breathing. "Ma! Can you hear me?!"

"Ohhh..." Her blanched face winced with pain. Her eyelids weakly fluttered.

"Piotr!" she whispered. "Call the ambulance."

I frantically phoned St. John's ambulance, then hurried back to her aid. I grabbed a towel and wiped the blood from her face. She painfully clutched her side and whispered again, "Piotr, straighten the house. I don't want the men to see a mess. And please, wash the ceiling."

I went with her in the ambulance to Western Suburbs Hospital. They wanted to keep her overnight for observation, but my 56-year-old mother would hear nothing of it. She abhorred hospitals. Once the x-rays showed she had suffered a contusion on the head and four broken ribs, she demanded to go home. The bewildered doctor strapped her up, and Pa arrived from work to drive us home.

I felt guilty as hell. Why couldn't she have waited? I told her I'd clean the goddamn ceiling later in the day. I kept her company during the evening while she watched the telly. Viewing Ossie Ostrich on "Hey, Hey It's Saturday " wasn't exactly my idea of a fun night. Then again, I was grateful she was alive.

JOURNAL CLUB
CONFERENCE ROOM
🐦

FRIDAY, SEPTEMBER 16

Rejuvenated by his Italian trip, Dr. Smelder stood in front of the whiteboard. The bronze tones on his skin gave evidence that his six weeks were not all spent listening to lectures indoors. He adjusted his slipping glasses and imparted a professorial grin. "I realize I've only been back a few days, but I want to impart this valuable information while it's still fresh. On the table, you'll find a number of articles on brief, systemic family therapy. You can read them at your leisure."

Leela rummaged through the stack of articles. She was back to her old self since Gerard's return. Her designer clothes reappeared while her cold sores disappeared. She selected an article and passed the rest around the table counter-clockwise.

Violet, once again blessing us with her presence on her off day, leafed through the bunch. Not finding anything of interest, she passed them all to me and went back to browsing her *Women's Day* magazine. I picked an article on triangularity and handed the rest to Maxine who promptly shoved the stack to Theresa who passed them to Henry. He selected one from the pile then handed Earl the remainder.

Gerard patted his rotund stomach still bloated from the Italian pasta and vino. "I'm very excited about this short-term model of family therapy. Once you learn how to develop hypotheses about family problems and begin to utilize triangular questioning, you'll discover quicker solutions. After experiencing repeated success in a brief amount of time, you'll never want to conduct therapy any other way. I'm absolutely convinced this model will make this department more advanced than any other unit in Sydney–who knows, even Australia. But first, you'll have to change your epistemology."

"Episte what?" asked Violet Struthers, sporting a new pinkish gray wig.

"Epistemology!" glared Gerard. "How we organize our thinking."

"I don't want to learn philosophy," answered the geriatric psychiatrist whose thinking was becoming increasingly disorganized. Although she had ceased interviewing clients, Violet was now spending her one-and-a-half days, whenever she arrived, reading magazines and knitting baby booties. Terminating public servants, especially one with as many years and connections as Violet, was no easy matter.

"Let's not get hung up on the word," snapped Smelder. "I mean that you have to change the way you think. Most of you conceptualize problems in a linear fashion."

Violet furrowed her brow. "What's that?" she asked as she scratched her head, tilting her wig off center.

Our teacher picked up a marker and drew on the whiteboard. "Linear means A causes B. You must think in a triangular fashion where A causes B which causes C which then causes A."

I wasn't game to ask for any clarification, for Gerard had become pretty aggro since his return. Leela must've informed him how, during his absence, Maxine had returned the department to an emphasis on long-term individual psychotherapy especially for sexual abuse victims.

"By questioning the family about their attempted solutions, the therapist opens the system to new information, new ways of viewing their problem and, ultimately, new ways to solve their problem. This can be done briefly without years of therapy. Triangular questioning is the technique that allows the therapist to draw out the triangular nature of interactional patterns. I'll demonstrate. 'Pinowski, what do you think Maxine thinks about this model?'"

I looked at Gerard standing at the head of the table, then peered at Maxine, sitting at the opposite end. "Uh... I don't know."

"You don't have to ask him what I think," she scoffed. "You'd get much further if you just asked me straight out."

Gerard pointed the black marker toward her. "I'm trying to show that triangular questioning explores differences between family members. You find that out by asking individuals what they think other members think about certain issues or problems."

With a smirk on her face, Maxine folded her arms tightly. I'm sure we all knew what she was thinking.

"The literature that I've passed out explains the theoretical underpinning of this line of questioning. Once you've read it, I'm sure you'll agree that the old methods of interviewing are outdated."

Leela fluttered her eyes. "Can you explain the role of the therapist as the detached investigator?"

Gerard paused and sucked on the capped marker. "In this brief, systemic model, a detached, investigative therapist can access more information."

Maxine sniggered, "The idea of the therapist being detached is as useless as pockets on underpants."

"What don't you agree with?" asked Gerard calmly, modeling detachment.

"As far as I can understand this, the therapist must not side with any family member or anyone's point of view."

"That's correct. When the therapist acts as a non-judgmental, detached investigator, he's less invested in the outcome. This enables the family to discover their own solutions rather than resist the therapist's expectations about change."

"I think you've had too much sun in Italy," admonished Maxine.

"What are you talking about?"

"Haven't you noticed our increasing caseload of patients who've been sexually abused? How the hell are you going to be detached with a child molester? The bastard has to be physically removed from the family."

Smelder's face turned scarlet. "You're not even trying to understand these concepts."

"Frankly, Gerard, I don't give a damn. There's nothing in my contract that says I have to give up my way of thinking. Since you've been away, this department has been running quite smoothly."

Putting aside any thoughts of non-judgmental detachment, our director glowered. "I want everyone to get one thing straight. This is *my* department. If I say we adopt this model, then that's what we'll do. I didn't spend six weeks in Italy for nothing. I'm expecting everyone to be enthusiastic about practicing these new techniques of brief treatment."

The nurse bristled. "Who taught you this Italian crap? Mussolini? You can't force us to change our clinical practice. Traumatized victims of abuse need a committed, attached therapist who can provide long-term psychotherapy to help in the recovery process."

Gerard tossed the marker on the table. "I understand there have been quite a few changes during my absence. I want to know who else objects to using this innovative model?"

The tension crackled in the room. My chest tightened; my heart palpitated.

Theresa eventually spoke. "I agree with Maxine. We have the right to choose whichever method we think is appropriate for our clients. We shouldn't be forced to adopt anyone's approach."

Violet straightened her wig. "I've developed my style over the past 30 years. I'm too old to learn geometry."

"I for one, support Gerard," endorsed Leela. "He's giving us a unique opportunity to..."

"Cut the crap," snapped Maxine. "We know you'd do anything for and with him. God only knows why."

Henry shuffled the articles. "We should be open to new ideas while, at the same time, remain tolerant to the wishes of others."

"Who's side are you on?" yelled Gerard and Maxine simultaneously.

His head turned to one, then to the other. "I don't think we should be promoting sides. We should be advocating an attitude which accepts diversity."

"A load of tripe," scolded the nurse.

"This systemic model sounds beaut!" exclaimed an over-enthusiastic Earl Jacobi. "I can't wait to try it out on my clients." After all, Smelder was his supervisor. The psychiatric intern wasn't about to take any chances at losing his accreditation.

"Where do you stand, Pinowski?" asked our agitated director.

I glanced around the room, frantically weighing up the sides. Didn't want to get into further hot water with Smelder. Yet, if I advocated his model, I might have to give up my only real expertise, the bell and pad technique with my bed wetters. Didn't want to see that go down the drain. My palms became clammy and my chest tightened in a vice-like grip. I struggled to breathe.

"I... ugh..." Couldn't get the words out.

"Come on, Peter," Maxine prodded. "Spit it out. Whose side are you on?"

A wave of anxiety cascaded through my body. My thinking stalled. My knees began to shake. I opened my mouth to say, "Not sure." The words could not escape.

Gerard glared angrily across the table. "I've thought about this long enough. Short-term, systemic family therapy will be incorporated into our clinical practice. I expect full cooperation from everyone. If we're really on about caring for clients, then we should be interested in improving our professional standards."

"I'll have you know," prided Theresa, "I regularly attend lectures at the Psychoanalytic Institute. I've spent countless dollars–mind you, my own money–to develop therapeutic skills."

"We're talking about brief, systemic family therapy, not your individual nonsense."

Her face grimaced. "It just so happens that some of us believe individual psychotherapy is far more important than your brief fix-it model."

"Working this way will be quicker and more cost effective," defended Leela.

"Bulldust!" countered Maxine. "This unit had a very successful track record before you arrived, and most of the staff worked with individuals. Since you've been perving on those families behind the one-way mirror, I've seen scores of families drop out."

Smelder fumed, "I'm not copping any of the goddamn blame for those clients. Families dropped out because inexperienced therapists didn't know what the hell to do with them."

I avoided his fiery gaze. The throbbing muscle in my chest pounded. It felt as if it was ready to burst.

The burly nurse pushed back her chair and brazenly stood up. "As far as I'm concerned, you know where you can stuff your brief, systemic model. I don't want any part of it."

Maxine Benton stormed out in a huff.

"Come back here right now!"

The sound of footsteps faded down the hall.

A phantom. In white surgical gown. Chasing me!
I frantically run. Panting for air. Into elevator.
Doors close. Safe at last! Elevator plummets. Base-
ment. Door opens. Footsteps. I slam buttons.
Surgical gloves reach in. I scream. No sound. Yell
louder. Silence. I bite fingers. They snap off. El-
evator moves. Safe again! Scraping sounds.
Coming from above. Hatch opens. White phan-
tom. Peering down. Gaping mouth, dripping
saliva. Powerful jaws crush my chest. I gasp for
air. Creature wraps me in silk. Entombed in co-
coon. Still alive, yet dead!

Stricken with terror, I awoke, shaking and sweating.
I nestled back into my *pierzyna* and thought of the kitchen
lights. I hoped they were turned off. I puffed up my pillow and thought of the hospital.

The team was deteriorating further while the tension thickened. With Maxine and Theresa refusing to
attend family therapy consultations, Gerard was behav-
ing like a raging bull. "Pinowski," he would yell, "when
are you going to wake up and learn to be a therapist?"

He directed his anger primarily toward Henry and
me because we didn't fully support him on his brief,

systemic model. As punishment, we were forced to sit in silence during the one-way mirror presentations while he and Leela discussed the benefits of triangular questioning with Earl Jacobi, who was more preoccupied in watching the female clients.

To show further spite, Smelder was assigning me additional cases, not just the easy ones. I was handed a delusional 14-year-old boy who, believing he had the power to heal, had approached a girl on crutches at a bus stop. Intending to cure her broken leg, he placed his hands above her head, repeating, "I heal thee of all thy sins." Apparently, the girl picked up a crutch to hit him, but in the process, fell over and broke her other leg. Should've referred him to Henry because of the religious implications, but he was snowed under just like me.

Henry was particularly upset because he was being inundated with cases involving sexually assaulted children. "With these troubled victims, I feel like Job," he told me. "God has allowed Satan to send trials and tribulations. Happy is the man whom God correcteth; therefore despise not the chastening of the Almighty."

I could do without the chastening. I began wondering how long I could last. My childhood anxieties, like a series of bad dreams, were returning to haunt me once more. As a 10-year-old boy, I used to be obsessed with electricity, forever checking that the lights in the house were turned off. I was now regressing back to that time when I woke three and four times a night to check on the outlets. Reassuring myself that everything was safe had little effect. I became increasingly anxious about going to bed, and stayed up till two in the morning in the hope that fatigue would stop me from obsessing or dreaming. When I finally conked out, exhausted, monsters of horror haunted my sleep. Terrified, I'd awaken only to experience another wave of anxiety about the light globes overheating and starting a fire. Another vigilant search around the house to insure that the outlets were safe merely continued the vicious cycle.

I took a couple of sickies to get away from the tension. Even searched the *Sydney Morning Herald* for a new job. Ma, slowly recuperating from her fall, had noticed my tiredness and irritability and offered me a dose of Combantrin, her favorite worm remedy.

"Restless sleep and crankiness are the early signs of worms," she warned. "When you were crabby and restless as a little boy, I would inspect your bottom while you were asleep. Many times I spotted them with the flashlight. The medicine always cleared you up."

Still suffering the guilts about causing her fall, I took the Combantrin to please her.

The night terrors persisted.

DOCTOR'S SURGERY

TUESDAY MORNING, OCTOBER 4

"What's the problem, Peter?" asked Dr. Wojtecko as he sat in his white coat behind the cluttered desk.

"I thought I was going to have a heart attack when I woke up this morning. Heart palpitations, chest pains, dizziness. I couldn't breathe."

"Take it easy," comforted the gray-haired family doctor. "You're much too young to have a heart attack."

"My chest is really aching, like it's caving in. I must be having a heart attack. Can't go to work like this. I'll collapse."

"Let's examine you and see what we find."

In a grandfatherly way, Dr. Wojtecko ushered me to the medical table where I removed my shirt and lay down. He checked my pulse, monitored my blood pressure, listened to my chest, and, after much pleading, took an electrocardiogram.

He held the readout. "There is considerable tension. But you are not suffering from a heart attack. Are you under any pressure at work?"

I sat up and buttoned my shirt. "I've been having a rough time lately. The staff are having lots of hassles. I'm worried about the chest pains. I'm terrified I'll freak out in a meeting."

"You look tired. Are you getting enough sleep?"

"Can't sleep."

"Is it similar to the time you were at the university and had your panic attacks?"

"Guess so. But I didn't think they'd come back. I need something to stop me from falling apart."

"Pull yourself together. Think of your mother. She worries enough about you, and she's not young anymore. That nasty fall has..."

"Please, Doctor! I need something to cope with the anxiety."

"Last time you didn't want medication."

"That was the last time. I can't go through another experience like that. I'm feeling desperate!"

Dr. Wojtecko led me back to the patient's chair in front of his desk. "I don't like suggesting this, Peter, but possibly a psychiatrist could help."

"I don't need one of them! All I need is some medication to overcome my anxiety. You'll see. Once the pressure's eased, I'll be back to my normal self."

He hesitated.

"Please, Doctor! Give me a script," I begged. "It'll make me feel better. I promise. I need something for today. I have clients to see."

Dr. Wojtecko lifted his pen over the prescription pad. "All right, Peter. These should settle you down. Take them three times a day."

"Thanks! What are they?"

"Tablets to make you feel better." He handed me the prescription. "These will lessen your anxiety."

I couldn't read his scribbling. "What are they?"

"Xanax. If you have any further difficulties, let me know."

"What's the dose?"

Dr. Wojtecko stood up. "It's a minimal dosage. Don't worry about it."

I remained in the chair. "What are the side effects?"

He patted my shoulder reassuringly. "Don't worry about it. They'll make you feel much better." He opened the door and ushered me out of his office. "Come back in a couple of weeks."

As I walked past the receptionist, nagging doubts plagued my mind. Dr. Wojtecko had said it twice: "Don't worry about it." Did that mean there really *was* something to worry about?

POSTSCRIPT
🐦

The early morning tablet of Xanax brought me relief. I definitely felt more relaxed. Even the crowded train to the hospital didn't phase me.

When I arrived at work, I checked the reference book on drugs–just to be on the safe side. Xanax, a benzodiazepine, was one of the anti-anxiety drugs which acted on the central nervous system as a muscle relaxant. The recommended starting dosage was .25 to .5 mg three times per day. Dr. Wojtecko had prescribed .5 mg three times a day. Why hadn't he started me on .25 mg? Was I more anxious than I should've been?

I read that the dosage could be increased but there was some risk of dependence especially for those with panic disorders. I scanned the list of possible adverse reactions–drowsiness, lightheadedness, headache, depression, nervousness, confusion, and insomnia. As I continued to read the litany of other possible side effects–constipation, nausea, dermatitis, diarrhea, lethargy, and irritability, I began to panic. Strewth! I didn't want to contract more symptoms from taking the bloody pills.

There was a clear warning that the dosage should be terminated gradually. An abrupt cessation could result in withdrawal symptoms such as cramps, diarrhea, seizures, sweating, irritability, insomnia, weight loss or gain, and a return of panic attacks. Christ! If I managed to avoid the side effects, I might just get hit with a host of symptoms *after* I stopped the medication. And Dr. Wojtecko told me *not* to worry!

Deep down, however, I knew that I couldn't continue without some help. I wasn't prepared to revisit my old therapist, Melody Mill, not after she booted me out of therapy. I felt there was little choice. Medication offered a temporary solution. And this morning's tablet did provide some immediate relief.

NEW CLIENT
🦟

THURSDAY, OCTOBER 13

"... Kamal and Dursen are six-year-old identical twins?"

"This is right," answered the mustached 42-year-old father, Mustafa Memisoglu. The huge, unkempt man, reeking of alcohol, wore a black T-shirt.

Bang! Clang! His two scruffy sons dumped the colored wooden blocks on the floor.

"Ouch!" cried the black-haired Kamal after being punched by his brother.

The 33-year-old mother belted Dursen across the back. "Sit still while the doctor talks," yelled Gwenda Memisoglu. Clothed in a faded brown dress, the slightly-built woman with massive streaks of gray hair looked the part of a worn and haggard mother.

"This is daughter," spoke the father through a half-smile.

"Her name's Yasamin," added Mrs. Memisoglu.

I turned toward the scrawny adolescent wearing beat-up red thongs. "How old are you?"

Her voice was barely audible. "Seventeen."

"Are you in school?"

Yasamin stared at her red toenail polish.

"My daughter. She very shy," mouthed the father. "She stay at home, help with house."

"Put those crayons down!" screamed the mother. "You're not allowed to draw on the walls!"

Avoiding the distractions, I asked Mr. Memisoglu, "What do you do for a living?"

"No work now. Hurt back at work. Must go for treatment. Every week."

"Sorry to hear that."

"This is right."

"Waagh!" wailed Kamal. His brother had knocked down his pile of blocks.

Dursen received another thump from the mother. "You leave your brother alone. I'm warning you."

The scrappy boy merely shrugged off her blow and began pulling the arms off a doll.

"How long have you been out of work?"

"Too long."

"It's been more like three years," interjected the disgruntled wife. "We're still waiting for the compensation case to be settled. Till then, we have to live off welfare."

The holes in the boys' shoes and the patches on their pants reflected a desperate need to pinch pennies.

"When the money finally comes, my husband plans to visit his family in Turkey."

"This is right," confirmed Mustafa as he forlornly picked at his fingernails.

I asked the mother, "Where were you born?"

"England. My parents migrated here when I was very young. My children were born here. Yasamin and Mustafa were born in Turkey."

"So Yasamin isn't..."

"Kamal and Dursen are ours. I have a 16-year-old daughter, Magda, from my first husband. He was a terrible man. Beat me up all the time."

"What happened to him?"

"He went crazy. One evening, Victor was drinking heavily and began hitting me in front of Magda. When I phoned the police, Victor poured petrol on himself and threatened to burn the house down. I didn't believe the stupid man would light a cigarette. Everything went up in flames. Magda and I were lucky to escape without burns."

"Where's Magda?"

"She couldn't face her emotional problems and became addicted to drugs, heroin mostly. I couldn't handle her continual lying and stealing. Had to throw her out. She's now living in a youth refuge."

A block of wood went flying past my left ear.

Gwenda grabbed Dursen by his threadbare pants and delivered another hiding. She didn't let up until he was wailing. For good measure, she gave the other boy a smack. "Sit still and be quiet!"

She shouted at her husband, "Damn it, Mustafa, do something about your sons!"

He pulled out a big bar of chocolate, broke it in half, and handed each boy a portion. Like ravenous rats, they tore through the paper.

"Since his accident at the steel works," she moaned, "Mustafa mopes around the house, feeling sorry for himself. Does nothing except complain about the pain."

I faced the man still picking his nails. "Are you in much pain?"

"This is right. Take medicine."

"He takes more than just medicine," sneered the wife. "After he hurt his back, Mustafa's been only good at complaining, drinking, and gambling. If I didn't hide the money, we'd have nothing to eat. We've been forced to move that many times because our rent wasn't paid. Last month, our car was repossessed. I work my guts out in a stinking fish and chips shop while Yasamin minds the boys."

I looked at the two feral kids whose mouths and hands were smeared with melted chocolate. When they returned to constructing a castle, the wooden blocks became all smudged.

I wondered whether my morning dose of Xanax would last. I checked the wall clock–10:15. Still had thirty-five minutes left in the interview. I faced the sullen daughter, her eyes transfixed on her toes. "Your mother tells me you care for the boys when she's working. Is that hard?"

The 17-year-old grunted.

"She's not that smart," confided Gwenda. "She has epilepsy. Has never done well in school and hasn't any friends. She came with Mustafa from Turkey eight years ago."

"Where's her biological mother?"

"Turkey. Mustafa left her in a mental institution when she attacked him with a butcher's knife. We don't know where she is. Could still be locked up."

"This is right," echoed her husband.

"I met Mustafa shortly after he arrived in Australia, and we got married."

"Waagh!" cried Kamal. A fight erupted with fists and brown smudges landing everywhere. Mustafa reached for another bar of chocolate to appease the boys while Gwenda lashed out with her hands.

When I tried calming the couple, who were in desperate need of parenting skills, Kamal approached me. The six-year-old boy wiped his snotty nose with his sleeve. "Can I... (sniff, sniff) ... sit on your lap?"

My eyes veered from the chocolate stains on his fingers to my tan trousers. I quickly pointed toward the wooden blocks. "Why don't you make me something?"

His brother brought me a stack of red logs. "You can help me build a house."

"Hang on, I was talking to Kamal."

"We can use these for our house," persisted Dursen.

Kamal edged closer to my pants. I grabbed him before he sat on my lap. Dursen whacked him in the head with a red log.

"Waagh!" blubbered Kamal. He wiped his nose with his hands then slopped them across my pants.

I glared angrily at Dursen. "You seem pretty angry!"

He replied by kicking Kamal's leg.

"Waagh!"

I looked at Mustafa, whose head was nodding. He was fast asleep! The mother came to the rescue and whacked Dursen in the fanny. "I can't take the boys anymore," she sobbed. "They're always fighting. I don't know what to do."

"Are there any relatives who could help you out?"

"Mum used to. But she had a heart attack last month. She's recovering in hospital." Gwenda dissolved into tears. "When I was a little girl, my father beat me. I left home when I was 16. That's when I met Victor. I got pregnant and we married. Mum would have nothing to do with me. After Victor died and I married Mustafa, Mum came good and helped me out. She'd watch the boys while Yasamin and I did the shopping. Now she's in hospital. There's no one to help..."

As she wept uncontrollably, I passed the tissues. "You sure had it rough. What about neighbors?"

"We've moved so many times. Now, the woman in the house next to us causes nothing but trouble."

"Why?"

"Mustafa's always fighting with her about her dogs. They poo in Mustafa's garden. He once threatened to poison them, so she reported us to the child welfare. Now we're being investigated for neglect."

This family didn't need therapy–they needed a major overhaul! I didn't have a clue where to begin with them, and I wasn't game to ask Smelder for help. No more one-way mirrors, thank you very much.

"Do the boys wet the bed?" I asked.

"Yes, Dursen does," she sniffled. "Almost every night."

"Would you like me to help you with Dursen's bed wetting?"

Gwenda reached for another Kleenex. "The pediatric ward referred us here. Kamal has undescended testicles. The doctor suggested we receive family counseling. I don't know why. They said you could help us."

"If we could stop Dursen from wetting the bed, one problem would be solved, wouldn't it?"

She dabbed her reddened eye. "I guess I wouldn't have to wash the sheets as often."

Kamal pointed to his brother's genitals. "Pssss..."

Dursen thumped him on the back.

"Waagh!"

I offered the mother some help. "I have this gadget, a pad that you put under Dursen's sheets at night. An alarm will sound every time he wets the bed. All you have to do is..."

PLAGUE OF THE BOGONG

SUNDAY, OCTOBER 16

She turned off the T.V. and handed me the Mortine bug spray. "Quick, Piotr! Spritz the ugly creatures."

"Hang on, Ma. the Evening News is almost over."

She angrily grabbed for the can and winced with pain. Her hand reached for her side.

I was fed up with her constant whining. Over six weeks had passed since her fall. The ribs were slow to heal. With every new ache and pain, she sought my aid to complete yet another lengthy list of chores. I was tired, not only of being her errand boy, but of her perpetual reminder "If only you had done what I asked, I never would have fallen." Six weeks was more than enough penance. My guilt was quickly dissolving.

"Hurry, Piotr," she shouted. "I don't want them messing my house."

"Yea! Yea! I'll do it now."

With insect spray in hand, I stalked the dreaded bogong moths that had infested the house. This spring massive numbers of the charcoal-gray moths migrated south from Queensland. Attracted by the lights in the house, they managed to evade all our screens and caused Ma great consternation by whirling around the light globes, crawling on the walls, and appearing in places no one would ever suspect.

"*Tutaj!* Here!" she yelled, spotting another.

I pointed the Mortine toward the bogong flying near Ma. I was keen to get rid of the pest.

YET ANOTHER
MANAGEMENT MEETING
🐾

MONDAY, OCTOBER 17

Wearing a neck brace, a very glum Theresa sat upright in her chair. Last week she totaled her red Honda and incurred a mild whiplash. She seemed more unhappy, however, about missing her bodybuilding than losing a car.

Earl was off with yet another sickie while the rest of us were still recovering from the flu.

"We must discuss the Jenson/Murray family," coughed Maxine. "The court hearing is coming up within the next couple of weeks. Some of us may be testifying."

"Are the reports ready?" asked Dr. Smelder.

"Just about. We don't have actual testimony from the two boys implicating the father, but I'm prepared to give evidence he was the sexual perpetrator."

Gerard reached for the case file. "I'll need to review the videotapes of my interviews with Mr. Jenson."

"We don't have them," added Henry sheepishly. "When you were sick last week, we received a call from the mother's solicitor. The court wanted access to all of the videotapes. Since you weren't here, Maxine and I decided to hand them over."

"You w-w-what?"

"Don't get your knickers in a knot," rasped Maxine. "They could have issued a court order for their release." "Did you check the tapes before handing them over?" Henry blanched white. "No."

"Christ Almighty!" stormed Gerard. "You could've released incriminating evidence!"

Leela kindled the flames. "One of the videotapes, showing you interviewing Mr. Jenson in front to the mirror, contained the team's discussion which followed the session."

"Goddamn it! Does anyone remember what we said?"

Leela obliged. "Maxine remarked that the father was guilty as hell."

Smelder slammed the file on the floor. "That does it, Benton! I'll have your ass for this!"

"We had to surrender those tapes!" defended the nurse. "If you weren't so obsessed with filming everything, there wouldn't be any videotapes."

"Don't blame the video-equipment. Relinquishing those tapes without even checking them was sheer stupidity."

Maxine wheezed, "What the hell would you have me do? They would've subpoenaed them."

"The least you could've done was edit the sessions. Any dodo would've done that. I don't want my department looking like a bunch of incompetent fools. Word spreads quickly. Our reputation's at stake."

Maxine's eyes blazed with fury. "Your reputation is always at stake!"

"I'm not taking anymore of your crap," growled Smelder. "I've already seen the Medical Superintendent."

"And I've spoken with the Nurses' Union," she retaliated. "As a matter of fact, my grievances will be taken before the hospital board. We'll see who has the last laugh!"

"Don't threaten me! You've never liked the fact that I brought professionalism to this department."

Theresa held her neck brace. "Before you arrived, Gerard, our team was cohesive. You've continually provoked staff dissension."

"That's not true," defended Leela. She reached to comfort Smelder's arm. "His expertise has strengthened our reputation. We receive referrals all the way from Newcastle."

"He probably gets a kick-back," sneered Maxine.

The battle was on once again. This time, holy Henry didn't even attempt to make peace. Daylight was fast becoming a nightmare. The walls were closing in. My chest tightened. I found it difficult to breathe. My legs wobbled like jelly. I was losing control. The stress... overwhelming. I needed another Xanax. And our team needed help. Now!

My cup of tea fell to the carpet. "Excuse me," I blurted, gulping for air. "But... ugh... I... that is,we... need help. Maybe one of our consultants could... er... help sort this out. I'm... ugh... finding it hard to breathe, er, think, with all this fighting."

Eyes turned toward me. The walls moved closer. The knot squeezing my stomach squeezed tighter. My heart pounded louder tom-toms.

"I wouldn't call it fighting," rebuked Smelder. "Just team conflict. Your suggestion, however, does have some merit. Our family therapy consultant, Frank King, could help us resolve these team issues once and for all."

"Hang on," defied Maxine. "What's he going to do? Perform a strategic paradox on us? Fiona Crompton would be a far better facilitator."

Gerard stamped his foot. "I, sure as hell, will not sit around with an analyst and free-associate about dreams and fantasies."

Maxine became equally entrenched. "I won't tolerate Frank King!"

I panicked. "We need help! Can't we find someone else us? Please?!"

"I agree with Peter," supported Henry. "The tension is becoming unbearable. We should decide on someone neutral, one who could instill us with hope."

Despite the mumbling and moaning, everyone, to my great relief, agreed to think about it and suggest names at the next management meeting. All we had to do was find someone courageous or stupid enough to treat our team.

We never did return to the discussion about the Jenson/Murray family. Gerard aborted the rest of the meeting. Just as well. I reached for another Xanax. Obviously three tablets a day wasn't enough.

HORNSBY SHOPPING MALL

THURSDAY, OCTOBER 20

5:34 p.m. I waited at the chemist for my new prescription. I had increased the dosage to four times a day. The anxiety attacks had subsided, but my supply was perilously low. I found another doctor, not far from the hospital, who remedied my distress with a new script. Wasn't prepared to visit Dr. Wojtecko again. He would've raved on about seeing a psychiatrist, the last person I needed.

"Remember me?" asked a stocky boy pulling on my arm.

He looked vaguely familiar stuffed in his khaki school shorts. I guessed that he was eight or nine years old, but I couldn't quite place him.

"Where do I know you?" I asked.

"I'm Angelo Tortelli. I saw you at the hospital."

The Italian encopretic! I hadn't seen him since our last interview. How could I forget? It was on my birthday, February 16th.

"How are you doing?"

"Good," he answered.

I motioned for him to join me away from the crowd. "How's your problem?"

He shrugged his shoulders. "All fixed."

"Really?" I couldn't believe it. "How?"

"Mum took me to one of them back doctors, a kiro-hactic."

"Not a chiropractor?"

"Yea. One of them. She took x-rays then bunged a machine on me neck."

"And?"

"It stopped."

"What?"

Angelo's eyes darted around the store as if to make sure no one could hear. "The poodling," he whispered.

"You're not soiling anymore?!"

His eyes dropped to his shoes. "Naw."

"It stopped altogether?!"

"If it ever happens, Mum takes me back. The lady bungs me neck with a machine and the problem's fixed again."

That was the most outrageous thing I ever heard–a chiropractor curing an encopretic. This kid had psychological problems, not spinal injuries. It must've been a spontaneous remission.

"Pinowski!" called the chemist. "You're prescription's ready."

"I have to go. How's your mother?"

Once more, he shrugged his shoulders. "She has migraines. Sent me to get some aspirin. She's buying some veggies at the green grocer if you want to see her."

"Maybe another time," I said. "Just say hello. I have to run."

I paid for the Xanax and left with the parcel of peach-colored tablets clutched tightly in my hand.

SUPREME COURT

WEDNESDAY, OCTOBER 26

After several postponements, the hearing for the Jenson/Murray case finally proceeded this morning. Since the couple had never been married, this custody dispute could not be heard in Family Court and had to be scheduled before the Supreme Court. Today's hearing would determine the legal guardian.

Our department held evidence which weighted heavily against the father. Therefore Gerard, Maxine, and Henry were subpoenaed along with the hospital pediatrician, Dr. Helen Towers. Smelder allowed me to take a flexi-day and offer support for Henry who, worrying obsessively about his first court appearance, had deteriorated into a blob of jelly. "There's an evil presence lurking in the shadows," he warned. I offered him a Xanax, but he refused.

I quietly unwrapped a stick of Juicy Fruit gum then, pretending to cough, snuck the morsel into my mouth. Chewing wasn't sanctioned in these dignified surroundings which still bore the resemblance of 18th century England. An austere Judge Anthony Stanton, black-robed and white-wigged, was perched high on his throne while, well below him, sat the court's secretary and court reporter. The barristers were already in possession of the long Bar Table which formed the boundary between them and the judge.

As I sucked on the Juicy Fruit, I spotted the father's counsel, the renowned Sydney barrister, Mr. Nicholas Fulster. The tall, stout man with a weathered, wrinkled face—indicating countless battles of jurisprudence—presented an impressive figure in his jet-black robe, bone-colored wig, and white bib. The cunning barrister had already earned his pay by having the case transferred from a female judge who may have been less sympathetic to his client. It was obvious that, as a solicitor himself, Richard Jenson had hired one of the best.

Opposing Mr. Fulster was the much younger barrister, Victoria Phelan. Make-up couldn't hide her fresh, youthful face which looked more like that of a university student. A sprocket of light brown hair trailed under the curly horsehair wig which helped add an air of maturity and respect. Recently procured by legal aid, she was acting on behalf of the mother, Gayle Murray.

The testimony of the parents painstakingly unfolded as each side sought legal custody of the two boys, four-year-old Conrad and eight-year-old Richard Jr. The couple had been separated one-and-a-half years, and each accused the other of gross neglect and contributing to the sexual abuse of the children.

Sporting a brown and black pantsuit, the 29-year-old mother, Gayle Murray, offered her evidence first. She painted a picture of a perverted father who molested the boys at his home. She was convinced his custodial weekends were spent playing sexually perverse games with the children. To substantiate her claims, she described an incident, when they once lived together, where he painted the naked boys with markers. She speculated that the children must've been sworn to secrecy with threats by the father that they or he would be taken away.

In contrast, the 35-year-old Richard Jenson, immaculately groomed in a gray three-piece suit, testified that the mother was more interested in drugs and other men than in the care of the children. He vehemently denied any wrongdoing and postulated that the sexual abuse occurred at the hands of a boyfriend who frequented the mother's house. According to the father, the boys couldn't reveal the truth because they were petrified with fear for their lives. The boyfriend, an ex-boxer, was physically abusive and had threatened to punch Mr. Jenson when he picked up his children.

With the charges and counter-charges flying back and forth, it became obvious the testimony of our department would affect the outcome of the case. The pediatrician, Dr. Helen Towers, was the first one from the hospital to take the side witness box. The short, trim woman was sworn in. She reminded me of a stern schoolmarm prepared to address a class.

Victoria Phelan, standing pompously behind the Bar Table, first established Dr. Towers' credentials. The barrister elicited from the 36-year-old doctor that she was the pediatrician-in-charge for the past three years at the Royal Prince Andrew Hospital, and that she graduated with class honors from the University of Sydney.

Victoria Phelan continued, "When did you first have contact with Ms. Murray and her two boys?"

"They were referred to me this year on Tuesday, the 31st of May," answered the fastidious pediatrician.

"What was the reason for the referral?"

"The mother had cause to believe her boys were sexually molested and had notified the police, who then referred the youngsters to the sexual assault unit at the hospital. Later, the children were brought to me on the pediatric ward."

"Did you examine the boys?"

"Yes."

"And what were your findings?"

Dr. Towers cleared her throat. "The four-year-old boy, Conrad, complained that his bottom was continually hurting, and it was hard to go to the toilet. I conducted a physical examination and concluded, after using the Reflex Anal Dilation Test, also known as R.A.D., that the boy's anus reflexively dilated to produce a positive assessment. This pathology was consistent with anal penetration as a consequence of sexual abuse."

"Did you also examine his brother, Richard Jr.?"

"Yes."

"And your findings?"

"The results of the R.A.D. Test were also positive. There was traumatic dilation of the anus."

"And your conclusions, Dr. Towers?"

"Based on the medical evidence, both boys were sexually abused."

"Thank you, Doctor," said the young barrister. "I have no further questions, Your Honor." She dispensed a flourish with her charcoal gown and sat down.

Judge Stanton directed the defense to begin cross-examination. Nicholas Fulster slowly rose and peered over the Bar Table as the short pediatrician pulled out a hanky.

"I want to clarify a few points, Doctor. This examination you mentioned. Is this the same test, also called the Anal Wink Reflex?"

"Yes it is."

"Doctor, I'd like you to explain to the Court, in layman's terms if you please, how you would specifically conduct this examination."

Helen Towers wiped her forehead. "Basically, the patient is asked to bend over and touch his toes in order to expose the anus which is then manually checked to determine if the anal ring is tight. If there has been an incidence of sexual abuse, the anus would contract then expand, in anticipation of some penetration."

"Was the Anal Wink Reflex your only indicator of sexual abuse on the two boys in question?"

"Physically, yes."

The barrister, still focusing his gaze on the witness box, paused to accentuate his next question. "What percentage of sexual abuse cases actually reveal physical evidence?"

The pediatrician shook her head. "I don't have an exact percentage."

"Isn't it true that, according to the research, *less* than 40% of such cases show physical evidence that a child has been sexually assaulted?"

"Quite possibly."

"And that with the majority of children, it's very difficult to actually show, in the way of physical evidence, that a child has been sexually abused."

Dr. Towers' voice crackled. "The physical exam is only one part of the assessment. We take into account the child's report, plus the social and psychological..."

"Excuse me for interrupting, Doctor. But we need to establish the validity of this so-called medical test. Is it not possible that an anal rupture could occur as a result of chronic constipation?"

"I suppose so."

"Wasn't Conrad complaining about constipation?"

"Yes."

"Tell me, Doctor. What are the differences, validated in the literature, between the results of the Anal Wink Reflex Test due to chronic constipation and the results due to sexual abuse?"

Helen Towers looked up at the judge, then glared at the barrister who was becoming a pain in the ass.

"We're waiting!" boomed the deep baritone voice. *"What* are the differences?"

"They're not really all that different. But when you take into account..."

"Would you say that assessing a sexually abused child *only* by anal dilation would be, quite simply, bad medicine?"

"Obviously you have to take into consideration all the other factors..."

"So evidence based solely on the Anal Wink would be inadequate."

"Well... yes."

"Thank you, Doctor. That will be all. No further questions, Your Honor."

Nicholas Fulster swished his robes and smugly sat down. A dour Helen Towers climbed down from the witness box.

The younger barrister appeared visibly shaken by her opponent's cross-examination. She scanned her notes and called Maxine to the stand.

After Maxine was sworn-in and her credentials were established, Victoria Phelan's voice grew stronger. "I understand you've been counseling the mother, Ms. Murray, for quite some time. Can you tell us exactly how long?"

"Gayle Murray and her boys were referred to our department after seeing Dr. Towers on the 31st of May. I've been counseling the mother twice a week for the past five months."

"What is your impression of Ms. Murray?"

"When she came to our department, she was emotionally distressed. She was in a state of shock and grief about the sexual abuse and needed intensive counseling and support."

"Has she been helped by the counseling?"

"Definitely!"

"In your assessment, do you think the mother is competent to raise the children?"

Maxine looked at the mother and smiled. "Yes. I have no hesitation in stating she is a very competent mother."

Gayle Murray returned the smile.

"What about the accusation that she's a drug addict?"

"She openly admits that, at one time, she was addicted to Valium. It seems that the many years of living with Mr. Jenson had placed her under an inordinate amount of stress. Taking Valium was her escape. When she left him, the main cause of her distress was gone, and she kicked the habit."

"So, in your professional judgment, you would say that Ms. Murray would be a very competent mother."

"Yes. Absolutely!"

Mr. Fulster leapt to his feet. "Objection, Your Honor."

"What is the objection?" asked the judge.

"This witness has reached a conclusion not related to any of the evidence she's just given. The witness was just talking about the mother's addiction. She cannot make a conclusion, based on the drug involvement, that she'd be a better mother."

"Objection sustained."

Victoria Phelan glared at her antagonist. She tried another question. "Speaking as a professional who's been involved with this case for five months, who do you think committed the sexual offenses?"

"The father, Mr. Jenson."

"Please explain your reasons to His Honor."

Maxine cleared her throat. "The boys acknowledged that a man interfered with them but wouldn't say who. The person appears to be a trusted figure. Considering that, at one time, the father had drawn pictures with colored markers across his sons' naked bodies, and considering that he is trusted by his boys, I could only conclude that his behavior is consistent with that of a perpetrator."

The young barrister accentuated the point by turning around and staring at Mr. Jenson. "Thank you. No further questions, Your Honor."

I pulled out another stick of Juicy Fruit as the serve passed to the weathered Nicholas Fulster. He began a fast-paced interrogation.

"How frequently have you been seeing the mother?"

"Several times a week," responded Maxine.

"How many times has that actually been?"

"Approximately 43 sessions."

"Did you talk to her on the phone in between interviews?"

"Yes. If she was in crisis or needed support."

"Well, exactly how often did you talk to her during the week?"

"As I said, there were two sessions a week and sometimes the occasional phone call."

"Have there been times when, in fact, you've talked to Gayle Murray every day?"

Maxine glared at the man in black. "During the initial crisis, it was necessary to give her emotional support."

Nicholas Fulster hesitated a moment while he pondered his next move. "Nurse Benton. Is it often that you give your personal phone number to clients?"

"Only in emergencies."

"Was Gayle Murray such an emotional wreck that she needed your home phone number?"

"I gave her my number because she was devastated after..."

The barrister interrupted by raising his voice. "Did you ever call Gayle Murray from your home over the weekend?!"

"As I said, when she first came for counseling, I wanted to make sure she was okay."

"Do you spend many of your weekends checking whether clients are all right?"

"Of course not."

"Let me ask you this. Do you *ever* phone male clients on the weekend?"

"Not usually."

"Have you *ever* phoned a male client from your home on a weekend?"

The nurse was silent.

Nicholas Fulster tapped his pencil on the table. "I repeat: have you ever called a male client from your home on a weekend? Yes or no?"

"No."

"Have you ever called other women clients over the weekend?"

"On occasion. I have."

"I ask you. Why do you need to phone female clients on weekends from your home, but somehow don't ever see the need to call male clients?"

Small beads of perspiration settled on Maxine's brow. "Because I work primarily with female clients," she sneered. "They're usually the victims of sexual abuse."

The pencil tapping increased. "Let me ask you this. Do you spend much time with men socially?"

"I object to this line of questioning!" shouted Victoria Phelan, jumping to her feet. "This line of questioning has no bearing on the case."

Her adversary faced the judge. "Your Honor, I'm merely trying to establish that Nurse Benton is extremely biased toward women. As a result, she's become overly involved with her client which extends into the weekends. I want to establish that it's impossible for Nurse Benton to offer an objective assessment about the case."

Judge Stanton peered over his glasses, first at Maxine, then at the wily barrister. "I'm satisfied as to its relevancy. I'll allow the questioning to continue."

Nicholas Fulster's eyes blazed. "Nurse Benton, to get the record straight, are you a lesbian?"

"I object!" cried the female barrister.

So did Maxine. "How dare you ask me that question?" she blasted. "Just because I work with women doesn't mean I'm a lesbian. You men always jump to the conclusion there has to be something sexual about women supporting each another emotionally. If most of your clients are men, which I presume they are, does that mean you're homosexual? You're only after the fat paycheck you'll receive when the father's off scot-free. What about the boys?! Who's interested in their..."

"Mr. Fulster!" the impatient Judge announced sharply. "This witness is not here on trial. Confine your questions to the evidence for which this witness is being called."

Judge Stanton then faced the witness. "Mrs. Benton. Please confine your remarks to the questions asked."

Nicholas Fulster offered a quick riposte. "I would have thought a simple *yes* or *no* would do, Nurse Benton. However, I'll withdraw the question. It's quite obvious you're sensitive about your social life. I'll ask you something less threatening."

"Mr. Fulster!" chastised the judge. "Just ask the question."

"I'm sorry, Your Honor. Nurse Benton, you mentioned that the mother used drugs to cope with the stress from living with my client?"

Her chest puffed out indignantly. "That's right!"

"Did Gayle Murray ever abuse herself with drugs *prior* to her relationship with Mr. Jenson?"

"I don't know."

"You don't know?" asked the barrister in mock horror. "Why you just stated earlier that Gayle Murray took drugs to cope with her relationship. One would assume that if she wasn't with Mr. Jenson, there wouldn't be any need to take drugs at all. That is, if we're talking about a stable woman! Isn't it a fact that when she was 19 years old, Gayle Murray was picked up for growing cannabis? And isn't it also true that her solicitor was able to have the charges dropped because of illegal entry by the police? That solicitor—my client—eventually fathered her children. Let's get the record straight. Gayle Murray began abusing herself with drugs before my client ever entered her life."

Maxine folded her arms tightly. "The marijuana was a minor..."

"Let's talk about your accusation. You indicated that my client was responsible for sexually abusing his children. How many sessions have you had with Mr. Jenson?"

"None. Those sessions were handled by our director, Dr. Smelder."

"So, in fact, you've never even interviewed Mr. Jenson?"

"No. It's the department's practice to..."

"How many interviews have you had with his sons?"

"As I was trying to say earlier, for sexual assault cases we allocate individual family members to different therapists. Henry Snart counseled the boys."

"So, in fact, the only person you've actually seen in your professional capacity, not including your weekend social phone calls, is the mother?"

Maxine seethed, "Those weren't social..."

"To get the record straight, you've never actually interviewed Mr. Jenson or the two boys."

"No."

"It appears that with your close intimate relationship with Gayle Murray, you would obviously be biased toward her point of view."

"Not necessarily..."

"No further questions." Nicholas Fulster swished back his robes and triumphantly lowered himself into his chair.

Maxine remained open-mouthed in the witness box until the judge released her. "You may step down."

Victoria Phelan was visibly distressed about Fulster's performance. She shuffled her papers and stammered, "M-m-my next witness is Henry Snart."

"Pray for me, Peter," he pleaded as his long legs stumbled to get past me. He fell on my lap and I pushed him onward. He fumbled to the front and tripped over the step into the witness box. His hands visibly shook while he took the oath. He should've taken my advice and popped a pill.

Victoria Phelan took a deep breath and corroborated that Henry was the pastoral care counselor at the Royal Prince Andrew Hospital. "You're the boys' therapist. Is that correct?"

"Uh, yes."

"And how long have you been counseling Conrad and Richard Jr.?"

"Approximately five months. I've, uh... had about 16 sessions with them."

"Do you think you know them pretty well?"

"I... uh... think so. They're... uh... beginning to open up and trust me."

She picked up a folder. "In your written assessment, you've indicated that the boys were sexually abused."

"Y-y-yes. They... uh... acknowledged that a man had interfered with their bottoms and played with their... uh... penises. Their behavior was also, uh, highly sexualized."

"What exactly do you mean by sexualized?"

Henry coughed and cleared his throat. He spoke as if by rote. "Sexualization is a state of mind or behavior that is inappropriately or unwittingly created in a child exposed to either sexual thoughts, feelings, or behavior."

"Can you elaborate?"

He crossed, then uncrossed his legs. "A young child that displays an advanced knowledge of sexual behavior suggests he's, uh, been subjected to sexual attentions by an adult."

"Can you give us examples of Conrad's and Richard's sexualization?"

Henry gazed at the floor and crossed his legs once more.

"Conrad was more explicit. During the therapy session with our anatomical dolls, he... uh... used the large male doll, which he called 'daddy dolly', to stuff a pencil into the smaller male doll's bottom. In addition, the mother caught Conrad... uh... fondling their dog's penis. Another time he was seen poking sticks into the dog's anus."

"What about Richard Jr.," asked Victoria Phelan.

Perspiration trickled down his cheek. "The school reported that Richard had asked one of the children if he," Henry coughed, "wanted to be sucked off."

"Where do you think the children learned this behavior?"

"From a trusted male."

"In your professional opinion, who do you think that trusted person was?"

"The father, Mr. Jenson."

"Can you elaborate?"

Henry cleared his throat once more. "Conrad and Richard Jr. continued to demonstrate through the anatomical dolls that the father was the abuser. The boys, when playing with 'daddy dolly', consistently exposed the doll's genitals and periodically penetrated the young male doll."

"Thank you. No further questions."

Nicholas Fulster stood and stared. Henry's own two eyes reacted by wandering in opposite directions while he nervously uncrossed then crossed his legs. Had the court permitted the barrister to step from behind the Bar Table, Henry surely would've turned into royal jelly.

"It's Dr. Snart, isn't it?"

"No sir. I'm not a doctor."

He feigned surprise and apologized. "Oh, I'm sorry. You said in your evidence to my learned colleague that you are a pastoral care counselor."

"Yes."

"Exactly what kind of training does one of these pastoral counselors receive?"

"Usually we, uh, have a degree in divinity. In addition, we take numerous courses in psychology and counseling."

"I see," pondered the barrister. He fingered a button on his robe. "Exactly how many formal courses in child psychology have you completed?"

"I've, uh, attended quite a few at Macquarie University."

"Have you had more training in theology or psychology?"

"I've definitely studied more theology."

"I understand you've written several papers analyzing Emil Brunner's work, *Eternal Hope.*"

Henry blinked in astonishment. "Why, yes."

"And it seems you've become fairly knowledgeable about hope and it's effect on clients. In fact, you've given several talks on the subject."

Henry seemed flattered. "Yes, I have." He uncrossed his legs and sat upright.

Nicholas Fulster pondered for a moment. "Tell me, Reverend. How many papers have you written on child sexual abuse?"

"Uh... none."

"How many talks have you given on the subject of sexual abuse?"

Henry's hands fidgeted as he shook his head. "None."

The crafty barrister feigned laughter. "And we're supposed to believe you're an expert witness?!"

Nicholas Fulster faced the judge and mocked a look of horror. "How can we believe that someone who acknowledges that he himself knows more about theology than psychology and has never spoken or written about the field of sexual abuse, how can we believe that such a person can speak with authority on such a critical matter as this? I have no further questions."

Judge Stanton excused the shame-faced witness. The seasoned barrister hesitated. "Before you leave, Mr. Snart, there is one further question, with Your Honor's permission."

The judge nodded.

"Did the children, at any time during your interviews, did they ever state categorically that their father abused them physically or sexually?"

"Well... uh... no."

"Thank you! That will be all."

The judge announced a 15 minute adjournment, and our demoralized team filed out for a quick cuppa. Helen Towers rushed back to the pediatric ward, probably to re-examine her sexually abused patients.

"You two acted like a bunch of galahs," chastised our director. "God knows what the court will think of my department."

Maxine was livid. "That barrister's a bastard! He'll make that slimy father look like a saint."

"You should've been more prepared. I told you..."

The squabbling continued throughout recess.

When court resumed, Dr. Smelder was called. A rather worn and tired-looking Victoria Phelan scanned the child psychiatrist's report.

Having elicited that Smelder was an expert on family dynamics, and that he had interviewed Mr. Jenson over six sessions, she reviewed his findings that the father was often sexually provocative with the children. She finally asked the damning question. "Doctor, in your professional opinion, do you believe the father, Mr. Jenson, sexually abused his two sons?"

A confident Dr. Smelder declared, "No question about it. As you have it in my report, he fits the clinical picture of a man who would sexually molest children."

"Are you sure?"

"In my clinical opinion, based on well over 20 years of professional experience, Mr. Jenson's behavioral patterns, which include massive denial, demonstrate that he is the perpetrator."

"Thank you very much, Dr. Smelder. No further questions." Without even a hint of a flourish, she slouched into her chair.

An air of expectancy filled the courtroom as Nicholas Fulster rose. I removed my gum and furtively stuck it under the wooden bench.

"Dr. Smelder, how many years have you been director of the Child and Adolescent Psychiatry Department?"

"Approximately five years."

"I gather you're interested in finding the truth in this case?"

"Naturally."

"Would you leave no stone unturned to seek the truth?"

"I'm primarily interested in helping those boys," countered Gerard. "They need a safe environment."

"In the course of gaining your information, did you interview the mother's boyfriend, the ex-pugilist?"

"No."

"And why not?" mused the barrister. "I thought you were concerned about the boys' safety."

"Since the boyfriend wasn't living with the mother, it wasn't our brief to see him. That was the job of the Department of Family and Children Services."

"Surely, if you were interested in the truth, you would have made provisions to interview him?"

"Our brief was to assess and counsel only the family members."

"Couldn't it be possible that the boyfriend, an ex-boxer, might be responsible for the sexual abuse? He did have direct access to the children."

"It seemed highly unlikely. According to the mother, there were very few times when he was alone with the children."

"But can you absolutely rule out the possibility that he never had the opportunity to molest the boys, especially since you've never interviewed him? My client continually expressed concern that the boyfriend was the perpetrator."

"As I said, that was a matter for the Department of Family and Children Services."

For the first time, Nicholas Fulster seemed frustrated. "Let's leave that for now," he said testily. "How long have you known Nurse Benton?"

"About five years."

"Would you describe her as competent?"

"She's very conscientious with her clients, if that's what you're trying to get at."

"Would you describe her as professional?"

"Yes."

"Do you think she's been very professional with this case?"

"Of course."

The black-robed man tapped a pencil on his writing pad. "Would you ever have disagreements with her?"

"Obviously, there will be times when colleagues disagree," came Gerard's retort. He smiled and added, "I assume you would have healthy disagreements with your colleagues."

The barrister wasn't amused. His pencil rapping quickened. "Have you ever disagreed with Nurse Benton over this case?"

"Occasionally."

"Could you tell the court what your disagreements were about?"

"Probably about case management. I may have thought Nurse Benton needn't have seen the mother as frequently. But as I mentioned, disagreements occur in any profession. I personally believe differences foster a healthy critical attitude."

Sitting on my left, Maxine gasped at Gerard's statement.

"That's all very interesting. But I'm puzzled about your methods of assessments. Surely there must be a science to all this."

"Absolutely. During our management meetings we discuss our cases and develop hypotheses about the diagnosis and prognosis. After we synthesize the material, our team arrives at a conclusion."

The pencil tapping stopped. "Sounds very impressive. I'm reassured this case is in such competent hands. Your Honor, I wish to show a videotape excerpt of the therapy team assessing this case. Their discussion follows an interview with my client."

Victoria Phelan jumped to her feet. "I strongly object, Your Honor! If that procedure is allowed, my client's confidentiality will be sorely abused. My colleague has already seen Dr. Smelder's report. That's all that's relevant."

The judge sought clarification. "Mr. Fulster?"

"Your Honor, this evidence is vital because it establishes the basis and method in which this report was created."

"Overruled."

A trolley with a television and VCR were wheeled into the courtroom. The barrister inserted a videotape and the television flickered. Our team, in the midst of a heated discussion, burst onto the screen.

Maxine was yelling at Gerard. "That sleaze bag is guilty as hell!"

Smelder berated her. "Don't go off half-cocked, for Christ sake. You're always blaming the men."

Maxine's face flushed bright red. "Are you blind? This mongrel is screwing his kids under your nose."

"I'm not totally convinced he's the guilty party. It could have been the mother's boyfriend."

"He could be guilty too. But I can feel it in my bones. This fucking bastard's been abusing his sons."

"Hang on one goddamn minute! You've blown a few cases in the past with your rabid crusade against men. The mother's not totally innocent. She dumped her sons with the father on the weekend so she could screw around with that pea-brain boxer. At least the father cared enough to look after his kids."

"And look what happened?..."

"We've seen enough!" bellowed the baritone voice. "Your Honor, this is an example of our *expert* witnesses at work. We need to seriously question the merit of their evidence." He gestured toward Maxine. "We have a nurse who obviously hates men." Then pointed at Gerard. "And a child psychiatrist who, in addition to questioning his nurse's competence, alternates between stating on videotape that my client is a caring father, then suggesting, here in court, that he's a molester."

Gerard snorted, "I object to your insinuation that..."

The barrister's hand waved toward Henry. "Plus, we have a minister who knows more about the theology of hope than the psychology of sexual abuse. What and whom are we to believe? And I again point out, there are no concrete statements from the children implicating my client."

"Just hang on a minute!" fumed the witness.

"No further questions!" shouted Nicholas Fulster.

Our team was well and truly done like a turkey.

The one day truce between Gerard and Maxine came to an abrupt end. "You bitch," seethed the psychiatrist as he departed from the building. "Before you released those tapes to the court, you should've edited them. You made me look like a goddamn fool."

"It's your own bloody fault," shouted Maxine. "Why the hell were you recording the team's discussion?"

Henry and I meekly followed. It was time for another peach tablet.

Henry and I were chatting in the secretary's office when Maxine arrived like a raging bull.

"The bastard! Just got off the phone with Gayle Murray. The court handed down its decision. She was awarded custody, but the father was allowed access on alternate weekends. The bastard! On top of that, the sexual abuse allegations against him were dropped because of insufficient evidence. Thanks to our legal system, another two boys get screwed. The only saving grace was the court's recommendation that the two children continue therapy."

Maxine jabbed her finger at Henry. "You better monitor the boys' visits with their father. Protecting them rests in your hands!"

MELBOURNE CUP DAY

TUESDAY, NOVEMBER 1

Why couldn't we have a public holiday like Melbourne so we could watch the two-mile horse race? While the rest of the hospital partied and cheered their favorite steeds, our department did bugger-all. No bets. No party. No one was talking.

VIOLET STRUTHERS' FAREWELL
FULL MOON
🦃

With staff conflict zooming past 10 on the Richter scale, we reluctantly gathered in the conference room. The mounting tension within the team finally forced the geriatric psychiatrist to tender her resignation. "Now I can visit the mud people in New Guinea," she proclaimed. "They remind me of the clay people in Flash Gordon."

The strain in the department had taken its toll. During the past two weeks, Violet had completely forgotten to wear her wig. On occasion, she had been seen scouring the halls and, while pointing to her tatty gray mess, asking our clients if they'd found any spare hair.

I doubted anyone would miss her. Recently, she spent her one-and-a-half days reading cook books. Not a bad way to earn a few quid, especially if she picked up an extra recipe or two. For today's occasion, she brought her special version of microwaved devil's food cake.

While paying tribute to Violet's 30-plus years in psychiatry seemed the right thing to do, we were hardly enthusiastic. With very little to say to one another, we just sat around and picked at the soggy dough. Smelder presented a gift of a small crystal vase and managed to say a few words in her honor. "Violet, you've finally gained your freedom from the responsibilities of psychiatry..."

"Look!" she exclaimed. "Outside! The jacaranda tree! The blue flowers are blooming. They're gorgeous..."

GROUP CONSULTATION

T

TUESDAY, NOVEMBER 22

2:33 p.m. Like a family waiting for their therapist, we fidgeted in the sweltering conference room. With summer nearly upon us, the air conditioning had failed, and the spell of sultry weather slowly baked the department. Theresa, still wearing a white neck brace for whiplash, huddled with Maxine while Gerard, having regressed to an oral fixation on his smelly pipe, whispered with Leela. Henry and I were sandwiched between the two camps and made idle chatter about the heat. Coincidentally, Earl called in earlier, too sick to attend. Lying bastard!

Wasn't sure how I, or we for that matter, made it this far. The departmental tremors, while splitting the team, still left the group intact–except for Violet who fell into the large crevasse. Deciding on a consultant to help resolve the tension created an untold number of quakes. Gerard was dead-set against a female facilitator; Maxine didn't want a man. Smelder pushed for a psychiatrist; Theresa requested a psychologist. Leela preferred Gerard's office for the consultation while Maxine demanded neutral turf–the conference room. Meanwhile, I was now consuming five tablets a day to steady my feet.

After intensive negotiations and bartering, the psychologist, Dr. Noel Christofferson, was chosen by default from the dwindling list of contenders. His recent article, "The Razor's Edge–Combining Psychoanalysis with Family Systems Theory," assisted his selection as it gave the impression he could work with two camps.

"I'm thorry I'm late," spoke a bald, bearded man. "There wath a pile-up of traffic on the Harbour Bridge."

Our consultant shuffled into the room. "Could I trouble thomeone here for a cuppa tea before we begin?"

When Leela went to satisfy his request, Noel Christofferson removed his brown suitcoat and placed it on the chair which bridged the gulf between Gerard and Maxine. He fiddled with his paisley tie and smiled apprehensively.

Leela returned with his cuppa. "Tathe wonderful," he murmured, then faced the group. "I talked to Leela about helping your team with thom problemth. Can you thare what you want to work on?"

He was supposed to help us with *our* communication?! Thank God, I had popped an extra Xanax before he arrived.

Wearing a lavender outfit, Leela fluttered her eyes at Smelder. "Our director has many innovative ideas which some members have resisted. We need to support Gerard in adopting a common framework for working with clients."

Gerard tapped his pipe with a metal prod. "I agree with Leela. As head of this department, I want everyone's cooperation. We must develop a unified therapeutic program."

"I've been here longer than anyone else in the room," added Maxine. "Before Gerard arrived, we saw most clients in long-term individual therapy. That worked very well. I disagree that we should all be working the same way. I support democracy, not autocracy."

Theresa adjusted her neck brace. "We should all be treated as competent professionals and be allowed the freedom of choice. This department has become extremely rigid."

Henry stretched his long, gangling legs into the vacant space within the circle. "I would like to decrease the divisiveness and develop greater harmony among the staff. We need to value and appreciate one another."

I took a long, deep breath. "I'm... uh... feeling uptight working here. I'd like our tension to feel better... I mean, for us as a team to feel better."

Gerard struck a match to re-light his pipe. "I want to address the critical issue here. Brief family therapy has been proven to be cost effective, whereas long-term individual psychotherapy merely creates client dependence and a low turnover of cases. Besides, research shows that therapists who prefer to work with clients individually do so because they feel uncomfortable with groups. Just can't handle them."

"If family therapists are so goddamn secure," bristled Maxine, "why do they need a team who hides behind a one-way mirror?"

Smelder blew a puff of smoke toward Noel Christofferson. "You can see what I have to put up with. I am continually undermined by the instigators on the team."

The burly nurse put on her best boxing gloves and faced the consultant. "He's calling me an instigator? Ever since he returned from Italy, he's been strutting around like a bloody dictator. Learn this model! Abandon that approach! The bastard even threatened to sack me!"

In the hot, sticky room, the slugging match was on between the two heavyweights. "That's because you were insubordinate," punched Gerard. "You kept on walking out when I was talking. No department head would take that kind of crap..."

"No employee with any self-worth would take the bulldust you've been dishing out!"

Theresa and Leela joined the fray while Henry attempted to referee. I glanced at our facilitator who was stroking his beard and watching the gladiators.

He should be stopping this! Perspiration trickled past my eyes. My chest tightened. Knees trembled. Heart palpitations thumped louder.

"Ugh... Excuse me, Dr. Christofferson... ugh... we need some help. I can't take these fights anymore."

He maintained the stroking rhythm on his chin. "Do you want to tell uth how you feel?"

"Huh? I just want all this fighting to stop... It's making me extremely nervous. It's like the parents are constantly fighting."

"Doth it remind you of home?"

"No. My parents don't fight anymore."

"When you were thmall, can you remember when your parenth fought?"

I glanced at the feuding couple. "If I wanted to... but the hostility here is unbearable!"

"Was your parenth' conflict thimilar to the fighting in the team?"

"I don't know. Never could stand conflict."

"What did you do ath a little child?"

"I went to my bedroom."

Christofferson nodded his head. "We often create a thimilar pattern with our colleagueth that we had in our family environment."

The brawling stopped. Like detective lamps, eyes were staring, forcing me to confess. Was he saying it was my fault that everyone was fighting? I wiped the sweat from my face. A gurgling sensation burned in my stomach–probably an ulcer. My hand went to my heaving chest. My mind whirled. Did I cause my parents to argue? Pa often yelled, "Quit mollycoddling. Let P.P. grow up and be a man!" Ma always retaliated, "Don't bully him! He's a sensitive child." Didn't want them to fight over me. I tried getting close to Pa, but he never wanted me around when he worked on the cars. Said he'd get into trouble if my clothes got dirty. I played alone in the backyard and dug ditches for my toy soldiers, preparing for battle.

"Peter?... Peter?!"

"Huh?"

"It might be helpful to thare your feelingth with uth?"

"Huh?"

"Listen, Christofferson," interrupted Gerard. "You're going off on a wrong tangent. Pinowski's a little fish." He pointed his pipe at Maxine and Theresa. "They're the real trouble mongers. Ask them about their family relationships, especially their fathers. They have a major hang-up with authority figures!"

"Us?" they howled. Theresa waved her finger. "You're exhibiting classic symptoms of insecurity and inferiority! You have an overwhelming need to be in control, and you're overcompensating for your feelings of powerlessness."

Maxine put it another way. "You're scared you can't get it up. You probably need a splint for your dick."

"That's not true!" protested Leela. "He's a terrific director!"

Smelder clenched his teeth. "Do you *now* see the problem I have, Noel?"

"Yeth, but I wath wondering about Peterth feelingth."

"Forget *his* feelings for Christ sake. Do something about those two bitches! They need the goddamn help!"

The heat was becoming intolerable. My chest wanted to scream. Felt dizzy, light-headed. Needed fresh air. And maybe another Xanax. I rushed out of my seat. "Have to visit the loo."

I removed my glasses and splashed cold water on my face. When I looked in the mirror, I was horrified. My hair was disheveled, my eyes were bloodshot, and an ugly red rash appeared on my neck. What a mess! I cringed at the thought of returning. I decided to pop another tablet to settle my nerves and bolster my courage. I then walked back to the raging battle.

In the center ring, Gerard and Maxine were slugging it out toe to toe. Leela and Theresa were cheering on their champions while our consultant, having removed his paisley tie, was sweating profusely to keep the fight clean. I joined Henry on the sidelines and watched helplessly.

"... You've always had it in for me," swiped Gerard. "Ever since I took over this unit, you've been sticking it in my back. You couldn't face the fact that I was your boss!"

Maxine returned with an upper-cut. "You've had as much success here as you've had with your marriages— all three of them. Women despise you!"

The psychiatrist staggered from the low blow and turned to Noel Christofferson who interceded, "There theemth to be thupprethed anger..."

"You're goddamn right there's thupprethed anger!" mocked Gerard. "Listen, Christofferson. Iif you can't control this consultation, we might as well end it right here and now. I'm not taking any more from that castrating bitch!"

Maxine huffed, "You don't have the balls to handle assertive women."

"Take it easy," soothed Theresa as she patted the sweating combatant. "Don't give him the satisfaction."

"Assertive? You call what you're doing assertive?" challenged Gerard. "No wonder your husband left you. He must've been fed up having his balls continually served on a platter."

"Don't let her rile you," Leela coached. "She wants to make you look bad."

I moved my chair further away from the group.

The consultant caught sight of me. "Doth the conflict frighten you, Peter?"

I wiped my glasses. "Don't like seeing people... ugh... yell at one another."

"Doth it remind you of your parenth?"

"When I was young, my father would often shout at my mother. I was scared he'd..."

"What the hell are you doing, Christofferson?!" Gerard screamed. "Goddamn it, I told you Pinowski's not the instigator. You're asking him about his family of origin while I'm being attacked by my head nurse. Who the hell trained you?"

The referee reeled. "I wath merely exploring hith feelingth."

"I'm not interested in feelings. I'm interested in results. Your job was to improve communication. That means getting my staff to support me. That's what I'm paying you for."

Henry slid his chair next to mine, prompting the wide-eyed Smelder to start throwing wild punches.

"Snart! I haven't heard one goddamn word of support from you. Don't sit there like a wimp! Why haven't you defended me against these accusations?"

"Face it, Gerard," pummeled Maxine. "You've got as many supporters in this department as a horse has arse-holes."

Leela blushed beetroot red. "You referring to me?"

"That does it!" cried Smelder. He threw his pipe on the floor, smashing it in half. "No one calls my social worker an arse-hole! Christofferson, you have plenty of evidence that Nurse Benton is creating the chaos. I want you to submit a report indicating gross insubordination!"

"He wasn't hired to write reports," bopped Theresa. "He's here to help us resolve our problems. Dictating demands won't improve the situation!"

"Are you going to listen to them, Christofferson, or are you man enough to support me? I need a full report implicating these two bitches. The only solution to the problem is to terminate their employment."

Maxine clenched her fist. "You can't do that!"

The flushed psychiatrist called on the referee. "What do you say, Noel?"

Christofferson's face looked punchy and drawn. He lisped more than ever. "I underthand your conthern, Dr. Thmelder, but I wath hired to fathilitate team building. A report would not be conthructive."

Maxine went for the knockout. "Face it! You've just been delivered a vote of no confidence. You have no support!"

Gerard staggered on the ropes. With a ghostly scowl, he scanned our faces. Leela's showed a grimace of defeat.

Having copped one thump too many, he struggled wearily to his feet. "I must've been in a fog," he said. "How could I have been so stupid? I see it now. A conspiracy! You've hired this man so you could take over my department. It's becoming clear. Christ, I should've seen it. When I was away in Italy, my troops back home were plotting to stab me in the back. You pretended Christofferson wasn't your first choice when, in actual fact, he was. You knew I wouldn't have considered him if he was at the top of your list. So you planted him toward the bottom. Clever. *Very* clever. I fell for the trap."

He stumbled toward his social worker. *"Et tu,* Leela?"

"No, Gerard. It wasn't like that! It wasn't like that at all!!"

"You spiteful little bitch! Just because I didn't take you to Italy. Well, I can assure you, I didn't spend all my time there alone."

"Gerard, don't. Please don't."

"Shut up!"

With bulging eyes and his puffy face contorted into a grotesque demonic sneer, Smelder growled, "I can assure each and every one of you that your attempted takeover hasn't worked. I will remain in charge here! No one's going to take away my department. No one! As far as I'm concerned, this consultation is over. I've tried it your way. Now, I'm warning you. Do it my way, or get out of the way!"

He staggered out, a commander without troops.

Tears splashed from Leela's eyes; her mascara began to run. She glanced around the room, seemingly in agony about her decision–stay with the team or follow the leader. She sighed deeply, wiped away the tears, then departed shamefaced from the room.

I sat there in silence. A swelling lump gnawed at my stomach. With Gerard's state of mind, only God knew what would happen.

SATURDAY, NOVEMBER 26

Midnight. Roaming in the department. Noises.
Crash! In Smelder's office. Door ajar. See scuffling.
Maxine strangling Gerard. Choking him with black
tie. His mouth foams. He claws at her clothes. Then
breasts. I scream, "Stop!" They tumble onto floor.
Spill crystal ashtray. Pipe still burning. Fire! "Stop!"
Smelder's paws grasp ashtray, smash Maxine's
head. Blood, spurting everywhere. I shriek, "Stop
killing me!" I thrust long blade. First at Gerard. In
the back. Then Maxine. In her chest. Again. And
again. Footsteps coming, running. The night
watchman. I escape through window. Shouts.
Gunfire. Arrive back home. Feel unsafe. Steal Com-
modore. Speeding on expressway. Road blocks.
Lights flashing. Police! Guns pointed. "Don't
shoot!" They blast. "No-o-o-o!" Blood! Oozing
down legs. Wet. Warm. Wet!

Bloody hell! I drenched the bed. It was bad enough
having nightmares, but wetting the sheets was going too
far. What the hell would I tell the grand inquisitor?
Clothes weren't allowed in the washing machine without first passing her inspection.

I lay in the soggy bed, depressed as hell. My life was falling apart. Not only did I work at a demented hospital, but I lived in a prison where I confined myself to the bedroom. Either that, or listen to Ma's constant complaints about her sore ribs, the fucking chores, or my inconsiderateness. Caught the bloody woman spritzing my room with more holy water, her latest attempt to cure my agitated state. Should've grabbed the fucking bottle and smashed it over her head.

My social life was ziltcho–couldn't handle any more rejections. And I was forever cranky, forgetful, jumpy, and depressed. Thank God for the Xanax. The six tablets a day enabled me to keep my head above water. I visited several other doctors to insure a steady supply. One of them had the nerve to caution me about getting addicted. Hell, I just needed another prescription, not a lecture.

To make matters worse, the rash on my neck was red and raw, weeping constantly. Had to get a script for cortisone ointment. And now my bladder!

Thought of going walkabout to Western Australia, but my erratic mind wouldn't allow the luxury. Couldn't think straight. Needed more sleep. I swallowed another tablet and pushed aside the clammy sheets. Please, God, no more nightmares.

PING-PONG

WEDNESDAY, NOVEMBER 30

I slammed another ball past my opponent.

"Can I have the next game?"

"Surjit! Where the hell you been keeping yourself?"

He joked, "Locked on the ward."

"I should polish off this bloke in a few minutes."

I whacked the final point past the sprawling player and announced, "I'm ready for some hot competition! Be prepared, Surjit. I've had lots of practice lately."

He bounced the ball on the table. "What happened to your neck?"

"It's nothing. A bloody rash."

"You all right? You look pale and tired."

"Don't worry about it. Been working extra hard. You can serve first."

"You're hands are shaking."

"Not to worry. As I said, I'm over-worked."

Surjit's brown eyes pierced my mind. "What's wrong, Peter?"

"What's this, a bloody medical? Serve the ball."

"We'll play it your way," he said, then sent a spinner across the table.

I netted the damn ball.

He served again. I netted another.

"You're not playing very well today."

"Just keep serving. My game will come back."

"I can see your problem."

"What are you talking about?"

Surjit pointed to my hands. "Every time you swing with your right, your left hand immediately moves to correct the paddle. You're off balance."

"My left hand never touches the paddle!"

He sent a topspin. "Be aware of your hands."

I managed to return the serve.

"Stop!" he shouted. "What are you doing?"

I spotted my left hand automatically repositioning the paddle in my right. "Strewth! Never realized I did that."

"That's what friends are for. To help us see what we cannot see."

"Don't need any of that rubbish today."

"I'm worried about you, Peter. You need help."

"Save it for your clients! The only help I need is for you to bloody well mind your own business. Give me the ball! I don't want to play anymore."

He tossed the white disc on the floor and crushed it under his shoe.

"What the hell did you do that for?!"

He said nothing.

"That was a special ball. It cost me two dollars! Why'd you smash it?"

"The old ball must crack before a new one can be played."

I grabbed my paddle and stormed out. "Rack off!"

MANAGEMENT MEETING?

MONDAY, DECEMBER 5

"Theresa," hissed Dr. Smelder, "tell us about your cases."

She continued writing on her notepad. "They're doing very well, thank you."

He pounded his fist on the desk. "As head of this department, I want to know what you're doing!"

Theresa eyed the crazed psychiatrist. "I've submitted my weekly case log as requested. Those clients requiring supervision have already been discussed with our analyst, Fiona Crompton."

"Don't you think I know what you're doing? I found out about the letter you and Maxine sent to the Medical Superintendent. Bob Gross and I go back a long way. Telling him I'm incompetent and dangerous to staff and clients merely revealed your own paranoia. I can assure you, that letter won't get very far. Bob has received my own report outlining every single infraction you and Maxine have committed. You've blatantly refused to attend family therapy consultations or the sessions behind the one-way mirror. Both of you refuse to present case material at management meetings, and you have flagrantly disregarded my directives. You're both marked for termination."

Maxine brazenly rose from her chair. "I've been in-ormed by the Nurses' Union that if I receive further harassment from you, I should inform you of such and exercise my right to leave the room. I'm giving you notice that I am being harassed, and, as of now, I'm exercising my rights."

Maxine bolted. Theresa followed.

"Come back here this instant!" shouted Smelder. He followed them down the hall. "You can't leave! I didn't give you permission..."

Like a man possessed, he returned snorting fire. "Rotten bitches!"

His eyes blazed fiendishly at the rest of us. "If any of you even *think* of going to the Medical Superintendent, I'll make your life unbearably miserable. Now get the hell out of here!"

A MAJOR DISASTER!

🦗

THURSDAY, DECEMBER 15

Blackie died this evening from tick poisoning. I had taken him for a run last Saturday at the National Park near Audley where he must've picked up the ticks. Several of the bastards lodged themselves in the back of his neck. A few others burrowed in his chest. On Tuesday, his back legs were paralyzed, and his mouth was frothing. I rushed him to the vet who injected a serum. It was too late. My best friend and companion for the past 13 years would bark no more. Why did he have to die? At a time when I needed him the most.

"You should've checked him!" Pa chastised as he watched the Evening News. "You've become very absent-minded. Didn't I always tell you? When you return from the bush, check the fur. Your dog might still be alive."

"Don't rub his nose in it," said Ma while she ironed the underwear. "Piotr, what's the matter? You're not yourself."

I stared at the telly.

"Look at you," she said. "The rash on your neck is worse. You're cranky most of the time, and you lock yourself in your bedroom. I worry about you. What's the matter?"

"Nothing! Leave me alone!"

Pa shouted, "Don't you yell at Ma! In my house, I demand respect!"

Ma stopped ironing. "Are you having those crazy attacks like you had at university?"

"No."

Pa switched channels. "You should move out and find a place of your own. Then you'll see how hard it is."

"Shush! There's no need to rush! Go heat the cabbage rolls, Piotr. You hardly touched your dinner."

"Not hungry."

I moped back to my bedroom and closed the door. My mind tossed and turned. Pa was right about one thing. I used to comb and inspect Blackie after every bushwalk. As of late, I was continually confused and irritated. And the bloody rash wasn't getting any better. Blackie's death *was* my fault. If it weren't for me, my dog would still be alive.

I lay on the bed wanting to cry. I couldn't. Did the next best thing and tore at my *pierzyna*. The seam burst, scattering thousands of feathers across the room. Then I cried.

ANOTHER HOT SUMMER DAY

FRIDAY, DECEMBER 16

I left the tablets at home, locked in the top drawer of my desk. As my penance for Blackie's death, I had decided to withdraw cold turkey from Xanax. I knew withdrawals could be difficult and quite possibly dangerous, especially if there were a seizure. But my dog had depended on me for his survival. It seemed a just punishment that I should no longer depend on medication.

"Bring on the family!" shouted Gerard. "It's past 10 o'clock."

Henry, the therapist in front of the one-way mirror, was the lucky one today. With Smelder becoming increasingly paranoid, it was better to be on the firing line with the clients than to be closeted behind the screen. While Theresa and Maxine continued their boycott, Leela had conveniently planned a previous engagement. Ever since Christofferson's effort at team building, she and Gerard had ceased all communication. Meanwhile, Earl and I were left to contend with a volatile commander.

With his smoking habit getting worse, he lit his pipe in the small, dark room. "Our numbers have dropped. I won't tolerate either of you leaving during the session."

"I would never think of missing such a golden opportunity to learn," crawled Earl.

"All right, Pinowski. Show me how much you know."

My stomach groaned. I shouldn't have eaten Ma's *golabki* late last night. Cabbage rolls with sauerkraut didn't quite mix with close confinements. And without my medication, I was overwhelmed with anxiety as my head throbbed with a god-awful headache. To make matters worse, being cooped up in the hot, stuffy, smoke-filled room made me claustrophobic. With the black drapes drawn across the window to keep the light out, there was little fresh air.

"Pinowski, you listening?"

"Uh... Yes, Dr. Smelder."

He blew the pipe smoke toward my face. "Tell me about the Mounser family."

My heart increased its thumping. I clutched my chest. "It's their first interview. Fifteen-year-old Simon is the identified patient. His brother Clarence is 13. The 43-year-old father is Benjamin."

"I know their goddamn names! What are the family dynamics?"

My intestines somersaulted. The smoke and the heat, added to the tension in the room and Ma's *golabki*, fomented a lethal brew. The pockets of gas gurgled. Maybe this wasn't the right time to withdraw from anti-anxiety drugs.

"Pinowski?!"

"Uh... The presenting problem..."

"Shhhh," he hissed. "They're entering the room. Now what the hell is that doing here?"

Clothed in an oversized speckled-gray tracksuit, Simon was holding a restless brown Chihuahua.

Smelder ripped the phone off the hook and buzzed the interviewing room. "Snart! Why the hell did you allow a dog into the department?"

Henry whispered awkwardly into the receiver. "The dog means a lot to Simon."

"Pedro is me boy's constant companion," added Mr. Mounser's gravely voice. "Me son goes nowhere without 'im. Even got permission from the school. They let Pedro wait in the courtyard."

The Chihuahua yapped noisily.

"For Christ sake, keep that mutt quiet!" He slammed down the phone. "Snart's an imbecile, letting the family bring in a pet. Next thing, he'll be counseling the animal. Pinowski, what's your hypothesis? Why does the boy desperately need his dog?"

My body prevented me from focusing on the question. Stomach juices, acting like a kitchen blender, whizzed turbulently around the *golabki*. Have mercy!

"Pinowski! You deaf?"

"Ugh... The boy's lonely... He needs a friend, a companion."

Smelder puffed hard on his pipe. "That's pretty goddamn obvious, isn't it, Jacobi?"

Earl nodded affirmative. "I wonder if it's related to the absent mother?"

"That's what Henry should damn well be finding out!"

In front of the mirror, Henry was asking the brawny father, "Can you tell me how Simon attempted to kill himself?"

"One morning, he wrapped one of me ties around his neck. He pulled one end with each hand until his face turned blue. Scared the bleedin' daylights out of me Clarence, who phoned me at work."

"Where do you work?" asked Henry.

"The abattoirs. I hang the meat on hooks. Me boss doesn't like the phone calls. When I came home, I gave Simon a smack around the ears. He stopped for awhile. Last week he tried the the same nonsense. Me Clarence gets frantic and keeps phoning the abattoir. I'll lose me job!"

Henry faced the 13-year-old brother who was wearing an old sweatshirt with a large red emblem of K Mart. "Do you worry about Simon?"

"Of course the kid worries!" berated Smelder. "Why else would he call his father on the phone? Pinowski, Henry needs a phone-in. He's wasting valuable time. What's your suggestion?"

I grasped my noisy churning stomach. "Excuse me, Dr. Smelder, but I have to visit the..."

"You're not going anywhere! What's your answer?"

"Ugh... What was the question?"

"Are you with us today? Snart needs a goddamn phone-in, you moron! What should it be?"

The nausea and cramps worsened. "Ugh... Should we ask about the absent mother?"

The furious psychiatrist snatched the phone. "Snart! You're wasting our time! Ask Clarence a triangular question. Why does he think his brother wants to kill himself?"

Henry hung up and repeated the question.

"I don't know," the boy answered.

Smelder fumed. "What do I have here? A bunch of clowns? Whenever a client says, 'I don't know,' it means the therapist hasn't asked the question properly. Didn't they teach you anything, Pinowski?"

My pounding heart tightened within my chest. The volume of gas begged for release. My legs started shaking. My stomach muscles contracted. The walls closed in again. Needed air. I pinched my thighs, trying to forget the pain.

Gerard bounced his hand off the mirror. "What's this moron doing?!"

Henry was comforting Simon, whose eyes were streaming with tears. Pedro was licking the boy's face.

The father blew into his handkerchief. "Me Simon's been very depressed since his bleedin' mother left with me best mate. He's never been the same. I keep telling 'im, it's not his fault his mother's a bleedin' scumbag. Me son keeps saying he wants to cash in his chips."

The father placed his large hand on the boy's knee. "Pull yourself together, mate."

Perspiration covered my face. I gripped my chest, my stomach.

Pedro jumped from Simon's lap.

"Watch that damn dog!" Smelder bellowed at the glass.

The Chihuahua sniffed the one-way mirror.

"Snart!" he shouted, reaching for the phone. Too late. The dog's hind quarters were already arched.

I lost control and bolted out of the room. Didn't quite make it to the loo on time.

SATURDAY, DECEMBER 17

4:18 a.m. Perched in our fig tree, the koel is driving me crazy with its piercing call. Its repetitive shrill began tormenting me at midnight and never let up. The bloody cuckoo should've stayed in Indonesia. We don't need any more migrating birds abandoning eggs for others to roost.

I check the mirror on my dresser. The rash on my neck was spreading to my arms. Wasn't sure what was happening to me. All I knew was that the diarrhea, dermatitis, headaches, confusion, and irritability were getting worse. Couldn't figure if the symptoms were the result of the increased stress, my attempted withdrawal, or God knows what else.

After the one-way mirror fiasco, I tried calling my old therapist, Melody Mill, at the university. Kept getting her bloody voice mail. She should have returned my cry for help. Even if it was the weekend. I yelled at the bloody operator who refused to give me Melody's unlisted phone number. Hell, this was an emergency!

The shrill of the red-eyed black cuckoo pierces the still night.

I throw a book out the window. "Get outa here!"

Christmas is only eight days away. Santa, sweltering in the December heat, has appeared at every shopping mall. Ba humbug! Can't be bothered about presents. I'll give Ma the money and have her pick them out. It'll get her off my back for a while. The crazy ol' lady's been driving me nuts with her constant banging on my bedroom door, yapping about my moodiness.

Another high pitched shrill shatters the morning. "Stupid bird," I screech. Another sleepless night.

I sit exhausted and delirious at my desk talking with Siggy, the bronze plaster bust of Freud. "Read," he instructs. I reach for the works of Edgar Allen Poe. The pages flutter open to "The Raven." The words haunt my mind. Siggy gives another directive. "Let your unconsciousness flow onto the computer." Past the point of fatigue, I could only obey.

Once upon a midnight dreary, while I ponder weak and weary.

Suddenly there comes a rapping, rapping, a cuckoo rapping, against the window...

"Who are you?"

I nod, nearly napping. Again there comes that sudden tapping, tapping, tapping...

"What do you want?"

I open wide the window. In there steps a jet-black cuckoo, red eyes piercing, piercing, my inner core.

"Why are you here?"

His right eye blinks, his left eye winks, winks, keeps winking...

"How much longer must this madness continue? I can't take it anymore!"

Quoth the cuckoo, "Forevermore!"

CLIENTS, COMING AND GOING

MONDAY, DECEMBER 19

"Do you have any children?"

The distraught Mrs. Bliss started crying.

Another bloody whimpering client.

I raised my voice. "Do you have any children?!"

"I told you last week," she sobbed. "My son... drowned six months ago... I'm not coping with his death... I don't feel like living."

Neither did I...

DAY BEFORE CHRISTMAS EVE

🔨

Another scorcher. My body, already clammy from the heat, lumbered out of bed. It felt as if I were dragging a ball and chain. Even on the eve of Christmas, our department loomed like Long Bay Jail.

I stopped off at the chemist to renew my prescription for the holidays. Despite my best effort, I couldn't withdraw from the anti-anxiety medication. I still desperately needed the peach tablets to provide relief from the ongoing tension. Figured the break over Christmas would lessen the anxiety and would provide a better space to decrease the dosage.

The bloody queue at the checkout was a mile long. Christ, I hated Christmas! And those soppy carols playing nonstop to induce shopping mania–what a rip-off!

I arrived late at the hospital. A scraggly plastic tree in the waiting room was the only sign of our holiday spirit. I hadn't scheduled any clients. No sense making the day any worse. I spotted Earl and Leela laughing and giggling down the corridor. He squeezed her ass and led her into his office. They closed the door.

I left the department to give Surjit a card. He was nowhere to be found. The staff on the Karen Horney Unit were already stuck into the champagne, celebrating with the patients. Couldn't distinguish who was administering to whom. When everyone started with the bloody Christmas carols, I split.

Lunchtime. I ate my soggy sandwich in the cafeteria. Afterwards, I wandered around the hospital to waste more time. Most of the departments were partying. In ours, Earl and Leela were probably the only ones experiencing Christmas cheer.

At 3:37, I decided to nick off early. When I headed back for my briefcase, I spotted a squad car parked in front of the department. Most likely a wacko suicide in the throes of holiday depression. Thank God, I wasn't in my office.

I walked into the waiting area. Bloody hell! Two policemen were dragging someone. I moved closer. Henry? What the hell were they doing with him? Handcuffed?!

"Henry!"

His eyes veered away.

The policemen brushed me aside. "Move it!"

They pushed the crumpled figure out the door. I followed. "Henry!" His shoulders twitched. He mumbled, "I was teaching them protective behaviors."

"Move it!" ordered the policeman. He shoved the manacled prisoner into the blue-and-white car. The door slammed shut and the squad pulled away. I watched in horror as the vehicle turned the corner and disappeared out of sight.

Back inside, Maxine was flailing her arms and shrieking, "That rotten bastard! Those boys were only eight and four!"

"What happened?"

"Where the hell have you been?" she screamed. "I caught your friend molesting the Jenson/Murray boys. The bastard! Said he was teaching the boys protective behaviors, showing them how to say 'No'. The past month, I sensed something was wrong. Henry was acting weird. Before he brought Richard and Conrad into the interviewing room, I arranged a small crack between the curtains in front of the one-way screen. I hid behind the mirror and watched. Disgusting! He had the boys pull down their pants. I barged into the room and caught him red-handed. God only knows what else he's done. The preaching bastard! I called the police straight away."

A couple of nurses entered the reception area. "Is it true?!"

Maxine raged, "When I interviewed the boys, they admitted it was happening over the past several weeks..."

As she continued to rehash the story, I rushed to the loo. My shaking hands struggled to remove a tablet from the plastic container. I turned on the tap and looked up at the mirror. The muscles around my left eye were twitching uncontrollably. I gasped. A dark, menacing shadow appeared.

"Who are you?" I hissed.

Strident laughter echoed in the room.

"Stay away from me!"

The phantom cackled and faded into my image on the glass. I gazed in horror at brown sweaty hair, white pasty skin, bloodshot eyes, ugly red blotches oozing clear liquid on my neck and arms, and my left eye twitching uncontrollably.

"No!" I cried. "That's not me!"

I flew out of the hospital, pushing my way past the scurrying crowds. More than ever, I desperately needed the safety of my bedroom. The insides of my stomach churned. I stopped by the gutter and heaved.

"You all right, son?"

I looked up at an officer of the Salvation Army standing by his red collection bucket. I vomited once more.

"Can I help?"

"Leave me alone!" I wiped my mouth and dashed toward the train.

Once safe at home, I flung the bedroom door shut and collapsed on the bed. My heart thumped; my head pounded. Henry and those two boys kept flashing through my head. Jesus! Not Holy Henry.

The others in the department filled my mind like a black balloon stretching and expanding: muscle-bound Theresa spread-eagle on her bench press; Earl Jacobi, stoned while playing with nubile adolescents; the storm trooper, Gerard, ordering the Nazi salute; Leela materializing, then Maxine...

My head ached. Stop! No more! Please, God. No more!

"Piotr? You home?"

Not Ma. Not now.

"Piotr? You finished work so soon?"

"I need to be alone!"

She banged on the door. "Why, what's wrong?"

"For Christ sake, leave me alone!"

For once, she listened.

CHRISTMAS EVE

♟

While *Dzisiaj W Betlejem* played on the phonograph, Stella, Stan, and their two children arrived from Melbourne. I was in no shape to greet them. I stayed in my bedroom most of the day, sick to my stomach. Thoughts of Henry and the two boys kept flashing in my mind, making me nauseous.

It was after eight o'clock when Aunt Adele and Uncle Janek appeared for the traditional wigilia supper. My stomach convulsed at the thought of eating Ma's *pierogis*.

A knock on the door. "Everyone's here, P.P."

I peeped out of my bedroom. "Feel dreadful, Pa. I'm still sick. Can't make it."

His eyes widened. "You look awful!"

"Yea."

"Ma will be very upset."

"Tell everyone I can't join them. I need to sleep."

"You can't miss midnight mass with the family. Wash up and rest. I'll call you when it's time for church."

I crashed on the bed and blocked out the rest of the world.

The clock said 11:16 p.m. when Pa yanked on my arms. "Wake up. Get ready for midnight mass. The church will be crowded."

Don't know how I made it, but I found myself standing with the other latecomers in the aisle of St. Vincent's. With the pews tightly packed, only the brown Christmas beetles whizzing around the high ceiling had enough space. The six open windows high on the walls offered little relief for the capacity crowd. While the choir sang *Gdy sie Chrystus Rodzi,* Ma fingered her black rosary beads and mumbled her Hail Marys. I stared blankly at the words on the front wall. *Ego Sum Nolite Timere.* I am without fear.

At midnight, the altar boys, wearing thongs beneath their white robes, led Fr. Czarnecki to the altar. With his golden jubilee under his belt, the ancient priest rambled through the mass. Stagnant air hung above our heads like heavy clouds. Patches of sweat formed across parishioners' backs. A beetle buzzed my right ear. Nauseated, I prayed for strength.

Communion lasted forever. The sole priest distributed white hosts to the long queue of hungry believers. I leaned against a pew. My head began spinning. Sister Margaret, dressed in a black habit, stood in front of the class. "Peter, this Holy Eucharist is sacred. Remember the nasty little boy? When he took the blessed host out of his mouth and stuck it with a pin, the Eucharist began to bleed. Don't ever chew it. You would hurt Jesus..."

"His mouth's bleeding! Give him some room!"

I lay on the floor. Faces staring. Ceiling spinning. Blood oozing from my lips. God, let me die!

"Your teeth cut a nasty gash in your tongue when you collapsed." It was Pa's voice.

2:37 a.m. Western Suburbs Hospital. I received seven stitches. Merry Christmas!

HAPPY NEW YEAR

✠

SUNDAY, JANUARY 1, 1995

Not much to celebrate. I printed out all of my journal entries for 1994. Seemed the right thing to do, like purging out the old year. Wasn't sure whether to burn the pages, so I dumped them in the bottom drawer of my desk. Good riddance!

I made another resolution to withdraw from the anti-anxiety medication. I knew I should've consulted a doctor, but after my experience in the department, my trust level with healing professionals was lower than a slug's navel. I had to do it alone, to sink or swim through the tortuous maze of withdrawal.

TUESDAY, JANUARY 10

I continued to wage a valiant battle to get off the medication. Withdrawal was touch and go, especially when the sweats, shakes, nausea, and headaches wrenched my aching body. After taking several sickies, I decided on the more gentle approach of curbing my intake of pills with one less tablet every three to four days. Wasn't sure which was worse though, the withdrawal or Ma's incessant nagging, "You're sick because you're not eating properly."

FRIDAY THE 13TH

JANUARY, 1995

The batteries in the wall clocks throughout the department stopped working, and the caged doves near the pediatric ward vanished without a trace. Must've been an omen.

I handed in my notice to Dr. Smelder. He couldn't care less. He was still embroiled with the furor unleashed by Henry's horrific sins. The irate parents reconciled for the sake of the boys, or so they said. They were jointly suing the hospital for big bucks. Gerard feverishly tried to salvage his tattered reputation as he responded to the incriminating evidence in the press.

I was given a month to complete my reports and terminate with clients. I realized that if I stayed at the hospital much longer, I'd either wind up in the psychiatric ward or at the drug clinic. Although an overdose offered a quick way out, quitting my job seemed the better solution. Wasn't sure what to do next, but I had stashed away a fair bit of cash during the year for such an emergency. In the meantime, I'd live at home until I got back on my feet.

FRIDAY, FEBRUARY 10

Over the past six weeks, and one relapse, I finally managed to be medication free. I wouldn't have made it without the help of Dr. Claire Moody's audiotape on managing anxiety. Practically memorized her lecture, word for word. The rash on my neck was clearing and my appetite was slowly returning. I vowed that the peach tablets would never again control my life. I locked the remaining few securely in the top drawer of my desk.

Having brought Ma's bagged lunch, I parked myself on the wooden bench outside the department. I finished my tuna salad and basked in the sun's warm rays.

"We haven't played table tennis in a long time."

I looked up at the smiling psychiatrist. "Not since you crushed my ball. You must've known this would happen."

"The signs were there," said Surjit.

"Have a seat. You must've heard that I'm leaving."

He nodded.

"Our department's disintegrating. Leela and Theresa have applied for jobs elsewhere, and Earl will move on once his placement has completed. As for Gerard and Maxine, they'll probably survive the hospital enquiry surrounding Henry. Like two stubborn bulls, neither one will quit."

Surjit sighed, "The head of our department, Jules Eaglesham, suffered another manic depressive episode yesterday. He was rushed to casualty after swallowing his bottle of lithium."

"This place is just like that book you gave me, *One Flew Over the Cuckoo's Nest*. Except we're the mad ones, not the patients." I thought again of that delirious morning of December 17th, conversing with a red-eyed black cuckoo. If my life continued like the past year, I might just end up cuckoo forevermore.

Surjit interrupted my thoughts. "What are your plans?"

"I don't know. These past two months have ripped me apart. I need time to piece myself together again. I'm not even sure if I want to stay in the field.

"Don't sell yourself short," soothed his voice. "You've learned a great lesson here."

"What? That my whole world was on the verge of collapse?"

He unfastened his tie. "In Hindu, we have three gods: Shiva, the lord of destruction; Brahma, the lord of creation; and Vishnu, the lord of preservation. These three powers represent the cycle of life. Destruction continually makes way for creation."

"That's a reassuring thought," I added sarcastically.

"Think of the drought we've just had. The intense heat of a bushfire is needed to split open the pods of the banksia tree. Its seeds can then be hurtled back to earth for regeneration."

"That's easy for you to say, but your life hasn't been turned inside out."

Surjit patted my shoulder. "Don't despair, Peter. A new path will open for you."

"It better happen soon. I've had more than my share of bad luck."

My mustached friend from India reached around his neck and unfastened a gold chain with a dangling old medallion the size of a 20-cent coin. "I want you to have this."

I examined the disc. "It's an elephant!"

"It's Ganesha," corrected Surjit, "the elephant-headed son of Lord Shiva and his consort, Parvati. He's the destroyer of obstacles and can assist you in removing barriers."

I had a hard enough time accepting Catholic mumbo jumbo about St. Christopher. How could I believe in an elephant man?

"The medallion is merely a reminder to believe," he said.

I hated it when he read my mind.

"Believe in yourself, Peter. That's the lesson we must all learn."

"Are you sure you want me to have this?"

"It's time Ganesha found a new home." Surjit rose and offered his hand. "Our paths will cross again. It is our destiny."

With a wave, my friend disappeared across the lawn.

As I left the Royal Prince Andrew far behind, my train roared across the Sydney Harbour Bridge. Dark gray clouds, gliding across the sky, reflected ominous shadows off the tiled roof of the opera house. I reached into my pocket and pulled out the the gold chain with the metal disc. That was bloody nice of Surjit to give me this present. Even though I didn't believe in its so-called powers to remove obstacles, I fastened it around my neck. Would've preferred to be comforted by a real pet instead of a metal insignia of an elephant man. I glanced at Ganesha who seemed to almost smile.

I could get another pet. The Royal Society for the Prevention of Cruelty to Animals was always begging for people to care for unwanted animals. In fact, the RSPCA might still be open. Maybe Surjit was right. Now was the time to begin a new life. Who knows, I might even talk my parents into family counseling. We could all change!

A black-and-white puppy, a cross between a bull-terrier and a short-haired pointer, jumped with excitement when I passed his cage. Large white spots adorned three of its paws, and his cute charcoal body sported a white zig-zag painted across the tail. You beauty! I named him Ganesha. My spirits soared.

The southerly winds were blowing when I rushed into the house. I was eager to show off the new pet snuggled in my arms.

"Look what I have!"

No one was in the kitchen. My bedroom door was ajar.

"What are you doing?"

Ma spun around. Her mouth belched fire. *"Psiakrew!* How could you?"

The frightened Ganesha piddled on my arm and jumped to the floor.

"What?"

"This!" she yelled.

"Hey!" I shouted. "That's private! You had no right searching my desk!"

She slammed down the printout. "I knew something was wrong! This is filth!"

"You had no fucking right reading my journal!"

Her face whitened. "Don't you swear at me!"

The volcano within rumbled. "For Christ sake, you searched my room like I'm a goddamn criminal!"

"You sound like a criminal. Drugs! Sex! This isn't my son!"

"You don't know who the fuck I am!"

She slapped my face. "I won't have you swearing in my home!"

My fingernails pierced the palms of my clenched fist. "I'll swear wherever I goddamn want to. That was my private journal! Those were my fucking thoughts!"

She went to slap me again. I grabbed her hand. "Don't *ever* hit me!"

"You'll go to hell!" she spewed. "You've written smut! Dirty trash! That computer is evil!"

Outside, lightning flashed. Thunder clapped. The winds howled and rain spanked the roof.

"This filth has to go!" She moved toward the computer. "This won't be used again. Not for smut. Not in my house!"

Enraged, I stepped in front of her. "You can't take it. It's mine!"

"Get out of the way! It's sinful."

I clutched her arm. We scuffled. I shoved her toward the dresser. She reached for my mug of yesterday's oxtail soup. I grabbed for it. She hurled the cup at the screen. *Crash!* Shards of glass and orange liquid flew across the room. My Macintosh was destroyed.

Tears welled in my eyes. Another companion taken away by my mother. Quivering with fury, I picked up the plaster bust of Freud. I tightly grasped Siggy, turning my knuckles white.

Ma stumbled back against the dresser, shrieking, "Put that down!"

I saw the back of her head reflecting off the mirror. The volcano erupted. "You've taken away my life! *I hate you!*"

My hand released the projectile–SMASH–against the dresser mirror. Plaster and glass splattered everywhere.

I walked out sobbing into the raging storm.

MY 30TH BIRTHDAY
A DREAM – OR A VISION?

Tossing and turning in the middle of the night. My psyche tortured, still fighting with Ma. A dazzling blue light flashes around a brown-skinned yogi, clothed in saffron robes, sitting in a lotus position. A red dot marks his third eye. The light glows and shimmers around the guru as he speaks. "Forgive yourself. Only then can you be healed. Love and accept yourself. You are perfect as God created you."

His hand reaches out and touches my chest. A shimmering blue beam streams into my swelling heart. Loving energy pulsates through every cell— releasing anger, guilt, hatred. Warmth and peace cloak and surround me. Healing. The smiling face glows with love and acceptance. I recognize the guru as he vanishes. Surjit was bidding farewell.

ELECTION DAY

🦃

SATURDAY, MARCH 25, 1995

A light sprinkle speckled the asphalt street with tiny dots. The recent rain seemed to be easing the drought.

The Budget rent-a-truck was already loaded. Pa closed the metal doors and climbed inside the cab. I had accepted his offer to help me move. Funny about his offer, though. I was expecting a glad-to-get-rid-of-you response. Instead Pa acted, almost in a way, like he was proud I was finally making it on my own. Not that he would ever utter those words.

Frightened and excited, sad yet happy, I cast one last look at my Ashfield home of 21 years. Ma was peeping though the lace curtains. We were still barely speaking. To add insult to injury, I was leaving her before the Easter holidays.

With Ganesha nudging his nose under my left arm, and my new Macintosh computer in my right arm, I walked toward the driver's seat. I started the engine and headed toward my rented flat, 582 North Steyne, across from the beach in Manly.

Today was a state election. Normally I would vote just because it was compulsory; however, it seemed fitting that I take a stand on this momentous occasion.

While Ma and Pa traditionally voted Liberal, I planned to cast a ballot for the Labour Party in *my* new district.

Next week I have a job interview for a counseling position. Don't know what the future will promise, but one thing I know, "This is not the last journal entry of the rest of my life."